THE TEARS OF ARTAMON TRILOGY

Lord of Snow and Shadows

"There are handsome young princes, beautiful princesses, cagey kings, evil magicians, subtle spymasters, loyal retainers and plenty of backstory to keep things hopping."
—*Contra Costa Times*

"Stands out from the pack . . . a very interesting and entertaining first novel, and perhaps the sign of a new star rising in the fantasy firmament."
—*Chronicle*

Prisoner of the Iron Tower

**ONE OF THE TOP SCIENCE FICTION TITLES
OF THE YEAR FROM THE *KANSAS CITY STAR***

"Solid, wonderful fantasy, sparkling and imaginative!"
—*Booklist*

"Ash takes her large and colorful cast of characters from horror to pathos, from triumph to betrayal, smoothly and convincingly. A roller-coaster ride of events and emotions in the best modern fantasy manner."
—*Kirkus Reviews*

Children of the Serpent Gate

"Uniformly well-developed and convincing, as is the whole world of the trilogy, with its vivid eighteenth-century European flavor and fallen angels who evoke *Paradise Lost*. Lovers of big, complex fantasy sagas (think Robert Jordan or George R. R. Martin) will be well pleased."
—*Publishers Weekly* (starred review)

FLIGHT
into
DARKNESS

Book Two of the Alchymist's Legacy

Sarah Ash

BANTAM BOOKS • NEW YORK

2010 Spectra Mass Market Edition

Copyright ©2009 by Sarah Ash
Map copyright © 2009 by Neil Gower

Published in the United States by Spectra, an imprint of The Random House Publishing Group, a division of Random House, Inc., New York.

SPECTRA and the portrayal of a boxed "s" are trademarks of Random House, Inc.

Originally published in hardcover in the United States by Spectra, an imprint of The Random House Publishing Group, a division of Random House, Inc., in 2009.

ISBN 978-0-553-58986-3

Cover illustration © Phillip Heffernan
Cover Design by Jamie S. Warren Youll

Printed in the United States of America

www.ballantinebooks.com

9 8 7 6 5 4 3 2 1

For Diana and Christopher Wallis

Acknowledgments

As the final credits roll for Alchymist's Legacy, it's time for me to express my warmest thanks to everyone who has helped me tell Celestine's tale:

First and foremost, my wonderful editor (and novelist herself), Anne Groell, for her boundless patience, understanding, and good humor, not to mention all her editorial expertise and experience.

My supportive agents, John Richard Parker and Merrilee Heifetz.

Three very talented artists: Phil Heffernan for the gorgeous cover art, and Jamie S. Warren Youll for the neat jacket design, and Neil Gower for the map.

David Pomerico for not only being my "Wise Reader" (that invaluable adviser as advocated by Orson Scott Card) but also for stage-managing the later stages of production.

Sara Schwager for a very thorough copy edit, and Josh Pasternak for his invaluable help in the early stages.

My two webmasters: Darren Turpin and Paul Raven.

Janet Barrett, headmistress of Oak Lodge Primary School, and all my colleagues and parent librarians for their continuing interest and support.

And last—though by no means least—my husband, Michael, for . . . well . . . everything!

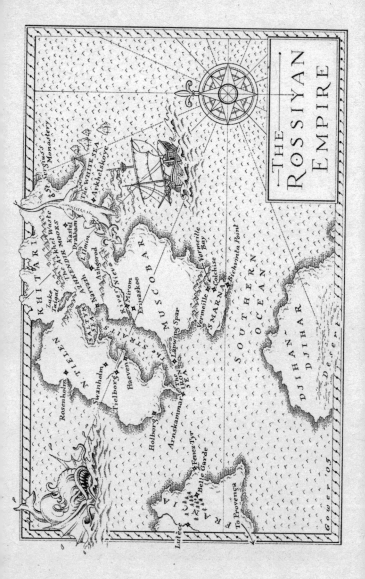

Foreword

In the secret history of the conflict between Tielen and Francia (as described in the Tears of Artamon) the mischief created by Francian agents Celestine de Joyeuse and Jagu de Rustéphan threatens to bring down an empire. *Flight into Darkness* recounts those events—but from the perspective of the Francian "enemy"—and reveals the hitherto untold story of what ensues in the turbulent months after the conclusion of *Children of the Serpent Gate*.

Prologue

SEVEN, THEY WERE SEVEN,
THE DARK ANGELS OF DESTRUCTION

Sardion, Arkhan of Enhirre, stared up at the watch fires burning on the battlements of the ancient fortress of Ondhessar. For centuries it had towered over the desert, his country's strongest bastion against invaders, concealing a priceless treasure in its vaults: the shrine dedicated to Azilis, the Eternal Singer. For centuries it had been his family's sacred duty to protect the sacred Lodestar that housed her spirit, aided by the secret sect of the magi of Ondhessar, his Emissaries.

But he had failed. After a bitter and bloody siege in which many of his magi had fallen, the Francian Commanderie had seized the fortress. His first attempt to take back Ondhessar had cost him dear; his beloved eldest son, Alarion, had died in the conflict and the Francians had beaten back his forces. The next attempt to take back the fortress, by stealth and magic, would have succeeded, had it not been for the untimely arrival of the Allegondan Commanderie, the Rosecoeurs. And now the hated banner of the rose fluttered from every turret of the fortress.

He had sent a mage-assassin to exact his revenge against the Francian royal family. First the Crown Prince, Aubrey, had died—and then his father, King Gobain. But it was not enough, not nearly enough to sate the grief or the emptiness in his soul.

A dry, cold wind suddenly gusted across the desert and the Arkhan pulled his burnous up to cover his nose and mouth as granules of choking sand swirled into the night air.

"I must take Ondhessar back," he murmured to the stars, "by whatever means I can, no matter how high the cost." His generals had failed him. Even his magi had failed him.

"My lord Arkhan? You have a visitor. A most . . . unexpected visitor."

Sardion turned, startled out of his dreams of revenge, to see Lord Estael, the commander of his few surviving magi, standing behind him.

"Who is it?"

"Lord Volkh Nagarian. The Drakhaon of Azhkendir."

So the legends are true, Estael thought, as he gazed at the Arkhan's unexpected guest.

Lord Volkh was tall, broad-shouldered, his black hair and beard sprinkled with the first threads of silver. Yet it was the darkness of his aura that compelled Estael's attention; the instant the stranger entered the Arkhan's audience chamber, the elder magus felt a shiver of warning.

We're in the presence of a powerful and ancient daemon. Is this why Sardion asked me to stay? To protect him? I fear my powers are no match for the creature of darkness that has concealed itself within this man.

"This is an unexpected honor, Lord Drakhaon," Sardion said guardedly.

"I've traveled a long way to see you, Lord Arkhan." The Drakhaon turned to stare at Estael and Estael saw that the Drakhaon's eyes were piercingly, luminously blue. Unlike the magi of Ondhessar, Lord Volkh did not hide the evidence of his daemon blood behind thick spectacle lenses. "This is a matter of the utmost confidentiality; I'd prefer it if we could talk in private."

"This is Estael, the eldest of the magi of Ondhessar; he has knowledge that may be of use to you."

"If he stays, then Bogatyr Kostya stays too." Behind the Drakhaon stood a single retainer, scarred arms folded, his iron-grey hair braided, Azhkendi-style. He had been obliged to hand over his weapons before being admitted to the Arkhan's presence, but his aggressive, menacing stance was enough to instill respect as he moved closer to his master, glaring suspiciously at Estael.

"What brings you so far from Azhkendir?" Sardion gestured to Lord Volkh to sit opposite him.

"I want to be-rid of the Drakhaoul."

"To be rid of it?" Sardion repeated and Estael heard the astonishment in his voice. "You inherited the powers of a Drakhaoul—and you want to be rid of it?"

"Have you no idea what it means to use these daemonic powers?" Lord Volkh cried. "Or what becomes of a mortal man's body when it is forced to host a Drakhaoul? Look at me. Look more closely." He lifted his hands to reveal sharp talons where the nails should have been, each one a dark cobalt. "And my hair." In the muted light filtering from behind the linen blinds drawn to shade the chamber from the fierce sun, Estael could just make out now that the Drakhaon's hair was more dark blue than black.

"Surely a small price to pay?" Sardion seemed unimpressed. "I heard that you defeated Stavyomir Arkhel's men and laid waste to his lands single-handed."

"This is merely the outward manifestation of its presence." Lord Volkh's voice grew so quiet that Estael had to lean forward to catch his words. "There is a legend in my country. It tells of the Drakhaoul's Brides, young women who were given to my ancestors . . . and were never seen alive again. It is no legend. Using the Drakhaoul's powers takes a terrible toll on a mortal body. It creates a terrible hunger that can only be assuaged by . . ." The Drakhaon's powerful voice dropped to a hoarse whisper. "By drinking fresh human blood."

So those hooked talons had torn innocent flesh . . .

"The priests of Nagazdiel summoned the Drakhaouls by blood sacrifice," Estael said. "The only way to bring a daemon into our world from the Realm of Shadows is to dispatch another soul to take its place."

Lord Volkh turned to him, and his eyes burned so piercingly blue that Estael could not hold his gaze and looked swiftly away. "How do you know all this, Magus?"

"It's one of the Seven Arcane Secrets of Ondhessar that have been handed down from one elder magus to another since our order was founded."

"I don't suppose that such knowledge would have helped my father." Lord Volkh no longer gazed at Estael but through him at some far-distant point. "The hunger eventually drives us mad. He grew so desperate that he abandoned me and my mother and sailed far into unchartered waters, searching for the lost island of Ty Nagar."

"Estael, have you ever heard of this Ty Nagar?" The Arkhan asked the question idly enough, but Estael, who knew his master well, sensed that he was taking far too keen an interest in the matter.

"Is that where the portal to the Realm of Shadows is said to be?" Estael said guardedly. "The place known as the Serpent Gate?"

Lord Volkh gave a brusque nod. "My father's last wish was to send the Drakhaoul back to the Realm of Shadows and end the curse on our family. But he died, far from home, before he could fulfill his quest and the Drakhaoul returned, passing the curse on to me. The truth is, Lord Arkhan, that I don't know how much longer I can endure this burden."

Estael heard the weary desperation in Lord Volkh's deep voice. It must have taken a great deal of courage for such a proud warlord to bare his soul to two strangers.

"And why, my lord, do you believe that I can help you?" asked Sardion.

"I've spent many years researching the history of the Drakhaouls"—Lord Volkh turned his burning blue gaze on Sardion—"and I discovered that your ancestors, Lord Arkhan, were once priests of Nagazdiel, the prince of the Drakhaouls. I believe that you and your magi may possess the lost knowledge that I'm seeking."

Estael realized that both men were staring expectantly at him. As elder magus, he had guarded the secrets of the Rift that lay hidden below Ondhessar for many years and he was not prepared to reveal them so freely to a stranger.

"It was the priests of Nagazdiel who first brought the Drakhaouls from the Realm of Shadows through the Serpent Gate to serve the sons of the Emperor Artamon," continued Lord Volkh. "So you must know of a way to send the Drakhaoul back."

"What other means have you tried, my lord? Exorcism?"

Lord Volkh let out a bitter laugh. "Oh, the monks at Saint Sergius's Monastery tried—to their cost. It was far too powerful for them."

"And what will become of this Drakhaoul, Lord Volkh, when you die?" The Arkhan's question sounded innocent enough, but Estael, to his alarm, detected an underlying hint of interest.

"It will seek out my son, Gavril. It attaches itself only to the male bloodline. I'd do anything to save my son from inheriting this curse. Gavril is a gentle, artistic boy who's studying to be a painter." To Estael's surprise, a sad, almost wistful look entered Lord Volkh's blue eyes. "He knows nothing of me . . . or the Drakhaoul."

"And if you had no son?"

Bogatyr Kostya, who had stood listening, as still and silent as a statue, unfolded his scarred arms and took a step forward.

"Is that a threat, Lord Arkhan?" He stared challengingly at Sardion.

"Stand down, Kostya," Lord Volkh growled, as if addressing a disobedient mastiff.

"Join with me, Lord Volkh," said Sardion suddenly. "Help me drive the Allegondans out of my lands. Lend me your powers."

Lord Volkh's fist came down on the table like a thunderclap, making Estael jump. "Have you any idea what you're asking?" In the uncomfortable silence that followed, Estael saw his master's gaze harden. Sardion's moods were unpredictable and Estael inwardly prayed that the Arkhan would not provoke the Drakhaon into transforming into his Drakhaoul-form. But then, to Estael's surprise, the blue fire faded from Lord Volkh's eyes and his expression became distant, almost sad. "I had hoped that you would understand, Lord Arkhan. But I see I was mistaken."

"All I know," volunteered Estael bravely, "is that the Serpent Gate was sealed by Saint Sergius and the key to opening it, the fabled ruby known as Nagar's Eye, was divided up centuries ago by Artamon's sons. Even if we discovered where Ty Nagar lies, Lord Volkh, there is no way to reopen the Gate—unless the divided shards of ruby could somehow be found and reunited . . ."

Lord Volkh let out a harsh sigh. "So even you are unable to help me."

"I fear you have had a wasted journey, my lord." Sardion smiled, yet there was no warmth in his expression. "But please stay with us tonight and let us entertain you. The sun will soon be setting and the desert nights are cold."

"I'll not prevail upon your hospitality any longer." Lord Volkh rose abruptly. "Come, Kostya."

Estael still sat at the table, unable to move. He realized that his hands were shaking. So even without revealing the daemon sleeping within him, the Drakhaon could induce this deep, visceral fear in everyone he encountered.

"He possesses the power of the last of the Seven," he heard Sardion mutter, "and he wants to be rid of it?"

A sudden burst of daemonic energy rippled through the air. Heart thudding with apprehension, Estael got up, knocking over his chair, and ran out onto the balcony. Surely Lord Volkh would not attack the palace?

"What is it, Estael?" Sardion cried, following him.

"My lord, look. *Look up!*"

Darker than the night itself, a great dragon wheeled overhead, the glittering scales on its body shedding a fine trail, like powdered stardust. As it winged away, Estael saw it gaze back down at them, and he recognized the proud, bitter look in its moon-blue, slanting eyes.

"Volkh is a fool." Sardion was still muttering under his breath as he followed the Drakhaon's flight across the moonlit desert until the dragon could no longer be seen against the stars. "He could rule the quadrant." The Arkhan swung round and gripped Estael by the shoulder. "Do you give me your word never to reveal anything of what I'm going to show you? On pain of death?"

Estael saw the crazed gleam in Sardion's eyes and knew that it would be madness to refuse his master's request.

"Follow me, Estael."

"Sentient stone?" Estael murmured, watching as the Arkhan made a cut with his dagger in his palm and smeared a little of his blood on the wall. A hidden carving appeared, sigils and the arcane hieroglyphs of Ancient Enhirran. So the hidden door could only be opened by a drop of the Arkhan's blood.

"Now you. Or else the chamber will never let you out again. And you wouldn't want to end your days walled in belowground, would you?"

Estael silently offered his palm to the Arkhan's blade and let a drop or two of his blood trickle down the dark, worn stone. A grinding, groaning noise began and a small doorway opened. Sardion led the way, the magus following down the dark passageway until they came to a second door, where the same blood ritual was repeated.

The chamber beyond was lined in black marble: Even in lanternlight, the atmosphere was somber and stifling.

"My father first brought me down here when I was eight," said Sardion. "I was terrified. I thought it was a tomb. I imagined there would be dead bodies."

Estael was gazing around him. "No bodies . . . but there are carvings in an ancient script." He began to translate. " 'Seven, they were Seven, the Dark Angels of Destruction.' " He broke off. "What is this place?"

"It's a shrine to Nagazdiel, the Prince of the Realm of Shadows," said Sardion. He drew aside a curtain that concealed a mosaic portraying a winged man, fashioned from chips of obsidian, garnet, and ruby. "The most powerful of the Drakhaouls."

"And this door?" Estael began to feel apprehensive. What was the Arkhan's true motive in revealing these ancient secrets to him?

"It leads into the Rift. My ancestors believed that it also led to the Realm of Shadows. And that anyone who could find his way into the Shadows could summon Nagazdiel to do his bidding."

"Did any of your ancestors ever attempt such a rash act?"

"We cannot enter the Rift. Those who tried, perished. In agony. Only those with mage blood can survive in the unstable atmosphere of the Rift." Sardion gazed pointedly at Estael.

"You don't mean *me*, Lord Arkhan?" Estael stared back at him, aghast. "Surely one of the younger Emissaries would be a better choice . . ."

"Rieuk Mordiern, then. He's the most powerful of you all."

"Rieuk is still recovering from his injuries. But I beg you to reconsider. If you set Nagazdiel free, can you be sure that such a powerful Drakhaoul would obey you? After all, he—"

"Are you daring to suggest that I am not as strong as Lord Nagarian? That I'm not capable of controlling a daemon from the Realm of Shadows?"

"No, Lord Arkhan, but I was reminding you that the Drakhaoul of Azhkendir was merely one of Nagazdiel's warriors. Nagazdiel himself—"

Sardion quelled his objections with a single look. "Test this doorway for me, Estael."

Estael steeled himself and passed through the doorway. If the Arkhan was wrong, he would suffocate in the unstable atmosphere. Veil upon veil of shadows parted, like gauzy spiderwebs, as he reluctantly moved forward, not wanting to leave the safety of the doorway. As his eyes became accustomed to the gloom, he saw a dreary wasteland stretching away into the far distance. Everything was the color of dust. From time to time a chill wind gusted across the emptiness but otherwise nothing stirred.

"What a terrible place," Estael murmured aloud.

And then he sensed it. A mighty power, darker than a stormcloud, was approaching. He shrank back. His sole instinct was to flee, to get away before it discovered him. Two stars had appeared in the dun light, crimson as fire. No, not stars—eyes, slanted, cruel eyes. And they were coming toward him, bearing down on him, relentless and swift. Estael turned to run back toward the doorway.

"*What are you doing here, Magus?*" The voice pierced him like an icy spear. Trembling, Estael dropped to his knees. "*Have you come to set me free?*"

Estael dared to look up. The Drakhaoul towered over him, its crimson eyes burning into him, reading him to the most secret recesses of his soul. Its powerful body was sheathed in scales of black jet that shimmered in the dull light. A mane of charcoal-black hair streamed down its back.

"*You're not strong enough to host me, old man,*" it said scornfully. Estael felt its hold over him relax and he fell forward into the dust. And as it strode away into the darkness, he heard it murmur, "*Am I never to escape?*"

PART I

CHAPTER 1

Rieuk Mordiern's damaged eye leaked a constant trickle of black blood that ran down his cheek, searing his skin as if laced with acid. And the young magus's good eye leaked salty fluid, as if weeping in sympathy with its ruined twin. He could see little more than a blur of images. Sunlight was a torment, making him seek the shadows.

And scored across his mind's vision was the blinding image of Azilis, her beautiful face superimposed over Celestine's, distorted with rage and loss. He could still hear her cry, harsh enough to lacerate his ears.

"*What children would keep their mother imprisoned against her will?*"

In his delirium, he relived again and again the moment when Azilis had attacked him, half-blinding him with a single burst of aethyrial energy, whiter than lightning.

I failed. I found Azilis, and she rejected me. After all these years of searching for her. The feeling of failure was almost as painful as the physical mutilation she had inflicted upon him. For many centuries, Azilis's spirit had kept the balance between the mortal world and the Ways Beyond. But since, as an inexperienced apprentice, he had inadvertently set her free, not knowing who or what she was, the boundaries between the two had begun to break down. And after that his life had become an arduous, unsuccessful quest to bring her back. Bound to protect Celestine de Joyeuse, Azilis seemed to have forgotten her role as the guardian of the gateway between life and death.

* * *

"Rieuk, I'm cold . . . "

Rieuk slowly turns around. There, in the gloom behind him, stands Imri . . . or a semblance of Imri, his black hair loose about his shoulders, his face half-veiled in shadow.

"Imri? Is it really you?" He has longed to see him so much . . . yet this feels terribly wrong. "What have they done to you?" Even as he reaches out to the revenant, it begins to fade, leaving him clutching empty air.

As Rieuk burned in fever, he sometimes thought he caught the distant sound of music in the night. Someone was pensively plucking old, sad melodies on an aludh or a dombra, each note falling on Rieuk's consciousness like a drop of cooling rain. Once he called out, "Who's there?" and the music ceased. Perhaps it was a dream . . .

Someone was gently sponging his damaged face with a soft, damp cloth. It felt unexpectedly, blissfully soothing, as if the water contained some healing balm that was drawing out the infection and lowering his fever.

A shadowy form was bending low over him, turning away from time to time to rinse out the cloth. Rieuk tried to focus with his one good eye to identify who was tending him. A subtle scent arose from the water: cleansing and refreshing, reminding Rieuk of the astringent smell of cucumbers and watercress.

"Where . . . am I?" Rieuk managed to whisper.

"You're awake!" The voice, a young man's, was soft and dark-toned, slightly spiced with a trace of a foreign accent; familiar, yet Rieuk could not identify the speaker. "I must tell Aqil."

"Wait." Rieuk heard his own voice, hoarse and urgent, as if from far away. He reached out blindly, catching hold of his carer's robe, pulling him closer.

"Don't you recognize me, Emissary Mordiern?" The blur loomed closer until Rieuk could make out a bespectacled face gazing curiously into his. Dark olive skin, framed by long, curling locks of crow-black hair, one side braided with crimson thread, Djihari-fashion. The young man removed his spectacles and Rieuk caught the unmistakable glimmer of mage eyes, liquid obsidian, flecked with the scarlet veins of the earth's fires. "I'm Oranir."

"But you were just a boy when we last . . ." How long had he been sick?

"I'm nearly eighteen," Oranir said stiffly, with the slightest hint of offended pride. "Old enough to become an Emissary."

The age I was when I first met Imri. Only then did the realization strike him—that he was almost double Oranir's age and had spent most of the young mage's lifetime traveling alone, forced to act as the Arkhan's Emissary, to protect dead Imri's immortal soul.

"Let me see my face." His fingertips tentatively moved upward over his right cheekbone. Oranir hesitated. "*Show me.*" The skin felt puckered and tender; even touching it made Rieuk squeamish. He had to see for himself. He had to know the worst. Teeth gritted with the effort of pushing himself up from the pillows, he took the little round mirror Oranir gave him and forced himself to look at his reflection.

They had skillfully sewn the eyelids together to cover the void behind, leaving a jagged scar where his eye had been. The burned skin was still an angry shade of red.

"Magister Aqil says that the scarring will slowly fade, but never disappear." Oranir spoke without expression.

"My eye . . ." The words came out in a whispered sob; Rieuk had known that his sight was impaired, but not until that moment just how serious the wound had been.

"Magister Aqil tried to save it. But it had become infected and the infection was poisoning your body. If he hadn't operated, you would have died."

Rieuk said nothing. The knowledge that he was disfigured and half blind was difficult enough to assimilate, but there was another, deeper concern.

If one eye is gone, then have half my mage powers gone too?

"Ormas?" Rieuk called to his shadow hawk. Ormas had fallen into a deep trance after Azilis's attack and Rieuk had begun to fear that he would never recover.

"*Master . . . ?*" For the first time in many weeks he heard a faint answer to his call. His heart swelled with fresh hope.

"How is it with you, Ormas?" His voice shook. Ormas had been his only companion in his long years of wandering, and the last weeks of silence had proved almost too great a burden to endure.

"*I'm sorry, Master. I failed you.*"

Rieuk placed one hand over his breast where Ormas's image was tattooed, seeking for the beating of the hawk's heart. "Let there be no talk of failure." There it was, a thrumming, weak but steady—a confirmation of Ormas's presence. "*She* was too strong for us."

He felt a sudden convulsive shiver within his body and Ormas emerged, fluttering down to perch on his outstretched arm. The smoke hawk lowered his head, swiveling it to one side to regard him with one bright amber eye. But Rieuk saw with shame that Ormas's other eye was burned away. His beautiful Emissary was maimed and half-blind too.

Rieuk woke in the night to the sound of music—the same sweet, plaintive air he had heard before in his fevered dreams, plucked from the darkly deep, resonant strings of an aludh. He sat up. The dry, sweet scent of the desert night perfumed the air. His turret room was silvered with fragile moonlight; out on the balcony he could see a man seated, his back against the parapet wall, his head tilted to one side as he leaned over the instrument, placing each note with infinite care.

Rieuk swung his legs over the side of the bed and attempted a few shaky steps toward him. The player stopped and looked around. It was Oranir.

"Don't stop."

"I'm not very good." Was there a hint of a blush in Oranir's words?

"It sounded fine to my ears." Rieuk reached the balcony and eased himself down to sit beside Oranir. "I've heard you playing that song before, haven't I?"

"I didn't mean to disturb you."

"So it was you." Rieuk was touched. "You were watching over me while I was ill."

Oranir laid the aludh down. "I—I've been watching over you for a long time." He turned suddenly to Rieuk. "Make me your apprentice. Please, Magister." His voice was low and urgent. "I'll do anything you want. Anything. I'll—"

"Stop. You don't want to get involved with me." Rieuk pushed Oranir away, holding him at arm's length. "I'm an assassin. I've blood on my hands."

"Do you think I'm not aware of that?" Oranir's eyes burned into his. "I'm not a child. Why don't you let me make up my own mind? Or do you think I'm not worthy?"

"I'm bad luck, Oranir." Rieuk forced a laugh. "I seem to bring misfortune on all those I care about. Why do you think I've worked alone for all these years?"

"It's him, isn't it? You're still in thrall to your dead master, Imri Boldiszar. He must have been a remarkable man for you still to be in love with him after so many years."

"Imri?" Rieuk's hands dropped to his sides. He tried to speak and found that the words were choked in his throat.

"I heard you calling his name when you were feverish."

"I was dreaming about him, that was all . . . Wait!" But Oranir got to his feet and pushed past him, hurrying away before Rieuk could stop him.

I've been watching over you for a long time. Had there been an unspoken confession in Oranir's words? There was no denying the fact that Rieuk felt attracted to the young magus. If he had not checked Oranir then, there was no telling where things might have led.

Rieuk drew in a shuddering breath. *So many years.* Of course it seemed an eternity to Oranir; Imri had died before he was born. Rieuk gazed up at the blue brilliance of the stars overhead.

"I have to move on. And I can't move on unless I know that you're at peace, Imri," he said softly to the night. *I've been alone too long.*

"I've altered the lenses in your spectacles to improve the acuity of your remaining eye." Aqil leaned forward to adjust the fit and Rieuk tried his best not to shy away. He still could not bear anyone's touching his face. His instincts had become so sensitive since he was injured that even the slightest movement close by made him flinch.

"Is there nothing else you can do?" He had lain awake night after night, unable to sleep for the constant pain, obsessed with one thought: *Surely the Magi of Ondhessar will be able to heal me.* Yet not until now had he dared to ask the question. Perhaps he didn't want to know the answer. Perhaps he didn't want the dream that had first brought him to Ondhessar at seventeen to be shattered.

"We did what we could. But by the time you reached us, it was too late," Aqil said bluntly. "The infection was so advanced that it was all I could do to save your life."

Rieuk gazed at his reflection. It was a face to frighten children. The spectacles did nothing to hide the scar. If anything they made it look more grotesque.

"What's the point?" he said aloud, tearing them off and hurling them to the floor. "Wearing a blank lens on the right side, when everyone can see that I'm disfigured?" He sat down on the bed and covered his face in his hands. He was shaking with rage. Why had he been so confident that Aqil could restore his sight?

He heard someone enter the room and raised his head to see Oranir picking up his discarded spectacles. He turned his face away, not wanting Oranir to know how volatile his feelings were. Oranir came closer, holding out the spectacles.

Rieuk pushed his hand away. "It won't make any difference. I'm disfigured. Damaged goods."

"Do you think you're the only one who's damaged?" Oranir's voice burned, low and furious. "What gives you the right to tell *me* how it feels?" He tore open his loose shirt, baring his lean upper body. Beneath the dark, delicate-feathered tattoo of his Emissary, Zophas, Rieuk saw the seams of old scars marring the smooth sheen of his olive skin.

"Turn around," Rieuk ordered.

Mutely, Oranir obeyed. More scars, like serrated stripes, were flayed into his back.

"Who did this to you?" The words caught at the back of Rieuk's throat.

Still Oranir said nothing. But his defiant stance, the stiffness of his shoulders, the shoulder blades, told Rieuk more than any explanation.

Before Rieuk was fully aware of what he was doing, he had reached out and drifted his fingertips down Oranir's back, parting the long locks of glossy black hair to trace the seamed skin. He half expected Oranir to flinch at his touch, to strike his hand away. But Oranir just stood there unmoving.

"The mage blood is a hard burden to be born with." Rieuk was still angry, but no longer just at his own disfigurement. He could not bear to think that Oranir had suffered so much pain and rejection when he was a child. Yet as his fingertips grazed Oranir's skin, he felt a slow, dark heat begin to burn within him.

What was he doing? His hand had come to a halt over the small of Oranir's back. What was this feeling? It was as fierce and intense as anger, and it had come to him as swiftly. But it was not anger. It was desire. And, unlike anger, he was not so sure that he could control it. Or even that he wanted to.

"Rieuk." Oranir turned to gaze at him, his face so much closer, a look at once vulnerable yet provocative smoldering in his eyes. So close that if Rieuk exerted the slightest pressure through the hand that rested on Oranir's back, their bodies would touch and their mouths would meet. Even as an ache of longing swept through him, Rieuk let his hand drop away and took a step back. This was all happening too quickly. His body had reacted before his mind had had time to assess the risks involved.

"Rieuk," said Oranir again, his voice low, urgent. "*Rieuk . . .* " It was as if he were conjuring a spell of binding, saying his name hypnotically again and again, and Rieuk could feel his willpower weakening.

"No," he heard himself saying. Another step back. *I can't do this to him. Or to myself. I can't afford to get involved with anyone again. Especially someone as vulnerable as Oranir . . .* He could see the look of blank incomprehension in Oranir's eyes. "I—I'm sorry, Oranir. Forgive me." And he turned and fled.

CHAPTER 2

"So you're up and about at last, Rieuk." Lord Estael nodded to him absently. He seemed preoccupied, scarcely glancing up from the ancient document he was studying. "You're stronger than you look; we feared at first that you might be past saving."

"But my right eye is gone. I'm half-blind." Rieuk leaned on Estael's desk. "Tell me the truth, my lord. Does this mean that I've lost half my powers as well?"

"The eyes are merely the outward manifestation of a magus's gifts." Estael gazed calmly back at him. "I have no way of telling if your innate powers have been affected as well. It seems, though, that you're well enough to resume your duties as the Arkhan's Emissary."

Rieuk drew back. That was not what he wanted to hear at all. "What use am I to the Arkhan in this condition?" The thought of having to carry out any more of Sardion's missions sickened him.

"He still has Imri's soul glass," said Estael bluntly. "How much do you care about saving Imri's immortal soul?"

Rieuk brought his fist crashing down on Estael's desk. "How can you let that madman take control of such a precious thing? Your own apprentice's soul? Don't you care about anything anymore, Lord Estael?"

Estael shrugged. "He is the Arkhan."

"Perhaps he's been Arkhan too long," said Rieuk darkly.

"Treasonable words, Rieuk." Estael's head was bent over the manuscript again. "It's lucky for you that only I heard them."

"I'd hoped for more from you, my lord." Rieuk could see

that Estael was not prepared to give him even the slightest support. As he left Estael's study, he knew that he would have to act alone. "I'm coming to pay you a visit, Lord Arkhan," he said under his breath. "But not quite in the way that you're expecting."

Rieuk, his face half-concealed by his burnous, settled himself in the shade of a tamarind tree outside the palace walls. Ormas perched on his forearm. In the merciless brightness of the late-afternoon sun, the smoke hawk's form was so faint as to be almost invisible, as though sketched on the burning air.

"Ormas, be careful," Rieuk murmured. "You'll have to penetrate the most secret places of the palace, where only the Arkhan himself goes. There may be traps or wards. The only thing that's certain is that Imri's soul glass is locked away somewhere obscure, where he thinks I'll never be able to find it."

"I'll do my best, Master."

It was perilous to be employing the very methods he'd used to carry out Sardion's missions on his royal master. But as he leaned back against the tree trunk, concentrating on seeing through Ormas's one good eye, he didn't care any longer. Deep within his heart he knew that he was doing something that he should have dared a long time ago.

Ormas fluttered from one palace window to the next. Ornate grilles and thick gauzes protected the rooms inside from the worst of the day's heat but were difficult to see through. Through Ormas, Rieuk caught glimpses of the daily life of Sardion's servants: thickset guards slowly patrolling the corridors; secretaries toiling with ink and paper; veiled women carrying trays of food.

"Go farther in," Rieuk ordered. Ormas skimmed over the inner courtyards, where the Arkhys sat in a shady summerhouse, drinking mint tea with her ladies-in-waiting, and darted into the inner palace. As Ormas flitted onward from room to room, Rieuk recognized the Arkhan's private apartments from the gilded decorations on the walls: a motif of lotus flowers and palm leaves. Soon Rieuk saw the Arkhan conferring with his ministers. As Ormas silently passed overhead, Sardion glanced upward as though he had sensed the hawk's presence, but Ormas continued onward. Rieuk saw the Arkhan's bedchamber—an austerely furnished room, dominated by a portrait of his dead son, Prince Alarion. Then Ormas penetrated the Arkhan's library, going from shelf to shelf of exquisite leather-bound volumes, all tooled in silver and gold.

"*There's nothing here, Master.*"

"Search again." Rieuk was growing more agitated with every room that Ormas passed through. There had to be a concealed door somewhere close by, a secret place known only to the Arkhan. But if Sardion had spotted the winged intruder, it could only be a short while before Ormas was discovered.

Ormas suddenly flew out through a shuttered window and hovered outside before returning to the library. "*Do you see it, Master? The extra window outside? There must be a door behind these shelves.*" Ormas launched himself at the wall of books and emerged in a dark little room beyond. Inside was a desk covered with maps; Rieuk recognized, even in the dim light, that they were detailed plans of Ondhessar. Was Sardion planning another assault on the fortress to win back Azilis's shrine from the Commanderie? But Ormas had perched on top of an ebony cabinet, inlaid with ivory, tortoiseshell, and gold. Rieuk tensed, his whole body rigid with concentration.

"Can you see inside, Ormas?"

The interior of the cabinet was dark as shadow, yet as the hawk's keen eye scanned the shelves, something glimmered dully in the gloom. A glass of aethyr crystal, fashioned in the shape of a lotus.

A soul glass.

And it was empty.

Rieuk left the shade of the tamarind and strode swiftly to the palace gate. The guards, stirring from their late-afternoon torpor, barred his way with their spears.

"Emissary Mordiern," Rieuk said, showing them his signet ring; the Arkhan had given rings to all his Emissaries, granting them access to the palace. And then, when the guard hesitated, he pulled off his burnous, revealing his damaged face.

The guard waved his hand and the sentries uncrossed their spears. Rieuk hurried through. The faster he moved, the less likely he was to be caught. Nevertheless he pulled out the little pouch he had concealed in his pocket, ready to disable anyone who tried to stop him. Granules of sleep-dust lay inside—a potent and fast-working narcotic drug. And he would use them, even on the Arkhan himself if need be. In the somnolent heat of late afternoon, most of the courtiers and servants were resting, and those Rieuk passed moved listlessly about their tasks.

Following Ormas's trail, he crossed the first of the inner courtyards, where only the refreshing trickle of the ornamental fountains could be heard. Entering the Arkhan's apartments, he made directly for the library. He pressed spine after spine along the book-lined wall, certain that one would prove to be the trigger to open the hidden door. The air in the library was hot and dustily dry, and his probing fingers were soon sticky with sweat. Any moment he could be discovered. At last he spotted the fake volumes and fumbled to find the catch; with a creak, the concealed door swung inward and Rieuk went in.

Ormas fluttered down from his perch on the cabinet.

Rieuk hesitated, then he forced the cabinet door open. His fingers closed around the lotus glass. He lifted it close to his left eye to examine it. Even in the shuttered darkness he could see that it was empty; a mortal soul would have given off a faint iridescent shimmer.

"What are you doing in my private study, Emissary Mordiern?" The Arkhan stood in the doorway. "No one is allowed in here. Not even my secretary."

Rieuk didn't care. He only knew that the Arkhan had betrayed him.

"Tell me, my lord, that Imri's soul is safe." Rieuk heard his own voice, low, trembling, on the verge of breaking.

"Guards! Help!"

The guards came running at their master's call; Rieuk flung a fistful of sleepdust toward them and one by one they crumpled to the floor, unconscious.

"This is treason." Sardion showed no sign of fear. "How dare you threaten your lord and master? You know what the punishment is for disobeying me? Your Emissary will be stripped from your body, one feather at a time, you will die screaming in agony—"

Rieuk wasn't listening to Sardion's threats. He came close to the Arkhan, staring unafraid into his chill eyes. "I've been your loyal servant, my lord, for many years. I've taken lives because you ordered me to, and all to preserve Imri's soul. And now I find I've been played for a fool! How long has this deception been going on?"

Sardion had stood his ground while Rieuk poured out his fury. He took a step back, only a small step, but Rieuk sensed that the Arkhan was genuinely alarmed. He came closer still, knowing that he risked death for such an offense, yet no longer caring as long as he could die knowing the truth. He drew in a slow, jagged breath. "I'm waiting to hear, my lord."

Sardion swallowed, almost imperceptibly, but Rieuk saw his throat muscles move. "Has it ever occurred to you that your quarrel might be with your fellow magi and not with me?"

"Please don't forget, my lord, that I've already caused the death of one king."

"Are you threatening me?" A little smile twisted Sardion's lips.

Rieuk had heard enough of the Arkhan's diversionary tactics. He held the empty soul glass up in front of Sardion's cold blue eyes. "Tell me that this glass is a fake and the real one is still kept safe elsewhere."

"Is that what you want to hear?"

"When did it happen? Tell me!"

"When the Rift began to fail, Lord Estael came to me. He begged me to release Imri's soul. You were far away in Francia at the time—"

"No." Rieuk's fingers closed around the empty glass, clutching it to his heart. "No . . . " The word escaped his lips, more a moan of pain than a gesture of denial. He had stolen souls. Was this his punishment—to undergo the same suffering he had inflicted upon Celestine de Joyeuse and Jagu de Rustéphan?

The rage that he had long held suppressed began to surge up within him, a dark, bitter fury.

You deceived me. He felt his whole body begin to tremble with the effort of controlling it. *You used me.* But it would not be controlled. It was a raw volcanic force. It spoke to the living earth deep below out of which rock and crystal were formed, it drew on ancient energies long buried and untapped since the making of the world.

The marble floor of the palace began to shiver beneath his feet. From far beyond the cloud of anger that enveloped him, he heard shrieks and cries of fear as the ground shook. He saw the Arkhan grasp at his desk to keep himself upright.

"*Master, no!*" Ormas's voice penetrated the turmoil in his brain. "*Don't do this. Don't destroy any more lives.*"

As if from a great way off, Rieuk found himself looking down at Sardion, who had crawled beneath his desk to protect himself from the shaking of the earth. The powerful Arkhan cowered, his hands clasped over his head.

Why have I been in awe of this man for so long? Why have I let him control my life?

"I should have you tortured for this," cried Sardion, "but it seems to me that no excruciation my torturers could inflict on your body could touch you as deeply as the pain you are suffering now."

"Where is Imri?" Rieuk thrust the empty soul glass in Lord Estael's face. "This glass is empty. *Where is he?*"

Lord Estael made a sudden move but Rieuk grabbed his wrist, yanking his arm up behind his back so that he could not perform a conjuration.

"Almiras!" Estael cried to his Emissary. But Rieuk had been expecting this and clicked his fingers to summon

Ormas. As Almiras emerged from Lord Estael's body, Ormas darted out, beating him back with an unstoppable fury.

"Take me into the Rift," Rieuk said into Lord Estael's ear. The shadow hawks dived and dodged in the air, Ormas deftly keeping Almiras at bay. "I want proof. No matter how painful, I want the truth."

Rieuk instantly sensed the change in the air of the Rift. It had always been so still and calm, a place of verdant stillness, except for the breeze stirring the boughs of the eternal trees. But now he could feel the gusting of an erratic, dust-dry wind, that seemed to blow from some desolate pit of hell. The faint vanilla-sweet scent emanating from the haoma trees had gone. The boughs overhead were ragged, as though the mean wind had torn through, shredding leaves and scattering green needles all around. Even the light from the emerald moon was so faint that when Rieuk raised his head, he saw that it was waning, veiled in tattered clouds. A sense of disquiet had replaced the soothing calm, fueled by the sinister gusting of the errant wind, as though a thunderstorm were brewing.

"You've stolen souls, Rieuk. You know what becomes of the physical body once the two are separated for too long . . . or the soul glass is shattered. Did it never occur to you that even a mage's soul could not be preserved intact all this time?"

"But we are magi. And we are bonded with our Emissaries. You told me—" Rieuk made an effort to control himself. Estael despised any display of weakness; he must not break down or he would lose his advantage. "You told me that we are different. You told me that Tabris was protecting Imri's soul. You *lied*."

"Yes, I lied." Lord Estael's voice was dry, emotionless. "It happened when the Rift became unstable. Tabris began to weaken and fade. You were far away, in Francia. I did what I could to restore Imri to his body. But it was too late, and I lost him."

"Lost him?" Rieuk repeated, saying the words aloud but not understanding them. "You *lost* Imri's soul?"

"Tabris fled deep into the Ways Beyond, leaving Imri's soul unprotected. If the Rift had stayed stable, then maybe we could have brought Imri back." In the lurid light Lord Estael's features suddenly looked old and drawn. "But the atmosphere in the Rift has become more and more unstable as time passes. Azilis was the only one who could keep the balance—"

"Azilis. Always Azilis." Rieuk could not bear to be reminded of her—or the damage she had done to him. "So it's my fault, for not being powerful enough to bring her back?" He came close to Lord Estael. "Aren't we straying from the point here? You used me. You played on my love for Imri. You *manipulated* me."

Estael did not even flinch. "Have you forgotten the vow you took on the day you became an Emissary?"

"So when Imri's ghost came to me, it was not a trick of the Rift as you so callously told me." The memory sent shivers through Rieuk. *I'm cold, Rieuk,* the revenant had said to him. Imri had been crying out to him for help, and he had believed Estael's lie. "Enough!" Rieuk's patience was burned out. He didn't care what became of his own life any longer, he only wanted to fulfill his debt to Imri. And he was prepared to risk anything, even if it meant traveling into the Ways Beyond to find him. "Where is Imri's tomb?" Rieuk turned around in the darkness, aware that he had lost his bearings.

"In that glade."

Rieuk caught a crystalline glimmer in the turbulent air. Hurrying down the slope, leaving Lord Estael behind, he came to a sudden stop. The tomb, fashioned from aethyric crystal, looked as though it were encrusted with layers of ice. It was impossible to distinguish what lay within anymore . . . a mere suggestion, a shadow of a human form seen through hoarfrosted glass.

Rieuk could hear Lord Estael following him down the slope, breathing hard as if the air was too thin. If he didn't act instantly, Estael would try to stop him.

"Forgive me, Imri, but I have to know." Rieuk focused all his power on the crystal casket. *No one else can do this. I am the only crystal magus left in this world.*

"Rieuk, stop!"

He channeled the power in one single, concentrated wave. The tomb lit up, radiating a light of dazzling purity that filled the darkness, pulsing ever brighter, until the crystal split apart in a rain of icy shards.

"No!" cried Lord Estael, too late.

Rieuk stared as the fine mist of aethyric crystal slowly dispersed. There lay Imri's body, perfectly preserved by the aethyric crystal.

He couldn't help himself. Even though every instinct shrieked that he should hold back, he fell to his knees and reached into the open tomb. His fingers caressed the chill contours of the beloved face, the cold lips that had once awoken his nascent powers with a kiss. It was like touching a statue fashioned out of ice.

And the instant his fingertips made contact, Imri's body began to disintegrate, vanishing so swiftly before his horrified gaze that even as he blinked away involuntary tears, there was nothing left but dust.

A barren wind shivered through the trees.

"What have you done, you fool? What hope is there to restore him, now that his body is destroyed!"

"Hope?" Rieuk rounded on Estael. "How can there be any possibility of hope left when his soul is gone?" His voice burned with rage and despair. That one last glimpse had broken him. "From the moment Tabris vanished, Imri was lost to us."

"Have you never heard of the Spirit Singers of Azhkendir?" Estael spat back.

Rieuk was beyond patience. "What new nonsense is this?" He was not sure if he was entirely sane any longer; he knelt amid the melting mist of dust and ice that had once been Imri Boldiszar, wondering.

"Shamans who travel through their songs to the Ways Beyond."

Rieuk looked at him blankly.

"They summon the souls of dead clan warriors to possess the living in battle, to give them supernatural strength. Guslyars, the Azhkendi call them."

"They summon the dead?" Was that what Lord Estael had been scheming? "And whose body were you planning on using for this spirit possession?" The possibilities filled him with a blaze of conflicting emotions; Imri restored, but in someone else's body?

"It's a practice not so different from soul-stealing."

"Then why have I never heard of them till now?" Rieuk heard his own voice asking as if from a great distance away.

"Because the Drakhaon, Lord Volkh, slaughtered them when he took his revenge on the Arkhel clan for killing his mother. Although I now have reason to believe that one may have escaped the Drakhaon's purge."

"How can I believe another thing you ever tell me, my lord?" Rieuk rose unsteadily to his feet. "You made me the Arkhan's tool. You groomed me to serve him. You spun me lie after lie." He drew closer to him. "I'm leaving Ondhessar."

"Sardion won't let you go. You know too much. If you were to sell his secrets to his enemies—"

"I really don't care anymore." At that moment, it felt as if the fast-melting ice crystals of Imri's body had chilled all feeling in Rieuk's heart.

"He may even send one of us to destroy you."

Rieuk shrugged. "I'll take my chances."

"I won't be able to protect you if you break your bond." Lord Estael's face looked suddenly drawn and old; the fierce mage fire in his eyes had dimmed. "But then, what does it matter now, anyway?" he said. Rieuk heard a bone-deep weariness in the magus's voice. "It's all over for us. The longer *she* is absent from the Rift, the weaker we become. Our Emissaries will fade first . . . and once they're gone, our powers will diminish too. Our time is over, Rieuk."

"Magister! Emissary Mordiern! Wait!"

Rieuk turned, shading his vision against the harsh sun. The crimson dunes still reflected the fierce heat, even in the late afternoon, making the desert air shimmer with a blood-ied haze. A man was coming toward him over the sands, his head and face protected by a loosely wrapped burnous. Below him, the strange excrescences of earth-colored rock, the Towers of the Ghaouls, wavered in the dry heat.

"Where are you going?" As the man came nearer, Rieuk recognized the dark eyes burning accusingly above the folds of the black burnous. Oranir.

"I haven't decided yet." He turned away, knowing that he was lying.

"You and Lord Estael quarreled. Didn't you?" Oranir had almost caught up with him, walking with the loose, swift stride of those accustomed to desert life. On the ridge, Ondhessar loomed above them, the hated crimson flag of the Rosecoeurs fluttering from every watchtower, a constant reminder of the foreigners' presence. "What happened?"

"That's between me and Lord Estael." Rieuk didn't want to pick over the bones of that painful encounter just yet.

"You're leaving." It was an accusation, not a question.

Rieuk kept on walking.

"Answer me! Don't I deserve an answer?"

Rieuk stopped and turned to confront him. Oranir would not be satisfied with half-formed excuses. "Yes. I'm leav-ing. I can't stay here and you know why."

"Then take me with you." He heard the breathless ea-gerness in Oranir's voice, and caught the echo of another passionate young man begging Imri Boldiszar to take him as his apprentice. He banished the memory from his mind; such strong emotions would only cloud his judgment.

"If you come with me now, you throw away everything you've worked so hard for. You become an outcast. A wanted man."

"I want to go with you." There was a stubborn note in Oranir's words that Rieuk had not heard before. "Besides, you're not fully healed yet. You need me."

Rieuk almost smiled. "So you have Lord Aqil's permis-sion to accompany me?"

Oranir shot him a sullen, defensive look.

"And what of your vow to the Arkhan?" Oranir did not

reply. Rieuk took a step closer to him. "You have such a promising career ahead of you, Oranir. Don't ruin your life for my sake." He let his hand rest on Oranir's shoulder. "Forgive me. I should have told you I was leaving. You've taken such good care of me. Thank you."

Oranir struck his hand away. "I don't want thanks." He backed away, feet slipping in the sand. "Why don't you understand? Why must you be so stubborn? Why can't you share your troubles?"

Rieuk turned away with a regretful little shrug. "Too many years of working alone, I guess. Farewell, Oranir." He slung his travel bag over his shoulder and set off again, climbing up the side of the ridge without once looking back.

Rieuk had plenty of time to reflect on what Oranir had said as he took the merchant route to the Djihari port of Tyriana. He passed himself off as an itinerant jeweler, making use of his skill with crystals to hire himself out to merchants and traders along the way.

He ended up working for Barjik, a diamond merchant from Serindher. From time to time, Barjik's wife, Serah, would shuffle into the stuffy back room of the shop, bringing little cups of bittersweet coffee, or date-and-almond cakes shaped like shells. From time to time, the heavy curtain separating the workroom from the shop would twitch, yet no one came in. He knew that he was being watched. And yet he did not mind. He was handling a precious commodity, after all, and no merchant could afford to be too trusting.

As Rieuk concentrated on the rough stones before him, seeking to expose their hidden potential, he kept seeing the look of wounded incomprehension in Oranir's dark eyes.

Why did I reject him again? I'm free now. Was I trying to protect him, or myself?

He selected a diamond from the pile and examined it.

At that time he had been in a daze, still trying to come to terms with the loss of Imri. Yet the moment when Imri's crystallized body had melted into a million glittering grains of ice, he had felt as if a shadow had lifted from his mind and his heart—and a heavy burden from his shoulders. He had been carrying the guilt of Imri's death for far too long.

So why had he turned away from Oranir? It had seemed the selfless thing to do. Yet the truth was that he had been traveling alone for so long that the thought of having a companion terrified him.

Not ready. I'm just not ready.

The dry aroma of turmeric and frying onions wafted into the room; Serah must have begun preparations for dinner. Sometimes the old couple invited him to share their evening meal; their own sons were far away in Serindher, looking after the business there, and Rieuk suspected that Serah missed her boys. Sometimes she'd murmur that he was about the same height as Chorpan . . . or that Itakh liked to drink his coffee sweetened with honey and cinnamon.

Rieuk became aware that he had been staring unseeing at the diamond for some while. He laid it down and wiped the sticky sweat from his forehead and fingers. The air in the back street was stiflingly hot by late afternoon.

Why couldn't I bring myself to accept Imri's death until now? Because Lord Estael fed me false hope? And if I've finally accepted that he's dead, why am I going to Azhkendir?

"To make certain that his soul is truly free," he muttered to himself. It was the last thing he could do for Imri. He concentrated on the rough diamond before him, piercing to the heart of the stone with his mind's eye. A swift burst of energy, sliver-sharp . . . and the first flawless facet was revealed. "I have to do this alone."

"You want a passage to Azhkendir?" The ship's captain shook the contents of Rieuk's money bag out on the table. "Why d'you want to visit that godforsaken country?"

Barrels of Smarnan wine were being unloaded from the ship moored alongside with much shouting and whistling from the crew. Rieuk had to raise his voice to make himself heard. "Trade must be good for you to venture so far north."

The captain shrugged as he counted out the coins. "It's a living."

The midday sunlight sparkled on the dark azure of the sea, impossibly bright. In this intense, burnished heat it was difficult to imagine the desolate snows of Azhkendir, cut off by frozen seas for a third of the year.

A shadow flitted across the sun. Rieuk glanced up, feeling Ormas stir uneasily within him. An Emissary? Were the magi tracking him? White-winged gulls were wheeling overhead but, as he shaded his damaged sight against the dazzle, he could see no trace of a shadow hawk. *Perhaps I imagined it.* Even though he was in Djihan-Djihar and out of the Arkhan's jurisdiction, his escape seemed to be going just a little too smoothly.

The captain of the *Satrina* had taken on a number of passengers, mostly merchants bound for the port of Vermeille in Smarna. Thanks to Barjik's contacts, Rieuk was traveling as a merchant too, trusted to carry out one final errand for his master.

As the ship left the port, Rieuk stood on deck, gazing back at the haze of heat hanging like a dusty fog above the ochre-and-sand-red buildings.

Gulls still wheeled and screamed overhead as the sails filled with wind. Out beyond the calm waters of the port, the waves grew choppy and the *Satrina* began to pitch and roll.

Once Rieuk would have been unable to stay on deck, relishing the fierce gusts that left a tang of salt on his lips and tongue. He would have slunk below, groaning as the first pangs of seasickness overcame him. But Imri had cured him of that curse, opening up a whole new world of experiences to him, and for that alone, he would always be thankful.

As the *Satrina* sailed into the turquoise vasts of the Southern Ocean and the coastline of Djihan-Djihar dwindled to a twilit blur on the horizon, Rieuk felt as if he was finally leaving behind all the long years of servitude. He leaned on the ship's rail, watching the sinking sun set the waves on fire.

Time to study the maps of Azhkendir he had bought from a dusty bookseller's in Tyriana.

He turned from the rail to make his way below, taking care where he placed his feet; coils of thick rope lay strewn across the deck as the crewmen changed tack. A man was coming directly toward him from the lower deck, his tall frame silhouetted against the fiery glow of the setting sun. Rieuk stopped.

"O—Oranir?" he stammered.

"Did you think that I would let you go without me?" Oranir's face was in shadow, although Rieuk caught a smolder of scarlet from behind his lenses. "You can't send me back now. The *Satrina*'s not putting in to port until we reach Smarna. I checked with the captain."

"How long have you been following me?"

"Long enough. You covered your trail well."

"So did you, for me not to have noticed." And for some reason not wholly clear to himself, Rieuk began to laugh. As the last gilded rays of the setting sun faded, the sea darkened from blue to inky purple and the sailors began to light the lanterns on the rigging.

Oranir moved closer. "I'm coming with you. To Azhkendir. Or wherever you go."

"Even though you'll be a fugitive too?"

Oranir's mouth took on a stubborn set. "I'd rather be on the run with you than back in Ondhessar serving a madman." He glanced at Rieuk over the top of his spectacles and Rieuk caught another warning glint from his fire-riven eyes. "So don't try to talk me out of it."

"You can still take a ship back from Smarna—" Rieuk began.

"And didn't you do the same?" Oranir drew closer still, his voice softer. "Didn't you abandon your college to follow Imri Boldiszar? Lord Estael told me so once. That must have taken some courage."

"Courage?" Rieuk heard the taint of ironic laughter in his voice. He was about to say, *I was all but expelled for disobeying my first master,* but for some reason, the confession would not come. Only then did he realize that he wanted to look good in Oranir's eyes.

"Make me your apprentice." Oranir reached out, placing his hands on Rieuk's shoulders.

"But you're already apprenticed to Aqil—"

"Make a new bond with me now." Oranir's face was so close to Rieuk's that he could smell the faint sweetness of caraway on his breath.

"Is this truly what you want?" Rieuk murmured.

"Do it."

Rieuk drew Oranir's head toward his and gently pressed his lips to Oranir's. As he did so, he felt a shiver catch fire within him as he sensed Oranir's powers.

"Teach me," Oranir said softly. "Teach me everything you know."

CHAPTER 3

The empty moorlands, stretching into the misty horizon, were a living tapestry embroidered with the vivid purples of heather and the coppery brown of the dying bracken.

Rieuk and Oranir had been tramping across the moors for days, skirting the barren, burned land the locals called the Arkhel Waste. At night they had taken shelter in ruined crofts or shepherd's huts.

Whenever they asked anyone they met—a lone shepherd herding his ragged sheep, or a hunter with a brace of rabbits slung over his shoulder, the answer was always the same. "The old shaman woman? They say you can only find her if she wants you to."

"Look." Oranir pointed to the sky. "Is that smoke?"

A thin plume rose into the pale sky, so faint that it could have been mistaken for a trail of mist or cloud. They hurried toward it but soon stopped, bewildered, seeing no sign of a hut or a cottage.

"I know you're here, Spirit Singer!" Rieuk cried into the desolate landscape. As if in answer, there came the distant peeping of a small heathland bird, perched on top of a tall clump of reeds. "I won't give up. I'll go on searching until I find you."

A breeze, tinged with the sulfurous tang of marsh mud, suddenly stirred the white wispy heads of bog cotton.

"Rieuk." Oranir nudged him. He turned to see the air rippling as though a heat haze were lifting from the mossy ground. Where there had been nothing but gorse bushes, Rieuk saw a little cottage, with a thin ribbon of blue smoke rising from its awry chimney. Hens scuttled about in the stony yard, scratching for food.

"You young mages need better training," said a querulous voice. "It took you long enough to find me!" An old woman with a shock of windblown grey hair was leaning on the cottage gate, watching them with beady eyes.

"Are you the Spirit Singer?" Rieuk asked cautiously.

"Malusha's the name, and I'll be frank with you. I don't like your kind. Never have. Not that I've seen one of your tainted mage blood in many a long year. Not that I see that much of anyone, these days. My lords and ladies keep me too busy."

"Your lords and ladies?"

She jerked a thumb up toward the dilapidated roof of the cottage. Hunched close together perched a row of sleeping owls, their feathers white as the snow on the distant peaks.

"The owls?" Rieuk caught Oranir's sidelong warning glance. Were they wasting their time? "Eccentric" seemed a polite description of Malusha; "out of her wits" seemed closer to the truth.

"Not just any owls." She glared at him and he flinched, riven by the malice of her bright, mad eyes. "Arkhel's Owls. D'you know nothing, Magus? They can host the spirits of the dead."

The spirits of the dead. Had she read his mind?

"Well, there's no sense us all catching cold in this wind; you'd better come inside, seeing as you've traveled halfway across the world to consult me." She beckoned them to follow her, shooing clucking hens from their path.

Inside the cluttered cottage, it was so murky that it took Rieuk a while to get his bearings. Oranir slipped his hand under his arm and guided him into the center of the room.

"You can take your spectacles off. There's no need to pretend around me," she said, pouring water into the battered kettle suspended over the fire. It was more an order than a suggestion. As she straightened up, she turned to gaze keenly first at Rieuk, then at Oranir. "Crystal magus," she said, "and earthfire magus. Two rare talents."

"I see that there's little we can hide from you," Rieuk said, wondering what else her sharp brown eyes had spotted.

"Sit down," she ordered, moving a pile of crumpled, stained blankets from a wooden settle near the fire. Glancing up, Rieuk saw white-feathered bodies huddled close together on one of the beams: more owls. Her familiars.

"So, while the kettle's on the boil for tea, tell me: What brings you halfway across the world from Ondhessar?"

By the time steam was puffing from the kettle's spout, Rieuk had given away rather more about himself than he'd intended. There was something about the smoky warmth of the cottage and her open manner that made him feel he was able to confide in her.

"If your dead master's soul was preserved in a soul glass, that means there's something else you're not telling me." Malusha got up, bones creaking, and went to make tea. The firelight illuminated the grave expression on her wrinkled face as she concentrated on measuring out the dry leaves into the pot and Rieuk saw how wrong his initial impression of her had been. Beneath the wild hair and the owl feathers, a wise and perceptive mind had been assessing them both. But how far could he trust her?

"You practice soul-stealing, don't you?" She shuffled back, carefully carrying mugs of tea. "There's no point denying it. I've heard the legends about Ondhessar." She settled down opposite them, cradling her mug between gnarled fingers. "I can't say I approve. There're too many Lost Souls wandering around the Ways Beyond as it is, without you adding to them."

Rieuk set the tea down, untasted. "Could that be what became of Imri?" He could not hide the tremor in his voice.

She shook her head. "Can't say for sure."

"But what does that mean? To be a Lost Soul?"

"Listen, Master Mage, what you're asking of me is unusual and highly risky—to the both of us. There're two options: one, to go looking for him far into the Ways Beyond, or two, to try to charm your dead master's soul here so that you can ask him what you need to."

One last chance to speak to Imri after so many years . . . Rieuk felt a jagged blade twisting in his heart. What would

Imri say to him? Would he be filled with bitterness that his last chance to return to life had been dashed forever? Could he endure such a bitter reunion? But he had traveled this far to complete this one last rite for Imri, so he knew he must find the courage.

"To do a summoning, I need a lock of hair, a possession, a relic of some kind."

"I—I have nothing." Why had that not occurred to him before?

"The soul glass?" Oranir said softly.

"Of course." Rieuk brought out the lotus glass from the soft leather pouch he wore around his neck and handed it to Malusha.

A shrewd little smile was glimmering in her eyes. "You do realize, don't you, that for this to work, you're going to have to tell me your real name."

Unable to look away from her penetrating gaze, Rieuk felt his cheeks burning.

"We didn't intend to deceive you. It's just . . . we've been traveling for so long, it seems more natural to use assumed names. My name is Mordiern; Rieuk Mordiern."

"And your kind are no more welcome these days, I imagine, than when I was a girl. It's a curse to be born with powers as strong as yours." Again Rieuk felt that bright, incisive gleam pierce through his defenses, reading deep into his soul.

Malusha brought out a stringed wooden instrument shaped a little like the ancient dulcimer Rieuk remembered from childhood in the village schoolroom.

"This is a gusly," she said, answering his unspoken question as she began to test the wire strings that filled the cottage with a resonant jangling. "Some call us Spirit Singers because we charm the spirits of the dead to us with our singing. There's a little more to it than minstrelsy, of course . . ."

As she played a long, slow succession of notes, the cottage began to grow darker, as if with each note she were weaving a protective veil of sound around them. But then each string began to toll like a bell—a somber, funereal sound that seemed to draw the darkness closer still. Rieuk sensed Oranir shift a little closer to him, as if instinctively seeking his protection. His head felt strange, as if his senses were altering; his sight was dimming yet his hearing was growing more acute. A drug . . . poison . . .

"What was in that tea, Malusha?" His tongue moved sluggishly, the words coming out clumsily.

"Nothing harmful. Just a few herbs to help you relax . . ."

Malusha began to sing, a soft, deep-throated crooning at first, wordless, blending with the bell-like reverberations of the strings. The walls of the firelit cottage slowly receded, melting into rushing darkness. Rieuk felt a shiver run through his body as he heard the Spirit Singer call a name, her voice suddenly strong, compelling, commanding. "Imri! Imri Boldiszar!"

For a moment the swirling confusion around Rieuk stilled and he saw, to his bewilderment, the indistinct, spectral faces of the dead, each one staring at him in mute appeal.

Rieuk followed Malusha through hall after lofty hall where indistinct figures wandered aimlessly. Time and again, she called on Imri's name. Many of the wandering souls looked up when they heard her voice, their eyes filled with longing. Then he saw the hope fade as they turned away.

"So many," he heard himself murmuring in horror. "So very many . . ."

Yet not one had answered Malusha's command and as she struck another flurry of notes, the pale faces were gone, swept away into the airy dark.

"So very many . . ." Rieuk was still repeating the words as he opened his eyes to see that he was back in his own body. Malusha was watching him intently, her gnarled hands resting on the silent strings of her gusly.

"What was that terrible place?" Rieuk could not rid his mind of the sight of the wandering, aimless dead, nor lose the dry taste of dust in his mouth. "And who were they? All those—"

"Those unhappy, unfortunate ones?" She finished the question for him. "You saw some of the Lost Souls, those who can't find their path to the Ways Beyond."

"But he wasn't there. Imri wasn't there. That has to be a

good sign, doesn't it? It means that he's not one of the Lost?"

Malusha did not answer straightaway. And her silence did nothing to calm Rieuk's growing sense of apprehension.

"Or does being lost mean that you no longer remember who you were?" He went over and knelt before her. "Malusha, *tell me the truth*."

"The Lady," she said at last. "The one who watches over the ways between our world and the worlds beyond. She's been gone too long. Where is she?" She fixed him with a penetrating stare. "I think you may know."

"The Lady?" said Oranir. "You mean Azilis?"

"Elesstar, Azilis, Azilia . . . she has many names. But things are beginning to unravel without her. Can't you sense it? The balance between the worlds is shifting. The place you call the Rift is unstable. If she doesn't go back soon, the souls of the dead will start to return. How can they find peace if she isn't there to guide them?"

Rieuk let out a sigh. "I tried," he said. "I tried to persuade her to go back. But she did this to me." He ripped off his eye patch, revealing his damaged face to Malusha. She did not flinch, but merely put out her hand and gently stroked his cheek.

"I have no more answers for you; I'm only a foolish old woman who's outlived her time."

Rieuk hung his head. He had placed so many of his hopes in Malusha's skills and all he had gained was more questions.

"So your journey isn't over yet!" She let out a chuckle. "I'm sending you to see an old friend of mine. He's a shaman. He owes me a favor or two."

"Chinua's the name." The tea merchant bowed, smiling, to Rieuk and Oranir. "It will be an honor to help a friend of Malusha's. Any friend of the Spirit Singer is a friend of mine."

Malusha had sent them to the market in the city of Azhgorod. And there, amid the hectic bustle of shoppers and farmers, they had spotted the little shop selling tea at the far corner of the square. Reaching the stall was another matter, for pigs were rooting around in the cabbage leaves, formidable Azhkendi matrons were jostling to get to the best produce first, and the air was filled with the deafening cries of the stallholders proclaiming their wares. The customers waiting in line to purchase black, green, or jasmine tea at the open window of the Khitari tea merchant's shop were quite decorous by comparison.

"Meet me here when the market closes," Chinua said, turning to serve an elderly lady, who was impatiently tapping her coin on the counter.

When they returned, Chinua led them into the back room of the little shop; it was dark and the air was fragrant with tea dust. They sat around a low table on rugs while Chinua poured them bowls of green tea. Nodding from time to time, he sipped his tea as Rieuk told him the bones of his story. When Rieuk had finished, Chinua was silent for a while, his broad face expressionless so that Rieuk could not tell what he was thinking.

"Are you prepared to travel to the roof of the world?" Chinua asked at last. "This matter is far beyond my skills. But there's a place on the northern shores of Lake Taigal, in the mountains, where you may find the answers you're seeking. Have you ever heard of the Jade Springs?"

"The Jade Springs of Eternal Life? I thought they were just a legend."

A slow smile spread across the shaman's face. "Ah. But haven't you found yourselves that there is a grain of truth embedded in all the ancient legends? If you can discover the hidden path to the Jade Springs, the Guardian will surely enlighten you. But it's not a journey to be undertaken lightly. However"—and he leaned forward to refill their bowls— "I'll be returning to Khitari to replenish our stocks in a couple of weeks. If you don't mind traveling on a cart, I'll be happy to take you as far as the steppes."

Rieuk consulted Oranir with a look; Oranir glared stubbornly back at him.

"I've come this far with you; I'm not going to abandon you now."

CHAPTER 4

"The roof of the world, Chinua called it." Oranir shivered as they stopped on the mountain path to gaze down at the blue-green waters of Lake Taigal far below.

"How can you still feel the cold after climbing all this way?" Rieuk was hot, and he leaned against a crooked larch trunk to catch his breath. "Is it me, or is the air growing thinner?"

"Maybe it's too hard a journey for an old man like you." Oranir let the little taunt slip with a straight face. "Perhaps you should ask the Guardian to make you young again?"

"Show some respect for your elders!" Rieuk said, laughing. And Oranir turned to him with a smile. There was some quality to the clean, clear mountain air that lifted their spirits. In the many months since they left Enhirre, Oranir had slowly begun to open up. No longer the wary, unsmiling, intense young man Rieuk remembered from Ondhessar, he had even begun to reveal a dry, playful sense of humor.

Yet as they set out once more up the rocky path, Rieuk was aware that the encounter to come with the Guardian of the Jade Springs might change their relationship forever. He glanced at Oranir's straight back going steadily on ahead of him and realized that he didn't want that to happen. Would it be better to turn back and leave his questions unanswered?

From time to time they stopped, listening in vain for the sound of fast-flowing water. As the sun began to dip toward the west, Rieuk called on Ormas and sent the hawk to search while he and Oranir shared some of the dried fruit they had bought in the village far below.

"It has to be the right way," Rieuk said, slowly chewing on a dried apricot, savoring the honeyed taste. "Chinua said the path wound up toward the two horned peaks, opposite the island."

"*I've found it, Master.*"

Looking through Ormas's keen sight, Rieuk saw that the hawk had spotted a waterfall whose fast-spilling waters churned up a froth of white foam. Beyond the falls a natural archway had been hewn in the mountain, and as Ormas soared up over the rocks, a hidden pool was revealed. Its luminous waters were colored the delicate green of river jade and half-obscured by clouds of rising steam.

"The Jade Springs." Rieuk stood up, infused with new energy at the sight of his goal. "Ormas has found them."

"It's getting dark," protested Oranir as Rieuk started off again. "If you miss your footing this high up, you'll—"

"Wait for me here, then," Rieuk called back down the track. His first glimpse of the springs only made him eager to consult the Guardian as soon as possible. He heard Oranir curse viciously in Djihari and set out after him.

It was almost night by the time Rieuk and Oranir passed beneath the rocky archway. The roar of the waterfall dwindled as they approached the springs and the steamy mist, tinged green by the glow emanating from the bubbling waters, enveloped them. Rieuk knelt and dipped in his hand. The springwater was hot, though not too hot to bear, and felt slightly effervescent against his skin.

"Rieuk!" Oranir was pointing into the heart of the steam where the waters issued from a gaping fissure in the mountain rock. Far out in the pool, Rieuk thought that he caught a glimmer of phosphorescence, livid as poison. A dark form could be seen moving toward them through the water. "What *is* that?"

Rieuk swiftly withdrew his hand. He sensed a powerful presence. "The Guardian?"

Breaking through the floating mist came a water serpent, its scales glittering jade and black, its head held high. Its emerald eyes fixed on them, it moved through the waters at astonishing speed. As it drew nearer, they saw that a third eye had opened in its scaly forehead.

Rieuk stayed kneeling, mesmerized, but Oranir launched himself forward, placing himself between Rieuk and the serpent.

"Two magi?" The serpent spoke and its voice was that of a woman, soft and sensuous. "I will only speak with one of you. Which shall it be?"

"Me." Rieuk rose.

"No!" cried Oranir, holding him back. "It could be a trap."

The serpent turned its glittering eyes on Oranir. "You must leave us alone," she said, adding slyly, "Don't worry. I don't intend to devour your master."

"I'll be all right, Oranir." Rieuk pressed his shoulder, speaking with a confidence that he did not feel. "Wait for me beyond the waterfall."

Oranir stood a moment, his eyes sullen, rebellious. Then he shook off Rieuk's hand and walked back toward the way they had come without a backward glance.

Rieuk turned to the Guardian. Where the jade-scaled serpent had been, he saw a slender woman, clothed only in her long green hair, which trailed over her naked body like strands of waterweed.

"Are—are you the Guardian of the Springs?" he stammered.

She rose out of the springs, the water dripping off her like a liquid veil. "My name is Anagini," she said. "What is yours?"

"Rieuk. Rieuk Mordiern." Mesmerized by her beauty, he stood staring as she glided toward him.

"Your eye." She touched his face and he felt his skin tingle. "Have you come to ask me to restore your eye?"

Rieuk had never imagined that such a thing was possible, believing himself to be disfigured for life. "Could you do it?" Distracted, he began to imagine how wonderful it would be to be whole again, to present an unscarred face to the world, and, best gift of all, to see clearly once more.

"These are no ordinary healing springs. But the price for

granting such a wish would cost you dear. There is always a price, Rieuk Mordiern."

"And what is that price?" He had begun to hope again in spite of himself.

"Your shadow hawk."

The dream died. He could never give up Ormas. He should have known it was pointless to wish to be restored; he would go scarred and half-blind to his grave.

"Your price is too high," he said sadly, resignedly. "I came here to ask you what has become of the soul of my dead master."

"Your master who was a magus?" Her soft voice could only just be heard above the hissing of the steam. "So you know nothing of the true nature of the shadow hawks of the emerald moon?"

"My master, not my Emissary." Rieuk thought that she had misheard him.

"Have you never asked Ormas who he is? Or . . ." Anagini's voice grew softer still, "or who he once was, before you claimed him?"

"I never thought to . . ." Rieuk suddenly began to understand what the Guardian was implying.

"I will give you an answer to your question," said Anagini and her eyes darkened until he felt as if he were gazing into fathomless waters, "but you must be prepared to live with the consequences. It may not be the answer you wish to hear. You may even come to wish you had never made this journey."

Was she testing him? "I am prepared," he said.

"Then summon Ormas and ask him yourself. But be careful; there is always a risk that you may lose him."

Oranir leaned back against the rocks beyond the waterfall, arms folded. From time to time he turned to glance uneasily toward the mist-wreathed springs. He didn't trust the serpent woman. And the longer Rieuk was gone, the more suspicious he became as to what her true motives might be. The light began to fade, and the luminous glow emanating from the effervescent waters grew more intense.

Suddenly a cry rang out, chilling and inhuman, echoing around the barren mountainside. The cry of a shadow hawk. Oranir turned and ran back beneath the arch.

Ormas fluttered down to alight on Rieuk's outstretched forearm so that Rieuk could gaze searchingly into his Emissary's smoky eyes of topaz flame.

"Ormas, who *are* you?"

"*I am Ormas, your Emissary.*"

"But before we were bonded together?" Rieuk had to know, even if the knowledge was going to shatter his most cherished beliefs.

"*I was a shadow hawk. I hunted with my kin in the place you call the Rift. I flew from haoma tree to tree, drinking the nectar from its flowers.*"

"And before that?"

Ormas blinked.

"Ormas, forgive me for what I'm about to do."

"*Master?*" Ormas stared at him trustingly.

"Lady Anagini?"

The Guardian suddenly raised her hands and flung a skein of phosphorescent mist from the jade waters over the hawk.

Ormas let out a cry, and in a dark shudder of wings, took to the air. Trapped in the net of mist, he fell back to the ground. Glimmering particles drifted down, forming a gauzy curtain, behind which Rieuk saw a shadowy form beginning to take shape, writhing and twisting as though in silent agony.

What have I done to him? A terrible cramping pain gripped his heart. It felt as if Ormas were trying to claw his way out of his body, out from under his skin. Rieuk slipped to his knees, clutching his arms across his breast to try to hold in the agony.

"Rieuk!" He heard Oranir's alarmed cry, and felt his hands close around his shoulders, supporting him.

"No, stay back." Rieuk managed to grit out the warning between clenched teeth. But Oranir stayed there, bracing him against his body as the flickering shadow shape that had been Ormas grew taller, looming over them both as they crouched on the ground.

"Who *are* you?" Rieuk whispered. Rising out of the darkness was a smoke-winged figure, as tall as he, gazing at him through wild eyes of topaz and jet, just as he had seen the night of his initiation.

"I no longer remember my mortal name." The voice was still Ormas's but deeper, riven with anguish.

"Show me your mortal form, Ormas," commanded Anagini. In the swirling mists, her eyes gleamed, three emerald stars. *That green, unearthly shimmer.* It was like the light cast by the emerald moon over the Rift . . .

The mists melted away and Rieuk saw a man staring at him, a man clothed in the ceremonial robes of a magus of Ondhessar, with long, dark brown hair and beard touched with threads of silver.

"Ormas?" Rieuk said uncertainly. The magus gazed back at him, frowning, as if he were a stranger.

"Who are you?" he said in bewildered tones. "What am I doing here?" He turned to Anagini. "Why have you summoned me, lady?"

"Ormas, don't you know me?" Rieuk demanded. The topaz eyes still stared at him and he saw the faintest flicker of madness at their heart.

"I have no idea who you are. How come you know my name?"

Rieuk could feel every etched mark of the hawk tattoo throbbing as though the blood-ink that linked him to his familiar was being slowly drawn out through his skin. He doubled up as the pain took hold.

"Enough!" Oranir shouted to Anagini as Rieuk sagged against him. "Stop this now. He can't take any more."

"Have I answered your question, Rieuk?" Anagini asked.

Rieuk nodded, unable to speak. He could feel Ormas's image begin to bleed out of him, as the tiny puncture wounds sealed so long ago opened, one by one.

Anagini drew a veil of mist around them and, at its darkest core, he saw Ormas's mortal form dwindle. And as it faded, the excruciating pain in his chest faded too. The hawk came winging toward him and, as Rieuk reached out to him, he melted back into his body.

"This is what becomes of a magus's soul." The Guardian's voice was harsh, each word like a hammerblow, piercing Rieuk's consciousness. "This is what you will become when you die."

"A shadow hawk?" Rieuk laid a hand over his breast, instinctively checking for Ormas's heartbeat close to his own.

"You are born with angel blood in your veins. So when your body dies, your soul cannot follow the path taken by other mortals. Neither can it ascend to be one with the Heavenly Guardians. So it is transmuted, changed in the Rift, to a winged spirit. But during that transmutation, all mortal memories are washed away. The soul is reborn as a winged spirit, a hawk of the shadows."

"So when Imri died, his soul . . ." Rieuk could still not fully grasp what Anagini had told them.

"Imri has been reborn as a shadow hawk."

Rieuk fell silent. At last he had learned the truth. He felt empty . . . yet he also felt a certain sense of release.

"Even if you were to find him in the Rift, he would remember nothing of you or his mortal life."

Anagini's words were frank to the point of cruelty.

"Nothing?" Rieuk repeated, hearing his own voice as if from far away.

"I have answered your question, Rieuk," she said softly. "And now you must fulfill your part of our pact."

Pact? Rieuk was fully awake again. "But we never agreed—"

She pressed her fingertips to his forehead, and her touch made him shiver. "Your powers are already weakening. Can't you feel it? And as the Rift grows more unstable, so your powers will slowly leak away . . . as will mine too. Go after her, and bring her back to the Rift."

"Azilis." This was not what Rieuk wanted to hear. "Why must it always come back to Azilis?"

"Azilis is an aethyrial spirit. She draws her strength from

the Rift. But she has been away so long that she too is growing weak. To survive, she has begun to draw on the life essence of the very child she was bound to protect."

"She's been living off Celestine's life force?" What happened to a mortal body when its essence was slowly drained away? Would Celestine begin to age too swiftly? She had been such a beautiful young woman when last he saw her; would he find her withered and feeble?

"When mortals bond with aethyrial spirits, there is always a price to pay. This is something the Dragon Lords of Azhkendir know to their cost."

"So . . . unless I bring Azilis back to the Rift, our Emissaries will die and we will lose our powers?"

"You are the last surviving crystal magus, Rieuk." She leaned toward him so close that he felt as if he were drowning in the liquid depths of her emerald eyes. "There is no one else with the skill to make a new Lodestar. Are you brave enough to do this? Even though it means returning to risk the dangers of the Rift?"

Rieuk swallowed. The mere thought of venturing back into that chaotic darkness disturbed him. But for the sake of Ormas and Imri's reborn soul, he knew there was no alternative. "If I must, then I must."

Anagini took his face in her hands and kissed his forehead. As she did so, he heard her voice whispering softly in his mind.

"I've seen that you care for that beautiful mage boy, but how far can you trust him? Take care."

The stars burned bright over the mountainside. While Oranir gathered brushwood and lit a small fire, Rieuk drank some water and, wrapping himself in his cloak, lay down close to the warmth, turning on his side away from Oranir. He was too depressed to talk or eat.

Yet he could not sleep. The same morbid thoughts kept churning around his mind, keeping him awake. Somewhere in the chaotic darkness of the Rift was Imri, reborn as a shadow hawk. Unless he brought Azilis back to stem the chaos, Imri would be lost a second time. And then there had been Anagini's warning. What did she know about Oranir? Why had she warned Rieuk not to trust him?

"I know you're not asleep," Oranir whispered, his lips brushing Rieuk's ear. Rieuk kept his eyes shut, pretending that he hadn't heard. But Oranir could be very persistent when he wanted to. "I'm here, Rieuk. I'm alive. How long can you go on loving a ghost?" Still Rieuk lay unmoving, wondering how long he could continue to resist. "He's never coming back to you."

Rieuk had begun to shiver, whether because of the cold of the mountain night or the chill that had pervaded his soul since Anagini had revealed the truth to him.

Oranir peeled back one side of the cloak, snuggling down beneath it, his body pressed close to Rieuk's. And this time, Rieuk did not push him away.

But later, much later, as the stars began to fade and Oranir lay, sound asleep, beside him, Rieuk sat up, staring into the embers of the dying fire.

I don't want to go back into the Rift. Rieuk knew that the turbulence, the darkness leaking from the Realm of Shadows, would drive him mad.

CHAPTER 5

The main border post between Djihan-Djihar and Enhirre was manned by the Rosecoeur Guerriers. All the other
entry points were patrolled by the Arkhan's guards. But the
magi had long ago devised their own secret routes through
the dusty foothills that avoided the necessity of passports
or papers. Yet as they drew near to the Enhirran border,
Oranir seemed to withdraw into himself, saying less and
less. Rieuk glanced at him frequently, troubled by his silence. Did the young magus feel as apprehensive as he did
about returning? They had both rebelled against the Arkhan,
and if they were caught, Sardion would not treat them
kindly for their disobedience.

They stopped near midday in a windy gully, high above
the Hidden Valley. Below, sinister even by day, stood the
twisted Towers of the Ghaouls. The searingly dry air made
it difficult to exchange more than a few words. The sun was
approaching its highest point in the sky and seasoned travelers like Rieuk knew that this was the time to seek out
whatever shade was available and rest until the sun began
to set. Sheltered by an overhang in the rock face, Rieuk unwound his headdress, which he had wrapped over nose and
mouth to keep out the sand and grit, and uncorked his water bottle, offering it to Oranir. Oranir took it and drank,
passing it back. As he did so, the wild, keening cry of a bird
of prey echoed around the gully. Looking up, Rieuk
glimpsed a shadowy shape against the harsh dazzle of the
noonday sun, wings outspread, circling high above.

"Have they found us already?" Oranir shaded his eyes to
see more clearly.

"Ormas," Rieuk said softly, "is that one of your kin?"
He felt Ormas slowly return to consciousness within him.

"*I cannot tell; it is too far off,*" came the listless reply.

"Then go and spy out the valley for us. Take care . . ."

Ormas took off, disappearing into the heat haze. Suddenly uneasy, Rieuk stood up, trying to see what was happening through Ormas's clear sight.

"All I need is a distraction to draw the others away from the entrance to the Rift. Can you do it, Ran? Just long enough for me to slip down the stairs . . ."

He turned around, but Oranir was no longer there.

"Ran?" he called.

They came at him from his blind side. Before he had time to defend himself, he felt the blow to the back of his skull, harsh as a thunderclap. Then, nothing but the dark.

"Have you forgotten the vow you made when you became my Emissary, Rieuk Mordiern?"

The harsh voice brought Rieuk back to consciousness. He hung, his hands shackled above his head, pinned to a wall. The air around him was dark and dank; he must be far belowground. He tried to raise his drooping head. A hand slipped beneath his chin and lifted it. Sardion was standing before him, staring at him with a look so cold and penetrating that he felt as if the Arkhan was reading his innermost thoughts.

"Answer me!" The hand tightened around his throat. Rieuk began to choke.

"N—no, Lord Arkhan," he managed to whisper.

"I have your hawk."

Ormas! Rieuk silently called out to his Emissary, hearing only the feeblest of answering cries.

"What have you done to him?"

"You betrayed my trust, Rieuk." Sardion's eyes bored into his. "You played me false. Do you think that you and your hawk deserve to live?"

Rieuk could feel nothing but the weak beat of Ormas's heart, echoed by his own. A grey film seemed to float between him and the torchlit dungeon.

"Please, don't hurt him." It was humiliating to have to beg but he could not bear to endure the hawk's agony.

"Shouldn't you be more concerned for yourself?" At last Sardion let go of Rieuk's throat, leaving Rieuk gasping for air. "The punishment for breaking your vow is to have your Emissary stripped out from your body, feather by feather."

"But I haven't broken my vow!"

"You revealed our secrets to an Azhkendi shaman woman." Lord Estael came out of the gloom to stand at the Arkhan's side.

How did Lord Estael know? Had they used some glamour to draw the truth from him? "She discovered them for herself. I could hide nothing from her. And she is no threat to us. She did all in her power to help me. I learned far more from her than I ever learned from you—"

Lord Estael struck him across the face. Rieuk, cheek on fire from the blow, stared defiantly back at his onetime master.

"Can't you see I'm trying to save you, you ungrateful boy?"

"Can't you see that I was trying to save us all?" Rieuk no longer cared if the Arkhan heard or not. "Why else would we have returned? I have to go back into the Rift and make a new Lodestar, an aethyr crystal as perfect as the first."

"A new Lodestar? You know very well that I have other plans for Rieuk Mordiern." Sardion's restless pacing was making Estael uneasy. "Why else would I have sent Oranir to bring him back?"

Estael knew all too well how Sardion wanted to use Rieuk. The Arkhan's obsession with the Drakhaoul Nagazdiel had grown with every day that passed. If Sardion set the daemon lord free, the ensuing consequences for Enhirre were too terrible to imagine. "My lord, I beg you to postpone your plan for a little longer. If Rieuk can fashion a new Lodestar—"

"And how long will that take?"

Estael had no idea. "A few days, I imagine, once he has found a suitable crystal—"

"Very well," said Sardion curtly. "I'll indulge you and your magi just this once. But don't think that I'll let Rieuk off so lightly. The instant that the Lodestar is complete, I'm sending him into the Rift to summon Nagazdiel."

Two of the Arkhan's guards forced Rieuk to prostrate himself before Sardion on the polished sheen of the marble floor. Behind him knelt Aqil and Oranir.

"I will vouch for Rieuk, Lord Arkhan," he heard Lord Estael say. "He won't betray your trust again."

"I want to hear him ask for my forgiveness," said Sardion coldly. "I want to hear him beg."

Rieuk swallowed back his anger. If that was the only way to get Sardion's permission to go back into the Rift, then he would have to obey.

"Please forgive me, Lord Arkhan." The words stuck in his throat.

"Louder."

"I beg you, Lord Arkhan, to forgive me for betraying you." Rieuk scowled at the polished marble.

"I will let you live this time, Rieuk, because Lord Estael tells me you are going to create a new Lodestar and bring Azilis back to Ondhessar."

"My lord is merciful."

"You've done well, Oranir," said Sardion. "Come and sit by me. I've missed you."

"Oranir?" Rieuk raised his head, not caring if Sardion punished him for doing so. "What does this mean?"

"I've missed you too, my lord." Oranir rose and without even a glance at Rieuk, went over to Sardion's chair. Sardion stood and, raising the young magus's face to his own, kissed him on the lips.

Rieuk stared. The earlier humiliation was nothing, compared with this. He could not bear to watch the familiar way Oranir returned the Arkhan's kiss.

Taking Oranir by the hand, Sardion made him sit beside him. Both gazed down at Rieuk, with a look that said blatantly, *You poor deluded fool, didn't you have any idea?*

CHAPTER 6

In the Rift, it was as if everything had been reversed, like an engraver's plate. The sky was black as charcoal yet the Emerald Tower and the skeletal branches of the great trees were etched in ghostly acid white. And the emerald moon was waning; only the thinnest sliver of a pale crescent showed from time to time from behind fast-scudding clouds, blown across the sky by the wind that was gusting in from the Realm of Shadows.

"Can you see any hawks?" Rieuk called to Ormas over the whine of the wind. "*Not one . . .*" Ormas's desolate cry was borne back to Rieuk from the turbulent darkness.

"Come back to me now, Ormas." The farther Ormas flew away from him, the more Rieuk feared that he might find it impossible to return. The distance between them felt as if it were growing greater by the second.

"Ormas!" he cried again.

The hawk came skimming down over the treetops, battling the wind, and perched on his shoulder.

Rieuk put his head down and set off into the Rift. But there was a dull, bitter ache around his heart. Oranir had betrayed him. *Did all the time we spent together mean nothing to him? Was he playing me for a fool the whole time?* Oranir had gone to Sardion's side as soon as he was bidden without even a backward glance.

Find the aethyr crystals, and get out as fast as possible. But he didn't know where to begin to look. Lord Estael had spoken of a mine that lay far beyond the Tower, deep in the Rift. But it was many centuries since any magus had dared venture so far in to seek out the source of the Lodestar.

"*You're a crystal magus; you'll be able to sniff the crystals out, like a pig scenting truffles,*" Estael had said to him as he left him in the Rift. The analogy was not at all flattering and Rieuk had resented the comparison.

"Yet here I am, rooting about in a forest; I might as well be a pig," he muttered to himself.

He notched a mark on the trunk of each tall tree that he passed, so that he could find his way out again. Already he could feel the disorienting effect of the atmosphere in the Rift seeping into his mind. The fitful light from the waning moon cast verdant shadows across his path from time to time; whenever the slender crescent reappeared from behind the clouds, he looked back to see if he could still make out the stark silhouette of the tower. He must have penetrated deep into the forest, for the moon had vanished from sight.

"Where can the hawks have gone?" he asked Ormas. "And is Imri among them?"

"*I cannot tell. If they were blown far away on this wind, they may have become lost in the shadows.*"

Lost in the Realm of Shadows. There was such a bleak, hopeless ring to Ormas's words. But Rieuk felt nothing but anger as he struggled onward.

Why must it be I who has to put this right? Linnaius stole the Lodestar. Why must I pay for his crimes?

Buffeted by a sudden violent gust of wind, Ormas was flung violently away from him into the dark air.

"Return!"

It was then that he felt it: a stab of clear energy that pierced his brain like a needle of ice. He stood still, concentrating on identifying the source. The thin light of the moon faded and died, leaving him stranded in the pitch black. The only solution was to stumble on blind through the forest, guided by the crystalline sound.

The intensity of the vibrations was growing stronger with every step he took until his mind was filled with a jangle of different clear pitches, like the ringing of hundreds of glass bells.

"*Careful, Master!*" Ormas's warning cry made him stop dead in his tracks. He gazed down. The moonlight shone out again as the clouds parted, revealing that he stood on the rim of an abyss.

The crystals had been leading him directly toward a crevasse.

Rieuk hastily stepped back, away from the edge. If he had fallen—

He felt himself break out in a chill sweat. He sank to his knees, shaking.

"Ormas. You saved me."

The high, clear ringing was so loud that it lit up his mind with a crystalline shimmer. He forced himself to crawl to the edge and gazed into fathomless darkness. "How am I supposed to get down there? *Fly?*" He sat back on his heels and began to laugh.

"*Let me go down into the ravine. Let me be your eyes.*"

Rieuk didn't want to let go of Ormas again, but there was little choice in the matter. With the crystals' song ringing in his head, he observed through Ormas's one good eye the jagged contours of the side of the ravine as the hawk flew downward, fighting against the sudden gusts of wind.

"*There's an opening not far below, a cleft in the rock. You can let yourself down. There are footholds. I'll guide you.*"

Rieuk had never conceived of such a cavern, where crystals bloomed like flowers, encrusting the walls and floor, each stone vibrating at its own unique pitch, filling his ears with a symphony of bright sound. There must surely be one among them that was kin to the first Lodestar in its perfection and clarity, one that was fit to contain Azilis and reflect the purity of her song. A crystal that could be both star and lotus . . .

The song of the aethyr crystals wound itself into Rieuk's brain, enchanting and beguiling him. He touched one after another, delighting as his body resonated in tune with their individual vibrations. Some spread warmth throughout his limbs, others sharpened his thoughts, and others still spread a slow, twilit calm . . .

He was in his element at last, in harmony with the source of his powers. He lost all idea of time, obsessively pursuing his search as Ormas slumbered within him, until he found a single crystal that pleased him in a way he did not at first understand. He coaxed it from the cavern wall, cradling it gently in his hands. Its facets were so clear that he could look right through them, yet even as he did, it seemed to him that he could see an evanescent trace of iridescence, like sunlight seen through falling rain.

"This is the one," he said aloud. His voice sounded strange to his own ears. He had not spoken aloud, even to Ormas, in a long, long while. He looked at his water bottle and saw that it was empty.

It was time to go back.

But a dulled weariness spread through his whole body; he had been so intent on his quest that he had not slept in many hours. His head began to droop. Ormas dozed within him. Surely it couldn't hurt to rest for a little while and regain his strength before he set out again to find the Emerald Tower . . .

"Rieuk! Rieuk!" Oranir stood on the top of the Emerald Tower shouting Rieuk's name into the void until his throat ached.

"Zophas." He summoned his shadow hawk and sent him out into the Rift. "Go and find Ormas."

He stood, his face raised to the lashing of the wind, waiting for Zophas to come winging back.

The look of betrayal on Rieuk's face still tormented him.

How could I tell you that I did it to save your life? For my plan to work, you had to hate me, to revile me. Sardion's moods have become so capricious that if he had once suspected how much you mean to me, he would have had you put to death in the most cruel and perverted way he could devise.

But now he feared that the plan had worked far too well and Rieuk had gone off into the Rift, never to return.

"*I can't sense Ormas*"—Zophas swooped down, borne on a gust of wind, to perch on Oranir's shoulder—"*or any of my brothers. The hawks have gone.*"

Lord Estael appeared below, tramping up the hill from the endless forest, leaning heavily on his staff.

Oranir went running down the spiral stairs to meet him, but the instant he saw the grim expression in Estael's eyes, he knew that the news was not good.

"There's no trace of him," Estael said. "It's as if the Rift has swallowed him up completely. Or worse still, he's lost his way and wandered into the Realm of Shadows."

"Let me go." Oranir tried to push past him.

"I forbid it!" Estael's hand shot out, grasping him by the arm. "With Rieuk lost, there's only the four of us left." Then his tone softened. "Don't throw your life away needlessly. It's not what Rieuk would have wanted."

"How can you possibly know what Rieuk would have wanted?" Oranir wrenched his arm from Estael's grasp. Was Lord Estael deliberately trying to make him feel guilty? He felt wretched enough already. He had learned far too young that to survive in a harsh world you had to deceive—or be trodden underfoot.

"I wonder how you can still sleep at night," Estael said, walking on past him with slow, weary steps. Oranir scowled down at the ground. He had his own reasons for betraying Rieuk, but he wasn't going to explain himself to Lord Estael. He had never imagined that matters would turn out so badly, with Rieuk disappearing into the Rift. And as for sleeping . . . the nights had never seemed so long or so empty without the steady sound of Rieuk's breathing beside him in the darkness.

Lord Estael let out a sigh. "I fear we are the very last of the magi," Oranir heard him say, his voice echoing back to him in the void, "and it will be our sadness to live on as our powers slowly fade away."

PART II

CHAPTER 1

Burning braziers warmed the shadows in the crypt of Saint Meriadec's, yet Celestine de Joyeuse could not repress a shiver as she followed Jagu de Rustéphan down the worn steps. Although perhaps that was as much due to the sleety snow falling outside as the eerie chill of the ancient crypt. The dusty tombs of long-dead exorcist priests lay in the alcoves below, surmounted by stone effigies, the features eroded by the passing of time and the reverent caresses of their grateful parishioners, a reminder, she knew all too well, of the brevity of life.

"Jagu!" Kilian was warming his hands at a brazier, beside their fellow officer, the taciturn Philippe Viaud. "And Celestine too? Well, this is quite the reunion of the old team. Any idea why the Maistre has summoned us here?"

"I have no idea what this is about," Jagu said, stamping the snow from his boots.

Ruaud de Lanvaux, Grand Maistre of the Commanderie, came down the stairs, brushing the sleet from his cloak; at his side, a slim, dark young man in priest's robes removed his spectacles to wipe the condensation from the lenses.

"His majesty," Celestine hissed, hastily curtsying. The men bowed, Jagu murmuring in her ear as he did so, "This must be important for the king to attend in person."

"Thank you all for coming so promptly," King Enguerrand said, peering shortsightedly at the assembled members of Ruaud's elite squad of exorcists. "Some disturbing news has reached us from Azhkendir." He replaced his spectacles. "The Drakhaoul has reawakened."

Celestine had learned the legend of their patron saint,

Sergius, the Drakhaoul-Slayer, as a child at Saint Azilia's Convent. She glanced questioningly at the other Guerriers, and saw that they looked as bemused as she.

"For years we've heard nothing about the Drakhaoul of Azhkendir," said the Maistre. "Then, just as the snows began, Eugene of Tielen invaded Azhkendir. The new Drakhaon of Azhkendir, Gavril Nagarian, retaliated. It seems that he used his Drakhaoul to repel Eugene's army, defeating him in what was—by the few garbled accounts we've gleaned—a bitter battle."

"*Used* his Drakhaoul?" echoed Jagu.

"This Drakhaoul merges with his master to take on the form of a powerful dragon that breathes poisoned fire. Its breath is lethal. The secret dispatch our agents intercepted described how hundreds of men—and weapons—had been reduced to ashes."

"A dragon?" Kilian said, his voice dry with sarcasm. "Oh, come now, Maistre, are we really to believe the old legend? Weren't we taught at the seminary, Jagu, that the name 'Drakhaoul' is nothing but a metaphor for the forces of evil?"

"It is our duty, as Saint Sergius's disciples, to take up our patron saint's fight against the Drakhaoul," said the king earnestly, ignoring Kilian's cynical comment. Celestine saw that Enguerrand's eyes shone as he spoke. She was touched by his fervor although she wondered what they could possibly do against a daemon powerful enough to decimate a whole army.

"With respect, sire," said Jagu, "if even Sergius was not strong enough to defeat the Drakhaoul of Azhkendir, what can we do?"

Ruaud undid the top buttons of his cloak and habit and drew out a crystal on a gilded chain.

"The Angelstone?" said Jagu. The other members of the squad drew nearer to look. Celestine saw that its clear facets were marred by a trace of midnight shadow, deep within.

"This crystal has been in the Commanderie's keeping since Saint Sergius's time," said the Maistre.

"Does it mean that the Drakhaoul is close by?" Celestine asked uneasily.

"No," said Jagu. "The stone goes dark when a daemon is near."

"We need to learn a great deal more about the daemon before we make our move," continued Ruaud, tucking the crystal out of sight beneath his robes, "and so we're planning to—" He broke off as footsteps could be heard on the spiral stair. Captain Friard appeared, breathless, his brown hair speckled with melting snow.

"I beg your majesty's pardon," he said, holding out a sealed dispatch, "but I was told to deliver this to you without delay."

"It's from Ambassador d'Abrissard in Mirom," said Enguerrand in puzzled tones. He broke the seal and moved closer to one of the burning torches to read. Celestine watched his face as he read and saw a puzzled frown appear that changed all too soon to a look of bemused anger.

"What is it, sire?" Ruaud asked. Enguerrand thrust the letter into his hands.

"It seems that Eugene of Tielen is indestructible. In spite of his injuries, he has not only taken Azhkendir, but Muscobar as well—and annexed Smarna. He has seized the five rubies known as the Tears of Artamon and declared himself Emperor!"

Celestine glanced at Jagu.

"This doesn't bode well for Francia," he said softly. "Will it be our turn next?"

"You mean *war*?" Just saying the word aloud made Celestine feel disquieted. "Could it come to that?" For as long as she could remember, Francia had maintained an uneasy peace with Tielen, and she hated the thought of the bloodshed and heartbreak that war would inevitably bring.

"We must call the council together at once, Ruaud," said Enguerrand, hurrying toward the stair; Ruaud and Alain Friard followed.

"So even a Drakhaoul can't stop Eugene's ambitions," said Kilian wryly.

"Which begs the question," said Celestine, drawing her cloak closer to her as the snow-laden chill seeped into the crypt, "where is the Drakhaoul now? And what does the king intend us to do about it?"

"I'm off for a glass of mulled wine at the Pomme de Pin," Kilian called back, as he walked toward the spiral stair. "Anyone care to join me?"

"Sorry—I'm late for guard duty at the Forteresse." Jagu sped ahead, two steps at a time.

"You'll come, won't you, Viaud?" Kilian dragged Philippe Viaud after him.

Celestine followed them slowly, waiting until their footfalls had faded away and she was alone in the church with her memories. She never left Saint Meriadec's without lighting a candle for the soul of the man who had been the Maistre de Chapelle there, and the one most dear to her in the whole world.

She put a coin in the box and took out a candle of smooth white wax. In the grey sleety light filtering through the arched window, the little chapel dedicated to the saint was bright with votive candles and after she had added her single flame, she knelt awhile, watching it burn.

"Can it be six years since I last sang for you here, dearest Henri?" she whispered, seeing the shadow of his beloved face looking up from his music stand, smiling at her with those soft, warm grey eyes, as his expressive hands sustained and shaped the choir's tempo, nodding to her to begin. "Six years since that magus stole your soul." The chapel seemed to grow darker as the bitterness of her grief returned. "Yet I still miss you so . . ."

She stayed there, lost in memories of her dead love, until she heard the door open and a cold, wintry blast announced the arrival of the sacristan to make ready for vespers.

The salon de musique, like many of the public rooms in the Palace of Plaisaunces, had not been redecorated since the time of King Enguerrand's grandfather, and the dark oak paneling and heavy painted beams, coupled with the leaded lozenges of yellowing glass in the narrow windows, gave the whole chamber a dreary and oppressive air.

Jagu dragged the fortepiano closer to a window, so that what little daylight was penetrating the thick glass could illuminate his music.

As Celestine handed Jagu the new song she had brought to rehearse, she could not shake off the ominous feeling that had haunted her since their secret meeting with the king a few days ago. "To think that a daemon with the power to destroy a whole army so swiftly, so ruthlessly, is at large." She couldn't help shuddering, as she imagined the devastation the Drakhaoul could wreak if it attacked Francia. "A creature of destruction so powerful that its breath could reduce hundreds of living beings to ashes . . ."

"And the Tielens, with all their advanced military weaponry, were no match for it." Jagu propped the music up on the fortepiano, turning down the corners of the pages to facilitate a quick turn. He looked up at her, a little frown shadowing his face. "Yet, Eugene has triumphed, against all the odds. He must have found a way to defeat the Drakhaoul."

Celestine gave a dry little laugh. "I don't know who to be more afraid of: the Drakhaoul or the new Emperor!"

"Perhaps we'll learn more tonight." Jagu turned back to the new piece. "What's this? 'O, Mon Amou'?"

"It's in the Provençan dialect. I've been practicing it all night."

They had been invited to give a recital before Duke Raimon de Provença on one of his rare visits to the capital, and Celestine had gone to some pains to seek out a song from his native province. She and Jagu had learned early on in their performing careers that thoughtful little touches like that pleased their patrons and could help smooth the way to good diplomatic relations. And what better way to collect useful information as secret agents of the Commanderie than by mingling with their distinguished audiences and listening discreetly? Over the last six years, such missions had taken them from Allegonde to Tourmalise, even to Mirom, to perform before the Grand Duke and Duchess of Muscobar.

Jagu peered at the music, leaning so close in the poor light as he sight-read the introduction that his nose almost grazed the paper, while she went through her customary vocal exercises to warm up her voice.

The door suddenly opened and Celestine broke off in mid-arpeggio to see that Ruaud de Lanvaux had let himself in and was leaning on a long metal staff.

"What brings you here, Maistre?"

"I was about to send for you when I heard such delightful sounds issuing from this room that I guessed you were already in the palace." He spoke lightly enough but she saw from his grave expression that this was not just a social visit. "I've just come from the council." He approached the fortepiano so that the three of them could speak quietly together. "His majesty is sending you to Azhkendir, Jagu, to Saint Serzhei's Monastery. He wants the monks to lend us the saint's golden crook, the one the Blessed Sergius used to defeat the Drakhaouls."

"The king intends to challenge the Drakhaoul of Azhkendir?" Shy, bookish Enguerrand setting out to confront this daemon of darkness? Celestine was touched that he should dare to envisage such a feat—yet, at the same time, her heart was filled with misgivings. And when she looked at Ruaud, she saw her fears mirrored in his eyes.

"Isn't Azhkendir completely cut off by ice at this time of year?" Jagu, ever practical, had already begun to think of potential hazards in the plan.

"By the time you've completed the sea journey up the coast of Muscobar, the thaw should have set in. And as proof to the monks of our good faith, you will take this with you." Ruaud placed the staff on the top of the fortepiano and began to unscrew the head. Tipping it, he carefully removed a long, charred piece of wood, so ancient and brittle that it had been reinforced with golden wire. "Do you recognize this?"

"Saint Sergius's Staff." Jagu spoke the words with reverence. "But what makes you think the monks in Azhkendir will agree to the king's request, even when they see this, the Commanderie's most precious relic?"

"I visited the monastery myself some ten years ago. I believe that Abbot Yephimy will take our request seriously when he sees the Staff."

"You gave a talk to us at Saint Azilia's about your experiences in Azhkendir." Celestine could not help smiling at the memory. All the girls were sighing over him for weeks; they thought him so good-looking in his Commanderie uniform . . .

"And the Commanderie trusts me to take care of the Staff?" Jagu sounded doubtful.

"We're sending one of the squad along with you. Viaud, probably."

"Why not me?" Celestine rounded on the Maistre. She was hurt that he had not even considered her.

"It's a monastery," Jagu said. "Women aren't permitted. Besides, it's too dangerous."

"More dangerous than protecting Princess Adèle from those magi-assassins in Bel'Esstar?" He had injured her pride and she wasn't going to let him get away with it so easily. "I don't remember Philippe Viaud being of much use on that occasion."

She saw Jagu shoot a look of mute appeal at the Maistre, who affected not to notice, leaning across the fortepiano to place the metal staff firmly in Jagu's hands. "Papers and passports are being prepared for you, and we'll let you know soon about your partner. Report to my office in the morning; we've booked passage for you on a merchant ship sailing to Arkhelskoye tomorrow." He turned to leave, pausing at the door to say, "And take care; Azhkendir is a dangerous and uncivilized country."

Ruaud finished decrypting the latest intelligence from the ambassador in Muscobar and sat back in his chair to reread his work.

" 'Eugene of Tielen has claimed the right, by ancient law, to be crowned Emperor because he has gathered together the five ancient rubies, known as the Tears of Artamon, from the surrounding kingdoms that he has conquered: Khitari, Azhkendir, Smarna, and Muscobar. And as no one has dared to claim this right since the death of Artamon the Great centuries ago, there seems to be no legal reason to stop him reestablishing the old empire under the name of New Rossiya.

" 'The night before the Emperor's coronation, an extraordinary phenomenon was witnessed throughout Muscobar. Five shafts of crimson light were seen emanating from the palace. Official sources at the palace said that they were fireworks to celebrate the completion of the imperial crown. But, having seen these mysterious lights myself, I can only state that I have never seen fireworks that burned so long or with such intense color that the night skies were bathed in red, like blood. Could it be a new alchymical weapon that the Tielens are testing? I feel most uneasy at the prospect.' "

Armed with this ominous news, Ruaud went in search of the king.

"His majesty is closeted with his mother," the guards on the doors to the king's private apartments told him, "and she says that no one is to be admitted."

She. Ruaud ground his teeth in frustration. For how much longer was Queen Aliénor going to try to keep control over her son's life? "Then would you be so good as to tell his majesty that I've come on an urgent matter of state that requires his immediate attention?" He placed strong emphasis on the last words.

One of the guards disappeared into the apartments while Ruaud paced the antechamber, aware that the others were watching him curiously. After a while, the doors opened again.

"His majesty will see you now, Grand Maistre."

Ruaud strode in to find Enguerrand seated beside his mother; on the table in front of them were placed several portrait miniatures which, Ruaud noted, were all of young women. Aliénor glanced up and gave Ruaud a stare so forbidding that it took all his nerve not to glance away. But he had learned long ago not to allow her to browbeat him; if he stood his ground patiently enough, she would eventually retreat.

"You're interrupting a very important family discussion, Maistre de Lanvaux," she said in a voice of ice. "This state business had better be as urgent as you implied."

"Mother." Enguerrand glared at her.

"What could possibly be more important than drawing up a list of potential brides for you? What about Astasia Orlova of Muscobar?"

"That young lady is already taken," said Ruaud, "by the Emperor Eugene. She was crowned Empress in Mirom at what was, by our ambassador's account, an impressive ceremony."

Aliénor's plucked eyebrows shot up but she carried on, undaunted. "I've always thought that Esclairmonde de Provença, my cousin Raimon's elder daughter, would make an excellent choice."

"I'm not ready to get married yet," said Enguerrand.

"Or there's her younger sister Aude—"

"Mother!"

"This really is most inconvenient. We shall continue our discussion after dinner tonight, Enguerrand." Aliénor rose at last and swept out of the chamber.

"I'm sorry." The flushed look of embarrassment on Enguerrand's face was revealing; the king had not yet learned to hide his feelings very successfully.

"I imagine that her majesty is merely anxious to see you happily settled," Ruaud said, unable to stop himself from adding, "with a bride who will give Francia a healthy heir to the throne."

The flush deepened. "The urgent state business?" Enguerrand said, swiftly changing the subject.

Ruaud repressed a little smile as he handed the decrypted letter to the king. Enguerrand was learning fast. "It's from Fabien d'Abrissard, our ambassador to the New Rossiyan Empire."

Enguerrand looked up. "These Tears of Artamon—what do we know about them, Ruaud?"

Ruaud had asked Père Judicael to research the ancient

history of Artamon's reign. "It seems that the Emperor Artamon's sons fought so bitterly over the succession that his empire was divided into five and the ruby in the emperor's crown was also divided into five, and one fifth given to each of the princes."

"So Eugene's claim is legitimate?"

"So it seems."

"But if anyone else were to seize the rubies, his claim to the throne would be equally valid?"

"That might prove difficult, sire," said Ruaud, smiling openly at his pupil's line of reasoning. Enguerrand was beginning to think like a statesman. "But technically, legally, yes."

CHAPTER 2

"Pilgrims?" The Rossiyan officer looked up from the travelers' papers to see a dark-haired priest and his servant—a fair-haired youth, pretty as a girl. "You've come a long way, Père Jagu. All the way from Francia! And you've got an arduous journey ahead of you. I hope you're both used to roughing it." He let out a brusque laugh as he stamped their passports. "Don't expect a warm welcome from the locals, either. They don't like foreigners—and they don't hide their feelings!" He handed the papers back. "Can't blame 'em, I suppose. They didn't ask to be part of the new empire. But be on your guard." He stared pointedly at the youth, who had not said a word, although his blue eyes had widened at the warning. "There're robbers . . . and worse . . . out there in the wilds."

"What a wretched place," Celestine muttered to Jagu as they set out, Jagu leaning on his sturdy metal staff. Dilapidated warehouses and wooden sheds lined the quay; every building they passed was weather-battered, with peeling paint, exuding a reek of damp and rotting timber.

"What can you expect? It's completely cut off by the ice all winter."

But just around the end of the quay, they found themselves caught up in a surging tide of people.

"Fish market," said Celestine as they passed fishwives, hoarsely crying out their wares. The stink of pickled herrings was making her eyes water. Jostled by traders, she was soon separated from Jagu, confused by the babble of voices in different tongues, mingled with the raucous screaming of seagulls overhead.

Jagu grabbed hold of her by one arm and pulled her into the doorway of a tavern. "Wishing you hadn't volunteered to come?"

"It's a little late for that. You know how important this mission is to me. And ever since the news leaked out about Lord Gavril's arrest—"

"Be careful what you say here."

She glowered up at him. "With the New Rossiyan Army in control, the Drakhaon's imprisonment isn't exactly a secret anymore."

All the inns surrounding the harbor at Arkhelskoye were filled with merchants and sailors. Jagu and Celestine tramped from one to another, only to be turned away every time.

"What did you expect, Father?" said the landlady of the last hostelry on the quay as she poured out ale for her noisy customers. "Once the thaw comes, this place is overrun. Now with the Tielens here as well . . ." She raised her eyes heavenward. "You could try the Osprey's Nest. Take the cliff path from the northern end of the harbor. Better hurry; looks as if sea fog's setting in. You don't want to miss your step; it's a long drop to the rocks down below," she added, wheezing with laughter at her own joke.

Celestine looked up at Jagu. He shrugged, as if to say, *What choice do we have?*

Celestine stubbed her toe on a loose stone as they tramped up the cliff path. Jagu caught her as she lost her balance and righted her.

"Thank you."

"Watch where you place your feet," he said sternly. "One false move and you're in the sea."

Did he think she wasn't aware of the sheer drop down the rugged cliff face to the churning White Sea below? Was he already wishing that Kilian—or dependable Viaud—had been his partner for this mission?

It had been difficult enough having to hide the fact that

she was a woman aboard ship, especially when the curse of her monthly bleed arrived. She had taken special herbs to suppress its effects and to calm the cramping pains, but having to pretend that she had eaten something that disagreed with her could only convince Jagu for so long. As she had lain curled up in her little bunk, it had occurred to her that this pretense was probably as much for her own benefit as his. Though she had never heard him mention sisters, he must have guessed that she was as vulnerable to "women's troubles" as any other girl.

She was determined to see the mission through, if only to prove to herself that she was strong enough to cope with its challenges. And because the Faie had whispered to her that there were ancient mysteries hidden in the wilds of Azhkendir.

It took a good quarter hour's tramp up the cliffs to reach the Osprey's Nest—a dilapidated little inn overlooking the White Sea. The keen breeze off the rough sea below was a constant reminder that the spring thaw had only just melted the ice and Celestine was soon shivering.

"It's rather remote," she said, gazing at the single lantern glowing in the gathering dusk.

Jagu set down his bag on the rocks and took out two of the books of prayer he was carrying. "Let's not take any risks," he said. Concealed within a secret compartment in each book lay a pistol, powder, and shot. "Here."

"Lucky the Tielens didn't search us too zealously," Celestine said, priming the second weapon. "Or should I call them Rossiyans now? That officer was a Tielen; I could tell from his accent."

"According to our sources, the troops currently occupying Azhkendir are from Field Marshal Karonen's Northern Army." Jagu finished loading his pistol and tucked it beneath his priest's robes. "Let's hope we're not obliged to use these."

The smoky fug in the inn made Celestine's eyes water. Blinking, she saw men staring at them from around the large tiled stove. A strong, unsavory odor assaulted them from a bubbling cooking pot. *Fish*, thought Celestine, her empty stomach contracting at the thought. *And none too fresh either.*

An old woman was stoking the stove and a gust of smoke billowed out from the glowing coals inside. She slammed the door shut, securing the latch with the handle of the shovel, and pushed herself to her feet, grunting with the effort.

"Priests?" she said in the common tongue.

"Can you put us up for the night?" Jagu asked, in a mild tone of voice. Was Jagu actually enjoying acting out the role of a shy, scholarly priest? "All the taverns in Arkhelskoye are full."

The old woman hobbled closer and stared up at him, hands on her hips. "You don't *sound* like Tielens," she said suspiciously. "Tielens aren't welcome here."

"We're from Francia. Our order was founded in memory of Saint Serzhei."

"Francia? That's all right, then. I can give you a room. Don't expect anything fancy, though. You're not in Azhgorod here. Oh, and you pay me first." One gnarled hand shot out, palm upward. "Dinner's herring stew. Extra for bread. And ale."

"Celestin, pay the landlady," said Jagu. They had agreed to keep her assumed boy's name as close to her own as possible, in case of the odd, unintentional slip. Celestine dropped the coins into the landlady's outstretched hand, aware that the other drinkers were watching her every move.

"So priests do pretty well for themselves in Francia?" The landlady bit a coin with yellowed teeth. Too late Celestine realized that they had both misread the situation. Azhkendi priests were probably too poor to stay in inns.

"My master will give you a blessing if you let us eat for free, lady."

"Nice try, boy." The landlady cackled, retreating to ladle out two bowls of stew from the steaming pot.

"We're on a pilgrimage to Saint Serzhei's Monastery," said Jagu as they ate, "and we're looking for someone to be our guide."

Celestine was prodding at the stew in the earthenware bowl with her spoon; she had spotted a piece of herring tail, but the other chunks floating in the oily water were most probably winter vegetables: turnips, maybe, and parsnips . . . The "herring" was only there to give flavor. She dipped a chunk of dry bread in and cautiously sucked the liquid out of it, trying not to wince.

"You've come a long way, Father," observed the landlady, adding with another cackle, "and you've still got a long way to go! It's several days' journey from here to the Kerjhenezh Forest."

"I could take you by boat to the samphire beaches," a grizzle-bearded fisherman said, puffing out an acrid waft of tobacco smoke from his pipe. "Though you need good sea legs; the seas are mighty rough around the Spines this time of year."

"By boat?" Jagu looked up from his bowl of stew.

"Most pilgrims from the capital take the route through the forest, but from Arkhelskoye it's far quicker to go by sea—once the ice has melted. It's hardly a day's journey on foot to the monastery from Seal Cove. Half a day for you hardy young people."

Jagu consulted Celestine with a look. She nodded, wondering how good her sea legs would prove in a little fishing smack.

"Let me buy you a drink," said Jagu to the fisherman. "An ale for my friend here."

"He's called Chaikin," said the landlady.

"Ugh. This room stinks of fish too." Celestine sniffed the air of the poky little room, searching out the source of the smell. "It's coming from the lamp! They must be burning fish oil."

"Herring fishing is one of Azhkendir's main sources of trade and income," said Jagu. "Alongside furs and mineral ores."

"Must you speak like a traveler's guidebook? And there's only one bed, or hadn't you noticed?"

He shrugged. "I'll sleep on the floor."

The harsh wind off the sea rattled the shutters, setting the lamp flame fluttering. Celestine threw down her cloak and ran her fingers through her cropped hair. She became aware that Jagu was staring at her in the dim light. "Well?"

"I still can't get used to seeing you this way."

"With short hair? How else was I to disguise myself as your servant? Priests don't usually travel about with young women—or boys with luxuriant tresses. Besides, it'll soon grow again." She tugged her fingers through the thick strands. "But it badly needs a wash. Oh, for a long soak in a hot bath . . ."

"I still don't understand why the Maistre sent you on this mission. Kilian or Philippe Viaud would have been a much safer choice."

"Safer for me, or for you, Jagu?" She saw him blink; the slightest of reactions, but enough to show that she had touched another sensitive spot. First the hair, now this. Yet it had taken weeks of travel to get him to begin to open up about his concerns; he had been even more reticent than usual. "I *asked* the Maistre to send me. You know I have skills that make me the best suited to this mission."

This was not the first time they had entered into this argument, and Jagu did not even bother to reply. Instead, he undid the top fastenings of his habit and drew out the chain concealed beneath, bringing the attached crystal out and holding it up to the flickering lamp flame.

"No change in the Angelstone," he said, as the facets reflected the yellowish glow.

"If anything the trace of darkness has grown fainter. It's almost as if we're moving farther away from the daemon," she said, puzzled.

"Or it's moving away from us." Jagu carefully unscrewed the head of his Staff and slid out the cylinder concealed inside.

Celestine watched Jagu check the brittle fragments of the ancient Staff, making sure that the delicate golden wire binding them together had not become dislodged.

"And the irony is that, thanks to the Emperor's conquests, it's never been easier to enter Azhkendir." Jagu gently slid the precious relic back and secured the end of the tube. "I never thought I'd have any reason to be grateful to the Tielens, but they've already made the ports and roads much safer for travelers."

"As long as they don't suspect us." Celestine drew her feet up onto the narrow bed, hugging her knees to her chest.

"Of what? We're members of the Francian church, here on pilgrimage. What's suspicious about that?"

"Let's not underestimate the Tielen agents. Have you noticed, Jagu? News travels remarkably fast in this new empire." She had been thinking about this during the long sea voyage.

"Tielen is a remarkably efficient nation. Their communications network functions far better than ours."

"Suspiciously better. We're still dependent on carrier pigeons and swift horses."

"And your theory?" Jagu sounded drowsy. Maybe the local beer was more potent than he was accustomed to.

"My father's invention. The one Kaspar Linnaius stole. The Vox Aethyria," she whispered. "The device that enables the human voice to be carried hundreds of miles through the air. If only we could find out . . ."

"Lend me your cloak."

"What are you doing, Jagu?"

"Just making sure we're not disturbed." He rolled up her cloak and inserted the precious metal cylinder in the middle. Then he lay down by the door, pillowing his head on the bundle. "Now that we're ashore, we'll have to take precautions to make sure they don't try to rob us in the night."

She stared at him. "You can't go to sleep down there," she said after a few minutes. "There's a howling draft. Your back will be so stiff by morning that you won't be able to move."

"I'm fine." He turned on his side, away from her, and snuffed out the lamp wick. Why did he have to be so stubborn?

"Listen to the wind. Such a lonely sound. There's nothing out there but the sea and the night." Suddenly she felt so small, so vulnerable, an insignificant grain of sand blown along on the fast-flowing current of time. "We're so far from anywhere here, on the edge of the known world. If you get sick, how can I carry on this mission alone?" she said into the darkness. He did not answer. "I'm cold." Which was true. "I need my cloak. What's the harm in sharing the bed? It's not as if we're going to take our clothes off and lie naked together. It's just to keep warm."

She heard him sit up. He let out a sigh. Next moment she felt the wooden frame creak, then shudder as he sat on the edge of the bed.

"Move over," he said in resigned tones. He wrapped her cloak around her, then lay down beside her. She snuggled down, her earlier sense of desolation melting away in the warm shadow of his long, lean body. The bed was so narrow it was impossible to lie side by side without touching.

"Jagu?" she said softly. All she heard was his breathing: slow, regular, reassuringly soothing. *Asleep already? Or just feigning it?* She closed her eyes, smiling to herself in the darkness.

The sharp light of dawn pierced the cracks in the shutters. Jagu opened his eyes. For a moment he lost all sense of where he was, aware only of an unfamiliar feeling of warmth and contentment. Then he saw the golden head lying so close to his.

Gently yet swiftly, he drew back his arm which in sleep he had unconsciously, protectively, wound around her. She was so deeply asleep that she only murmured like a dreaming child, nestling closer to him. She must have cuddled up to him in the night, instinctively drawn to the warmth of his body.

He pushed himself up on one elbow, gazing down at her as she slept on, oblivious to his presence. The urge to touch those tousled strands of golden hair was almost too much to endure.

His hand crept out, hovering over her.

What am I doing? Surely I'm old enough now to control these urges! It's not as if I'm still a boy, cursed with wet dreams.

"You awake, Father?" The innkeeper's shrill voice called.

He started, hastily withdrawing his hand. "Chaikin's ready to leave!"

"We'll be down right away," he called back.

"I want a bath," grumbled Celestine, sitting up and rubbing her eyes. "I stink of travel. So do you," she added pointedly.

"They have communal bathhouses in Azhkendir," Jagu said, suspecting that she was trying to provoke him. "If you went in with me, *Celestin*, it wouldn't be long before—"

"Yes, yes, I understand."

Celestine had no option but to settle for a perfunctory wash in a bucket of ice-cold well water that left her gasping but fully awake. *Will I ever get properly clean again?* Perhaps after a while, they would become used to the smell of each other's unwashed bodies.

She and Jagu chewed their way through a bowl apiece of gritty, glutinous porridge. Then they fetched their belongings and followed the old fisherman down a narrow, crumbling cliff path to the rocky shore far below.

They had to wade out through the freezing tide to reach Chaikin's fishing boat, which lay at anchor in the little inlet.

"Wind's a fresh northeasterly this morning," Chaikin told Jagu as he helped them clamber aboard. "Can your boy make himself useful? I could do with a couple of extra hands."

"We'll both help out," Celestine heard Jagu say as he stowed their bags and the precious Staff beneath an old piece of sailcloth. "Surely you don't sail her single-handed?" Jagu added as he pulled on the ropes to raise the boat's mainsail, a triangular expanse of canvas.

"When I drop you off at Seal Cove, farther up the coast, I'll be picking up my grandson." Chaikin jabbed the air with the stem of his pipe, then clamped it back between his teeth.

"Do you take many pilgrims to the monastery?"

"Not anymore. Not since the Arkhel Clan was slaughtered by Lord Volkh." Chaikin removed his pipe and spat. "Maybe that'll all change now."

Jagu brought out a notebook and did little pencil sketches

of the contours of the coast, marking the inlets and bays they passed. Celestine noticed that the raw northerly wind had brought a touch of color to his pale complexion; his cheeks and nose were red with the cold. She felt her own nose running and wiped it on her sleeve, as she had often seen the choirboys do at the cathedral in Lutèce. She saw him look at her in horror and stuck out her tongue at him.

"Seals!" Chaikin yelled, pointing with his pipe. Celestine forgot her own discomfort, gripping the side of the boat. Several sleek grey-brown heads were bobbing up and down between the waves, watching them. The fierce salt wind blowing her hair into her eyes, she followed their antics with delight as they swam effortlessly past through the choppy waters.

"There's a colony out on one of the Drakhaon's Spines." Chaikin pointed again to the line of jagged rocks protruding out of the sea; from their vantage point they looked remarkably like the back of a great dragon emerging from the waves.

"A word of advice for you, Father," Chaikin was saying to Jagu. "If you keep to the Pilgrims' Road through the forest, you'll find your way to Saint Serzhei's. The brothers mark certain trees every year to show the way. There are shrines and pilgrims' wells of clean water to make sure you're on the right route. But don't wander off the path. Wild boar and wolves often come down from the Kharzhgylls in winter, looking for food. Oh, and the robbers . . ."

"A day's journey inland," Jagu said as they tramped over the wet sand. The tide was going out, exposing a wide expanse of sandy beach, filled with little tidal streams, runnels, and rock pools. Gulls skimmed low over the shore. The air smelled of sea salt, mingled with the slightly sulfurous tang of mud.

"If only we had horses. We'll never reach the monastery before dark; it's already well past midday." Celestine pointed to the pale sun which was no longer directly overhead.

"Then we'll just have to find one of these pilgrims' shelters before nightfall."

* * *

The ancient forest of Kerjhenezh covered most of the eastern corner of Azhkendir, extending as far as the foothills of the snow-covered Kharzhgyll Mountains, the natural border between the Drakhaon's lands and the khanate of Khitari, now all united as part of Eugene's empire. New spring leaves on the thick-girthed oaks were only just beginning to unfurl, but the heavy branches of the firs—larch, pine, and cedar—kept the Pilgrims' Road well shaded and the sandy ground underfoot soft with a carpet of dried needles.

Jagu pointed to the faded white symbol of Sergius's crook daubed on the knotted trunk of a tall pine. "Ironic, isn't it? The very reason for our journey is going to show us the way." Celestine heard the faint, warning call of a bird, answered by another, farther off. She had been troubled by a strange sensation ever since they parted company with Chaikin. From time to time she shivered, even though she was not cold or feverish.

A current of silvery translucence snakes through the air . . .

The green branches overhead stirred, moved by a freak gust of wind.

She stopped, hugging her arms to her, suddenly chilled to the depths of her soul.

"Celestine?" Jagu, realizing that she was no longer walking beside him, turned and saw her standing, gazing up into the cloudy sky.

"What is *he* doing here?" she said, as if talking to herself.

"He? Who do you mean?" Jagu looked upward. All he could see above the interwoven branches of shaggy fir was the milky pallor of the cloud-veiled sky.

"Didn't you feel it?" Her eyes had a distant, unfocused look. "It was the Magus."

CHAPTER 3

"The Magus?" Jagu hastily pushed back his sleeve, checking the mark on his left wrist. "Are you sure?" He showed her; the sigil could only faintly be detected, like a pearlescent tattoo against the blue veins marking his pulse point. "If it's a magus, then it's not the one who did this to me."

"Why is Kaspar Linnaius in Azhkendir?" Celestine asked, kicking a pinecone out of her path. "Is he here on the Emperor's business? Or on some affair of his own?" She felt on edge now.

In a little clearing, they found the first shrine to the saint—a worn stone plinth, overgrown with ivy. Jagu bent down to clear away some of the clinging strands. Faint letters could just be made out, surmounted by the sign of the crook pointing the way to the monastery. The only sound was the twittering of birds and the occasional feathery flutter of wings as they flitted across the glade.

"Doesn't it strike you as ironic that Saint Sergius is venerated here," Jagu said, straightening up, "even though his murderer, the Drakhaoul, has lived on for centuries in the ruling house? How can the Azhkendis reconcile the two, the saint and the daemon?"

While he was speaking, Celestine noticed that a strange stillness had fallen over the green glade.

"The birds have stopped singing. Is someone watching us?"

"Show yourself!" Jagu drew his pistol. Back to back, heel to heel, they slowly turned around, checking for any sign of movement among the lichen-blotched trunks. But if anyone was shadowing them, he kept well hidden. She heard him let out a slow breath. "This is only the first of the shrines; there are four more to go before we reach the monastery."

"If we're going to reach the pilgrims' shelter before nightfall, we'd better make a move." Celestine was tired and her feet were hot and sore, but the knowledge that Kaspar Linnaius was close by gave her new determination to keep going. As they left the glade, she noticed Jagu glancing back over his shoulder. Had the Magus been shadowing them?

They stopped by the mossy banks of a forest stream to catch fish for supper. Celestine had learned on earlier missions that Jagu's stillness and quick eye made him a good fisherman.

"That's not a trick you learned at the seminary," she said, watching him dispatch the slippery, struggling char with an expertly judged blow to the head.

"My elder brother Markiz taught me," he said, laying it beside his two earlier catches.

"How many brothers do you have?" He so rarely spoke of his family that she couldn't resist the chance to tease out some information about his early life.

"Markiz took over the family estate when my father died three years ago. Léonor is a notary in Kemper. And I . . ."

"You showed an early gift for music, so your father sent you to a seminary."

He pulled a face. "My father never really understood," he said curtly, getting to his feet. "Time to go." He pointed to the sky. "We have to find the pilgrims' shelter before dusk."

The daylight was fading; glints of gold from the setting sun filtered through the branches. In the twilight, Celestine tripped on a knotted tree root.

"Ow!" She hopped to lean against a mossy trunk, nursing her stubbed toe.

"Watch where you place your feet. If you trip and sprain your ankle, I'm not going to carry you."

Why did Jagu always have to be so self-righteous? She glared at him. "It's getting a little hard to see my feet, or hadn't you noticed? It'll soon be dark. And then what do we do?"

"If we don't reach the pilgrims' shelter, we'll just have to make camp here."

She pulled a face. "Oh, wonderful! And be prey to all those ravenous wolves and boar Chaikin warned us about?"

"I'll light a fire." Jagu glowered back at her. "We're not exactly short of kindling."

"Then we might as well shout to any local brigands, 'Here we are, why don't you come and rob us?'"

He said nothing to her taunt, continuing along the path. She set off resignedly after him, dragging her sore foot.

"Smells of damp." Celestine sniffed as they investigated the shelter.

"It's been a while since any pilgrims stayed here." Jagu straightened up from the ash-stained hearthstone.

"Perhaps we're the first this year."

"At least there's a well with clean water. And a roof of sorts over our heads."

Having grown up in Saint Azilia's Convent, Celestine was accustomed to making do with such basic comforts. She wondered whether sleeping in drafty dormitories and rising before dawn each day to do backbreaking chores had toughened her, making her even better suited to enduring the hardships of life on the road than seminary-educated Jagu.

While Jagu laid and lit a fire, she drew water from the ancient well. By the time she was lugging the battered bucket back across the clearing to the shelter, it was dark and a spatter of sparks shot up into the darkening glade.

"Azhkendir, Saint Sergius's birthplace." Jagu leaned back, gazing into the flames. "Just think; this is the same forest in which he grew up. He might even have fished in the same stream. I wonder what made him decide to dedicate his life to God . . ."

Celestine glanced at him; he seemed to be unaware that she was watching him, lost in his own thoughts. His dark eyes burned, not just with the reflection of the firelight but with an inner passion. She had rarely known Jagu to speak of his beliefs; he had only told her that he had turned his back on a career in music and entered the Commanderie after Maistre de Lanvaux had saved him from a soul-stealing. But hearing him talk made her realize how little he ever revealed of himself to anyone, even to her, keeping so much bottled up inside.

"I found most of the texts that they made us study at the seminary boring . . . or difficult to understand. But when we read Argantel's *Life of the Blessed Sergius,* everything changed. It was inspiring. And when Maistre de Lanvaux rescued me from the magus"—he looked up at her through the leaping flames—"I remember thinking, '*This* is what Sergius must have been like. This desperate show of courage in the face of impossible odds.' "

"I wish I could have seen the Maistre in action," she said fondly. Jagu had never really spoken of his encounter with the magus before; all she knew was that it had left him scarred and wary. But Ruaud de Lanvaux was a bond they shared; he had rescued both of them from certain death: she, a starving, orphaned child, he, a schoolboy marked as a magus's prey.

"Careful, you'll burn your tongue," warned Jagu, handing Celestine the spitted fish, hot from the flames.

She was so hungry by then that she didn't care. The white flesh of the char, silvery skin crisped and charred by the fire, tasted delicious. She licked her sticky fingers when there was nothing left but bones and looked up to see him watching her. There was a rare hint of a grin on his face.

"What?"

"I was just thinking what your adoring public would think if they could see their idol now: hair hacked short, wiping the grease from her lips with the back of her hand."

"Is it so different from Gauzia playing a breeches role in an opera?" Celestine hadn't given Gauzia much thought till

then; circumstances had driven the two girls very far apart—
Gauzia to a prestigious career in opera, Celestine to a new
life as a secret agent of the Commanderie.

She and Jagu rarely spoke of Henri de Joyeuse, even
though it was he who had first brought them together. The
truth was that neither had ever fully recovered from his
death six years ago. But if Jagu had lost a beloved teacher
and mentor, Celestine had lost her first and only love. The
best way to keep his memory alive in their hearts was to ensure that his music was played wherever their Commanderie work took them. To the musical world they were
renowned as interpreters of his songs—and under this guise
they had traveled throughout the western quadrant, giving
concerts while at the same time gaining valuable information to feed back to the Commanderie about foreign affairs. Celestine had learned very early how to use her looks
to charm all manner of secrets from smitten diplomats and
politicians. And thus far no one had ever suspected her of
spying for Francia. Thus far . . .

The sound of distant bells ringing could be heard, oddly
sweet on the morning air.

Through the thinning tree trunks ahead, Celestine could
see whitewashed walls. A few minutes later, she and Jagu
emerged in a sun-dappled apple orchard where bees droned
in the pink and white blossoms. At the far end, Celestine
spotted two monks, one old, one young, tending beehives.

"At last," she said. "This must be it." Her blisters were
throbbing and she could no longer help limping. The
thought that there would be clean water and medicinal
salves to soothe her aching feet was the one thing that kept
her going.

"Wait." Jagu checked her, one hand on her shoulder.
"Let's make certain . . ." He pulled out the Angelstone and
held it up to the light. "No change," he said and concealed
it beneath his shirt again.

*I could have told you as much, Jagu. But you still don't
trust my powers . . .*

The young monk, hearing voices, looked up and came hurrying through the trees to greet them.

"Good day to you, brothers. It's early in the year for pilgrims," he said, grinning at them. "My name's Lyashko. Have you come far?"

"From Francia. My name is Jagu and this is my servant, Celestin."

"Francia!" echoed Brother Lyashko. "Do you hear that, Brother Beekeeper?"

The elder monk came hobbling over and peered at them shortsightedly. "Run on ahead, Lyashko, and tell Abbot Yephimy."

Lyashko set off at a run toward the white walls of the monastery.

"Welcome to Saint Sergius, my brothers," rang out a strong, vibrant voice.

Celestine saw a tall, broad-shouldered priest striding vigorously toward them, arms wide open. His brown hair and long beard were streaked with iron grey, but he bore himself more like a soldier than a monk.

"We are members of the Francian Commanderie, Abbot," said Jagu. "Is there anywhere more private that we could talk?"

Celestine noted that the abbot gave her a long, appraising glance as they entered the silent cloisters and knew that he had seen through her disguise; Yephimy was obviously not some doddery old country priest. It was not going to be easy to persuade him to part with the monastery's precious relic, no matter how noble the cause.

"Now, what is all this really about?" he asked, ushering them into his study.

"The leader of our order has been monitoring the disquieting growth of daemonic activity in this part of the world," said Jagu. "We have been sent to investigate."

"Ah," said Yephimy, folding his hands together. "The Drakhaoul."

"Is that its Azhkendi name?" Celestine asked, testing him.

Yephimy frowned at her. "It never revealed its true name. However, your leader will be pleased to learn that the daemon has been cast out from Lord Gavril's body."

"Cast out, maybe, but not destroyed," said Jagu. "Members of our order tracked it along the Straits. We believe it may have gone to ground in Muscobar."

"What? It's still at large?" From Abbot Yephimy's look of dismay, Celestine knew they had him at a disadvantage.

"We believe so. And that is why the Grand Master of our order has commissioned the reforging of Sergius's Staff."

"Sergius's Staff?" Yephimy repeated. "You have Sergius's Staff? But how? The Chronicles state that it was shattered in Sergius's last battle with the Drakhaoul." He rose, staring at them with suspicion. "Exactly who are you, and what is this Commanderie?"

"We are Companions of the Order of Saint Sergius, Abbot," said Jagu. "Our order is dedicated to the destruction of all daemonic influences in the world. As for the Staff, well, legend has it that Argantel, the founder of our order, fled Azhkendir with the shattered pieces and had it repaired in Francia. All the pieces save one: the crook, which we understand you keep here, in the shrine."

"Lord Argantel was indeed Sergius's friend," said Yephimy slowly. "But our Chronicles do not record what became of him. So. Show me this relic."

Jagu placed his metal Staff on Yephimy's desk and unscrewed the top. He tipped the shaft gently and out slid the charred fragments, bound into a whole with bands of golden wire.

Yephimy put out one hand and touched them reverently. "These should be kept here, with the saint's bones. Have you come to return it to the shrine?"

"You misunderstand our intentions, Abbot," said Jagu gravely. "We are on the trail of this daemon. We intend to use the Staff to destroy it."

"Will you give us Sergius's golden crook?" Seeing the look of alarm in the abbot's eyes, Celestine put the question they had traveled hundreds of miles to ask. "So that we can defeat the daemon and send it back to the Realm of Shadows?"

Yephimy let out a sigh. "I cannot answer for my brothers without consulting them," he said, "but I offer you the hospitality of the monastery while we discuss your proposition."

Jagu placed his hand on the abbot's arm, staring intently into his face. "This matter is urgent. I beg you, Abbot, do not discuss it too long."

Jagu and Celestine joined the monks for supper in the refectory, sitting with the abbot and the two beekeepers, Lyashko and old Osinin.

"We're self-sufficient here," said the abbot, gesturing to the food on the tables. "Everything you eat has been grown and harvested here, from the beetroot soup to the goats' cheese."

"This bread tastes so good," said Celestine, trying not to gulp it down too fast in her hunger.

"Try our special liqueur," said Brother Lyashko, lifting a stoneware bottle. "It's made with honey and mountain herbs."

"It's strong stuff for a young lad," warned the abbot. "But you must take a bottle when you leave; a drop or two will warm you up on cold nights."

"So the Clan Wars are finally at an end?" Jagu asked.

Yephimy nodded. "I never thought I would say it, but I give thanks to God for the Emperor's intervention. The Tielens have brought peace to our war-ravaged country at last. And now that the Drakhaoul is gone—"

"Did you see him in the forest?" asked Osinin suddenly as he slurped his soup. "You must have passed him on the pilgrim's route."

"We saw no one," said Celestine, wondering if Brother Beekeeper's wits were wandering.

"That old fellow who came here yesterday," persisted Brother Osinin. "Spent all day doing research in the library. You remember, Abbot? The one with the peculiar eyes. Gives you the chills when he looks at you. Colder than a winter blizzard."

"Peculiar eyes?" Celestine was only half-listening, intent on mopping up the last of her soup with her bread.

"If you're referring to Magister Linnaius, Brother," the abbot said pensively, "he left rather suddenly. I don't think he even came to bid me farewell."

"Kaspar Linnaius was here?" Celestine was all attention. "Could you show us the books he was reading?"

A luminous blue dusk was settling over the monastery as Celestine and Jagu followed the abbot across the courtyard, and there was a crisp chill in the air. From the darkness of the forest came the distant, eerie hooting of owls.

Yephimy lit a lantern and led them past shelf after shelf of old leather-bound volumes to a little door at the far end, which he stooped to unlock with a key from a chain worn around his neck. "We keep our oldest, most precious manuscripts in here," he said proudly.

Celestine stopped in the doorway to the little book room, sniffing. There was a hint of something lingering in the dusty air that reminded her of her father's study. She held up the lantern to illuminate the chained book lying open on the desk.

"*The Glorious Life and Martyr's Death of the Blessed Serzhei of Kerjhenezh*," said the abbot reverently. "This copy is hand-scribed; it dates from the time of Artamon."

"But what's this?" Celestine held the lantern closer to the yellowed vellum pages; something glittered faintly in the glow. She gently touched it and brought her fingertips close to her face.

Jagu, looking over her shoulder, began to read by the flickering light. "'Armed with the might of the Righteous Ones, Serzhei banished the Drakhaouls from Rossiya, and bound them in a place of torment for all eternity. Yet there was one who still defied him and all the hosts of heaven.'" He looked up. "The text is referring to the Drakhaoul of Azhkendir, isn't it, Abbot?"

The abbot nodded.

"I think that there was a secret text hidden on this page," Celestine said, "and this pretty alchymical dust has been used by the Magus to reveal it." She brushed the dust from her fingers onto the open volume but, to her disappointment, nothing happened. "So Linnaius must have come here—on the Emperor's orders—to discover the place where Sergius imprisoned the remaining Drakhaouls."

"The Magus is still close by." Celestine rounded on Jagu as they crossed the courtyard. "Why can't we go after him?"

"Because he has a significant advantage over us," said Jagu flatly, "in that he can fly. And we can't."

"So you're just going to ignore the fact that he's—"

"Now just wait a moment." Jagu caught hold of her by the arm. "What is our mission?" he said sternly.

"To destroy the Drakhaoul."

"And our orders are—"

"To return directly. With or without the golden crook." A sullen, almost rebellious look had appeared in her eyes.

"So you were just about to abandon the mission and go chasing off after Kaspar Linnaius?"

She pulled away from him and stood, staring at him defiantly. "We've never been this close to him before, Jagu. And you saw for yourself that he's been researching the history of the Drakhaouls. Even the abbot was shaken."

He let out a sigh. Sometimes she could be so headstrong. "We've only a couple of days before the *Dame Blanche* sails from Arkhelskoye. There's no time left."

"Have you forgotten?" She seized his left wrist and tugged back the sleeve, exposing the place where the magus had seared his mark on Jagu's wrist. "We made a pact together. In Saint Meriadec's. You vowed to hunt down the magus with me." In the dying light her eyes had darkened to the deep blue of the dusk. It was all he could do to resist her: her pale face upraised, pleadingly, to his.

"But that was before the Drakhaoul was set loose. This is an unprecedented situation. We both made another vow before God, remember? To act as the Knights of the Commanderie used to in olden times and fight the forces of evil."

"Fine." She let go of his wrist. "Follow the old chivalrous code if you must. But I say that we're making a grave mistake in not investigating this matter further."

* * *

The chanting of the monks of Kerjhenezh filled the white-washed dome of the chapel with a dark sonority that sent little shivers through Jagu's whole body. The sound resonated to the very core of his being. The ancient hymns to Saint Sergius exuded a raw, untrained energy that, though they had nothing of the refined beauty or complexity of the choral singing at Saint Meriadec's or the cathedral of Saint Eustache, spoke of the harsh truths of life and death. Many of the monks had beards as white as the snow on the jagged mountaintops beyond the forest, yet their voices were strong and deep-throated, filled with a vigor that belied their years. There was no organ to support them, just the occasional ringing of bronze-voiced bells.

Candles of ochre beeswax made from Brother Osinin's hives filled the dark Azhkendi night with light and gave off a musky, honeyed smoke, warming the cold air. Their flames gilded the fading colors of the frescoes depicting the life of the saint, making the gold leaf of his halo and the feathery wings of the guardian angels gleam.

This is just how it must have been in Sergius's time. The soft glow of the candles dimmed, and Jagu blinked the tears away unashamedly. This was what he had been trying to explain to Celestine in the courtyard earlier. This was why he had joined the Commanderie in the first place; to be a warrior for good against the forces of evil.

Why didn't she understand?

Even here he could not stop thinking about her.

"Blessed Sergius, help me to learn to live with this temptation," he prayed silently. "Show me how to be true to my vows."

Had Sergius ever fallen in love? If so, then Argantel's chronicles of his friend's life left no mention of it. But Mhir, the patron saint of the Allegondan Commanderie, had given his life to save Azilis, the woman he loved.

Jagu thought that he had come to terms with his feelings for Celestine. Like all Guerriers, they had both taken a vow of celibacy when they joined the Commanderie. Yet the deeper they journeyed into Azhkendir, the more his willpower had begun to weaken. They had undertaken many missions for the Commanderie, yet this was the first on which they had been alone.

Is this a test? Is this what it really means to try to tread the same path as Saint Sergius? That without temptation to resist, there's no chance of growing spiritually stronger?

Or have I been deceiving myself all this time?

"This is excellent work, Kaspar." The Emperor leafed through the information that Linnaius had extracted from the monastery library, his eyes alight. He had never lost the boyish enthusiasm that Linnaius had found so engaging when he first began to work for the royal house of Tielen. But the Magus was far from happy about Eugene's obsession with summoning a Drakhaoul of his own. "Now that you have discovered the location of the Serpent Gate, what's to stop us going to search for it?"

"Eugene, please read again—with great attention—that page that I translated from Lord Argantel's *The Life of the Blessed Sergius.*"

"Very well." Eugene began to read aloud. " 'Prince Nagazdiel must never be set free. For if this prison is breached, the darkness will cover your world in perpetual night and he and his kindred will lay waste to the earth.

" 'And then the seraph spoke to Sergius, saying, "To that end, the Warriors of Heaven have put a seal on the Door to the Realm of Shadows, that can only be breached by a crime so horrible that none would dare to undertake it. For only by the sacrifice of the Emperor's children in that far-distant place can that Door ever be opened again and the dread Prince Nagazdiel released. And no mortal would dare stoop to such a base and inhuman act." ' " He looked up at Linnaius. "Surely this is nothing more than one of those ancient prophecies that sound doom-laden, yet are merely a warning to the curious?" He laughed. "Even if they could break the cypher, who would go such lengths as to try to kidnap my daughter, Karila, and transport her thousands of leagues away to some obscure island that may—or may not—exist?"

Linnaius sighed. Eugene was right. The text had lain hidden for centuries; who else had the skills to decipher it, let alone make use of the information? Yet still he wished that Eugene would be content with what he had already achieved and not constantly yearn for more.

CHAPTER 4

"This mission has been a failure." Celestine threw down her heavy pack. "We've traveled all this way only to return empty-handed."

"Not entirely so." Jagu held up the stoneware bottle Brother Beekeeper had given him as a parting gift.

"The monastery's life-preserving liqueur? Strong enough to strip paint, I'll wager." They had endured bedbugs, inedible food, and all kinds of weather on their quest, only to be rewarded with a bottle of the local *eau-de-vie*.

"It's disappointing that Abbot Yephimy was unwilling to part with Sergius's crook," said Jagu distantly, "but not entirely unexpected."

"*Disappointing?*" Sometimes Jagu's refusal to show his feelings could be so irritating.

"Remember what the Maistre told us: Use every opportunity to record the lay of the land for future reference. Now that we know the monastery from the inside, we can plan our next move."

"To steal the crook?" She was surprised that Jagu would even suggest such a thing.

"The monks have lived under the Drakhaoul's shadow for so long that they have become blind to its powers." He took a sip from his water bottle. "They don't realize the danger they've set loose on the rest of the world in driving it from Lord Gavril's body."

"But just the two of us? Without backup?"

He shook his head. "Of course not. We'll need a whole detachment to pull this off."

"A detachment of pilgrims?" The image was so odd that it almost made her smile.

"And a swift cutter waiting in the cove nearby for a quick—" He broke off, as if listening.

"What is it?"

She only caught the flash of movement out of the corner of one eye. Jagu gave a muffled grunt and crumpled to the ground.

"Jag—" Her scream was stifled as someone clamped a hand over her mouth. Next moment, she was forced to her knees. Her unseen attacker pulled back her hood and, grabbing her by the chin, yanked her head upward. She heard him let out a low whistle of surprise—and then, with brutal swiftness, he pushed her onto her back on the rough ground. She was aware as she fell that another man was ripping open her bag, searching for anything worth stealing, she guessed. *The book.* The precious book was concealed inside, wrapped in a spare shirt.

"Faie!" She tried to call to her for help, but the pressure of the man's hand only increased. The fall had knocked the breath from her body. Her assailant forced himself on top of her, trying to subdue her with the weight of his body. He had guessed she was not a boy. She fought and struggled as, with his free hand, he tugged at her clothes. He was too strong for her.

Dizzy, angry, she attempted to knee him in the groin—but her desperate struggles only seemed to excite him the more. She could not even reach the little knife she wore tucked into her boot. And she could feel his breath against her throat, hot and panting, as he fumbled beneath her cloak, trying to tug down her breeches.

"*Faie!*" she cried again in terror. And suddenly the twilit glade was filled with a dazzle of shimmering light. Her attacker paused. The moment's distraction gave Celestine her chance. Up came her knee again, jabbing hard into his groin with all the fury she could muster. He fell back, gasping. And in that moment, she felt the Faie's protecting arms around her. Bathed in the pure, white light of her guardian spirit, she arose, staring down at her attacker. The Faie gave her strength, the Faie's power blazed through her eyes, flowing through her body until she felt as if she were glowing with aethyrial radiance.

Slowly, she raised her hand, pointing accusingly at the robber. She could see him clearly at last, crouching like a beast at bay, his face twisted, his bloodshot eyes bulging. She took a step toward him and saw, to her satisfaction, that he cringed away from her, one shaking hand rising to shield his eyes from her brilliance.

She heard his accomplice give an incoherent shout of fear. She took another step toward her would-be violator. Her fingers tingled with the Faie's power.

"Celestine, *no!*" Jagu's hoarse voice broke through the trance. "Don't do it!"

"*He deserves to die.*" She heard another voice, clear and hard as ice. It seemed to issue from her lips.

"You promised me." She saw Jagu slowly push himself to his knees. His head drooped. "*You gave me your word.*" He staggered to his feet, leaning against a tree trunk.

"You're all right." She slowly lowered her arm. A surge of relief flooded through her and the cold, murderous rage melted away; all she wanted was to run to his side.

Her attacker began to crawl away into the shadows; the accomplice had already fled.

One lurching step at a time, Jagu made his way toward her. Blood dripped from a jagged gash on the side of his head. His arms reached out and held her. Suddenly she felt faint and sick, and she clung to him as if he were a rock in a pounding sea. The aethyric light slowly dwindled as the Faie silently faded back into the book.

Jagu felt Celestine trembling as he held her, her face pressed against his shoulder. Dizzy from the blow, he closed his eyes, trying to calm his agitated mind, to think logically.

She's safe. That was all that mattered. But no thanks to him.

"I'm so sorry. I was careless," he said. "I let my guard down."

"It wasn't your fault, Jagu," she said, her voice muffled

in the thick folds of his robes. "They prey on poor pilgrims. They're scum."

A moment ago, she had dominated the glade, her eyes blazing with light, possessed by her guardian spirit. Now she was just a frightened, vulnerable girl again. He didn't want to admit it to himself, but the guardian spirit had saved them both. If it hadn't appeared to protect Celestine, he could not bear to think what the robbers might have done to her as he lay unconscious among the tangled tree roots. And yet were anyone to learn the secret of her innocuous-looking *Lives of the Saints*, the Inquisition would not hesitate to destroy her.

Celestine wanted to wash herself clean, to rid herself of the taint of her attacker's pawing hands, the lingering stink of his sweat, but Jagu's wound needed treating first. She went over to the stream and doused her handkerchief in the cold water, wringing it out. Then she began to dab at the congealing blood.

"What did he hit you with? A tree branch? It must have been quite a blow to lay *you* out cold." She chattered away, intent on distracting him, aware of the need to distract herself too. "It's swelling up. You'll have an impressive bruise there soon. At least the bleeding's stopped; it's quite a superficial wound. But he must have whacked you pretty hard." There were some basic medical supplies in her bag. She took out her little pot of arnica cream and smoothed some onto the contusion.

"You're going to have a headache," she said. "If you can get a fire going, I'll brew you an infusion of willow bark to dampen the pain. We don't have to worry about catching our supper tonight; we've plenty of cheese, honey, and bread left from what the brothers gave us."

"The Staff!" Jagu started up. "Is the Staff safe?"

In all the confusion of the attack, they had both forgotten their sacred treasure. But in the twilight, Jagu found it still lying where he had left it. The robbers had been after more valuable plunder than a priest's staff.

* * *

Jagu threw pinecones on the fire and as they burned, sending up blue smoke into the night, their strong, aromatic scent seemed to cleanse the air. Celestine sat hunched, cradling her mug of tea in both hands, gazing into the crackling flames.

What was going through her mind? She looked so distant, her gaze so abstracted that he wanted to put his arm around her, to comfort her. But the danger was past and he no longer had any excuse. Yet every time he remembered how she had clung to him, her body pressed close to his own, he felt an ache of desire so strong it almost overwhelmed him.

"Why is Linnaius so interested in the Drakhaoul?" she said suddenly. So she had been thinking about the Magus again. "Lord Gavril is the Emperor's prisoner, condemned to life imprisonment in the Iron Tower. He's no longer a threat." She tossed on another pinecone, watching it flare into bright flame in the heart of the blaze. "And to use his Dark Arts to pry secrets from that chained book in the monastery library . . . it stank of sorcery in there."

Jagu forced himself to ignore the confusion of feelings twisting his heart. Tracing and defeating the Drakhaoul was the aim of their mission, maybe the most dangerous one they had ever undertaken together.

"Yet if the Drakhaoul were to take a new mortal host, then that man would be a real threat to the Emperor," he said. "Eugene barely escaped with his life from their last encounter. He'll bear the scars to the grave."

"But the Drakhaoul can only meld with one of the Nagarian family." She turned to look at him, the flames staining her pale face with fiery shadows. "Or is that just a legend? Could it meld with anyone?"

"If Eugene wants the Drakhaoul's powers for himself, then Francia is in real danger." Jagu prodded at the fire with a stick, sending a sizzle of sparks up into the starry dark. "He's conquered the five princedoms of Old Rossiya; why would he stop there? His agents must know that our navy is half the size of his northern fleet . . . and no match for his alchymical weapons."

"But if we arrest Linnaius," she said, her voice low,

"Eugene's ingenieurs will soon find it impossible to continue to manufacture alchymical weapons."

"Our mission is to destroy the Drakhaoul, not to go after Linnaius," he said sternly. "No matter what our personal desires may be, we must obey the Maistre's orders."

To his surprise, she let out a little giggle. "Oh, Jagu, must you always be so punctilious? We're not at the Forteresse now." He saw her adding another dash of the monks' liqueur to her tea.

"Go easy there, Celestine," he said, reaching for the flask. "A little too much of that stuff and you'll wake up with a pounding headache."

"You're such a spoilsport," she said, snatching the flask away and dangling it just out of his reach. "If you want it, you'll have to come and get it."

He made a lunge and missed. Laughing triumphantly, she took another long sip of her tea.

"Give that here!" He lunged again, catching hold of the flask. But she wouldn't let go and he ended up almost falling into her lap.

"Ask nicely, Jagu." Her breath was sweet with the gentian liqueur. Was she drunk? Her cheeks were flushed in the firelight and she was looking at him with a teasing, provocative smile.

"Please." He knelt beside her.

"On one condition, then." Her speech was becoming slurred. "You have a little more too." She uncorked the flask and held it up to his lips; the liqueur poured out, trickling down his chin.

"Enough!" he said, trying to wrest the flask from her hands. In the tussle, she fell backward and he found himself lying sprawled on top of her. The flask rolled away across the dried leaves.

In the chilly Arkhelskoye tavern, he had managed to restrain himself. But now his self-restraint suddenly snapped and he pressed his mouth to hers. He heard her let out a muffled sound, more like surprise than protest.

What am I doing? Panicked, he pushed her away from him.

"Why did you stop?" she murmured. Her lids were drooping. "That was nice . . ."

Because if he didn't stop immediately, he'd never be able to hold himself back.

She nestled her head against his shoulder, like a sleepy, trusting child.

Taking advantage of her when she's had too much to drink? I'd never forgive myself.

When they boarded the *Dame Blanche,* Captain Peillac handed Jagu a sealed letter bearing the Commanderie's crest.

"It seems we have been engaged to perform before the Emperor and his new bride in Mirom." Jagu passed Celestine the message.

" 'The ship will put in at the port of Khazan, where you will disembark and receive further instructions,' " she read. "What does the Maistre want us to do in Muscobar? What can have happened while we've been away?"

But Jagu seemed in no mood to talk; he was busy transcribing the pencil sketches he had done aboard Chaikin's boat to make a rough map of the coastline between Arkhelskoye and Seal Cove.

"Must you do that now?" Celestine asked, kicking her heels against the wooden side of the bunk. "Can't this wait until we reach dry land?"

"We need something to show for this mission," he said, not even glancing up from his work. His face was drawn in a frown of what she assumed to be concentration. "I don't like to return empty-handed . . ."

So his simmering moodiness was caused by their failure to secure the golden crook? "The Maistre will understand. He knew that the monks were unlikely to hand over their prized relic. At least we've learned enough to prepare for a return visit." No, there had to be more to it than that. There was something else troubling him and, knowing Jagu, he was likely to keep brooding over it for days rather than share his fears with her. She tried a change of subject.

"I hope my hair will have grown enough to look presentable at court. Perhaps I'll have to buy a wig!"

"At least you can still practice," muttered Jagu. "I can't remember the last time I touched a keyboard. I'll need to lock myself in a music room when we reach Mirom. Maistre de Joyeuse always used to say—" He broke off. "I'm sorry."

"It's all right, Jagu." His comment had been entirely spontaneous. "You know it's better to talk of him, to keep him alive that way." She smiled, although her heart still ached whenever she thought of Henri. "In fact, I was going to suggest that we perform 'October Seas' at the recital. With words by Mirom's favorite poet, the Empress and her court will love it."

A large trunk was awaiting them at the Khazan customs house. Jagu had it carried to their lodgings and set about the task of trying to open the rusted catches with his pocket-knife.

"I can't wait to see what's inside!" Celestine hovered excitedly behind him.

"Damn!" Jagu shook his right hand. He had managed to open the final clasp, so Celestine threw open the lid as he knelt back on his heels, nursing his injured finger.

"Look, Jagu." There were clothes, neatly packed in layers of lavender-scented tissue, leather folders of music, and many other personal necessities they had been obliged to do without for so long. She plunged her hands in among the soft folds, drawing out her mulberry silk concert gown with a cry of delight. "There's a letter here. It's in code. Here; you're the cryptographer." She turned to pass it to him and saw that he was trying to trim the broken nail, just as if he were a fine lady of the court.

"It'll soon grow again," she said.

He hardly looked up, frowning at the damage. Over the years they had worked together, she had come to accept that the fastidious care Jagu took of his hands was one of his personal quirks. She rummaged in the trunk and found her ivory box of cosmetics; inside lay a porcelain pot of almond oil hand cream. "Here." She passed it to him. "This will restore a dewy softness to my lord's chapped skin."

He looked up at her, unsmiling at her little joke. "A keyboard player must always take good care of his hands," he said, scowling. "They are his livelihood."

"Just decipher the letter," she said, raising her eyes to heaven, "then when we know what our orders are, you can get back to your manicure."

With a sigh, he took up the letter and went to the desk to work out the encryption. About ten minutes later, he looked up and said, "We're to be guests of the Francian ambassador to Muscobar, Fabien d'Abrissard. A coach has been arranged to take us cross-country to the River Nieva. From there, we travel by ship to the capital."

The coach jolted violently and Celestine grabbed at the leather strap to keep herself from being flung into Jagu's lap.

"Another pothole," he said, grimacing. "The Emperor needs to put some money into improving the public highways in Muscobar."

"You'd rather be on horseback, wouldn't you?" Celestine said, righting herself and smoothing out her skirts. It felt odd to be wearing a dress after so many weeks dressed as a boy.

He gave a terse grunt. He was a Guerrier; of course he would rather be outside in the fresh air.

In Khazan, Celestine had indulged in the luxury of a long bath, scraping the ingrained dirt of travel from her body, lathering with sweet lavender-scented soap. Jagu had shaved off the many weeks' growth of dark beard and, with clean-washed hair and smartly dressed in a well-tailored jacket and breeches of charcoal grey, no longer looked like a vengeful prophet or mad Azhkendi monk.

"If only it were winter, then we could travel by troika. Wouldn't that be romantic? Wrapped up in furs, skimming over the snow, listening to the chiming of the sleigh bells . . ."

"It was good of the Francian ambassador to send this coach to bring us from Khazan to Mirom," Jagu allowed.

"Ambassador d'Abrissard and the Maistre are old friends, I believe," Celestine said. She couldn't help smiling as she remembered the first time Ruaud de Lanvaux had introduced them . . .

"Why are they doing that?" Jagu pointed out of the window at the farmworkers who had stopped at the side of the road as they drove past, all bowing respectfully. "We're not royalty."

"As I understand it, the peasants here are little more than bond slaves to their noble landlords. Or so Count Velemir told me once. That's why they behave so deferentially. I wonder if the new emperor will change all that . . . although it won't make him very popular with the Mirom aristocracy . . ."

Celestine joined Jagu up on deck as their ship slowly approached the city of Mirom, to hear Jagu let out a low whistle.

"Look over there."

A great number of five-masted men-o'-war lay at anchor in the naval dockyard close to the magnificent colonnaded facade of Admiralty House.

"They must be the Emperor's war fleet," she said. "Can you make out any names?"

Jagu took out his little spyglass and trained it on the forest of masts. "The *Rogned*." He turned to her. "The flagship of the Tielen Southern Fleet! Something's up, Celestine, can't you sense it?"

Celestine did not like to think what the presence of this vast fleet assembling so near the Straits might mean for Francia. "We must alert the ambassador."

"Yet it's so blatant." Jagu continued to scan the vessels. "Perhaps it's just a show of strength, designed to warn off any potential rivals."

"We can't assume anything when it comes to Eugene of Tielen."

It was a taxing piece of navigation for the ship's master to negotiate the narrow waterways, as the ship, jostled by the many merchantmen and smaller craft, eventually reached the city docks at Mirom.

"Our best plan is to head straight for the embassy and

consult Ambassador d'Abrissard." Celestine was leafing through the correspondence from the ambassador. A vile stench, so strong it almost made her retch, wafted across the bows. She clapped one hand to cover her mouth and nose. "What is *that*?"

"The tanneries, I'd guess," Jagu said. "Mirom has a thriving trade in fur and skins."

"Don't tell me, you endured far worse in Enhirre?"

"It's so hot there that dead flesh rots in a matter of—"

"Yes, yes." She raised one hand to silence him; he had regaled her on too many occasions with his tales of his time in the desert. "Now, when is our first engagement, tomorrow night?"

A sudden keen gust of wind almost blew the papers from her hand.

"You should go below," Jagu said sternly. "Breathing in this air is bad for your vocal cords."

She glared at him. They had been making music together since they were students, yet he still treated her as if she were a child. The fact that he was right only increased her annoyance.

"Welcome to Mirom." Fabien d'Abrissard rose from his desk to greet them. A couple of secretaries discreetly scuttled out a side door. Celestine curtsied and Jagu bowed to the ambassador. "Demoiselle, you look more lovely each time I see you."

She caught a sardonic glint in his keen glance. "You flatter me, Ambassador," she replied dryly.

"I meant it, dear Celestine." Abrissard abandoned the formal tone and reached out to shake Jagu's hand. "Lieutenant. It's good to see a familiar face from Lutèce. How is Maistre de Lanvaux?"

"He sends his warmest greetings," said Celestine, and handed him the folder of letters.

"Let's have some tea." Abrissard tugged the brocade bellpull and a tall, distinguished-looking butler brought in a silver tray of tea. "We'll serve ourselves, Claude," said Abrissard. "You can go."

Claude withdrew, his lips pursed in a slight curl of disdain.

"Claude is such a stickler for etiquette," said Abrissard, "but we need to talk, and if we'd waited until he had served tea in the correct manner, we'd have lost valuable time. Cream? Sugar?"

"Cream . . . and a little sugar," said Celestine, who had longed for such treats during their time on the road.

"Black for me, thank you." Jagu rose to take the delicate porcelain cup and saucer. Celestine saw that Abrissard was barely hiding a smile.

"Mortification of the flesh, even when it comes to tea, eh, Lieutenant? Be a little kind to your stomach in Muscobar; they take their tea very strong here. I thank God for Claude, who knows exactly how long to steep the leaves to extract the most subtle flavor."

"We caught sight of the Southern Fleet setting sail," said Jagu.

The playful little smile faded.

Jagu leaned forward in his chair. "It's not just assembling for show, is it? Is Francia in danger?"

"We know that Eugene has a significant tactical advantage over every other country in the quadrant." Fabien d'Abrissard lowered his voice. "The Tielens have developed a means of communicating directly over vast distances, just as I am talking to you now."

Celestine started, almost spilling her tea into the saucer. Her father's invention: the Vox Aethyria, stolen by Kaspar Linnaius.

"How does such a system work?" Jagu's habitual frown had reappeared.

"As far as we know, it involves two machines that send and convey the voice through the air."

Jagu's frown deepened. "That sounds suspiciously like a device that uses the Forbidden Arts."

"If we could capture one of these machines and discover its secrets, then Francia could be so much better placed to defend herself against Eugene's ambitions."

"You'd use Eugene's devices against him?" Celestine stared at the ambassador.

"We'd be foolish not to," Abrissard said bluntly. "So, make the most of your time in the Winter Palace to learn everything you can about the Emperor. It's an invaluable opportunity."

As Celestine descended the embassy staircase, the dark red silk of her concert gown whispering softly as she walked, Fabien d'Abrissard appeared to greet her.

"I hope you won't think it too forward of me," he said, holding out a little box tied with mulberry ribbons. She smiled at him as she opened the box. After so many months playing at being a boy, it was delightful to receive compliments and little gifts again.

"An orchid? Why thank you, Ambassador," she said, clasping the delicate bloom to her heart. "It's a perfect complement to the shade of my gown." And the crimson-spotted orchid would also help to disguise the fact that, even artfully arranged, her hair was still unfashionably short for a woman of society.

"You realize, don't you, that the Emperor is going to attend? He claims he has no ear for music, but he's indulging the wishes of his new bride."

"The Emperor himself?" Jagu appeared, stuffing the music into his leather case. "We've never performed before an emperor before."

"So make no mistakes, then, Jagu," said Celestine mischievously, "or we could cause an international incident."

The Emperor was waiting for the Empress to finish her toilette, reading through for the second time that day the latest dispatches from Smarna. The situation in the capital, Colchise, was becoming more tense by the day, with the students holding rallies to protest against the New Rossiyan regime. How was he expected to sit calmly through a musical recital when matters were unraveling so swiftly?

He was so on edge that when Gustave appeared, he started up, expecting the worst. But Gustave merely bowed and presented a sheet covered in an eccentrically looping hand.

"A letter from the Duchess of Rosenholm, highness."

"What does Aunt Greta want now?" Eugene said, sinking back on his chair.

"The duchess writes on behalf of her neighbor, Oskar Alvborg, recently invalided out of the army, asking your imperial highness to reinstate him."

"Count Alvborg?" Eugene frowned at the mere mention of the name. "The arrogance of the man, taking advantage of my aunt's sympathetic nature! He disobeyed my orders in action—and, as a result, the Drakhaoul destroyed his regiment. He's fortunate that I didn't have him executed on the battlefield for insubordination. Send the standard reply, Gustave. And, of course, my respects and good wishes to the duchess . . ." Gustave bowed again and was about to withdraw when Eugene suddenly said, "I want you to inform me the instant you hear any news from Smarna, Gustave. Understood?"

Gustave nodded and Eugene turned back to the dispatches.

"Are you ready to attend the recital, Eugene?" Astasia emerged from her dressing room, and Eugene could not help but gaze at her, distracted from his official papers by her pale beauty. She had chosen a simple gown of cream satin that complemented her dark hair; and, charming touch, he noted, she was wearing the amethysts he had given her as an engagement gift.

"You look . . . radiant," he said, wishing, as he stumbled over the words, that he could express himself better when it came to matters of the heart.

"You don't think this gown is too outmoded?" she said anxiously. "Demoiselle de Joyeuse has come from Lutèce, and the ladies of Lutèce are always so stylishly dressed."

"I think they will look to you to set the style." He could not help himself and reached out to take her in his arms. To his sadness, he sensed her flinch as his burned face drew near to hers—then make an effort to control herself to accept his kiss.

"We should go," she whispered, unable to meet his gaze. "It's time for the recital to start."

* * *

The music room in the Winter Palace had recently been re-decorated with Tielen restraint in muted shades of ivory and duck-egg blue. Porcelain bowls, overflowing with cream lilies and double peonies, had been placed on every little table and pillar, perfuming the air.

Celestine felt unaccountably nervous as they waited for the imperial couple to make their entrance. She had not sung in public for many months and, in spite of a program of intensive vocal exercises, felt unready for such a prestigious engagement.

"His imperial highness, Eugene of New Rossiya," announced the majordomo as the double doors opened, "and his consort, Astasia."

As she rose from her curtsy, Celestine could not help but steal a look at the Emperor, who had seated himself beside his young wife. Although she had heard of his disfiguring injuries, she was shocked to see how one whole side of his face and neck was seared and red, making the blue of his eyes all the more piercing by contrast.

What a fearsome creature the Drakhaoul must be, to have inflicted such terrible burns . . .

She pushed the intrusive thoughts to the back of her mind, smiled at the attentive audience, then turned to nod at Jagu.

Celestine de Joyeuse is so much younger than I had imagined from her illustrious reputation, thought Astasia. *And how elegant she looks in that gown of mulberry silk, with just a single orchid pinned in her golden hair; quite the epitome of fashionable Francian elegance. I must get my dressmaker to make me a gown in the same style.*

The singer's pure, delicate voice soared higher, each little cascade of notes like clear water falling, or a lone thrush fluting in the still, close air before rain.

The song came to an end, and for a moment the last perfect pitch hung in the air. Then the applause began. Astasia clapped and clapped, unable to restrain her enthusiasm.

Celestine sank into a deep curtsy, one hand clasped to her breast, murmuring her thanks before rising and gesturing to her accompanist.

The fortepiano player rose, unsmiling, and bowed. A tall, gaunt young man with pale skin and long, straight dark hair, he had more the air of an ascetic or a monk than a musician. She thought she caught a secret, subtle little glance that passed between singer and accompanist. *Can they be lovers?* Astasia wondered, thrilling to the idea.

"And now, we would like to perform for you one of Henri de Joyeuse's last compositions," Celestine announced in the Muscobite tongue. "The song 'October Seas,' set to the words of your celebrated poet, Solovei."

More applause greeted this tribute to Mirom's favorite author. But to Celestine's distress, the instant she heard Jagu playing the familiar introduction, the subtle and sad surge and fall of notes, brought unbidden tears to her eyes. *Why now?* She swallowed hard, trying to loosen the constriction in her throat. *What a foolish time to let Henri's music affect me so badly. I can't sing like this!*

She dug her nails into her palms, willing the emotion away. *I'm a professional. I owe it to Henri to bring his music to a greater public and keep his music alive. Every time I sing one of his songs, I feel his presence in every nuance, every phrase. If only I still didn't miss him so . . .*

Astasia glanced at her husband as the recital continued, but Eugene was staring beyond Celestine with a distant, slightly frowning expression. She could sense he was not enjoying himself. She had hoped that the visit of one of the most celebrated musicians of the day might change his opinion of the art and might even give them something to discuss together. Eugene had already confessed to her that he had no ear for music. Give him a rousing military march to whistle and he was happy. This was too subtle, too refined for his tastes. And then the artistry of Celestine's singing overwhelmed all other thoughts, and the music—wild, soulful, and free—possessed her.

During the applause, she saw Gustave, her husband's secretary, appear and make his way toward them. He whispered something to the Emperor she could not catch.

"Ah," said Eugene. He nodded and leaned toward Astasia. "Forgive me. Some official business I must attend to." He rose—and the rest of the audience rose too. Court etiquette. "Demoiselle de Joyeuse," he said, "you have enchanted us with your delightful voice. Please do not think me rude; state affairs intrude upon my pleasure and I must attend to them."

"Your imperial highness honors me." The singer sank into another deep curtsy as Eugene left the room with Gustave at his side.

The recital continued, but Astasia could no longer concentrate on the music or surrender to its spell. She knew it must be a matter of some import to have drawn Eugene away from such a prestigious gathering.

"So there's a revolt in Smarna?" Eugene cast the message Gustave had brought him on the desk beside the Vox Aethyria. Several of his secretaries in the communications room flinched.

"So it seems, imperial highness," Gustave said tactfully.

"I should never have put Armfeld in charge of the citadel in Colchise," Eugene muttered to himself. He had anticipated that Azhkendir would resist the Tielen invasion, but Smarna was proving the most rebellious of all his conquests. He would have to act swiftly to put down the rebellion before it got out of hand and spread throughout the whole country. He sighed. "There's nothing for it but to send in the Southern Fleet. Gustave, get me Admiral Janssen."

"And I thought you might want to read this." Gustave passed him a letter. Eugene took it, wondering what new dilemma it might contain. But as he swiftly skimmed the contents, he found himself at a loss for words. For it came from Baltzar, the Director of Arnskammar Asylum, and informed him that the prisoner, Gavril Nagarian, had fallen grievously sick of the typhus and was not expected by the prison physician to survive. His hand dropped to his side, still holding the letter. He knew that he should feel glad that the enemy who had destroyed so many of his soldiers and disfigured him was at death's door, yet he felt nothing but an unexpected and inexplicable sense of . . . regret. To die in prison of typhus fever seemed an ignoble end for such a redoubtable enemy.

If only we could have had the chance to meet again in battle . . .

"Highness." Gustave was addressing him from his seat at the Vox Aethyria. "Admiral Janssen is awaiting your orders."

CHAPTER 5

The instant Celestine closed the door of the dressing room and laid down the bouquet, the smiling mask she had somehow managed to sustain cracked.

Why did "October Seas" affect me so? I've sung it many times since Henri's death.

One hand rose shakily to cover her face, as if to hold the shattered pieces in place.

Did anyone notice?

Since she had left the music room, flashes of memory from the song's first performance kept returning to increase her distress: Count Velemir presenting her to Andrei Orlov; Prince Andrei's sulky expression transforming to a smile of dazzling warmth as he kissed her hand. And Henri glancing up at her from the fortepiano with such a look of pride and pleasure that it had made her heart melt.

How difficult to accept that all three were dead: the suave and charming count, slain by Gavril Nagarian; Prince Andrei drowned at sea in a freak storm; and Henri, her beloved Henri, destroyed by a soul-stealing magus.

We never said good-bye, Henri. If I could just see you one last time, talk to you one last time, then maybe I could move on . . .

But necromancy was one of the Forbidden Arts. And as an agent of the Commanderie she had sworn to eradicate all such practices.

The door opened and she whipped around, forcing a defensive smile. Jagu came in, the sheet music under one arm.

"It's only you, Jagu." Relieved, she sank onto a chair.

"*Only* me? Who were you hoping to see?"

"So"—she made herself concentrate on their present situation—"have you found out why the Emperor left in such a hurry?"

"The palace is buzzing with rumors." Jagu poured them both a glass of mineral water from the crystal jug that had been provided for the two performers. "One name I heard mentioned several times was 'Smarna.' "

"But not Francia." Celestine sipped the water. "Let's pray that—" A little tapping on the door interrupted her. She glanced questioningly at Jagu. "Come in."

A stout, grey-haired lady-in-waiting appeared in the doorway.

"I've come from her imperial majesty," she said in their own tongue. Celestine rose, recognizing her as the Empress's chaperone.

"Countess Eupraxia." She curtsied. "Please come in."

"The Empress would like to . . . speak with you, Demoiselle." The countess's plump cheeks were red and her full bosom heaved, as if she had run all the way through the palace. "If you would be so good as to accompany me . . ."

A private audience? Celestine glanced at Jagu and he gave a brief nod of assent. "I am honored to accept the Empress's invitation," she said and followed the countess out into the lofty, echoing corridor.

"You sang so beautifully," Empress Astasia said, smiling warmly at Celestine. "I felt utterly transported."

"Your imperial highness is too kind." *With velvety eyes that appealing, I wonder if the Emperor can refuse her anything.* Celestine was reminded of her first royal patron and friend, Princess Adèle, now married to Ilsevir of Allegonde. Was this imperial audience merely a gesture of appreciation . . . or did the Empress have an ulterior motive in inviting her?

"Please, come and sit beside me," said Astasia in Francian, gesturing to the blue-and-white-striped sofa.

"Your highness speaks our tongue like a native," Celestine said.

"I had a Francian nursemaid, didn't I, Praxia?"

"Indeed you did," said the countess, nodding fondly.

"Would you like some tea, Demoiselle de Joyeuse?"

Celestine nodded. "That would be most agreeable. Thank you."

While sipping a cup of strong tea sweetened in the local fashion with jam ("the damson is delicious"), Astasia suddenly turned to Celestine and said, "I have a request to make. I do hope you'll be able to accept. You see, Karila, my little stepdaughter, hasn't been very well. She doesn't have a strong constitution. And her eighth birthday is very soon." From the look of sadness that clouded the brilliance of Astasia's eyes, Celestine realized that, unlike some stepmothers, she genuinely cared for the little girl.

"I wondered if you would consider giving a recital for Karila at the Palace of Swanholm? There's to a be a masked ball there soon—a Tielen custom, my husband tells me—to celebrate the midsummer solstice."

It did not escape Celestine's notice that Astasia blushed when she said "my husband." Was theirs a love match? There was a difference of some sixteen years between Eugene and Astasia, yet all the court gossip throughout the quadrant had regarded the partnership as merely a marriage of convenience and political necessity. She could not help wondering how the young Empress felt about her husband's terrible injuries; perhaps she had nursed him back to health after he was burned by the Drakhaoul . . .

"Thank you; it would be an honor to sing for the little princess," Celestine said, carefully setting down her empty teacup on its delicate saucer. Her mind began to whirl with the possibilities such an invitation presented.

As Celestine and Countess Eupraxia left the Empress's rooms, they passed a portrait, half-draped in black. Celestine stopped, recognizing the charming, confident smile and distinctive violet-blue eyes.

"Isn't that a portrait of the Empress's late brother, Prince Andrei?" she asked.

"It is." The countess's eyes filled with tears. "It's many months now, but she's still not over his loss, none of us are. Such a tragedy . . ."

Celestine nodded, caught up in a vivid memory of the first time she had been presented to Andrei. His ready, infectious smile had instantly dispelled her nerves, putting her completely at her ease.

"Lost at sea," said the countess, dabbing her eyes, "in a terrible storm in the Straits. Such a waste. That dear, dear boy . . ."

And yet, Celestine wondered but did not dare say aloud as she followed Eupraxia to her waiting carriage, would Eugene have found it so easy to conquer Muscobar if Andrei were still alive?

"We've been invited to perform at Swanholm Palace," Celestine told Jagu as the ambassador's carriage jogged back toward the embassy. "*Swanholm,* Jagu!"

"Well, that's a great compliment, but I can hardly see why you're so excited." Jagu looked distinctly unenthusiastic. "A journey to Tielen and back is going to take at least six weeks out of our schedule. What about our concerts in Allegonde? And suppose the Maistre wants us back in Francia?"

She stamped her foot on the floor of the carriage, exasperated. "Who else resides at Swanholm? In the laboratories especially designed for him by Prince Karl? The Tielen Royal Artificier, no less, *Kaspar Linnaius.* We'll be able to spy on him firsthand. No one from the Commanderie has ever managed to get so close."

"Well, when you put it that way . . ."

He still seemed less than interested, so she folded her arms and stared out at the dark streets of Mirom, offended.

After a while he said with a sigh, "We can't just take matters into our own hands, Celestine. If you act rashly at the Emperor's court in Swanholm, you could spark off a diplomatic incident, and that's the last thing we need. We must get word to the Maistre and await his instructions."

"Fine! And while we sit around for days waiting for the Maistre's reply, we'll be losing valuable time. It's the *Magus,* Jagu."

"And that's precisely the reason we need to proceed with

caution. The man is very dangerous. You know that better than most."

It was her turn to sigh. Why must Jagu be so insistent on following the correct protocol at all times? "Very well," she said grudgingly. "We'll ask the ambassador to ensure that our message is sent by the swiftest diplomatic post available."

The trunks were packed and Celestine was waiting with Jagu in the hall of the embassy for their carriage to arrive. Claude suddenly appeared, walking stiffly as usual, carrying a folded paper on a silver tray.

"The ambassador sends his apologies that he is unable to bid you farewell in person." He bowed, presenting the tray. "He's been called away on urgent business. But he left you this note."

Jagu opened the letter and Celestine peeped over his shoulder to read it:

> Stay vigilant. I've yet to discover the reason why the Emperor left your recital so suddenly. His people are keeping something secret. Remember: Once you're in Tielen, you'll be on your own. I'll give you the name of one or two trustworthy contacts. If I've played my cards right, I'll be invited to the Dievona Ball at Swanholm. But until then, be on your guard . . .

The broad mouth of the Nieva was filled with warships. A great fleet of the New Rossiyan navy was under full sail, making for the Straits.

As the *Dame Blanche* followed in their wake, Jagu and Celestine went up onto the observation deck to take a closer look.

"There's the *Rogned* again," Jagu said, following the fleet with an eyeglass borrowed from Captain Peillac. "Where are they heading, I wonder?"

Celestine leaned out over the rail, straining to see. The wild salty wind whipped her hair into her eyes. "Not for Francia, I hope!"

"Hard to tell. But what a formidable sight they make. Each man-o'-war bristling with cannons . . ."

"Is that a fishing boat out there?" Celestine leaned out even farther. "It's being blown into the path of the fleet! The fishermen haven't a chance!"

The sound of rending timbers carried on the fierce gusting wind. With it came frantic shouts for help. Two men were in the water, threshing and bobbing in the wake of one vast warship as another bore down upon them.

"They'll be crushed!" Celestine turned to the ship's master to appeal for help, but Captain Peillac had already summoned up a rescue party and the sailors were lowering a rowboat into the churning waves.

And then a feeling of dread overwhelmed her, as if she had been swept overboard into the dark tide. She began to shiver uncontrollably. As she helplessly watched the drowning men, the sea around them began to spin like a waterspout, funneling upward. *Wings.* Something was rising from the waves on great, beating wings that were blue-black as a starlit night.

"Jagu." Celestine clutched at Jagu's arm, pointing. "Look. What in God's name is that?"

Jagu raised the eyeglass he had been using to observe the Tielen fleet and focused it on the wreck of the fishing boat.

"Whatever it is, it's not of this world." He swiftly passed her the glass.

"There were two men in the water. Now I see only one— and *that* abomination."

The sailors had nearly reached the wreckage.

"The Angelstone," she urged. "Check the Angelstone."

Jagu pulled out the crystal pendant from inside his shirt. The clear crystal had turned as dark as ink.

"A warrior daemon," she whispered, "from the Realm of Shadows. It's the Drakhaoul."

CHAPTER 6

"Turn back!" yelled Jagu to the rowers, but they were too far away to hear his voice.

"If only Abbot Yephimy hadn't been so stubborn, we could have used Sergius's Staff." Celestine could only stare at the dark-winged daemon, eaten up with frustration at their helplessness. And yet, even as she clutched the wet rail of the ship, the creature halted in midair.

It shuddered.

Suddenly, it let out a wailing cry, inhuman and desolate. Then it began to plummet toward the waves, losing its hold on its human burden.

"Can it sense the Angelstone?" Jagu leaned far out over the rail, straining to see what was happening.

"Be careful, Jagu!" Celestine grabbed hold of him, fearful that he might be swept overboard.

For a moment daemon and man disappeared below the surface. Then a whirlpool began to churn the waves. The sailors shouted out and cursed, gripping the sides of the rowboat as it was thrown sideways, almost capsizing. And out of the spinning water, Celestine saw a shadow rise, dark as smoke, and speed away, low across the waves.

The sailors gently laid the two fishermen down on the deck. Celestine went to help them but Jagu put a hand on her shoulder. "Wait."

The younger of the two began to retch, spewing up a lungful of seawater. He forced himself to his knees, turning to the older man who lay motionless beside him. Celestine watched in growing distress as he tried to revive him.

"Come on, Kuzko." The fisherman laid his head against the other's chest, as if listening for a heartbeat. "Don't desert me now!"

The old sailor's head lolled back, mouth gaping.

She saw the fisherman lay him back down on the deck and gently close his eyes. One of the sailors came up and wrapped a blanket around his shoulders. Only then did the fisherman crouch beside the still body and weep.

Celestine opened the cabin door and took a long, appraising look at the young fisherman, who lay deep in exhausted sleep. In spite of his untidy black curling hair, rough beard, and skin dark-tanned by wind and sun, there was something about him that suggested he was no ordinary fisherman.

Jagu was busy discussing their itinerary with Captain Peillac. She felt a little guilty acting on her own initiative, without his approval, but she was certain that the young man's features were familiar.

"I *know* you," she whispered. "We've met before. But when . . . and where . . ."

He began to mutter in his sleep, twisting and turning, as though in the grip of a nightmare. Mumbled words escaped his salt-dried lips.

"Drowning . . . I'm drowning!" He flailed wildly as though fighting to stay above the waves.

She caught hold of his hand. "You're safe now."

He sat bolt upright. Eyes of dark violet-blue stared into hers. "I—I'm so sorry. I was dreaming."

"It must have been quite a dream." Gently, she released his hand.

He nodded, still staring at her. "I've seen you before. You sang in Mirom last winter. You're Celestine—"

"De Joyeuse. I'm flattered you remember me." *I've seen eyes of that unique hue very recently. Can he be one of the Orlovs?*

"Celestial in voice as well as in name," he said. "How could I forget?"

"The daemon creature that attacked you," she said, ignoring the compliment. "That would be enough to give anyone nightmares."

"That was not what I was dreaming about. My ship went down in the Straits some months ago. The old man, Kuzko, rescued me. And now—" He choked on the words. "Now he's dead."

"You don't talk like a common sailor." She was looking at him curiously. "What's your name?"

"Andrei."

"Andrei?" she said, her mind racing. *My ship went down in the Straits* . . .

"Where are you bound?"

She made an effort to focus her thoughts. "Why, to Swanholm, to sing for Princess Karila's birthday at the request of the Emperor's wife, Astasia."

"Astasia," he repeated, pronouncing the name with affection, almost reverence. "Demoiselle de Joyeuse," he said in Francian, "may I confide in you?"

"He says he's Andrei Orlov, Crown Prince of Muscobar?" Jagu stared at Celestine, his brows drawn close in a frown of disbelief. "How can you be sure he's not an impostor? Or out of his mind?"

Celestine had been expecting this reaction. She forced herself to count to ten before replying. "You met Prince Andrei last year in Mirom, at Count Velemir's reception, Jagu, didn't you? Before the Revolt?" Their cramped cabin was not the best place for such a discussion; the sea was still choppy and, seasoned travelers though they were, the creaking and pitching of the *Dame Blanche* made it difficult to talk about such a sensitive subject without raising their voices. "You have to admit that the likeness is remarkable."

"The same Prince Andrei who went down with the *Sirin*?" Jagu crossed his arms defensively as he sometimes did when not wishing to admit that she might be right.

"Can't you see what a trump card has fallen into our hands?" she went on, trying to keep her voice low. "When

Eugene forced Muscobar to capitulate, Andrei was believed to be dead. Now that he's alive, there's a rival for the throne. And if he allies himself with Francia, Eugene will find himself in a very tricky situation indeed."

"And then there's the Drakhaoul." Jagu pulled out the precious Angelstone and showed it to Celestine; the trickle of darkness that had polluted its clarity had disappeared. "Is it gone for good? Or could he summon it back and destroy us? We have to interrogate him, Celestine. The Maistre would expect nothing less."

"Let's leave him to rest a little longer." She put on her most appealing tone, one that she knew Jagu could not refuse. "If we bombard him with questions when he's still in shock, we'll only make him more confused." Although the prospect that Prince Andrei might be able to summon the daemon to his aid was deeply unsettling.

"Help me . . . Drakhaoul . . ."

The prisoner was dying. Wasted with fever, the brilliance of his blue eyes dimming, the young man suddenly murmured a few words, barely intelligible. And his jailer had been ordered to summon the Director of Arnskammar Asylum if he said anything, so he dutifully locked the door and set out to fetch his master. For some reason, it seemed that the Emperor had a personal interest in the prisoner.

He had just reached the courtyard when he sensed the sky darken overhead. Glancing up, he saw a stormcloud speeding toward the tower. He stopped, terrified. For he had glimpsed eyes in the whirling darkness, eyes that burned with the piercing blue of lightning.

The director came running into the courtyard.

"What in God's name—?" he began, then fell silent as both men stared at the top of the tower. The prisoner's cell was shrouded in shadow and little flashes of energy crackled and flickered about the conical roof.

A flash of dazzling light seared their eyes and the top of the tower exploded, shattered stones and tiles showering down into the courtyard. The jailer pulled his stunned master to the ground, covering his head with his hands. As he glanced fearfully up, he saw—or thought he saw—a great winged creature, blue as midnight, wheeling away through the cloud-veiled sky.

"No one could have survived such a lightning strike," said the director, getting unsteadily to his feet, brushing the dust from his clothes. The jagged ruins of the broken tower were silhouetted all too clearly against the clearing sky.

"But d—didn't you see it, Director?" the jailer stammered. "The winged creature . . . like a dragon . . ."

"A dragon?" The director gave him a stern look. "I have no idea what you're babbling about. I will inform the Emperor straightaway that the prisoner died when lightning struck his cell."

"Captain Peillac has just informed me that we'll reach Tielen by dawn." Jagu ducked as he entered Andrei's cabin to avoid hitting his head. He set down a bottle of red wine and proceeded to pour with a steady hand. "So that gives us plenty of time to make the journey to Swanholm." He handed both Celestine and Andrei a glass, then lifted his own in a toast. "To your miraculous survival, my lord Andrei."

"Miraculous?" Andrei took a sip of the wine. "If you hadn't sent out your men to the rescue—"

"I was referring to the creature that plucked the old man from the waves," Jagu said.

Andrei set his glass down. "You saw it, then?" A lost, sad look clouded his eyes.

"What was it, Andrei?" Celestine was gazing sympathetically at him. Jagu leaned back against the cabin wall; it was best to let her charm the facts from the young prince.

"It healed me. Whether it was a spirit that haunted the place where I was shipwrecked, or it sought me out for some purpose of its own, I don't know. All I know is it healed my body and restored my mind."

"It healed you?" Celestine shot Jagu a swift, meaningful glance. "Did it ever reveal its purpose to you?"

"Not on Lapwing Spar, no. But in Mirom it spoke to me. It said, 'You were born to rule. But it is too soon.'"

" 'Born to rule,' " echoed Celestine. "And then it abandoned you?"

"I don't know why. For a moment I thought I heard a distant voice crying out for help." Andrei gulped down his wine. "But it might have been Kuzko." His voice faltered and Jagu refilled his glass. "Where was Eugene's war fleet going in such a hurry?"

"We asked ourselves the same question," Jagu replied. "Who knows where Eugene's ambitions will lead him next?"

"Our countries have always been allies, Andrei," Celestine said in Francian. "Your command of our language is excellent. We understand each other well, don't we? You've been deprived of your right to rule Muscobar by this new regime. Yet your family also claims descent from the Emperor Artamon. Had matters gone otherwise, you could have been Emperor of all Rossiya."

"I could be Emperor?" Andrei said slowly. "But how? I have no country, no name, no troops at my disposal. The Muscobite army and navy have been absorbed into Eugene's forces."

Celestine consulted Jagu with another glance. He nodded. Then she turned to Andrei and said, "We believe that our master, King Enguerrand, would be very interested in meeting you."

"I'm going to the council meeting," said Enguerrand. "Alone. Without my mother."

Ruaud de Lanvaux stared at his young protégé, astonished. "But with respect, sire, how can you keep her away?"

Enguerrand glanced round at Ruaud as Fragan, the king's valet, fussed about him, obsessively brushing his jacket and straightening his lace cravat. Ruaud caught a glint of a dark little smile behind Enguerrand's thick spectacle lenses. "I've contrived to send Maman on my behalf to open an orphanage. On the opposite side of the city."

So Enguerrand was beginning to stand up to his domineering mother at last. Ruaud offered up a silent prayer of thanks as he followed him into the council chamber. The councillors rose with a scraping of chairs and bowed, waiting to sit until Enguerrand had taken his place at the head of the long table.

Chancellor Aiguillon, first minister of Francia, addressed the council.

"Your majesty, gentlemen of the council, we have received an impassioned plea for help from Smarna. Eugene's forces have imposed martial law."

The councillors began to murmur among themselves. Ruaud was watching to see how Enguerrand would react to this disturbing news. He saw that the king's hands had tightened their grip on the arms of his chair until the knuckles were white.

"In view of the unstable situation," Aiguillon went on, "I think it would be prudent, sire, to postpone your pilgrimage to the Holy Land."

"Did my mother make that suggestion?" Enguerrand stared at Aiguillon and when he was a second or so late in replying, added, "Of course she did; your hesitation confirms it. But I tell you now, Aiguillon, that I will not let either my mother's overprotective nature or the Emperor's overweening ambitions interfere with my plans."

Ruaud was surprised to hear how forcefully the young king had spoken. The whole council was listening attentively.

Enguerrand turned to Ruaud. "The Second Fleet is under orders to act as our escort, isn't that right, Grand Maistre?"

"Indeed so," said Ruaud. "Your majesty will be traveling with an escort of twenty-five well-armed warships, under the command of Admiral Mercoeur."

"I like this plan!" The Duc de Craon, Enguerrand's uncle, thumped the table enthusiastically. "That will place our ships close to Smarna, should the need arise . . ."

"Where will Eugene's ambition and greed for power stop? Francia could well be next! But"—and Aiguillon leaned forward over the council table—"we are well prepared this time. Grand Maistre, if you would be so good . . ."

Ruaud rose. "Twenty years ago, the Tielens destroyed our fleet in the Straits, using alchymical weapons devised by Kaspar Linnaius. And now, at last, we're in a position to retaliate. Acting on the intelligence of our agents, we have a plan in place to arrest Kaspar Linnaius, then destroy the alchymical munitions factories. The Armel fleet is on maneuvers off Fenez-Tyr. Admiral Romorantin is standing by to launch an attack on Eugene's naval dockyards just as soon as you give the order, sire."

Enguerrand nodded.

"Arrest Kaspar Linnaius?" It was Inquisitor Visant who, until then, had not contributed anything to the meeting. "And how, precisely, are you going to achieve that, Maistre de Lanvaux? The self-styled Magus has persistently evaded all our attempts to bring him to justice. What makes you think you'll succeed where the Inquisition has failed?"

"I have every confidence in my agents," Ruaud said patiently.

"Isn't it a little rash to hazard so many sailors' lives on the assumption that your agents will capture Linnaius?"

"Isn't it more rash to sit passively by and wait for the Emperor to make his move against us?" Ruaud had not planned to oppose the Haute Inquisitor so openly in front of the council, but Visant had left him no choice.

"Then we will assure the Smarnan council that they can count on Francia's support." Aiguillon looked round at all the councillors. "Any objections, gentlemen?"

"Such an assurance will commit us to a needless war with the Emperor," protested Visant.

"Smarna today, Francia tomorrow," said Aiguillon. Ruaud looked around, surprised to find an unexpected ally in the chancellor. "Let's act now before the situation deteriorates any further." He turned to Enguerrand. "Sire?"

"I authorize the arrest of the Magus," Enguerrand said. "And once we have him in our custody, I say we strike at Eugene's dockyards."

The councillors rose to their feet, applauding. All except Visant, who sat, stone-faced, staring at the council papers in front of him.

Gavril Nagarian opened his eyes. He was lying on a cliff top, gazing up into the brilliance of a sun-warmed blue sky.

"Free," he whispered. "I'm *free . . .*" And then he remembered how he had come to escape the Iron Tower. "Why did you come back for me, Drakhaoul? I cast you out . . ."

"*You called for me. You were dying.*"

"And you rescued me . . . and healed me, in spite of what I did to you . . ."

"*We are bonded for life, bonded by your blood,*" whispered the daemon. "*I need you as much as you need me.*"

The image of Kiukiu's limp body still haunted Gavril, her throat marred by the ravages he had inflicted in his hunger. "I nearly killed her. The bloodlust was so strong, I couldn't control myself. Do you understand, Drakhaoul, why I sought the exorcism?"

"*I understand that she means more to you than Azh-kendir.*"

Gavril put his hands to his head. He had had too much time in Arnskammar to try to square matters with his conscience. He had saved Kiukiu's life, but in losing the Drakhaoul, he had also lost his country to Eugene. It was a bitter fact to live with. "I—I love her more than life itself. She accepted me unquestioningly for what I was, half-man, half-monster. But now that we are united again, Drakhaoul, how can I ask her to take me back?"

The distant sound of cannon fire disturbed the drowsy silence of the grassy cliff. Gavril Nagarian got shakily to his feet and went toward the cliff edge to gaze out to sea. "But this is Smarna," he said, astonished. "And what are all those warships doing in Vermeille Bay?" And then his surprise turned to anger as he recognized the Emperor's colors flying from the masts of every ship. They were bombarding the citadel of Colchise. Colchise, which had been his home for many years.

"No," he murmured, feeling the anger burn fiercer within him, "I can't let this happen. This must stop. Drakhaoul!" he called suddenly.

"*You are still weak, Gavril. Are you certain that you want to attack them?*"

"If I don't strike now," Gavril said, flinching as another

round of shot smashed into the citadel walls, "then it will be too late."

A few seconds later, a dark-winged dragon took to the air, darting straight toward the *Rogned*, the flagship of the Emperor's Southern Fleet.

CHAPTER 7

"Where is Andrei?" Celestine demanded. She had left Jagu alone with Andrei over the remains of their meal for only a few minutes while she collected a letter from the customs house, and now there was no sign of the prince.

"He went out for a walk along the jetty. Said he needed time to think. He's still cut up over the old man's death."

"How could you let him out of your sight?" Sometimes she did not understand Jagu at all.

Jagu sighed and pointed out of the window. The sun was setting over Haeven and had half sunk beneath the low clouds, illuminating the western horizon with a vivid dazzle of stormy gold. A lone figure stood silhouetted against the evening light. "He's not our prisoner, Celestine. We can't keep him confined."

"But if anyone were to recognize him—"

"Prince Andrei always went clean-shaven. With that fisherman's beard, no one will give him a second look."

"I'll go give this letter to him."

"Better wrap up, then. The air is damp tonight and you don't want to catch a chill before Swanholm."

She stuck out her tongue at him. Why did he have to treat her like a child? "As if I'd be so foolish . . ."

"What a dramatic sunset," Celestine said as she approached Andrei. "You're an experienced sailor; does such a sky herald another storm?"

"No," he said. He seemed distant, hardly turning to acknowledge her presence. "The weather can prove fickle off these shores, even for the most experienced sailor."

"I have news for you from King Enguerrand." She handed him a sealed letter.

He broke the seal and stared at the strange dashes and symbols, perplexed. "Is this some new Francian alphabet? It means nothing to me."

"It's encrypted," Celestine said, unable to repress a smile at his evident confusion. "Don't worry; Jagu has the key at the tavern." She slipped her hand beneath his arm. "Let's go back now before I catch cold out here and ruin my voice."

To our royal cousin, Andrei Orlov of Muscobar, from Enguerrand of Francia:

> We are most heartily relieved to hear of your miraculous rescue. Please rest assured that news of your survival will not be revealed until you judge the time is right to do so.

> We extend the hand of friendship to you and assure you of a warm welcome at our royal court. We also have new intelligence of events that took place toward the end of last year, which will both disturb and intrigue you.

> Our representative in New Rossiya, Ambassador d'Abrissard, has some proposals to make, which we believe will be to our mutual benefit . . .

Andrei was rowed out through a brisk dawn breeze to meet with Fabien d'Abrissard aboard ship.

"Eugene's agents are everywhere," the ambassador said as he welcomed Andrei into his paneled stateroom in the stern. "Here, at least, we are on Francian territory. Coffee to warm you this chilly morning?"

"Thank you." The square windowpanes afforded a view over the Straits: an expanse of rain-grey sea and pale clouds.

The ambassador clicked his fingers and his butler poured Andrei coffee in a delicate white-and-gold cup. After living so long in a poor fisherman's cottage, Andrei had grown unused to such refinements and handled the flimsy china nervously.

"And our guest might appreciate a dash of brandy." Had Abrissard seen his hands tremble? The ambassador's expression gave nothing away; although his lips smiled at Andrei, his manner was cool and detached. The butler added a measure of brandy to Andrei's cup and discreetly withdrew, closing the door softly behind him. For a moment the only sound was the lapping of the water against the ship as it bobbed gently at anchor.

"Were you aware that the power behind Eugene's empire is one Kaspar Linnaius, a renegade scientist, wanted for crimes in Francia?" Abrissard asked.

Andrei shook his head.

"We have reason to believe that this same Kaspar Linnaius was responsible for the sinking of your ship."

"Sinking the *Sirin*? But how? She went down in a storm."

"A storm that came out of nowhere on a calm night? A similar event occurred some years ago in the reign of Prince Karl, when the Francian fleet was wrecked by a disastrous storm."

"But what possible proof could you have?" burst out Andrei.

"The testimonies furnished by two of Linnaius's fellow mages some years back, under torture," said Abrissard smoothly. "They confirmed that this self-styled Magus can command and control the winds."

"But . . . that's preposterous."

"We have a witness. The night of the storm, one of the grooms at the Palace of Swanholm confirms that he saw Linnaius create a storm that brought down trees in the parkland. I should emphasize that this intelligence is of the highest confidentiality."

Andrei sat back, trying to grasp the full implications of what Abrissard was saying.

"This should not be so difficult for you to accept, Andrei Orlov," said Abrissard in the softest, smoothest of voices. "You, who have been touched by a daemon."

"You're implying that Eugene ordered Linnaius to sink my ship? Doesn't that count as assassination?" At first, the news had left him stunned; then anger began to burn through.

Abrissard shrugged eloquently. "In war, such terms do not apply."

"And my sister has married this man!" Andrei could sit still no longer; he rose and strode to the window to gaze out at the sea. A watery sun had begun to show beneath the clouds, catching the tops of the waves with flecks of silvery gold.

"You're an ambitious young man, Andrei Orlov. Do you care about the future of Muscobar?"

"Of course I do!" Andrei said hotly.

"Then come to Francia. King Enguerrand assures you of the warmest welcome at his court. He has great plans for the future. Those plans will include you, if you wish."

Andrei turned and stared at Abrissard. He heard what the ambassador was saying, yet not putting into words. Francia had old scores to settle with Tielen.

"And Astasia?"

Abrissard's proud gaze grew colder. "Your sister has committed herself to Eugene. It may be difficult to persuade her to change her allegiance."

"Your ambassador asked me to give you this." Andrei handed a sealed letter to Celestine.

"Thank you." Celestine felt a little shiver of excitement as she took it from him, recognizing from the firm handwriting that it came from Ruaud de Lanvaux. If the Maistre had given his blessing to her plan, then she would need all her courage and ingenuity to try to entrap the Magus. She was desperately eager to open it straightaway, but because of the sensitive nature of its subject matter, she retired to her room to read the Maistre's instructions.

Yet when she broke the seal, she found the message inside was frustratingly brief:

"Do whatever you judge is necessary to achieve your goal; but be discreet—and above all, be very careful. Extra funds will follow to cover any necessary expenses."

"So here you are at last!" A ginger-haired man came into the room, shaking the raindrops from his greatcoat.

"Kilian!" Jagu rose and hurried over to give him a welcoming hug. "What brings you to Tielen?"

"I've been chasing across half the quadrant to catch up with you two. Don't you ever stay more than a couple of days in one place?"

"And now you've found us," said Celestine, a little tartly. She had never entirely warmed to Kilian Guyomard's joshing manner. Yet because he and Jagu had been friends since their schooldays, she forced herself to put up with his banter.

"What brings me to this godforsaken country?" Kilian threw his wet coat down. "Since you failed so spectacularly in your mission to persuade the monks of Kerjhenezh to part with their sacred treasure, I'm here to ensure that the Staff is safely returned to the Forteresse."

Celestine opened her mouth to make a sharp retort but then thought better of it; she sensed that Kilian would have liked nothing better than to revel in her discomfort.

"Any chance of a drop of aquavit? I'm frozen." Kilian went over to the grate to warm his hands at the blaze. She poured a glass and handed it to him. He took a sip and nodded. "Ahh; that's better. Did you know that our agents have just learned of an intriguing turn of events? Lord Nagarian has escaped from Arnskammar Asylum." He took another slow sip.

Celestine caught Jagu's startled glance. "Does that mean that the Drakhaoul of Azhkendir has returned to protect its first master?" she said. "Was that where it was going when we saw it in the Straits?"

"Who knows?" replied Kilian with a wry smile. "Except that Arnskammar is supposed to be impregnable. No one has ever escaped from there before—and lived to tell the tale. Imagine the Emperor's expression when he was told the news . . ."

She left the two old school friends to reminisce and went to check on their royal guest, who was receiving the attentions of the local barber.

The barber had washed and cut Andrei's wild, salt-stiffened tangle of dark hair and was trimming his beard to an elegant style suitable for a man-about-town.

"The barber's done a good job," she said as Andrei looked critically at his reflection in a hand glass. "You look quite respectable now."

"Though I hear the nobles of the imperial court are going clean-shaven these days, like the Emperor."

"But the beard helps to preserve your anonymity," she reminded him.

He suddenly put the mirror down and got up, pacing the room like a caged animal. "All this waiting around is making me restless."

"Jagu's still occupied with the ambassador's business," she said. "Perhaps you could escort me about town?" It was important to keep Andrei busy in case, in his frustration, he did something rash and spoiled their plans. "With all these foreign sailors in port, I confess I'm a little nervous to venture out alone." How odd that false declaration sounded to her ears; hadn't she just traveled to Azhkendir and back disguised as a boy? She was glad that Jagu was not present to hear her play the role of the defenseless woman.

"I'm glad to be of use," Andrei said eagerly.

"Spring comes so much later in the north," Celestine said to Andrei, as the cherry blossom petals came fluttering down, blanketing the street with a covering of delicate pink snow. The squall had finally blown away and thin, misty clouds were parting to reveal blue sky behind.

A stroll was just the excuse she needed to draw more information from Andrei. Something in his story had been troubling her. "That spirit we saw. It was terrifying. A daemon." She chose her words with care; at present he knew her only as a singer, not as a member of an elite team of exorcists. "Yet you say it healed you of your injuries and restored your memory. That doesn't seem like the action of an evil spirit."

"It gave me courage. Confidence in myself." He stopped, gazing up into the clearing sky as if unconsciously searching for a lingering trace of its presence. "When it made itself a . . . a part of me, I felt so strong. As if I could accomplish anything I set my mind to. Now that it's gone, I feel . . . empty."

He could almost be describing what she had experienced when the Faie had left her body to return to the book. She looked at him with fresh sympathy. He had been possessed by the Drakhaoul, a daemon spirit that had wreaked unimaginable destruction, and yet it had used him kindly. Was there some kinship between the Faie and the Drakhaouls?

"Forgive me for unburdening myself to you. I've had so much on my mind since . . ." Andrei glanced at her, with the hint of an intimate smile.

His eyes are so warm when he smiles. "You must have been so lonely, all those long months after your memories returned." It was difficult not to feel sympathy for his current predicament.

"Not so lonely as when I returned to Mirom and walked the streets of my home as a stranger. It's a very peculiar sensation to stand in front of your own memorial and see your name engraved there with the dates of your short, insignificant life beside those of your dead friends and crewmates . . ." The haunted look had clouded his eyes again. "I felt like a ghost."

"Well, will you look over there!" Kilian nudged Jagu, pointing across the square. "Isn't that your charming partner?" Jagu looked and saw Celestine walking along the gravel path beneath the cherry trees with Andrei Orlov, one hand resting on his arm. The two seemed absorbed in their conversation, Celestine's golden head raised so that she could gaze attentively up at him.

"They seem to be getting on rather well, wouldn't you say?" There was an all-too-familiar hint of malice in Kilian's words. Jagu decided to ignore the sly dig, designed, he knew, to provoke him.

"Our orders are to gain as much information from him as possible. Celestine has a talent for putting people at their ease . . ." How lame it sounded. He couldn't even convince himself. "I'm content just to be with her. Near her. I don't ask for more."

"Such admirable self-restraint. Such a noble lack of self-interest. Most people would say that you're deluding yourself."

What possible satisfaction could Kilian get out of goading him like this? Jagu wondered. "Must you always see things from your own peculiarly warped perspective?"

"Only a damned fool would let himself be tormented day after day by a love that can never be fulfilled."

Was there more of an edge to Kilian's words than usual? Or did they seem sharper because of the raw wind off the Straits that suddenly stirred the cherry branches, dislodging the last tender blossoms?

"What, precisely, do you mean by—" Jagu began, but Kilian interrupted him.

"My ship leaves tomorrow on the dawn tide. I need those reports for the Maistre from you both—even if you have to stay up into the small hours to complete them."

Jagu went down to the docks in the dark before dawn to see Kilian off. It seemed odd to be handing Sergius's Staff into his care after so many months. It had made him feel strangely secure, as if the saint's presence had been protecting and guiding them.

"I fear the Maistre will be disappointed," Jagu said as they approached the harbor.

"Did you really think those old monks would give up their sacred treasure to a rival order?"

Jagu shook his head.

"It was a valuable reconnaissance mission. You mapped the coastline. You found the pilgrim trails through the forest to the monastery. Now we know what we're up against." There was no hint of jesting in Kilian's tone anymore.

"So we're not giving up?"

"It's the king's will," Kilian said. "Enguerrand has some grand project in mind. You may find yourself on the way back to Azhkendir very soon."

Jagu groaned. "I don't think I could endure the smell of herring again."

As they walked on, a crowd of Tielen sailors went hurrying past, moving in the direction of the naval dockyards.

"Something's up," said Kilian.

"Kilian! Jagu!" Celestine came running after them. "Have you heard the news? There's been a big sea battle off the coast of Smarna. It sounds as if Eugene's Southern Fleet has suffered a significant defeat."

"But the Smarnans have only a handful of warships," said Jagu. "How could so few overcome such a powerful navy?"

"Who knows?" said Kilian. "As long as they don't fire on my ship home, I couldn't give a damn. And here she is, the *Azénor*." He stopped alongside the three-master, which was bustling with crewmen, making ready for the crossing to Francia.

"Godspeed, then, and an uneventful voyage." Jagu gave Kilian a hug and placed the metal Staff in his hands. "And take good care of the Staff."

"You know you can rely on me," said Kilian.

"Tell the Maistre," added Celestine, "that we're going after the *big fish,* as he instructed; we may need extra support."

"By all the saints, you're formidable when you set your mind on something, Celestine. I'd hate to be on the opposing side!" Kilian feigned a shudder, a teasing light glinting in his green eyes.

"My Southern Fleet has been attacked by the Drakhaoul of Azhkendir." Eugene paced the Magus's laboratory, his hands clasped behind his back. Linnaius said nothing; it was best, he had learned from experience, to let the Emperor vent his rage first before offering any kind of counsel. "What will Lord Gavril attack next? Swanholm? We must make our move now, Linnaius." Eugene stopped and stabbed his finger at the chart that lay open on the table. "We must go to Ty Nagar and find this legendary Serpent Gate. I will summon a Drakhaoul of my own."

"Are you certain this is the only solution?" Bringing a

second Drakhaoul into the world seemed to Linnaius too drastic a response.

"Why wait any longer? I have the key, the Eye of Nagar."

"But if you succeed in opening the Serpent Gate, can you be certain that only one Drakhaoul will come to your call?"

Eugene looked up at him, a gleam in his eyes. "I can't. But should such a thing happen, I shall be relying on you, Kaspar, to close the Serpent Gate before the others can escape."

Linnaius had suspected that might be the case. "We're talking of prodigiously powerful daemons here. I've never attempted anything this dangerous before."

"The only way to fight fire is with fire," said Eugene stubbornly. "And the only way to defend the empire is to set free my ancestor's Drakhaoul, the Drakhaoul of Helmar."

"But the other five? 'Seven, they were Seven, the Dark Angels of Destruction,' " Linnaius quoted from the ancient curse he had uncovered in the monastery library in Azhkendir. "If they are all let loose through the Serpent Gate, they could bring about the end of the world."

"As I said before"—and Eugene placed one hand on Linnaius's shoulder—"I have complete confidence in you to prevent such a catastrophe from occurring."

"I appreciate the compliment, Eugene, but we are about to open a gate that leads to the Realm of Shadows. Even if it's only for a few brief seconds, we must prevent even the smallest trickle of darkness from leaking through into our world. Who knows what nameless horrors lurk near the Gate, waiting for just such an opportunity?"

"Where's your sense of adventure?" Eugene burst into laughter. "A search for a fabled island far beyond Serindher; an Emperor's rubies; it's the stuff of legends, Kaspar. How soon can we leave?"

CHAPTER 8

Celestine's little entourage took rooms at an inn in the village of Helmargård, which lay close to the Swanholm estate. The construction of the palace had attracted many craftsmen to the area and they in turn had brought their families, so that what had once been a huddle of farm cottages around a wooden church had grown into a bustling and prosperous small town.

It had been Celestine's inspiration to invent the role of concert manager for Andrei, and Ambassador d'Abrissard supplied the necessary papers for "Mr. Tikhon." The concert manager's first task was to send a letter informing the palace majordomo that Celestine de Joyeuse had arrived at the Empress's request and was awaiting further instructions. But when Celestine saw how poor his skills were, she composed the note herself, adding—at his request—an enigmatic postscript in Francian which she hoped would pique Astasia's curiosity.

The reply, which came promptly, was delivered by a neatly dressed flunkey wearing the blue-and-grey livery of the House of Tielen.

I regret to inform you that Princess Karila has been taken ill and so the birthday recital may have to be canceled. However, her imperial highness, while aware that you have postponed engagements abroad at her request, would not wish you to have been inconvenienced. She requests that you visit the palace at your earliest convenience to discuss rescheduling the concert.

Lovisa, Countess of Aspelin

The carriage began the long, winding descent into the valley, and Celestine let out a little gasp of delight as she caught her first glimpse of Eugene's palace. From the limpid waters of the lake in the landscaped park, to the geometrical designs of the formal gardens set out in the Francian style, all had been executed to impress. Even the carriage drive had been cleverly designed to reveal Swanholm's splendors to the visitor from different perspectives. But it was the facade of the central building, with its two subtly asymmetrical wings, that impressed her the most. Clean lines, the sheen of steel-grey slate tiles, and the many windows offsetting the soft pallor of the stone, with little ornamentation save the tall pillars supporting the magnificent portico, each one as smooth and slender as the birch trees in the surrounding woodlands.

And yet all this elegance conceals a malevolent and dangerous canker: the Magus's laboratory. Is he here, I wonder? Can I sense his presence? Or . . . can he sense mine? The thought sent a little frisson through her. *But then why should he suspect? He has no reason to know that I am on his trail . . . or even that I'm still alive. I have the advantage of surprise.*

"Don't do anything rash," Jagu had said to her before she left the inn. He had stopped her, one hand on her arm. The concerned look in his eyes had startled her.

"Don't worry, Jagu, this is merely a reconnaissance mission."

"So you're the Francian singer." Eyes the frosty blue of an ice-bound lake stared suspiciously at Celestine. "My name is Lovisa. Please follow me to the music room."

Celestine curtsied. She had not missed the note of disapproval in the way the Countess of Aspelin pronounced the word "Francian."

Alone, Celestine explored the music room. The fortepiano boasted a pretty marquetry case decorated with ornate clefs intertwined in a pattern of songbirds and lyres. When she tested a few keys and played a little run of notes, she discovered that the instrument was not just attractive to look at, it was also in tune.

The doors opened and Empress Astasia came in, accompanied by the countess. Celestine sank into a deep curtsy.

"Welcome to Swanholm, Demoiselle," Astasia said, smiling warmly.

"I am so sorry to hear of your stepdaughter's indisposition, highness. Would you prefer to cancel the recital?"

"After you have taken the trouble to alter your schedule to travel all this way? No, I won't hear of it." Astasia turned to her lady-in-waiting. "You can leave us now, Countess," she said pointedly.

As soon as they were alone, Astasia hurried over to Celestine. "You said you had something to impart to me," she said softly. "Something of personal significance."

Celestine nodded.

"I have little skill at the keyboard," said Astasia, "but if I were to attempt to accompany you, perhaps you could tell me the news you bring between verses?"

This was going better than Celestine could have hoped; her message must have piqued the young empress's curiosity. "An ingenious conceit, highness." She lifted a book of songs from the top of the fortepiano and began to leaf through the pages. "Do you know 'The Waterfall'?"

Astasia settled herself on the seat and took a look at the music. She pulled a wry face. "Too hard."

"This one is just right. 'Summer Evenings.' A beautiful melody, a deceptively simple accompaniment. And in my native tongue, which is not so familiar to the Tielens, I believe," Celestine added mischievously.

"I've never played this one before," Astasia stared at the notes, biting her lower lip as she concentrated, "so not too fast, Demoiselle, I beg you."

"*In summer . . . when the swallows swoop overhead . . .*" Celestine began. "*Empress,*" she sang, fitting the words to the melody, "*your brother is alive.*"

Astasia stopped playing abruptly. "Alive?" Celestine saw her violet eyes brimming with tears. "Where is he? In Francia? How is he?" She clutched Celestine's hands in her own. "And how do you know?"

"He is in remarkably good health, all things considered," Celestine said, touched by Astasia's response. "After his ship was wrecked, he was washed ashore nearly dead and was nursed back to health by an old fisherman."

"My poor Andrei." Astasia let Celestine's hands drop. "He must think that we abandoned him." She looked utterly stricken at the thought.

Celestine could not help but feel sorry for her. "Your brother finds himself in a very difficult situation. Your husband has taken the throne of Muscobar that was rightly his. If he were to come forward now, what would the Emperor do?"

"I'm sure Eugene would welcome him to court," Astasia said, her eyes brimming with unshed tears. "For my sake."

"Think again, imperial highness. Some dissident elements might see your brother as a significant rival to your husband's authority." With Andrei and Jagu, Celestine had very carefully rehearsed what she should say. "His reappearance could cause considerable damage to the stability of the empire."

"But Andrei would never do anything to hurt me," protested Astasia.

"The consequences could be disastrous," said Celestine firmly. "He was very reluctant to have me tell you the news—let alone your parents—for fear it would place you all in an impossible situation."

"So where will he go?"

"His wish," Celestine said, "is to see you once more, then to begin a new life. Far away from Muscobar."

"H-how far?" Astasia stammered.

"I have a letter for you." Celestine slid finger and thumb into her décolletage and discreetly extracted a thin sliver of folded paper from beneath her lace fichu.

Astasia opened the letter and read it; Celestine saw her wipe away a stray tear as she handed it back. "I daren't keep this, in case anyone was to find it. Especially Countess Lovisa."

Celestine nodded and swiftly slipped the paper back beneath her fichu.

"I want to see him so much." Astasia seemed to be talking to herself. "If only I could leave the palace. But I'm watched, day and night. It's just that I can't bear to think he's so close by and yet I can't, I daren't risk—" She broke off suddenly, looking directly at Celestine. "I have an idea, Demoiselle. There is to be a masked ball here at Swanholm for Dievona's Night—a Tielen tradition, I'm told. If I could arrange for you and your accompanist to be invited . . ."

"For Dievona's Night?" Celestine considered the proposition, wondering what plan Astasia was hatching. "Well, my next recital is to be given in Bel'Esstar. The weather is clement and the seas are calm. If we delay our departure to attend the ball, I think we shall still make Allegonde in good time."

"Would you say that we are about the same height?" Astasia asked. "And the same build?"

"Well, yes . . ."

"At a masked ball, everyone is in disguise. It can be hard to tell exactly who is who. If I were to provide identical costumes, we could pull off a little charade of our own."

"You—and I—in the same costume?" It was an ingenious idea—although not without its risks.

"And then you and I will secretly exchange masks for a little while, so that I can become Celestine de Joyeuse."

"Allowing us to smuggle your brother in, disguised as Jagu?"

Astasia laughed through her tears. "Just don't let anyone ask Andrei to play the fortepiano, or our charade will be discovered!"

Celestine laughed too, caught up in the Empress's infectious good humor. "And I will be Empress of New Rossiya! Or will I? For who'll be able to guess?"

"I don't know how to thank you, Demoiselle." Astasia

reached out and clasped the singer's hands in her own, pressing them warmly.

"Please, highness," and Celestine pressed Astasia's hands in return, "call me Celestine."

"How did she take the news?" Andrei hurried out to meet Celestine as she stepped down from the carriage that had brought her from Swanholm; he must have been keeping an anxious lookout for her. "Was she very upset? I didn't want to upset her. But she has to know the truth about her husband."

"Let's discuss this indoors, shall we?" Celestine cast a look up and down the little cobbled street; there were many people about in the village, all employed, it seemed, on some errand to do with the ball. But even the sweetest dairymaid carrying cream for the desserts or the humblest tailor staggering beneath the weight of masquerade costumes could be one of Eugene's agents, paid to watch and listen.

"Swapping places with the Empress?" Jagu said. The shutters were closed and in the gloom, his voice sounded strangely slurred. "I think it's too risky."

Celestine had guessed correctly that he would object to the plan. "It's a masked ball. Everyone will be in disguise."

"But if you're caught, you could be charged with treason."

"Why are you sitting in the dark, Jagu? It's a beautiful day." She went to open the shutters to let more daylight into the room and saw him wince.

"What's wrong with you?" She came closer, staring intently at him. "You look awful."

He sighed. "If you must know, Prince Andrei couldn't sleep again last night and insisted on playing cards into the small hours. And now I have a pounding headache."

"So you emptied a few bottles of wine at the same time? You don't deserve any sympathy." But she began to search in her reticule for a paper of powdered headache remedy.

"You try keeping his highness from leaving the inn! He's as restless as a caged beast. How much longer till Dievona's Night?"

"Drink this." She poured him a glass of water and emptied the powder into it. He looked at it suspiciously. "It's all right; it's not an alchymical potion. Just some feverfew."

"It sounds as if you've made a favorable impression on the Empress," he said, grimacing as he drank the bitter liquid.

"She's kind, trusting, and, I suspect, very lonely." Celestine took back the glass. "Why else would she confide in me?" She realized as she was speaking that she had developed a genuine liking for Astasia; she understood how her open, spontaneous nature, which set her apart from the other sophisticated and world-weary young noblewomen, must have bewitched Eugene . . .

"Are you having second thoughts?"

Why was Jagu able to read her so accurately? "I—I feel sorry for her, I suppose. Just imagine how traumatic it would be to hear from a stranger that your husband had a hand in your brother's death."

"Isn't it better that she should know the truth, however harsh?"

"Yes, except I believe that she genuinely loves Eugene," Celestine said, pensively twisting the feverfew paper between her fingers, "and that makes this all the harder."

"Remember," Jagu said, "it's for the good of Francia."

"Demoiselle de Joyeuse?" The innkeeper put his head around the door. "A message for you from the palace."

Celestine opened the letter and read aloud, " 'It is her imperial majesty's wish that you return to Swanholm to continue with her singing lessons. A coach will pick you up at three this afternoon.' " She looked up at Jagu over the crisp white paper. "What do you make of that?"

"It sounds to me as if the Empress is ready to go ahead with her plan."

Celestine nodded, although she still felt conflicted about her role in this charade. "I'd better make myself look presentable." As she passed Jagu, he caught hold of her by the hand.

"Promise me that you won't do anything rash," he said, his voice low, intense.

"Rash?" She forced a laugh. "You know me, Jagu."

"Yes. I do. And that's why I want you to give me your word that you won't act alone. Even if you meet . . . a certain magus."

She looked down at his hand, which was still wrapped around hers, pressing tightly. That touch, that firm pressure stirred something buried deep within her, a memory of a time that she had snuggled close to him and felt so safe, so cherished . . .

He must have realized it too for he swiftly withdrew his hand and walked away. "Just be careful," he said with his back to her so that she could not see his expression.

By three in the afternoon, the day had turned unseasonably sultry. When Celestine was shown into the music room, she saw the Empress sitting by the open window, dressed in a simple high-waisted summer gown.

"Your highness looks so charming in that sprigged muslin," Celestine said. "I'm sure you'll start a new fashion at Swanholm."

"Thank you! Countess Lovisa told me that it was démodé and inappropriate. But it's too hot today to wear a formal court dress. And as we'll be trying on costumes a little later, I thought there was little point in being laced into a boned corset. Now, what shall we play?"

"I've brought this song for you to try; it's an old love song from Provença . . ." Celestine placed the accompaniment to *"O Mon Amou"* on the music stand of the fortepiano. *If the Empress has something to confide in me and anyone walks past, they'll assume that we're discussing the music.* "Shall we give it a try?"

They managed a page and a half until Astasia lost control of the keyboard part and broke off, laughing helplessly. Celestine sang on for a bar or two, then joined in the laughter, leaning on the fortepiano to support herself.

Suddenly Astasia started up from the keyboard, staring out onto the terrace. "Hush," she said, wiping tears of laughter from her eyes, "we have an audience."

Celestine glanced around.

An elderly man stood outside the open window, his wisps of white hair and beard tousled by the breeze. He bowed but not before Celestine had seen the wintry glint in his pale eyes.

It's him. It has to be.

"Beautiful music, ladies," he said. "I must congratulate you." And he continued on his way along the terrace.

"There is no privacy to be had in Swanholm," said Astasia and all the merriment had gone from her voice.

Celestine felt as if a pit of shadows had opened at her feet. "Tell me, highness," she whispered, "who was that ancient gentleman we saw just now?"

Astasia pulled a grimace. "The Magus? His name is Kaspar Linnaius. He's a scientist, I believe, though he has an official court title like 'Royal Artificer' or some such."

It was Kaspar Linnaius. And he stared straight at me. If he recognized me, he gave no sign of it. "He looks at least a hundred years old!"

"I confess he gives me the shivers. It's his eyes: so lifeless, so cold . . ."

Celestine nodded, still shaken.

"He's busy arranging the fireworks for the ball. I'm told his displays are the most splendid to be seen in the whole quadrant."

"Does he make them here in the palace?" Celestine asked, recovering herself a little.

"He has his own laboratory, although I've never visited it."

"Isn't that a little risky, working with gunpowder so close to the royal apartments?"

"It's in the stable block, at some distance from the main wing. But rumor has it that he has set up invisible wards that repel any unwelcome visitors."

"Ow!" wailed the Empress as her maid Nadezhda struggled to lace her into the shepherdess's costume. "Must you pull quite so tight?"

Celestine watched in silence, wondering if they would ever be alone so that she could break the news to Astasia. If anyone were to overhear, she would be arrested for speaking treason against the Emperor. And if the cold-eyed countess was spying on them outside . . .

"Now the wig." Nadezhda eased the soft white curls into place.

"And a mask." Astasia took the gilded mask from Nadezhda and put it on. "Stand next to me, Celestine."

Celestine obeyed.

"We are a good match in stature. I think this costume will suit our needs very well."

Celestine nodded. "Then Jagu will come as a shepherd."

"Nadezhda," Astasia said. "You remember what we agreed?"

Nadezhda bobbed a little curtsy. "I'll go whisper your requests to the costumier straightaway."

Astasia made sure the door was firmly bolted after her. Then she handed a gilded mask identical to her own to Celestine and tied the golden ribbons securely behind her ears to stop it from slipping. Then they checked their reflections in the mirror, masked faces close together.

"Perfect," said Astasia. "Who would guess? We look like identical twins."

Now, before Nadezhda comes back.

"Did you know, highness," said Celestine, taking off the mask, "that Kaspar Linnaius, whom we saw earlier, is no ordinary scientist?"

"I had some notion, yes," Astasia said, fiddling with her wig. "I know that he has placed certain wards on the palace here and its grounds to protect us from harm."

"But were you also aware," and Celestine dropped her voice, "of his other talents? Or that his title is not a fanciful conceit? He is a wind mage, able to bend the winds to his will."

"I had no idea!"

Celestine could not see the Empress's expression clearly but she noticed that her hands had fallen away from the wig.

"In the conflict between Francia and Tielen, your husband's father, Prince Karl, won a decisive victory over my countrymen in a sea battle off the Saltyk Peninsula. At the height of the battle, a terrible storm broke and many of the Francian fleet were blown into the rocks."

"The seas around the Saltyk Peninsula can be treacherously unpredictable," Astasia said lightly, taking off the heavy wig and replacing it on its stand, "even in the best of weather."

"And Prince Karl was Kaspar Linnaius's patron."

"I don't think we should be talking of this, Celestine . . ."

I can't stop now; she must hear it all. "Your brother's ship, the *Sirin*, went down in a storm that blew up out of nowhere. On a calm, moonlit night."

There came a loud rap on the door. Someone rattled the door handle.

"Imperial highness!" It was Countess Lovisa's voice. "Why is your door bolted?"

"I'm in dishabille!" Astasia beckoned Celestine to the fireplace. She pressed the marble acanthus leaf on the right and as a panel slowly slid into the wall, Celestine heard the grating of hidden machinery.

"A secret passageway?"

Astasia's voice dropped to a whisper. "I'm desperate to hear more, but it's best if you leave now. I'm certain that Lovisa has been spying on me. We mustn't arouse her suspicions."

"I understand." Celestine bent low to enter the secret passage.

"It opens onto the shrubbery near the Orangery, but be careful there is no one about to see you."

"With so many people around for the ball, it won't be difficult to disappear into the crowd."

"Nadezhda will have the costumes delivered to your lodgings."

"Are you dressed yet, highness?" called a voice from the corridor.

Astasia gave a little groan. "Lovisa again. Go."

She touched the acanthus leaf again and the panel slid to, leaving Celestine in the dark of the secret passageway, frustrated that the prying countess had interrupted their conversation before she had finished warning Astasia about the Magus.

"Are all the arrangements made?" Andrei's eyes were dark-shadowed as if he had not slept.

"The *Melusine* is waiting at Haeven to take you to safety in Francia, highness," said Jagu. "We have a cabin prepared for your sister too, should she choose to leave with you."

"I can't bear to think of her sharing that man's bed a moment longer." Andrei rose and began to pace the little room restlessly.

Jagu exchanged a surreptitious glance with Celestine. Both were aware how risky a game they were playing and the strain of waiting was obviously beginning to tell on Andrei. Jagu had already had enough of humoring the Muscobite prince's unpredictable mood swings but was unwilling—for reasons he couldn't quite define—to leave Andrei and Celestine alone together.

"Delivery from the palace for Demoiselle de Joyeuse!" called the innkeeper. A moment later, he came puffing up the stairs, carrying a wicker hamper.

"Costumes!" Celestine flung open the lid and pulled out the silky flounces of the shepherdess's dress, followed by breeches and a silken jacket of the same powder blue.

"Wigs," announced the innkeeper, reappearing to deposit two boxes. Celestine took out a white-powdered wig and presented it to Andrei.

"You can't mean I have to wear this?" His dismayed expression was so comical that she burst into delighted laughter. "But I'll look like a *travesti*!"

"So will everyone else. And your true identity will be hidden under this mask." She placed the gilded mask over his face, tying the laces behind his ears. A slip of paper fluttered out and Jagu bent to retrieve it, trying to hide his disapproving expression. Was she consciously flirting with Andrei? He didn't like the way she was behaving so familiarly with him.

"It's addressed to you, Celestine." He handed her the note, stony-faced. "It's from the Empress."

* * *

The Empress was sitting at the keyboard when Celestine was admitted to the music room. But as Celestine rose from her curtsy, she realized that the Empress was silently weeping, a lace handkerchief pressed against her lips as though to hold in the sobs.

"Why, imperial highness, whatever is wrong?" Celestine said in her warmest, most sympathetic tones. She had begun to hate herself for having to play so cruelly on Astasia's feelings.

"I—I was prepared to forgive Eugene many things," Astasia said at last, dabbing at her eyes. "No one can reach his position without making enemies. But I couldn't sleep last night thinking of what you told me . . ." A fresh flow of tears stifled her words.

The sight of Astasia's face all red and blotched from crying only increased Celestine's sense of guilt. "Forgive me, highness, but are you referring to—?"

"The Magus. The sinking of the *Sirin*. How could Eugene have sanctioned such a thing? Muscobar wasn't even at war with Tielen when she went down in the Straits."

"It may be that the Magus acted alone for the good of Tielen . . . or to gain favor with your husband. The Emperor himself may have known nothing about the consequences of the storm until the news broke and it was too late to do anything."

"I only wish I could believe it to be so. But Eugene had everything to gain from my brother's death. I don't know if I can trust him anymore." Astasia was so distressed that her tears began to flow unchecked. Celestine felt so sorry for the young woman that she forgot court protocol and put her arms around her.

Dievona's Night arrived and the carriages of the illustrious guests began to roll through the village, heading toward the Swanholm estate. Celestine hired the innkeeper's daughter to act as her maid and help her with the intricate fastenings of the boned bodice and pannier overskirts of the shepherdess's costume. Tightly laced, she sat before her traveling mirror, making small adjustments to her wig so that not a single golden hair could escape and betray her identity. And she wondered if the Empress was feeling as apprehensive as she at that moment. She had developed a genuine liking for the Empress over the past days; Astasia had accepted her unquestioningly, treating her as a friend. "And a friend is a luxury that I haven't been able to afford for so very long," she said softly to her white-wigged reflection.

"Are you ready, Celestine?" Jagu called. "Your carriage is waiting."

"Coming." Celestine draped a black velvet cloak over her costume, took up her gilded mask, and went out onto the landing to find Jagu waiting for her. His eyes widened as he gazed at the beribboned vision in powder-blue satin.

"Does it suit me?" She performed a little pirouette for him, unable to hold back delighted laughter as she held the mask to her face, peering at him teasingly.

"It's certainly . . . different from your usual style of dress." He seemed at a loss for words.

"Ah, but can you be sure it's really me? I might be her imperial highness—"

He caught her by one lace-gloved hand. "How can you take this so lightly, Celestine? This isn't a charade. Forget the pretty costumes and the masks. Never forget that you're a foreign agent. If you're caught impersonating the Empress, it will mean imprisonment—maybe even execution."

She stared at him. The expression in his dark eyes was severe to the point of disapproval. Why didn't he trust her? "Lightly?" she repeated, hurt. "If you think—"

"Demoiselle." She turned to see Andrei in a suit of matching blue satin, his black curls hidden beneath his white-powdered wig. "How charming you look. Shall we go?" He offered her his arm and she placed her hand on it.

"I won't be there to back you up if anything goes wrong," Jagu muttered as she swept past him down the stairs. "Please be careful."

CHAPTER 9

"What is your will, Lord Arkhan?"

Oranir prostrated himself before Sardion. Beside him, Lord Estael, Magisters Aqil and Tilath, also bowed down. *So few of us left now, since Rieuk was lost in the Rift . . .*

"King Enguerrand of Francia is on his way to Ondhessar." There was a tremor of excitement in the Arkhan's voice. "He is on a pilgrimage, with only a small retinue of guards. I want you to assassinate him."

Lord Estael raised his head. "Lord Arkhan, is that wise? Such an act, on Djihari soil, could bring the most terrible retribution on you and your people."

"You dare to question my judgment, Estael?" The cold anger in Sardion's voice made Oranir flinch.

"I do." Estael gazed up at his royal master. "Why risk so much when we can achieve the same results by more subtle means?"

"And what means are you referring to?" Sardion stood over Estael, arms folded.

"You may remember we used a slow and subtle poison to eliminate Enguerrand's father, Gobain," said Magister Aqil.

"Slow? The king is only here to pay a brief visit to the shrine."

"We know from our intelligence that Enguerrand has never enjoyed good health," Estael said.

"Then one of you must infiltrate the king's entourage. You, Aqil."

"Not I!" said Aqil. "The Francian Guerriers have seen my face before; I can't risk jeopardizing the mission." He turned to Oranir. "But you will go in my stead. You were my apprentice for six years; you are better trained in physic than most western physicians."

Oranir had been staring at the floor, praying that they would not select him. He heard Aqil's words with a sinking feeling. "But won't they suspect me?"

"You've traveled abroad, you must have learned something about the Francians in that time. You're an excellent choice," said Estael.

"But, Lord Est—" Oranir began, but Estael silenced him with a look.

Oranir just managed to hold his tongue until they had left the Arkhan's apartments. But as soon as they had been escorted to the main gates of the palace, he could not restrain himself any longer.

"Why does the Arkhan wield so much power over us? Why did none of you dare to stand up to him? Only Rieuk had the courage to defy him, and what did we do? We turned our backs on him, abandoning him to his death in the Rift. We betrayed—"

"Quiet!" Estael turned on him with such a forbidding look that Oranir left his sentence unfinished. "Even out here his spies are watching, listening."

The great sandstone walls of the ancient fortress of Ondhessar towered above the king of Francia's entourage as they neared their goal. Enguerrand, his head and face loosely covered in a burnous, Djihari-style, to protect him from the stinging sand, gazed up in awed silence at the ancient citadel. At his side, Ruaud de Lanvaux gazed too, his heart heavy with memories. He had been not much older than Enguerrand when he had fought his way into Ondhessar and been the first to discover Saint Azilia's hidden shrine. The stairs and courtyards had been slippery with blood; the whole fortress had reeked of death and sorcery. In the desperate battle, the Commanderie had been forced to employ two of their precious Angelstones to defeat the black arts of the magi of Ondhessar.

Now the Allegondan Commanderie, the Rosecoeurs, had

command of Ondhessar. It was humiliating to have to ask their permission to visit the shrine.

"How long is it since you were last here, Maistre?" Enguerrand was asking him.

Ruaud had been lost in his recollections of the past. "Well over twenty years . . ."

"Just after I was born, then?"

Ruaud nodded, realizing that he must seem extremely old to Enguerrand. "We tore down the Arkhan's standard and hoisted our Commanderie flags that day." His vision was drawn upward into the burning blue of the sky to where the crimson banners of the Rosecoeurs hung limply from the flagpoles, not stirring for want of a breeze. A bird of prey was slowly circling high above the towers of the fortress, so faint against the brilliant sky that it seemed to his dazzled eyes as evanescent as a wisp of smoke.

"Why is Captain nel Macey making his majesty wait in this intolerable heat?" Ruaud demanded, turning around in the saddle to see if there was any sign of activity.

The great gates began to open with a grinding sound. The captain came striding out, followed by a column of Rosecoeur Guerriers, who lined up to form an honor guard for the king.

"I apologize for making you wait, sire," nel Macey said, bowing, "but we had intelligence of a possible attempt on your life. Let me offer you and your men some refreshment . . ."

The shrine is just a hollow shell without Azilis's presence. Ruaud, arms folded, stood watching Enguerrand's rapt expression. It brought back to him something of the burning excitement he had felt when, wounded and exhausted, he had first discovered the hidden cavern.

But then *she* had been here. Her ethereal voice had drawn him. Even if her singing had only been a natural phenomenon, currents of desert wind sighing through hidden vents, setting the crystals in the cave vibrating, it had lifted his weariness, making him forget the pain of his wounds. All that was left in the shrine were the ancient frescos and a gaping alcove where once the statue of Azilis had stood, a white apparition carved from translucent and flawless marble.

"Sacrilege," Ruaud muttered under his breath. "The Rosecoeurs had no business taking her away."

"What did you say, Ruaud?"

"So has it been worth such a grueling journey, sire?"

"Yes. Oh, yes." Enguerrand turned to face him, unwinding the spectacle wires from around his ears to wipe the tears from his eyes. "Of all the holy shrines that we've visited in the past weeks, this is by far the most affecting of all. There are too many peddlers and souvenir sellers crowding the other places. But here it feels as if time has stopped. We could climb the stairs and find ourselves back in Azilis's day . . ."

Ruaud had a sudden, disturbing flash of memory.

Père Laorans . . . the cache of dusty, hidden manuscripts . . . the lost texts pronounced as heretical by Donatien, leading to Laorans's banishment to found a mission in distant Serindher.

"Are you still alive, Laorans?" Ruaud murmured. It had been a long while since the order had received a report from the mission.

"What is it, Maistre?"

"I was just remembering an old friend, sire."

"Did he die at your side in the battle for the fortress?"

Ruaud shook his head slowly. "No, though many brave Guerriers never saw Francia again. But in some ways, it might have been better if he . . ." He left the sentence unfinished. Laorans's discovery had brought an untimely end to a promising career in the Commanderie. Though banished to the tropical heat of distant Serindher for his heresy, he had continued to serve the order faithfully.

What became of those ancient manuscripts, I wonder? Did Donatien really burn them? Or are they still locked away in some vault in the Commanderie?

Enguerrand awoke next morning with a fever. Ruaud took one look at him, shivering and white-faced, and knew that the pilgrimage was at an end. He paid the landlord of the inn a considerable sum of money on condition that he agree to entertain no other guests but the Francians. He sent a courier on ahead to warn the captain of the flagship, which was waiting at the port of Tyriana, and went to attend to the king.

As Ruaud approached the king's bed to administer a fever draft from the medical supplies he had brought, anticipating just such an occurrence, Enguerrand caught hold of him by the hand, his fingers hot and clammy.

"Whatever happens, my mother *must not know* of this. She was against the pilgrimage in the first place. She will never let me go again . . ."

"Don't forget that, as much respect as you have for your mother, you came of age last year. She may seek to influence you, but—"

"She'll say that I was irresponsible, to leave Francia for so many months . . ."

"You're in constant communication with the First Minister. Don't you trust him?"

"Of course I trust Aiguillon. But I know my mother's methods. She'll do everything she can to undermine his authority . . ."

Ruaud heard these last words in silence. Enguerrand was all too aware of his mother's ambitions; Aliénor was unwilling to relinquish her hold over her son, or the government of Francia.

But when, by nightfall, the fever was so high that Enguerrand's teeth chattered together, Ruaud consulted the innkeeper, who sent out for a physician.

The physician shook back the hood of his cape. Ruaud saw a dark-skinned young man, scarcely older than the king himself, his eyes concealed behind thick-lensed spectacles.

"Aren't you rather young?" Ruaud demanded.

"I served a six-year apprenticeship before I started to practice." The young man's command of the common tongue was impeccable, tinged only with a slight Enhirran accent. "But if you prefer, I could send for my master? Only he's in Tyriana, so it would take him several days to get here."

"No, that won't be necessary." Enguerrand needed physic immediately. Ruaud led the young physician to the king's bedside and watched closely as he checked Enguerrand's pulse.

"May I examine him further?"

Ruaud nodded. The physician pulled back the loose sheet and probed with his fingertips, feeling behind and below Enguerrand's jaw, then moving down to gently press on his stomach below the rib cage. Each time, Enguerrand winced.

"There are swellings here, and here . . ." The physician slowly shook his dark head.

"And that's bad because . . . ?"

"The glands are infected. We call this red sand fever. It can kill, if not treated correctly."

"His life is in danger?"

"Give him six drops of this tincture every two hours." He handed Ruaud a slender phial containing a viscous dark fluid. "And keep him cool. It's important to bring his fever down as soon as possible."

"Six drops," Ruaud muttered.

As the physician turned to leave, Enguerrand's hand moved and caught hold of his sleeve. Ruaud saw the king gather all his strength to smile at the young man.

"Thank you for coming all this way. You and your people have been . . . so kind and welcoming to me," he whispered.

Oranir's hands were shaking uncontrollably as he left the inn; he tried to conceal them in the sleeves of his robe. He had seen the friendly warmth of Enguerrand's smile and his courage had failed him. He remembered how bitterly Rieuk had railed at the crimes Sardion had forced him to commit in the name of vengeance. There was no honor in killing a sick man with poison.

I can't do it. He clenched his fists. *I won't.*

Halfway down the street, he turned and ran back, hoping he was not too late.

* * *

Ruaud was measuring out the drops into a glass when he heard footsteps approaching. He looked up to see the physician, his face flushed, in the doorway.

"Have you administered the drops?" he asked breathlessly.

"I was just about to. What's wrong?"

"I gave you the wrong phial. Please forgive my carelessness, my lord. Please let me make it up to you."

Ruaud, puzzled, took the second phial the young man held out. "Why, what's in the other one?"

The physician gave him an enigmatic look. "Throw the contents down the drain, my lord. You might kill a few rats." And without another word, he pulled up his hood and vanished into the night.

"You ungrateful boy." Sardion struck Oranir, the harsh blow sending him reeling. "You had Enguerrand of Francia in your power, and you showed him mercy. I should have you tortured for this. I should have you stripped of your Emissary!"

Oranir, dazed, wiped the blood from his cut lip.

"It is not your place to disobey my orders. It is not your place to decide who lives, who dies." He summoned the guards at the entrance. "Take this piece of filth to the dungeons and lock him away. I don't want to look on his treacherous face again."

The next day, the courier came from Tyriana with a folder full of official dispatches. Ruaud sat by the king's bedside, reading through them with a sense of increasing disquiet. One, from Admiral Romorantin, informed his majesty that the Armel fleet was making for the Straits in preparation for the planned attack on the Tielen dockyards, where the remainder of the Emperor's warships were being repaired.

Ruaud glanced at the sleeping king. Why had Enguerrand fallen sick at the very moment that they were about to make such a decisive move against their enemy? For once, although he hated to admit it, Aliénor had been right. Enguerrand should have postponed the pilgrimage. Francia had never been in a stronger position to assert herself against the Emperor.

Ruaud broke the seal on the final dispatch and saw to his surprise that it came from the First Minister of Smarna.

> To his royal majesty, Enguerrand of Francia.
>
> The unexpected arrival of your majesty's fleet on maneuvers off our shores has unnerved our Tielen oppressors. On behalf of the council, I beg you not to delay any further. We are ready to strike back at the invaders—and will make our move as soon as you are ready.
>
> Nina Vashteli

This was a God-sent opportunity; Francia's war fleets were positioned in exactly the right place to attack the Emperor where his forces were at their weakest—and Enguerrand lay gravely ill.

"Of all times, why must it be now?" Ruaud muttered.

Enguerrand must have heard him, for a voice asked drowsily from the gauze-draped bed, "What's wrong?"

"Majesty!" Ruaud raised the gauzes and saw that the king's skin was no longer pearled with sweat. His breathing seemed easier too and the hectic flush was fading from his face. "How are you feeling?"

"Not . . . quite awake yet." Enguerrand blinked owlishly, fumbling for his glasses; Ruaud pressed them into his hand. "Why were you sighing just now? Is it bad news?"

"On the contrary, sire, it could be very good news for Francia." Ruaud poured Enguerrand a glass of boiled water and helped him drink a sip or two. "Smarna has asked for our help."

"Then we must go to their aid." Enguerrand lay back on the pillows. "Tell Admiral Mercoeur to make straight for Colchise and give the Smarnans whatever help they need to drive out the Emperor's forces. We'll follow directly behind."

Ruaud stared at Enguerrand. Such decisive words! He pressed his fingers to the young man's wrist, checking his pulse, but the beat was firm and steady.

Enguerrand opened his eyes again. "You feared the fever was talking, didn't you?" he said, a little smile on his cracked lips. "But I feel quite clearheaded again. If you draw up the letter to Admiral Mercoeur, I'll sign and seal it."

As soon as the letter had been dispatched to Admiral Mercoeur, Ruaud returned to the king's bedside to find that Enguerrand was sleeping peacefully. Ruaud vowed to give the physician a generous reward, but the young man never returned to collect his payment, and as soon as Enguerrand was well enough, the royal party set out—not for Francia, as they had originally planned, but for their new ally, Smarna.

Time had no meaning in the Rift. Rieuk had no idea how long he had been trying to find his way out . . . and yet he was determined not to give up.

He had fashioned a new Lodestar, but it was of little use if he couldn't leave the Rift. Had Sardion sent the other magi in to search for him? The thought tormented him; he could have been stumbling on, while they called for him, just out of earshot.

Sometimes, exhausted, he collapsed to the ground and slept. But sleep was as much a torment as waking. In his dreams, phantoms arose out of the swirling dust and shadows.

Have I died and gone to hell? He could not remember dying. He could not recall falling sick, or being attacked.

Suppose Lord Estael has had my dying body entombed in aethyr crystal to preserve it, as he did with Imri, and trapped my soul in a soul glass?

Suddenly he felt sick and chill. He crouched shivering, his arms hugging his knees to his chest. Was it possible for a disembodied soul to feel the cold? Or any kind of physical sensation?

Time has no meaning in the Rift.

He felt no need or desire for food or water. That fact in itself was enough to make him question if he was trapped in an eternal sleep. *What is sustaining my life here? No mortal man could have survived for so long in here.*

But I'm not wholly mortal. I have angel blood in my veins . . . even if it is the cursed blood of a fallen angel.

Yet the magi were not immortal. Imri had died, just as Hervé, Gonery, and the others before him . . .

"Ormas?" He put his hand to his breast, but felt only a faint tremor of response; his hawk was still deep in sleep.

The haoma trees are dead and the smoke hawks have gone deeper into the Rift.

In his more lucid moments, Rieuk made himself repeat over and over everything he had ever learned as an apprentice at the College of Thaumaturgy: alchymical compounds, glamours, the constellations, even elemental magic. He recited the names of the places he had visited, country by country, trying to keep the images alive and vivid in his mind. Trying, above all, to preserve some sense of who Rieuk Mordiern was. He even sang to himself some of the old songs of Vasconie, learned by rote with the other children at the village school before . . . before . . .

The light of the emerald moon was so faint that it hardly cast enough light for him to see where he was going. He had carved signs on the thick, ridged trunks of the ancient cedars to mark his path. Yet no matter which way he went, he never found the marked trees again, almost as if the bark had erased all trace of his presence.

CHAPTER 10

Swanholm glimmered in the summer dusk, like a palace of enchantments from a fairy tale. Strings of pearlescent lanterns were festooned over every bower and alley, glowing like luminous spider-webs heavy with dew. Strains of dance music drifted out from the ballroom, where all the doors and windows had been opened to let in the balmy night air. Yet Celestine felt so jittery as she flitted through the torchlit courtyard that her hands were trembling. She knew she was being foolish, acting on impulse, without proper backup. But it was a chance not to be missed. And she had the advantage of surprise.

Exchanging places with the Empress had proved no more difficult than a game of charades, even though she knew that discovery carried considerable risks. She had even managed to reunite Andrei and Astasia at the very moment the fireworks display took place, when the guests' attentions were diverted. Yet as she waited in the shadowed archway by the door that led to the Magus's laboratory, she felt nothing but apprehension. But she had been waiting so many years for this opportunity. She would not back down just because she was afraid.

An old man came around the corner. In the faint lantern-light overhead she caught a glint of eyes as cold as winter ice and shivered involuntarily.

He was alone.

She stepped forward and, swallowing back her fear, said quietly, "Good evening, Magus."

Linnaius started. She had caught him by surprise. Emboldened, she took another step toward him. Faint fanfares drifted from the gardens, mingled with raucous bursts of cheering. They must be lighting the Dievona's Bonfires. She lifted one hand to her gilded mask and untied the ribbons.

"You have me at a d—disadvantage—" he began, stuttering a little.

"Let me introduce myself." She peeled off the white wig, shaking loose her hair. "My professional name is Celestine de Joyeuse. But Henri de Joyeuse was the name of my singing master, the man who adopted me, a poor orphan in a convent school."

He did not react when she pronounced Henri's name. "This is all very interesting, Demoiselle, but—"

She took in a deep breath and said, "My real name is Klervie de Maunoir."

She saw the shock in his face and knew with a thrill of triumph that she had the advantage.

"Hervé's child?" His voice trembled. "Impossible. You are too young."

"I was just five years old when the Commanderie took my father. That was twenty-one years ago."

Linnaius twitched his finger and thumb, and the lantern-light brightened overhead, illuminating her face. Such power in his fingertips; she must be very careful.

"But—my dear child—"

"I am no child, Kaspar Linnaius." Even though she had determined to stay calm, she could feel anger beginning to well up. "After they burned my father at the stake for heresy, I was forced to grow up all too fast."

"This is fascinating, my dear." A vague look had glazed his eyes; he seemed not to be paying attention to her any longer. "Let us arrange a tête-à-tête for tomorrow, and I will tell you everything I know about your father."

"I sail for Allegonde tomorrow."

He moved closer, gazing searchingly into her face. "Yes, I see the likeness now; your eyes are the same color as his," he murmured. Celestine tried to take a step backward and found that she could not move. How had he managed to bind her? She could sense his mind attempting to probe hers; it felt as if cold, invisible fingers were reaching into her brain, turning all her thoughts to ice. She was frozen; she could not move. She saw him slowly raise his right hand . . .

"Don't try any mage trickery on me," she said. "I took precautions to protect myself . . ." Her voice began to trail away as a little shimmering cloud drifted down around her. *Faie!* she called in panic as her senses began to dim. *Faie . . . help me . . .*

Flambeaux lit the lodge-house gates, elaborate ironwork grilles topped by gilded swans, the emblem of the reigning House of Helmar.

Where was Celestine? Andrei paced the gravel drive, wondering what was detaining her. It was time to go. He had already been recognized by Valery Vassian, his oldest friend. And being reunited with Astasia had stirred up so many emotions.

Can I trust you to keep my secret, Valery? But then, you were always devoted to Astasia. If her honor were at stake, I know that you'd give your life for her without a moment's thought . . .

The Dievona's Bonfires were burning in the valley below; flowers of scarlet flame springing into bloom in the palace gardens and around the lake. The sight of Eugene's magnificent palace, lit by many hundreds of candles, only served to increase Andrei's bitterness.

"Here I am, the heir to Muscobar, forced to skulk like a poor servant . . ."

But the Francians had reminded him that he had the advantage of surprise; he must bide his time a little longer.

The sound of hooves on the gravel distracted him; a lone horseman was riding at a slow trot up the drive toward him. By the guttering flambeaux, Andrei recognized his friend Valery Vassian. One of Valery's hands controlled the reins, the other gently supported the slender form of a young woman who lay slumped against him.

"Celestine?" Andrei reached up to take her as Valery reined his horse to a stop. "What's happened to her, Valery?" She weighed so little in his arms, in spite of the voluminous folds of her blue dress, her golden head drooping against his shoulder.

"Let's take her to her carriage." Valery swung down from the saddle to help him. "Coachman, do you have any smelling salts?"

Andrei gently propped Celestine up in the corner of the carriage. "Did she faint?" Anxiously he felt for a pulse in her wrist. "Her hands are cold." Ever since they first met, Celestine had been so resourceful, so strong, her determined attitude to her mission making him feel ashamed of his own indecisiveness.

"*He* said she was drunk, but I can't smell any trace of alcohol on her breath." Valery, leaning one arm against the carriage, peered inside.

"*He?*" Andrei swung around, alarmed. "Has someone drugged her? Has she been molested?"

"The Magus? It must be many a year since he was capable of such a thing," Valery said, amused.

"She was with the Magus?" Had Celestine dared to confront Kaspar Linnaius alone? Andrei's anxiety and admiration for her increased in equal measure. If anyone had a score to settle with the Magus, it should be he, acting on behalf of Muscobar and his drowned crewmates.

Celestine let out a shuddering sigh but did not open her eyes.

"She just seems to be very deeply asleep." Andrei turned back to her. "Although . . . what are these little specks of glitter on her clothes?"

"Spangles?" suggested Valery lamely. "Sequins?"

"Jagu will kill me for letting this happen," Andrei murmured under his breath.

"What's that?" Valery said.

"Hadn't you better be getting back, Valery? You don't want to raise any suspicions."

"Right-ho." Valery climbed back up into the saddle and saluted Andrei before turning his horse's head back toward the palace below.

* * *

The fireworks display had come to an end, but the Dievona's Bonfires had been lit all over the grounds of the palace, and the masked revelers were wandering toward them, accompanied by musicians from the surrounding villages; pipers and fiddlers, playing the age-old folk tunes, drowning out the more refined strains of the court orchestra.

Eugene had waited till then to make his excuses and slip away from his guests; he had instructed Gustave to tell anyone who asked that he was going hunting. Although he could not help but feel guilty when he glimpsed Astasia, all alone on the terrace.

"*I'm doing this for you, Astasia,*" he told her silently. "*It's the only way that I can protect you—and the empire—from the Drakhaoul of Azhkendir.*"

Earlier, he had removed the Tears of Artamon from his imperial crown and now carried them, safely stowed in a velvet pouch. From time to time he sensed a tremble of energy from the ancient rubies.

But where was Linnaius? Eugene gazed around impatiently, eager to be on his way. The Magus was late. He could hear the fiddlers playing, the wild music mingling with the delighted cries of the guests as the bonfire flames flared high into the night skies.

"F—forgive me, highness." Linnaius appeared, a little out of breath. There was something odd about his expression; it was highly unusual for the Magus to show any sign of emotion, but Eugene suspected instantly that something had disturbed him.

"What happened, Magus?"

"Nothing that need detain us." Linnaius led the way into the obscure shrubbery where he kept his sky craft hidden from curious eyes. "I dealt with it."

Eugene shrugged. There was no point in prying. "Then let's be on our way," he said, clambering into the craft as Linnaius raised one hand to the star-speckled sky. Seconds later, the trees and bushes around them began to sway and rustle as a fresh wind blew up and filled the sail. Soon they were rising high above the palace grounds until Eugene could gaze down at the red florets of fire far below, marking each summer bonfire.

And then as they headed toward the coast, he felt the rubies begin to vibrate, as though they contained a vital energy of their own.

Klervie de Maunoir was alive. Linnaius kept seeing her face superimposed against the clouds overhead, her blue eyes, so like her father Hervé's, staring accusingly into his. *If I had known that Hervé's family had survived the Inquisition's purge . . .*

As they passed above the Straits, he turned the craft toward the south.

"You look troubled, Kaspar," said Eugene. "Is all well?"

"I was just checking my charts," Linnaius said. It wasn't exactly a lie. He knew that it was no time to be distracted by a ghost from his past; Eugene needed transport, as swiftly as possible, for the consummation of his desires.

Linnaius glanced at Eugene's face, catching him in an unguarded moment as he gazed out across the blue of the Southern Ocean toward the horizon. In the heat, the Emperor had stripped off his jacket and tugged open his shirt. The disfiguring scars left by the Drakhaon's Fire could be seen only too well in the clear light, marring half his face and extending down one side of his body to the hand he had raised—in vain—to protect himself from the searing blast.

A Drakhaoul had injured him, but could a Drakhaoul use its powers to heal Eugene's damaged body and make him whole again? Linnaius, in all his long life, had never attempted anything so reckless. And even if Eugene succeeded in summoning one of the Drakhaouls, why would a daemon so powerful agree to serve a mortal master?

The low hum issuing from the rubies was growing louder and as the sun burned down more fiercely, Eugene took out the stones and began to bind them together with the length of gold wire Linnaius had prepared. As he was completing the task, Linnaius felt a sudden pulse of energy and a bolt of crimson light shot out, radiating far into the sky.

"What in God's name—" began Eugene.

"A beacon," said Linnaius, now as excited as his imperial master, "to show us the way to Ty Nagar."

"Can that really be Ty Nagar?" Eugene's voice was quiet but Linnaius saw how his whole body had tensed as he leaned forward to take a closer look. The smoke rising from the peaks of active volcanoes besmirched the clear blue of the sky.

Linnaius gazed up at the Serpent Gate and felt a rush of dark foreboding enshroud him, as if stormclouds had gathered to blot out the sun. The archway of writhing winged serpents loomed high above them, dominated by the head of Nagar himself, fanged jaws snarling defiance at the tangled jungle and ruined temples below.

"This must be the sacrificial stair," he murmured, "leading up to the gateway through which the priests sent their victims as sacrifices to Nagar. Until the day they summoned one of his daemons into this world . . ."

But he was talking to himself. Eugene had gone on ahead and was already beginning to clamber up the ancient archway.

"Take care, I beg you, highness!" Linnaius cried.

"Don't worry," came back Eugene's voice as he climbed, finding footholds on the shoulders and wing tips of the stone daemons. "I always enjoyed rock climbing . . ."

Linnaius could hardly bear to watch as his imperial master reached the top of the archway and leaned out precariously far to insert the rubies into the empty eye socket of the daemon's head.

"It's done," Eugene called down. "But why is nothing happening?"

A blood-red light had begun to emanate from the rubies, tainting the lichened grey stone with their glow. Linnaius felt the unsettling, disturbing sensation growing stronger within him. "Come down, I beg you."

"Very well." Eugene sounded disappointed. Minutes later he jumped the last few feet, landing on one knee. Linnaius saw the disillusionment in his face as he sank down on the worn sacrificial stone and wiped the sweat from his eyes on his shirtsleeve. "I failed," he said. "Maybe it was all for the best . . ."

"Wait." Linnaius had heard a deep rumble, as if the earth were groaning. "What's that sound?"

Eugene stood up. "An earthquake? Or is the volcano about to erupt?"

It was growing darker. Smoky fog began to issue from Nagar's maw, billowing out until the archway was filled with swirling darkness. And in that darkness, the rubies glowed more intensely, a daemon's eye, fixing its unblinking gaze upon them.

The ground suddenly shuddered violently beneath their feet. Linnaius lost his balance and fell heavily; beside him Eugene was flung forward onto his knees. As Linnaius tried to push himself up again, he glimpsed something twitch high above his head.

One of the stone daemon-dragons on the Gate had begun to uncurl itself from the tangle of twisted, contorted bodies. A shimmer of color flooded through the grey stone. Linnaius, helpless and terrified, saw the daemon slowly stretch its lithe body as though awakening after a long sleep. Then, opening its great wings, it flew down to alight beneath the Gate. Wild locks of hair—gold and copper and malachite green—streamed down its scaly back.

Eugene rose to his feet and began to move slowly toward the glittering creature.

Linnaius tried to call out to him to stop but, as in a waking dream, his voice would not obey him. As he watched, helpless, Eugene opened his arms wide to the daemon, as if to embrace it.

At one moment, Linnaius saw two figures: the mortal man and the Drakhaoul-daemon. The next, as he blinked the swirling smoke from his eyes, there was only Eugene. Then Eugene began to sway. "H—help me, Kaspar," he whispered, then pitched to the ground, insensible.

"*I know you now, mortal. You are powerful.*" The Drakhaoul's voice whispered in Eugene's brain. "*You are*

Emperor. And yet you bear scars, inflicted by one of my kin."

"Heal me." Eugene managed at last to stammer out the words. "Make me whole again."

"*You are a warrior, Eugene. Your instinct is to fight me. But if I am to heal you, you must surrender your will to mine.*"

Linnaius watched, powerless to intervene, as Eugene's prone body began to twitch and writhe on the sacrificial stone. A spiral of golden mist enwrapped him, and at its heart, a wave of flame arose, utterly enveloping the Emperor.

"No!" Linnaius cried out, but even as the cry was torn from his throat, the dazzling fire died away and he saw Eugene slowly raise his hand and gaze at it, turning it this way and that. He sat up and tentatively touched his face, then his scalp.

He let out a triumphant shout. "Look, Kaspar. Look at me!"

Linnaius stared at the Emperor. Eugene was just as he had been before the disastrous battle in Azhkendir: unblemished again, miraculously healed by the Drakhaoul he had freed.

"Highness." Linnaius ventured closer. "You—you've been restored."

Eugene was smiling at him. "And this is all thanks to your dedication, my friend." He held out his hand.

Linnaius hesitated, then took Eugene's outstretched hand and pressed it between his own, feeling the smooth sheen of the new skin. "Your highness honors me," he said quietly.

The Emperor suddenly turned his head away as if listening to a voice Linnaius could not hear. Then he said, "The Drakhaoul of Azhkendir is coming. The rubies must have drawn him to Ty Nagar." And as Linnaius watched, speechless, great shadow-wings unfurled from the Emperor's back. A creature of terrifying beauty stood before him: a daemon-dragon with scales that shimmered jade green, malachite, and gold in the sunlight.

The dragon flew to the top of the Serpent Gate and, hovering there, extracted the ruby eye with one of its talons. It tossed it down to Linnaius, who caught it, hugging it to him.

"I have unfinished business with Lord Gavril," it called with the Emperor's voice. "I'll distract him while you take the rubies safely back to Swanholm."

"Highness, wait, I beg you!" But the creature that had been Eugene turned and flew off toward the sea.

You've found the power you desired, imperial highness. But you've paid a high price for it, Linnaius found himself thinking, as he made his way wearily back to the sky craft. *And now, where will it end?*

As the sky craft rose slowly above the steamy warmth of the jungle, Linnaius sensed a sudden disturbance in the air. Gazing back down at the Serpent Gate far below, he saw a sight that made him shiver with terror, in spite of the oppressive heat.

The grey volcanic stone out of which the Gate was carved had begun to shimmer. Color was flooding through the twisted, agonized forms of the remaining three Drakhaouls, filling their wings and scaly bodies with vivid, jewel-bright ichor. As Linnaius watched, fascinated, he saw them begin to stretch their limbs, extending sharp-taloned fingers as though waking from a long sleep. One glimmered with the dark hues of an autumn twilight; a second burned fierce as a scarlet flame, while the third was so golden-bright that Linnaius could not look directly at it.

How had this happened? Eugene had summoned one Drakhaoul and one alone. Yet there was no escaping the fact that in replacing Nagar's Eye, even for so brief a time, he must have inadvertently set the others free from their stone prison.

In a sudden shudder of wings, they took to the air. Linnaius cowered in his craft as they streaked away overhead, like three fiery comets searing the deep blue of the sky.

"No," Linnaius heard himself murmuring, as if a mere word from a magus could stop such powerful daemons. "What have we done, Eugene? What abominations have we let loose on the world?"

CHAPTER 11

Astasia wandered forlornly through the palace looking for Eugene. Exhausted, upset, and confused, she was determined to learn the truth about the sinking of the *Sirin*.

The servants were yawning as they began the work of clearing away the detritus left after the last guests had departed: the empty ballroom was strewn with streamers, discarded dance cards, crushed flowers, and plates of half-finished food. The polished floor was puddled with spilled wine and melted ices. The lingering smell of stale alcohol and gunpowder fumes almost made her retch.

Why do I feel so sick? Have I eaten something that disagreed with my stomach?

No one had seen the Emperor and Astasia eventually found herself at the office of Gustave, Eugene's personal secretary.

"Imperial highness!" Even the usually meticulous Gustave looked a little the worse for wear, with a hint of stubble darkening his cheeks and chin. "Why didn't you send for me?"

"Where's my husband, Gustave?"

"He—" and it didn't escape her notice that Gustave faltered—"he's gone hunting."

"Hunting," she repeated incredulously. It was so obviously a pretext—but for what? *Does he have a mistress?* "You expect me to believe that after the celebrations last night he's gone hunting?" And then she felt the tears burning in her eyes again. It was unforgivable of Eugene to treat her, an Orlov, in that neglectful way. His indifference was too much to be borne! Too proud to let Gustave see her reaction, she turned on her heel and hurried out without another word, only to run almost directly into a tall young officer in the uniform of the Imperial Household Guard.

"Are you all right, highness?" he said in concerned tones.

Blinking back her tears, she looked up and saw that it was Valery Vassian.

"Valery," she said with relief, "I'm so glad to see a familiar face."

"Your brother told me to look after you," he said softly in their home tongue. "Shall I escort you back to your apartments?"

So Valery knew Andrei was alive. She put her hand on Valery's arm and let him lead her back through the hordes of sweeping and scrubbing servants. And as they walked, her anger at her absent husband began to grow. The *Melusine,* Andrei had said, would be sailing from Haeven—and a berth was booked for her. She glanced up at Valery and saw him blush and glance away. He had always looked out for her, even when they were children playing together at Erinaskoe, and she knew that his feelings for her were stronger than friendship.

Once safely back in her apartments, she sank down on a chair, all her energy exhausted.

"Can I get you anything: water, tea, coffee?" Valery offered. She pulled a face; even the thought of tea or coffee made her feel queasy.

"Valery," she said, looking up at him pleadingly. "Will you help me?"

He didn't even hesitate. "Tell me what you want to do," he said gallantly, "and I'll help you, no matter what."

"I can't stay here a moment longer. I want to go to join Andrei." She saw his eyes widen in surprise. "Valery, I shouldn't have asked this of you, I'm sorry—"

He went down on one knee before her. "I gave Andrei my word that I'd look after you and I never go back on my word. If that's what you wish, highness, then I'll make the arrangements straightaway. As discreetly as I can. Although until they've finished clearing up after the ball, no one will notice yet another carriage leaving the grounds."

Astasia was so touched at his words that the tears began to flow freely. "Thank you, Valery, I promise I'll make this up to you . . ."

He took her hand and kissed it reverently. "Just to be near you, highness, that's all I ask."

Celestine awoke to find daylight streaming into her room. "Too bright," she murmured. Her vision was blurry and her head felt thick and heavy, too heavy to lift off the pillows.

"Awake at last!" Jagu's voice was so loud that it made her temples throb. She closed her eyes and turned away from him.

"How long have I been asleep?"

"Asleep? The Magus drugged you." Jagu sat on the side of the bed. "Whatever possessed you to confront him on your own? You're lucky that he didn't do worse. And what's more, you've lost us our one advantage against him: the element of surprise. Now he'll be on his guard."

"I hate it when you preach, Jagu . . ." She pressed her fingertips to her aching forehead. "Ahh, my head hurts."

"Perhaps that'll teach you not to go charging in alone without making a proper plan."

"I shouldn't have expected any sympathy from you." She just wished he would stop talking and leave her alone to recover.

"*Now's* the time to go back and investigate, when the servants at the palace are fully occupied clearing up after the ball and all the remaining guests are asleep or too drunk to care."

"Now?" she said, reluctantly opening one eye. "In this condition?" She was still wearing the powder-blue shepherdess costume, only now its silky folds were crumpled and stained.

"I've ordered the carriage. We'll spin the guards at the gate some story about your leaving your music behind."

Celestine tried to push herself up to a sitting position. To her surprise, he slipped his arm around her and propped the pillows up behind her. "I'll fetch you some strong coffee. Or would the demoiselle prefer tea?"

* * *

Celestine approached Kaspar Linnaius's door a fourth time. Jagu lurked downstairs, keeping watch. Each of her earlier attempts to break in had failed. The Magus's wards repelled her, sending unpleasant shocks shooting up through her hand and arm.

This time, she was determined not to fail.

No one had challenged them as they made their way toward the laboratory. All the servants were busy clearing up after the ball. Many of the household were wandering dazedly around as if still in a drunken stupor. But then, she was already well-known as the Empress's intimate companion. Why should anyone wonder what she was doing?

For this attempt she had taught herself an incantation from her father's grimoire, "To Break Down Mysterious Barricades." After checking that the corridor was empty, she murmured the words three times, knocking on the invisible door in the initiate's fashion.

Although she saw nothing alter, she felt the air ripple as though an invisible curtain had been drawn back. And when she raised her gloved hand to open the door, she met no resistance. The gloves were another precaution; Linnaius was almost certain to have left some trace of alchymical poison on the handles to snare the unwary.

The door swung inward. She entered, muttering the incantation again just for good measure. Warily, she went through the neat laboratory toward a second door, which had been left ajar.

A young woman lay on the bed. Her skin was pallid, her eyes open and staring, as if at some horror only she could see.

"Jagu!" Celestine cried. "Come quickly!"

CHAPTER 12

Jagu appeared in the doorway. "Sweet Sergius," he muttered. "Is that a body? If so, we have more than enough evidence against him."

Celestine knelt and held a glass to her lips. "Look," she said, showing him the blurring made by the slight trace of breath. "She's alive." She touched the young woman's shoulder. She shook her. "Wake up!" she cried. The young woman made no response at all.

"Alive, yet not alive," said Jagu. "He's stolen her soul."

Soul-stealer. Their eyes met, locked.

"Is Linnaius the one, after all?" Her throat had gone dry.

"Is he the one who killed Maistre de Joyeuse?" Jagu put her suspicions into words.

Celestine didn't want to have to think about that most painful of subjects; she needed to stay strong and focused on their task. She rose. "We have much to do. He could return at any minute. Let's take as much evidence from here as we can get in the carriage."

"Are we just going to leave her like this?"

A sudden shaft of sunlight penetrated the Magus's laboratory, catching glittering fire in a glass case on his desk. Celestine shaded her eyes, wondering what was sparkling so brilliantly amid so many stoneware jars of alchymical substances and ancient, dusty volumes. "What is this, Jagu?" She went over to the desk. "Could it be . . . ?"

A device intricately engineered out of metal, wood, and crystal lay within the case. It looked like a timepiece or a chronometer, and yet there was something familiar about it that tugged at her memory. "Is this my father's Vox

Aethyria?" She had seen a device just like this in her father's study. *Don't touch, Klervie, it's very delicate* . . . warned a voice from the past, strong hands gently yet firmly removing her sticky fingers from the case.

She turned to Jagu. "We must take this with us."

"It looks far too fragile." Jagu had begun to pack books of alchymy into a trunk. "What is it?"

"It's a communications device. With this, our agents will be able to talk directly to the Emperor. Just imagine what an advantage this will give us in negotiations!" She lifted it, holding it close, sensing the faintest of vibrations within the sensitive mechanism.

It's all right, Papa, I'll be careful this time, I promise. I'll guard it with my life.

Celestine watched Jagu and the coachman carrying the box containing the Vox Aethyria and the books out of the courtyard. Still no one had challenged them. It was almost as though Linnaius had sprinkled his sleepdust over the whole palace. Perhaps the Emperor's servants had been ordered not to interfere with the Magus's experiments and had learned to stay away . . .

A sudden chill gust of wind pierced the balmy summer warmth. Celestine's skin tingled. She clutched her arms to her as the icy draft scored a warning across her mind.

He's here. For a moment she felt overwhelmed by panic. Suppose Linnaius unleashed the full force of his powers against them?

Sleepdust. She returned to the laboratory and slipped the little phial of iridescent granules into her bodice. What was the harm in using some of the Magus's own magic to subdue him?

Gathering up her skirts, Celestine ran down the stair and toward their carriage, calling out a warning. "Jagu! He's returned!"

Jagu felt the wind gust through the parkland trees, setting all the leaves trembling. He squared his shoulders, reminding

himself that hunting down magi was the principal reason
he had joined the Commanderie.

*I'm not just doing this for Francia, I'm doing this for
Celestine.*

Yet he had not been forced to confront a true-blood magus face-to-face since Paol's murderer had almost taken his
life too in the school chapel. And as he set out toward the
gardens, he was forced to clench his fists to stop his hands
from shaking.

He felt a faint prickling sensation in his left wrist. Looking
down, he saw that the skin where the magus had imprinted
his sigil on him was glimmering.

*It can't be the same magus. He was young, even well-
favored. And Linnaius is so old.*

He caught sight of an elderly man in the distance. He
was slowly coming toward him along one of the gravel
paths, stopping every now and then, as if to catch his breath,
one hand pressed to his chest, the other clutching a little
casket.

As Jagu watched, he reached the topiary gardens and, tot-
tering to a garden seat, lowered himself onto it. Emboldened, Jagu set out toward him, passing along a path of grey
gravel between clipped box beds. The Magus was sitting
slumped against the ironwork scrolls of the bench. His
breath came in shallow gasps and his eyes were shut.

"You don't look very well," said Jagu quietly. "Can I
help you?"

Linnaius slowly raised his head, squinting in the bright
sunlight. "I'm just a little . . . fatigued." He tried to get up
again, clinging to the side of the seat.

"Lean on me." Jagu took hold of him. "Are you going
into the palace?"

Linnaius nodded and they set off at a slow pace toward
the stables.

*As long as he doesn't notice that I'm steering him in the
opposite direction . . . "*

Just a little farther now," Jagu said aloud, as they reached
the stable courtyard, where their coach stood waiting, horses

harnessed, ready to leave. The coach door opened and Celestine emerged.

"Good day, Kaspar Linnaius," she said. "We have been waiting for you."

Jagu felt the Magus react and tightened his grip on Linnaius's arm.

"What do you want with me?" Linnaius demanded.

"Just to take a ride in this coach together," she said. "It's a lovely day for a ride, isn't it?"

"I will not be taken anywhere against my will—" Linnaius began.

"Please don't make a fuss," Jagu said as he drew his pistol from his belt, "or we will be obliged to compel you by other, less pleasant means."

"At least let me bring a few possessions . . ."

Jagu pressed the muzzle of a pistol against the back of the Magus's neck. "Into the coach," he whispered. "Now."

CHAPTER 13

Jagu hurtled across the cobbled quay toward where the ambassador's carriage stood waiting.

"Urgent, you say, Lieutenant?" Abrissard gave Jagu one of his frostiest looks. "This had better be urgent enough to make me delay my return to Muscobar."

Jagu, too breathless to reply, handed the casket to him.

"What's this?" Ambassador d'Abrissard opened the lid. A rich crimson glow emanated from inside, fierce as a winter's sunset, lighting his face with its fire.

"The Tears," Abrissard said in wondering tones. "The Tears of Artamon." He shut the lid swiftly and when he looked up, Jagu saw that his eyes gleamed. And the ambassador was usually so self-controlled. "How did you—"

"They were in the Magus's possession." Jagu, exultant that he and Celestine had pulled off such an outrageous feat, could not stop himself from smiling.

"And you weren't followed?" The ambassador glanced anxiously around. "You're certain no one saw you?"

Jagu gave a little shrug. "The palace servants were too busy tidying up after the ball."

"I will inform his majesty straightaway." Abrissard was once again the prudent diplomat.

"Isn't the king still in Djihan-Djihar?"

"Indeed. I'll get the rubies off Tielen soil as swiftly as possible." Abrissard's tone was brisk. "Where's Demoiselle Celestine?"

"Keeping guard over the Magus in case he wakes."

One of Abrissard's curving black brows quirked upward

and Jagu found himself wondering if it had been so prudent to leave Celestine alone with Linnaius.

"She'll be fine. Père Judicael taught us special techniques to subdue the magi." He spoke with a confidence he did not feel; he was anxious to get back to Celestine as soon as possible to make sure that she was still safe.

"Captain Peillac will take you and Linnaius to Francia on the *Dame Blanche*. As to the Tears, I can assure you they will be delivered to the king directly."

"Very good, Ambassador." Jagu saluted and turned to leave when Abrissard stopped him.

"I'll be commending you both to his majesty. The contents of this simple casket could well change the tide of history. Well done, Lieutenant."

Jagu bowed, acknowledging the compliment. As he hurried back to the tavern, he still could not quite believe their good fortune in capturing both the Magus and the prized rubies together.

"This is where we must part company, your highness." Celestine curtsied to Prince Andrei. "I wish you a safe journey to Francia." She turned to board the *Dame Blanche* but Andrei seized hold of her hand.

"Are you certain you're feeling all right?" he asked in a low, intense voice. "I was so worried about you. Linnaius is dangerous—"

"I'm fine." She smiled at him, touched by his concern. "I was just careless and I let my guard down. Don't worry. I won't make such a foolish mistake again."

The crates containing the incriminating papers and alchymical equipment from the Magus's laboratories were being carefully loaded onto the *Dame Blanche* under Jagu's watchful eye.

"Maybe I should come with you." Still Andrei held her hand between his own.

"But you promised your sister that you would wait for her!"

"I don't know if she will come, though." Andrei looked so forlorn that her heart was touched.

"Oh, she'll come. Your sister feels very neglected by—"

"Celestine!" Jagu was standing at the top of the companionway watching them with a frown as dark and menacing as a thundercloud. "We're waiting for you."

The sky above the port of Haeven began to darken as if a tempest were blowing in across the Straits.

Celestine's ship, Andrei thought anxiously. *The Magus is on board. Suppose he's summoned a storm to help him escape? She could be in grave danger . . .*

And then his whole body chilled as if he had fallen into deep icy water. For what was coming straight toward them was no stormcloud. It dashed across the tops of the waves, whipping them up into a frenzy of foam. Eyes fixed on him, daemon eyes of dazzling intensity that seemed to pierce through him to the deepest core of his being.

"What's wrong, Andrei?" He heard Astasia's voice as if from a great distance.

"G—get on board, Astasia," he managed to stammer. For he knew what it was; it was kin to the spirit that had healed him: unimaginably powerful, filled with an untamable fury. He broke into a stumbling run, intent only on drawing the creature away from his sister, heading out along the jetty.

"*Why are you running from me, child of Artamon?*" He could hear its voice, and it was different from the voice of the Drakhaoul that had healed him. "*I am Adramelech.*" Soft, yet imbued with strength and understanding. "*I am your destiny. The blood of the Emperor Artamon runs in your veins. Merge with me . . . and I will fulfill your deepest desires.*"

"A—Adramelech?" Andrei stammered—and the creature enveloped him, enwrapping him in a cloud of twilit mist until he felt as if he were drowning in its empurpled depths.

Drenching rain blew in gusts across the deck of the *Dame Blanche.* The wind battered her sails and whipped the waves into great rolling breakers until she pitched and tossed helplessly.

Belowdecks, Celestine struggled toward the Magus's cabin.

Every lurch of the vessel flung her against the wooden walls, but she fought on until she reached the cabin door and unlocked it. The door flew open and she stumbled inside.

The Magus lay as they had left him, securely bound to the bunk. But one finger, his right index finger, was moving slowly. And though his eyes were closed, she saw a faint smile on his pallid lips by the light of the flickering lantern.

"This is your doing." Another great wave threw her against the wall of the cabin. She grabbed hold of the bunk head to steady herself. "Make it stop!"

"Release me," he murmured, his voice barely audible above the roar of the storm, "and I will do as you ask."

"But what good will it do if you sink the ship?"

"Release me . . . and no one will be harmed."

A sound of splitting timber came from abovedeck, followed by a great shout and a terrifying crash.

There was a spell she had read in her father's grimoire, a binding spell. It was very risky to use such a powerful trick of the Forbidden Arts on a Commanderie ship, but as the *Dame Blanche* shuddered, helpless in the blast of the storm, she had little alternative but to try.

She closed her eyes, concentrating with all her heart and will. *Faie, help me.*

Suddenly her whole body was infused, drenched with the Faie's pure light.

She raised one hand, pointing at the Magus.

"*In bonds invisible, I bind thee,*" she whispered, hearing the Faie's sweet, clear voice fused with her own. She could feel the coils of power slowly unraveling and rolling down the length of her arm into her wreathing fingertips, wrapping themselves about him. And she knew that Linnaius could feel them too. She heard him whisper "No!" even against the groaning and creaking of the timbers of the ship.

"Now, sleep." She dipped into the little phial of dustlike granules she had found in his laboratory, and softly blew on her fingertips, sending the dust to settle over him in a powdery cloud.

His lids began to close and his finger ceased to move as the protest died on his lips. The wind suddenly dropped and the waves stilled. The sickening pitching and rolling stopped and the ship lay becalmed.

Celestine let out a long, slow breath. She and the Faie had meshed him in a web of his own making; the sleepdust had worked on him, just as it had when he had used it on her at Swanholm. She had feared he might have made himself immune to his own devices. Just as long as no one from the Commanderie had witnessed what she had done . . .

It was only then that she realized the cabin door hung open and Jagu was standing in the doorway.

"How could you, Celestine?" Jagu's eyes burned dark in his pale face. He was soaked, wet locks of black hair plastered across his forehead. "You *promised* me."

The Faie's energy still pulsed in her veins, mingled with her own nascent powers. "There was no other way to subdue him. If I hadn't stopped him then, we could all have drowned." She felt exultant, intoxicated with the success of her actions.

"But if Maistre de Lanvaux hears what you have done—" Jagu broke off. He seemed to be searching for a reason that might sway her to his point of view. "Remember what they did to your father, Celestine."

"No one will know if you say nothing, Jagu," she said lightly. Could she still trust him? "No one knows what happened here but you."

The sun's first light pierced Ruaud's cabin early and he lay in his bunk, still half-asleep, remembering fragments of a strange dream. All that remained was the memory of a gilded glow that surrounded the ship, casting a trail of liquid gold across the dark sea . . .

As the flagship cut through the waves, a flash of morning light caught fire in the clear facets of the Angelstone, which he had hung above his bunk for safekeeping. Ruaud reached for the stone and gazed at it in consternation, not understanding what he saw. A flame of bright gold, pure as the sunlight, glinted within. Threads of other colors twisted and pulsed around it: violet, scarlet, blue, and malachite green.

"Maistre?" Frantic knocking jolted him completely awake. "It's the king!"

"I'll be right there." Ruaud hurried to the king's cabin in his nightshirt.

Enguerrand turned to greet him with an ecstatic smile; Fragan, his valet, hovered anxiously behind him. "There's nothing to worry about; I'm feeling well. Exceptionally well, in fact."

"I found his majesty lying unconscious on the floor of the cabin," said Fragan.

"Sire?" Ruaud said, inwardly praying that this was not a return of the red sand fever. He gazed intently at the king, trying to see if there was any outward sign of illness.

"Fragan, will you leave us?" Enguerrand's eyes seemed unusually bright but he spoke lucidly enough. The instant they were alone, he said, "I had the most wonderful dream, Ruaud. In fact, even now, I'm not certain if it was a dream. My guardian angel came to me. He said I had been chosen. Chosen to be Saint Sergius's successor."

Oskar Alvborg stared bitterly up at the portrait of his dead mother, Countess Ulla.

"Why am I left kicking my heels here, with only my father's title and gambling debts as legacy?" His footfall echoed through the empty mansion as he limped from room to room. Ignominiously discharged from the Tielen army after a disastrous battle with the Drakhaoul of Azhkendir, he had been eking out a miserable existence on his father's estate ever since. "Damn you, Eugene. Why did you have to treat me so shabbily? Was it my fault the Drakhaoul wiped out my regiment?"

A fiery shadow flickered through his mind. He stopped, aware that something was approaching him, something that felt like the terrifying aura of the Drakhaoul . . . yet was strikingly different.

The room suddenly shimmered with flame. Terrified, Oskar saw scarlet eyes staring at him from the darkness.

"The blood of Artamon runs in your veins, Oskar

Alvborg," whispered a dry voice. "*Let me heal your injuries. Become one with me and I will make your dreams come true.*"

"Who are you?" Oskar demanded.

"*You think yourself Gunnar Alvborg's son . . . but you are Prince Karl's illegitimate child, Eugene's unacknowledged brother. You have as equal a right to the throne of Tielen as Eugene.*"

"How can you know such a thing? Show me proof." Oskar was skeptical, although the thought of being Karl of Tielen's son inflamed his ambitions.

"*Hidden behind the canvas of your mother's portrait is a letter from the prince to your mother,*" whispered the voice. "*What more proof could you want?*" Oskar turned—and in that moment the shadow struck, enwrapping him in its fiery coils. He cried out in agony—and then, as it melted into him, he began to see clearly again.

"Who are you?" he gasped. "Are you a Drakhaoul?"

"*My name is Sahariel,*" said the voice within him, "*and I have come to help you fulfill your destiny, Oskar.*"

"The old man is still asleep," Jagu said to Celestine as he emerged from Linnaius's prison cell. He lowered his voice. "You need a story to cover yourself for the Inquisitors. They'll ask. You know they'll ask."

Celestine tossed her head impatiently. Since they had arrived at the Commanderie Forteresse to deliver their prisoner, Jagu had become increasingly jittery. And in their working partnership, she had always relied on him to be the levelheaded one.

"All I did was use his own magic to subdue him. A little sleepdust; what possible harm could there be in that?"

Men's voices could be heard farther along the dark stone passage. Jagu took hold of her arm and hurried her away in the other direction.

"Only you know what happened aboard ship. If I hadn't stopped him, we'd all have drowned."

"They won't see it that way." They stopped beneath the

uncertain light of a guttering lantern. "Take off the spell you placed on him, Celestine. Before they guess who is responsible and put you on trial too."

"If your vow is so important to you, Jagu, why don't you tell them yourself?"

He gripped hold of her by both arms. "How can he be tried in the Inquisition Court if he's in a coma?"

She hesitated, her anger dissipating a little. Was the spell she had used affecting her judgment?

He relaxed his grip. "I'll invent some excuse to keep Visant's men at bay. That'll give you the time to undo what you've done."

"Guerrier de Joyeuse." Celestine showed her papers to the guard outside Linnaius's cell. "I've come to interrogate the prisoner."

He scratched his head. "Interrogate an unconscious man?"

"I have reason to believe that he's been fooling us all. Give me a quarter hour or so . . . ."

"Good luck to you, then, Guerrier." He unlocked the cell door.

As soon as the cell door clanged shut, Celestine went straight over to the narrow bed where the Magus lay insensible and knelt beside him.

"*Sever,*" she whispered, holding her hands over the invisible bonds with which she had confined him. She heard him let out a faint, groaning sigh.

"Where . . . is this?"

"You're in the Forteresse in Lutèce," she said, sitting back on her heels to observe him.

"Klervie," he said in a whisper.

"Don't call me that!"

"I'm the only one alive who really knew your father. There's so much I could tell you about him."

"You'll have to do better than that, Magus." She had known he would try to win her sympathy with subtle words. And yet wasn't that the real reason she had come?

"Hervé was such a promising student. From the moment he first arrived at the college, I knew he would go far." Linnaius's eyes were closed and his voice drifted toward her, as if he were talking in his sleep. "I can see him now . . . an eager-eyed boy with a shock of untidy hair. So absentminded. When he was intent on his studies, he would forget everything else, especially his laboratory chores."

His words were working their spell; she knew she should leave, yet she stayed, entranced by the portrait he was painting of her father.

"If you liked and respected my father so much, why did you steal his invention?"

"Who told you that?"

"*He* did! Just before they dragged him onto the pyre in the Place du Trahoir."

A look of puzzlement crossed the Magus's pallid face. "But why would Hervé believe such a thing?"

"Because it was true!"

"I was not in Karantec when the Inquisition came because I was far away in Khitari. When I heard what happened to the college, I knew I could never return to Francia. So I stayed in the north and sought protection from Prince Karl of Tielen."

"Why should I believe you?"

"Have you never asked yourself if anyone else was responsible? My apprentice, Rieuk Mordiern, was the one who made the Vox Aethyria work, though it pains me to admit it. And he ran away to join the secret sect of the Magi of Ondhessar: the ones who practice the Forbidden Art of soul-stealing."

"Ondhessar?" Celestine had been well schooled by Ruaud de Lanvaux in the bloodstained history of Azilis's Holy Shrine. "The soul-stealers?" All of a sudden she felt a chill drench her. "Rieuk Mordiern became a soul-stealer?"

"Rieuk was a stubborn and willful boy." Linnaius let out a faint sigh. "He was also a powerful crystal magus. He was the one who energized the aethyr crystals in the Vox and established a sympathetic resonance between them."

"Was? Is he dead?" Doubts crept into her mind; the magus who had put his mark on Jagu was a soul-stealer, as was the one who took Henri's life. "But you also know how to steal souls!" She rounded on him. "That wretched girl we found in your rooms. You used her soul, and then left her for dead."

"But that was not a true soul-stealing. She was a Spirit Singer. Didn't you see her zither?"

A Spirit Singer. His story almost sounded convincing—and yet she could not bring herself to believe it.

"I employed her to search for a soul in the Ways Beyond . . . and she couldn't find her way back. That was when she fell into that trancelike state—"

"I don't want to hear your excuses."

"Why don't you listen to what I'm telling you, Celestine? Rieuk may still be alive. I saw him in Enhirre a year after the fall of the college. And he was the one who released the aethyrial spirit from the crystal. *The spirit that your father bound in his book*." The Faie. She could feel his eyes boring into her, two silver shafts of light.

"Rieuk Mordiern did that?" Celestine took a step back.

"That crystal was stolen from the Shrine of Azilis. I happen to know, because I stole it." Linnaius let out a little self-satisfied chuckle. "I needed it for our Vox Aethyria. We'd tried every other kind of crystal. I knew that the shrine crystal was unique; I just didn't know quite how unique . . ." Were these just the ramblings of a senile old man? Could she trust anything he said?

A strange radiance flickers like silver firelight burning in a tray on Papa's desk. The light sharply outlines in shadow-silhouette two men bending over the tray.

She had been just five years old. She had woken to hear a faint, desolate cry coming from her father's study, a cry that drew her from her bed to see what was the matter.

Fading in and out of clarity like a reflection in a wind-rippled lake, she glimpses a face, its features twisted into an expression of such agony that it pains her to look at it. And as she gazes, it fixes her with its anguish-riven eyes.

"Help me," gasps Rieuk Mordiern. "I can't control it . . ."

The soul-stealing magus with the hawk familiar had demanded that she give him back the Faie. He had called her Klervie. And he had described the Faie as an "aethyrial spirit," just as Linnaius had done. Why was Linnaius telling her that Rieuk Mordiern was the one who had set the spirit free from the crystal?

"Haven't you been pursuing the wrong man? Shouldn't you be seeking to take revenge on the man who condemned your father to the stake: Alois Visant?"

She looked at him, angry and bewildered. "You're just trying to confuse me!"

His hands parted in a gesture of denial and she noticed that they trembled, as if palsied. "What have I to gain from that? I'm your prisoner and certain to be condemned to death."

His words came like a dash of cold water, clearing her mind. "And you deserve to die for your crimes against Francia." She drew herself up, remembering that she was an agent of the Francian Commanderie. "Your alchymical weapons have killed countless Francian sailors. The storms you've created have drowned countless more—Muscobites as well as Francians."

Another little shrug. "I was merely serving my good friend and patron, Karl of Tielen. He made me a citizen of Tielen. In war, one fights to defend one's own country."

This was going nowhere. She made to leave, but one hand snaked out and gripped her by the wrist. "Be careful, Celestine." His pale eyes stared piercingly into hers. "The aethyrial spirit you are harboring is both dangerous and powerful."

She tried to pull away, but his grip was unexpectedly strong.

"How long do you think you can deceive the Inquisition?"

"What?"

"I can see the changes that she's wrought in you already. Take a good look at your eyes next time you pass a mirror."

What was he babbling about? Was he losing his wits? She snatched her hand back and retreated, glaring at him. "She's my guardian. She would never do anything to harm me."

But as soon as she had regained her room, she found herself snatching glances at her reflection every time she passed the little mirror propped up on her desk. Eventually she seized it and critically examined her reflection.

"Changes?" Her eyes glinted, but they were bright with

anger that the wily old man had almost succeeded in under-mining her confidence, manipulating her emotions through her precious memories of her father. "I won't let him get to me again."

Ruaud de Lanvaux retired to his study to go over the tran-script of the day's proceedings at Linnaius's trial.

When Celestine was called forward to be interrogated by Visant, he had felt a sudden inexplicable sense of unease. She had looked serene and had answered the Inquisitor's probing questions without showing the slightest hesitation or nerv-ousness. So why did he still feel so troubled? Was it the line of questioning that Visant had employed? Or was it a dis-turbing rumor he had been informed of earlier that day? Two of the crewmen had gone to Kilian Guyomard, claiming that they had seen her, at the height of the storm, bending over the Magus, murmuring a magical incantation—after which the storm had suddenly, dramatically, died down.

"Sailors are superstitious at the best of times," Kilian had said, laughing it off, "but I thought you should know, in case Inquisitor Visant chooses to use the allegation in his questioning."

And then there was the alchymical machine Jagu and Celestine had removed from the Magus's laboratory. What in Sergius's name was it? It stood on his desk, sparkling in the candlelight, an elaborate mechanical construction of metal and crystal. Perhaps Celestine had been mistaken as to its alchymical function and it was merely a new type of clock, not yet seen in Francia.

Yet the perfection of the clear crystal, fashioned in the shape of a flower with its petals open, reminded him of something he had seen long ago.

"The lotus crystal in the shrine," he murmured. Kaspar Linnaius had stolen the sacred treasure and he, young and stupidly eager, had tried to stop him, earning a broken col-larbone for his pains. On damp days like today, the old in-jury still ached. "Is it possible Linnaius used the crystal he stole to make this machine? And if so, why?"

A gentle tap on the door interrupted his musing.

"You wanted to speak with me, Maistre?" Celestine stood on the threshold.

He looked up, smiling, genuinely pleased to see her. "Come in. I'm sorry to summon you here so late."

"Just me, and not Jagu?"

Had she guessed the reason he had summoned her? He forced himself to keep smiling, wanting to put her at her ease.

"I wanted to have the opportunity to chat together, just as we used to, Celestine. I've been so busy that I was afraid you must have been thinking that I was neglecting you." Even though he had devoted his life to serving God, he had always cared for her as if she were his adopted daughter.

She sat opposite him, smoothing down her black uniform skirts.

"My dear child, it's been too long."

"You look tired, Maistre," she said. "Are you allowing yourself time to sleep? Are you remembering to eat?"

"Don't worry on my account; Alain Friard nags me if I neglect such necessities. No, tell me how you've been faring. This was a dangerous and delicate mission, capturing the Emperor's right-hand man and smuggling him out of Tielen."

"It had its tricky moments, I confess. Linnaius is a very powerful magus. But I'm certain now that he isn't the magus who took Henri from me."

Ruaud flinched, in spite of himself. "I thought as much." He had never been able to confess his terrible secret to her: that he had inadvertently—in his haste to catch the magus who had stolen her lover's soul—trodden on the alchymical glass in which it was contained. Even after so many years, his heart still ached whenever the subject arose, wondering if had he not misplaced his feet in the darkness of that attic room, he could have saved the musician's life and changed the course of Celestine's fate.

"But he was difficult to subdue. In his attempt to escape, he nearly sank the ship we were traveling on."

She had not once met his eyes as she spoke. She was with-holding something. And he felt his heart ache even more as he remembered the allegation the sailors had made against her. He must warn her that she was in danger. He must protect her as far as he could without compromising his role as Grand Maistre.

"Is it true that you used one of his own alchymical compounds to subdue him?"

"Who told you? *Jagu?*"

He had obviously hit a sensitive spot.

"It was remarked on by two of the crew."

"There was no other way." She looked at him at last, her gaze defiant.

"Celestine." So it was true. He feared for her now. "For Sergius's sake, what possessed you to do something so rash? Inquisitor Visant would condemn you as a sorceress if he came to hear of it."

"And if we had all drowned and Linnaius escaped? What then?"

He reached out across the desk and took her hand in his, pressing it. "Promise me, my dear child, that you will never act so foolishly again. I could not bear it if you were to fall into the hands of the Inquisition."

"You need not fear for me, dear Maistre. I'll be careful, I promise." The words, spoken so sincerely and in her sweetest, most heartfelt tone, almost set his mind at rest. Yet there was still something . . .

"And have you tried to use the Vox?" she asked.

"The Vox?" he repeated, feeling a little stupid that he had no idea what she was talking about.

"It's a communication device. A Vox Aethyria." She indicated the crystalline contraption. "This is how the Tielen generals exchange information over many hundreds of miles. It's one of their most closely guarded secrets. The one on your desk is almost certainly linked to another in the New Rossiyan Empire. Perhaps even to the Emperor himself."

"Celestine, how do you know so much about this?"

"It was originally commissioned from the College of Thaumaturgy by our own government. The records are all in the Inquisition archive." She spoke with such quiet authority that he felt ashamed of his ignorance. "But then the Inquisition intervened. Kaspar Linnaius escaped to Tielen with the plans and completed the work." She still had not fully answered his question.

"But this is an alchymical device. If Visant could hear you now, he'd have you arrested for possessing forbidden knowledge." His anxiety made his tone more harsh than he intended and he saw her blink, as though avoiding a blow. "How could you defend yourself if he put his interrogators to work on you?"

"There were papers and designs in Linnaius's study. It wouldn't take a genius to understand them." Again that calm, self-possessed air; why was he so worried on her account? Was it that her story didn't quite convince him? He had known her since she was a little child, and he couldn't help but suspect that she was still withholding some vital piece of information from him.

"Maistre," she said, leaning closer over the desk, "this Vox gives Francia an invaluable advantage over the Emperor. We have his magus and we have his communications device. For the first time in many years we can do more than defend ourselves against the Tielens. Let the Vox be used as its original inventor intended: to protect our nation."

Cleverly she had turned the conversation away from herself to the broader implications of the discovery. If this intelligence was true, then he must take the device to the king.

Jagu gazed at Celestine as she stood before the court in her black uniform robes, her golden hair drawn back under a simple linen coif, and thought how beautiful—and vulnerable—she looked. He no longer had any idea whether such thoughts were impure, only that he would run through fire rather than see her harmed.

"Celestine de Joyeuse," said Inquisitor Visant, pronouncing each syllable of her name with exaggerated care. "You have shown great zeal in your quest to track down Kaspar Linnaius."

Be careful. Jagu leaned forward. *He's out to trap you.*

"I acted only as any member of the Commanderie would in the circumstances," replied Celestine coolly. "I was given my orders and I carried them out."

Jagu relaxed a little. She had not fallen for Visant's first snare. But there would be more traps, and each one more subtle than the first.

Visant was consulting a sheaf of notes. "Considerable zeal," he said at last, looking up. "I see from the ship's log that the ship bringing the prisoner to Francia nearly foundered in a sudden, violent storm. Can you explain to the court what happened?"

"Linnaius used his arts to summon a storm wind and blow us off course, back to Tielen."

"You witnessed him performing this rite?"

"I did."

Jagu tensed. He alone knew what Celestine had done to ensure that Kaspar Linnaius did not work his Dark Arts. If anyone else had observed what had happened in the cabin and whispered the truth to the Inquisitor, they were both doomed.

"And if the accused is so powerful a magus, why did he not succeed in his endeavor?"

"He was weak," said Celestine with a little shrug. "The effort exhausted him. I saw his hand drop back and his eyes close. I believe he may have suffered some kind of stroke."

"I see," said Visant. "As a member of our order, you took certain vows?"

"Yes."

Jagu closed his eyes, dreading the next question Visant would surely ask her.

"Including a vow to abjure the use of the Forbidden Arts?"

"Yes."

Visant paused, as though going to ask another question, then suddenly turned away, returning to his desk. "I have no more questions for Guerrier de Joyeuse," he said, then added, "at the present time."

Ever since she left the courtroom, Celestine's mind had been in turmoil. She had been sure that she would feel nothing but satisfaction at having brought her father's betrayer to justice at last. Instead she found herself tormented by doubts and insecurities.

Did Linnaius work some kind of glamour on me?

The portrait he had created of her father had been so convincing that she had been able to think of little else. Had Hervé's relationship with Linnaius been in some way kin to her own with Maistre de Lanvaux? Suppose the old man had been telling the truth—and he had been as devastated by the execution of the mages as she?

She walked on through the streets, so wrapped up in her thoughts that she did not notice where her feet were taking her until she realized that she had—unconsciously—come to the Place du Trahoir.

There, in the center, stood the gibbet from which hung the twisted corpses of the condemned, executed that morning. Carrion crows gathered on top of the crossbar, waiting to peck and tear at the dead flesh. She shuddered, feeling the taste of bile in her mouth. In spite of the five years she had spent as a Guerrier, she had still not become hardened to the sight. Yet these were common criminals, convicted of robbery or murder. There had not been an Inquisition execution for heresy in a long while.

The exultant sense of triumph she had felt on the ship had seeped away. Confronted with the grim reality of the scaffold, she could only remember her father's bruised, bloodied face and his broken body. Surely it was just that the Magus should suffer the same punishment as his fellow magi?

But is this really what Papa would have wanted me to do? A dull chill passed through her body as she stood staring up at the scaffold and its grisly contents.

I've become a creature of the Commanderie. I've poured all my frustration and fury into hunting down Kaspar Linnaius. And now I can't even be sure that he betrayed my father.

Have I made a terrible mistake?

"There were moments in the courtroom yesterday," Ruaud de Lanvaux said, gazing intently at Celestine, "when I began to have doubts about your loyalty to our cause."

Jagu felt his heart stutter a beat or two.

"I can assure you, Maistre, that you need have no worries on my account," she said quietly.

"Is that so?" The Maistre still gazed at her, as though not entirely convinced, and Jagu's anxiety increased. "Well, I'm about to offer you the opportunity to prove yourself. I'm sending you both back to the monastery of Saint Sergius in Azhkendir. Your ship sails at dawn."

"To Abbot Yephimy?" Jagu glanced at Celestine, expecting her to protest. But she was staring into the middle distance, as if her thoughts were elsewhere. "But—but why?"

The Grand Maistre took out the Angelstone and held it up to the light. The purity of the crystal was sullied by swirls and surges of darkness, as if ink had leaked into clear water.

"*They* are here," he said. "In Francia."

"They? There's more than one Drakhaoul at large?" The daylight in the Maistre's study seemed to lose its brightness as Jagu remembered the terrifying shadow they had seen in the Straits. "But who set them free? Who found a way to summon them?"

"I have no idea who unleashed them—or how. All I know is that we must arm ourselves against them. Before it is too late."

"Too late?" Celestine repeated as if she had only just heard what the Maistre was telling them.

"You read the ancient warning for yourself in Azhkendir, didn't you? 'Prince Nagazdiel must never be set free,'" Ruaud quoted from *The Life of the Blessed Sergius*. "'For if his prison is breached, darkness will cover the world in perpetual night and he and his kindred will lay waste to the earth.'"

Jagu looked into Ruaud's eyes, hoping to catch a glimmer of reassurance there, but saw only stern resolve. "If we don't defeat the Drakhaouls, they will wreak havoc. That is their nature; they are angels of destruction. When we joined the Commanderie, we made a vow—each and every one of us—to continue the work of our patron saint and protect Francia against the powers of darkness. If we can't find a way to stop them—then who can?"

"So you still intend to reforge Sergius's Staff?" Jagu said. It seemed a vain hope in the face of such a daunting threat.

A sigh escaped Ruaud's lips. "That," he said, "is the king's plan."

The sigh did not escape Jagu's notice. "Even though the abbot refused to hand over the golden crook?"

"I'm sending a detachment of Guerriers with you," continued the Maistre, "to ensure that he doesn't refuse a second time. And as you'll be in the Drakhaon's lands, don't neglect to gather any intelligence that could be of use to us in the war to come."

War? Jagu looked blankly at the Maistre, not immediately understanding what he meant.

"We know so little about the Drakhaoul. But the Drakhaon's men, his *druzhina*, share a deep bond with their master: a bond sealed in blood. They'll defend him to the death." Jagu nodded and Ruaud put a hand on his shoulder. "The Commanderie has to make a stand," he said with a bleak smile, "a stand against the oncoming darkness."

Andrei retired to his bedchamber in Belle Garde to reread his orders. King Enguerrand had awarded him his own command: the *Aquilon,* a fast frigate, standing by to take part in Francia's covert operation against the Emperor's navy. In order to reach Fenez-Tyr in time, he would have to leave straightaway. He paused as he passed the mirror to check that his uniform was correctly buttoned and saw another face gazing back at him from the shadows.

"*Andrei,*" whispered a voice, soft as sleep. His Drakhaoul's shadow image was purple-hued like the dusk, yet its amethyst eyes were lit with an intense jewel-sharded brilliance that pierced him to the soul. "*You were born to rule Muscobar, Andrei. Your birthright was stolen from you by Eugene of Tielen. Let me help you take back the land that is rightfully yours.*" So it had already read his innermost thoughts; there would be no hiding anything from this daemon.

"But there's a price, isn't there?" The Drakhaoul was promising him what he had long dreamed of, saying the words he wanted to hear, recognizing his frustrated ambitions, but he was not fool enough to believe that such a prize would come free. "There's always a price."

"*In return, I only ask you to keep my presence a secret . . . until the time is right.*" Was there the hint of a smile in Adramelech's voice?

"The time is right for what?" Andrei asked, unable to quell his lingering suspicions.

"*Your sister, Astasia, is expecting Eugene's child. A very special child. You'd want to see her safely delivered first, wouldn't you?*"

"Astasia's *pregnant*?" Why hadn't she told him? Why was she keeping it a secret? "But this changes everything."

"*Until her child is born, you must be patient. Perhaps there are other dreams you wish to fulfill before then . . .*"

He suddenly saw Celestine de Joyeuse's sweet face, her soft blue eyes gazing appealingly back at him, as they parted at Haeven. "Celestine?" he whispered, not realizing until now how much he had been thinking about her. His face burned as he guessed what Adramelech must have read in his most intimate thoughts.

"*If you want her so badly, I can help you win her heart . . . and her body . . .*"

"That's enough!"

"Andrei? The carriage has come to take you to Fenez-Tyr."

Andrei started guiltily as he heard Vassian's voice outside his chamber door. He felt like a conspirator, whispering treason.

"Just a moment, Valery . . ." But when he glanced in the mirror, the Drakhaoul had withdrawn from sight and he saw only his own reflection.

CHAPTER 14

"Where's his majesty?" Ruaud had arrived at Enguerrand's apartments to accompany him to morning prayers in
the palace chapel and there was no sign of the king.

"Still abed," said Fragan, Enguerrand's valet. "Shall I tell
him you're here, Maistre?"

"I'll go rouse him myself." It was unlike Enguerrand to
sleep so late. "I hope he's not sickening again . . ."

The king's four-poster bed was hung with curtains of
thick dark brocade embroidered in gold thread with sala-
manders and lilies, another relic from the time of the king's
grandfather. Ruaud went to open the heavy curtains and let
light and fresh air into the stuffy chamber. As he did so he
heard the king murmur in his sleep, moving restlessly.

"Adramelech," he muttered, "Sahariel . . . where are
you?"

Ruaud paused, his hand on the wrought-iron window
catch, wondering what strange dream his pupil was having;
the names—if that was what they were—sounded like
Ancient Enhirran. He opened the window and, as he leaned
out to draw in a lungful of morning air, the Angelstone
dropped down on its chain, catching the sunlight. Ruaud
was about to replace it beneath his robes when he saw that
the crystal was alive with intertwining spirals of rich color
again: purple, blue, green, scarlet, and most vivid and brilliant of all, gold. And he felt that same inexplicable sense of
anxiety that had first afflicted him aboard ship.

"What time is it?" came the king's voice, slurred with sleep.

"Time you were in chapel, sire," Ruaud said, unable to
conceal a note of disapproval at the king's tardiness.

"I had another dream, Ruaud." Enguerrand's eyes were shining as he sat up and reached for his spectacles. "My guardian angel spoke to me again. He said that he would help me defeat the Drakhaoul of Azhkendir and—"

A sharp rap on the door interrupted him and Fragan appeared, bowing. "If you please, majesty, dispatches have just arrived that require your urgent attention."

Ruaud watched the king's face keenly as he read the first dispatch, wondering if Admiral Mercoeur had launched the attack on the Tielen dockyards.

"It sounds as if our ships have dealt the Emperor a severe blow," Enguerrand said, confirming Ruaud's suspicions. "Tielen munitions factories burned down, dockyards under bombardment . . ." He glanced up at Ruaud. "I wish my father could have lived to see this day. He would have been so proud." He opened the second dispatch, frowning as he scanned the contents. "A letter from my mother," Enguerrand said, handing the paper to Ruaud. "She is entertaining not one but two of the Orlovs at Belle Garde."

"We have an unexpected guest: the Empress Astasia, traveling incognito with her brother, Andrei," wrote Aliénor. "It seems that there has been a significant falling-out between her and her husband and she has fled the court at Swanholm. Unfortunately, it transpires that she is *enceinte*, so I can see no real advantage for Francia in keeping her here."

"The Empress is expecting a child? Eugene's heir?" Ruaud looked at Enguerrand.

"We must make the most of this, Ruaud." An uncharacteristically resolute look had hardened the king's gaze. "For the first time in this century, Francia has the chance to assert herself against Tielen. If only we could communicate directly with the Emperor. A letter setting out our demands will lose much of its impact, even if we use our swiftest couriers."

As the king was speaking, Ruaud could think of nothing but the Vox Aethyria. *This is how the Tielen generals exchange information over many hundreds of miles,* Celestine had told him. *This Vox is almost certainly linked to another in the New Rossiyan Empire. Perhaps even to the Emperor himself.*

"I believe we may be able to overcome that problem," he said, "by using one of the Tielens' devices against them."

The safety of your wife and unborn child must be of the utmost importance to you.

The Emperor clenched his fists as he reread the transcript of his earlier conversation, by Vox Aethyria, with Ruaud de Lanvaux, Grand Maistre of the Francian Commanderie. "Conversation?" One of his fists came thudding down on the desk, making the delicate mechanism of the Vox shudder. "Political blackmail, masquerading as diplomacy. No, worse. Holding Astasia against her will. How could matters have come to this?" Eugene went to the window of his quarters and gazed out toward the smoldering ruins of the Imperial Dockyards, billowing smoke still besmirching the pale evening sky. The Francians had not only sunk several of his warships in the Straits, they had attacked the dockyards too and destroyed the ships lying in dry dock.

"I was too bound up in my own concerns to notice how lonely you were, Astasia," he murmured. Only now did he realize how much she had come to mean to him. He was prepared to submit to the Francians' blackmail if only to ensure that she was safe. Even if it meant sacrificing a part of his empire.

The imperial carriage moved slowly away from the quay. Inside, Astasia sat staring in stunned disbelief at her husband. No longer disfigured by the terrible burns inflicted by the Drakhaoul of Azhkendir, Eugene looked just like his portrait in Swanholm, painted when he succeeded his father nearly ten years ago. His fair hair seemed to have deepened to a richer tint of gold and his skin was smooth, with a healthy glow.

"How did this miraculous cure happen, Eugene?" she asked guardedly. Throughout the voyage back to Mirom, she had been tormented by shame and remorse, knowing that Eugene had ceded Smarna to Francia to secure her safe return. But the instant she set foot on the quay at Mirom and saw him, the heartfelt apology she had rehearsed so carefully flew out of her head.

"You're well? And the baby?" he asked, and she heard a tremor of concern in his voice. He had every reason to be furious with her; this unexpected kindness unnerved her. After all, she was the one who had run away from court.

"I'm a little tired, but the baby is growing well, thank you," she said, blushing. He had skillfully diverted the conversation away from himself. "But you—how did you—?"

The sound of cheering voices outside the window startled her; gazing out, she saw that a crowd had gathered to welcome her home. Smiling, Eugene raised his healed hand to wave to them and nodded to her to do the same. Frustrated, she turned away to acknowledge the enthusiastic greetings.

As the carriage approached the Winter Palace and drew to a halt for the imperial guards to open the gilded ironwork gates, he turned back to her and she caught a sudden alien glint of green in his eyes, brief as a passing shadow. Had she imagined it? It left her feeling unsettled, as if she could not be sure that the man sitting beside her was exactly the same man she had married.

"Must we stay in Mirom?" she said. "I was planning to go to Erinaskoe to see Mama and Papa. The city is so oppressive in summer."

"If the country air will do you and the baby good, then of course you must go to Erinaskoe." He was still smiling at her. What was different about him? And why was it so disconcerting?

CHAPTER 15

"Arkhelskoye in summer." Jagu shaded his eyes against the sheen of bright sun reflected off the sparkling water to gaze at the port as the *Dame Blanche* sailed into the harbor. "How sunlight changes the look of a place."

Celestine was gazing back toward the headland where their escorts, three warships, had taken up their positions, standing ready to defend them if they were attacked yet keeping well out of sight from the mainland. "Do you think the port authorities will accept our story? Pilgrims in high summer when Saint Serzhei's Day falls in the depths of winter?"

Jagu shrugged one shoulder. "If we were to wait for the saint's day, we'd be ice-bound here until the thaw." He still dreamed of that cold night in the Osprey's Nest tavern when she had snuggled up to him for comfort, and he had come so close to breaking his vow. Even the memory sent a shiver of heat through his body. He stole a glance at her, wondering if she remembered that night too . . . and if it had meant as much to her as it had to him.

"Celestine," he began tentatively, "do you—"

"Lieutenant!" Philippe Viaud hailed him. "The men are ready to disembark." Twenty Guerriers, dressed in hooded pilgrim's robes of raven black, had lined up on deck.

"Let's go over the plan one more time." Jagu gazed at his fellow Guerriers. "Lieutenant Viaud, you're in charge of the horses and the lookouts. Make sure that we're covered for a quick escape. Adjutants Gurval and Vouvay, when we've secured the crook, you and your men will make your way back to the port through the forest."

"Lieutenant!" The young officers saluted him with alacrity. He hoped he had made the right decision in putting his trust in them.

"And me?" Celestine was regarding him with the faintest hint of a malicious sparkle in her eyes.

"As we discussed. Go straight into the shrine and find the relic. I'll be at your back to protect you."

Celestine made one last check before they left the ship for the raid on the monastery. Her pistols were primed and the powder was dry. She hoped she would not be forced to fire them. She wanted to avoid bloodshed at all costs.

She drew out the pouch of sleepdust that she had stolen from the Magus's laboratory in Swanholm. It was potent stuff, as she knew to her cost; it had rendered her unconscious for hours.

But how long does its potency last?

The fine crystals shimmered dully inside the little leather pouch. Celestine took great care not to look too closely, for fear of sending herself instantly into a deep trance.

I won't use it unless there is no other possible alternative. Yet when she remembered how vehemently Abbot Yephimy had refused their request back in the spring, she knew that she might be forced to employ this substance, created by forbidden alchymical magic. The last thing she wanted was to have to fight the monks for the sacred relic.

"I gave you my answer once before, Lieutenant." Abbot Yephimy placed himself on the steps in front of the doors to the shrine. The monks were assembling on either side of him, forming a human barrier between the Commanderie and their goal. "The crook stays here. With the Blessed Serzhei's bones."

Jagu looked into the abbot's eyes and saw the challenging stare of a warrior. Yephimy was ready to give his life rather than hand over the relic.

"It's so peaceful here in Kerjhenezh, isn't it?" Celestine's clear voice suddenly rang out, breaking the tense silence. "But the situation beyond your walls has changed, Abbot.

There are now five Drakhaouls at large. We must reforge the Staff and defeat them, or they will tear our world apart."

"Then let us repair the Staff here," said Yephimy equably. "We have a forge."

This was going nowhere. "I must ask you again, Abbot," said Jagu, "to hand over the crook."

"And I tell you again, Lieutenant, that I cannot do that."

"We have no wish to harm you or any of the brothers, but we have our orders from the Grand Maistre." As Jagu was speaking, he saw Yephimy gazing over his head to the main gateway. Gurval and Vouvay must have arrived with reinforcements. At that moment he also saw Brother Lyashko, the young beekeeper, hand the abbot a heavy broadsword.

"You'll have to kill us first, Lieutenant de Rustéphan," Yephimy said, placing himself in front of the shrine doors.

Jagu saw at once from the abbot's stance that he had used that sword before—and probably to lethal effect. Beside him, the brothers suddenly drew out weapons: wood-cutters' axes; ancient, rusty pikes; Azhkendi sabres. But many of the monks were white-bearded and stooped; their heavy blades wavered in palsied hands.

This was not going as Jagu had planned. He took Celestine by the arm and drew her to one side. "I don't want any bloodshed if we can avoid it. But they seem determined to put up a fight."

"Leave it to me," she said.

Celestine's hand closed around the leather pouch. If she could just edge close enough to the monks—

"Charge!" yelled Adjutant Gurval, running forward. The ringing clash of metal sent the crows sitting on the chapel roof scattering, cawing into the air.

Jagu wheeled round, his hand raised to stop the attack. But it was too late; the Guerriers had drawn their swords and followed Gurval. One of the monks fell to his knees, run through the throat by Gurval's blade. Jagu swore.

Celestine was staring, transfixed. She had never seen

action at such close quarters before. The shouting, the sudden stink of blood, terrified her. This was all going wrong.

Jagu drew his pistols. "If we get out of this alive, I'll have that young hothead demoted!"

The monks had formed a tight knot, attempting to beat back the Guerriers with pitchforks, hoes, and rusty swords. Only Abbot Yephimy wielded his weapon like a trained warrior. Before the dazzle of his scything blade, the Francians began to drop back.

A sudden explosion beyond the walls made Celestine flinch.

"Reinforcements?" Jagu, grim-faced, signaled frantically to Viaud to check it out.

I have to act now or it's all for nothing. Celestine plunged a hand into the pouch, feeling the sleepdust tingling faintly against her fingertips. *Faie. Protect me.*

"*I will be your shield.*" As the Faie's bright energy went sizzling through her body, she set out, zigzagging through the fighters, making straight for the abbot.

One moment Celestine was at Jagu's side. The next, she was gone. To his horror he saw her running into the very heart of the battle, right toward Abbot Yephimy.

His heart stopped.

And then he noticed the translucent shimmer of light about her. Her guardian spirit must be protecting her.

With a dexterous flick of the wrist, she cast a fine glittering powder into the air about the abbot's head. As the abbot's broadsword came slicing down, she neatly sidestepped the blow and darted clear.

The broadsword dropped from Abbot Yephimy's grip with a sonorous clang. The abbot fell to his knees, then crashed forward onto his face, his big body slowly rolling down the steps. The brothers nearest to Yephimy began to sway and collapse to their knees.

The Forbidden Arts.

Celestine turned and beckoned to him. Jagu had no choice but to follow her into the shrine.

* * *

The clatter of the Guerrier's boots shattered the candlelit peace of the shrine. Beneath the dark eyes of the painted saints staring down from overhead, Celestine lifted the lid of the wooden box containing the golden crook. She looked up at Jagu. In the gloom, her eyes blazed bright with that same strange crystalline gleam he had seen only when the spirit had taken possession of her body.

"It's ours," she said.

"Let's get out of here," Jagu said tersely. He hoped none of the other Guerriers had noticed her appearance. But as they came up the stairs into the main body of the chapel, the sound of frenzied shouting arose from the courtyard.

"Listen." Jagu put his hand on Celestine's shoulder, holding her back.

"Drakhaon! *Drakhaon!*" It was a war cry.

"Lord Gavril's men." He primed his pistols. "Get ready to fight your way out of here."

"Open the doors."

Jagu's men pulled the chapel doors open, revealing an extraordinary sight. Most of the monks lay unconscious. One of their lookouts was dead, a crossbow bolt through his throat. But instead of the hordes of *druzhina* Celestine had expected to find, there were only two, wielding their sabres like madmen as they attacked. And behind them, she spotted Viaud's men returning from their reconnoiter.

"Put down your weapons," she ordered in the common tongue. "You're surrounded."

Jagu stared at the carnage below. Bodies lay sprawled across the chapel entrance: both monks and his own Guerriers. He could see blood trickling slowly down the steps. The air stank of gunpowder.

"Drakhaon!" yelled a defiant voice again.

There, surrounded by his Guerriers, stood three strangers; one wore a Tielen uniform, the other two looked like barbarian warriors, with tattooed faces and war braids.

And Jagu remembered the enigmatic words that Ruaud had whispered to him before they set sail for Azhkendir.

"*You'll be in the Drakhaon's lands; don't neglect to gather any intelligence that could be of use to us in the war to come.*"

"The war to come," he repeated under his breath. He looked at the two warriors and saw that, in spite of their ferocious appearance, they were very young, one scarcely more than a boy.

What better way to learn about the Drakhaon than from his own men?

"Take those two alive."

"Are you mad, Jagu?" Celestine cried. "Let's just get out of here before reinforcements arrive."

"I'm merely obeying instructions."

"You'll never take us alive!" yelled the taller of the two Azhkendi warriors. Whirling his sabre about his head, he rushed toward the steps.

Jagu saw the Tielen raise his hand in a vain gesture, as if to stop the boy. He heard the dull thud of pistol-stock blows on flesh and bone. The two Azhkendi warriors toppled and fell at the feet of their attackers. The Tielen slumped to the ground, unconscious.

"Bind them, hand and foot," Jagu ordered, "but leave the Tielen behind."

"They'll only slow us down." Celestine pushed past him, daintily lifting the hem of her robes to avoid soiling them in the spilled blood. She turned at the gateway and said, "Well, what are you waiting for, Jagu? The Drakhaon? Didn't you hear? They called for him."

The sails of the *Dame Blanche* filled with the fresh evening wind, as Captain Peillac set off south toward Arkhelskoye.

"*The Drakhaon!*" Celestine suddenly heard the Faie cry out in warning. She ran to the ship's rail, gazing up into the sky, which was fading to the purpled hue of moorland heather as the sun sank.

"The Drakhaon's coming after us!" Her skin crawled and tingled as she sensed the Drakhaon approaching, even though she could not yet see the wings that were darker than night's shadows above the forest.

"It's just your imagination," Jagu said, more brusquely than usual.

She rounded on Jagu, her fear and fury spilling out. "We have the crook; we have what we came for. Why did you take the Drakhaon's men hostage?"

"Because the Maistre wanted me to." His voice came back to her gratingly.

"But we stand no chance against him out here on the open sea—"

Jagu reached out and caught hold of her by her shoulders. There was a grim and dangerous look in his eyes that silenced her. "He won't attack us while his men are on board."

"Can you be so sure?" Even as she challenged him, she sensed the dark vibrations of the Drakhaon's wings drawing nearer. Shouts came from the lookout; Philippe Viaud had taken out a telescope and was training it on the shore. She felt Jagu's hands tightening about her shoulders and saw a look of genuine dismay extinguish the anger in his eyes. "He will come for us and kill you all, you Francian filth," the red-haired boy had spat at them before Viaud struck him across the mouth, hard, to silence him.

"*He's here.*" The Faie's voice radiated through Celestine's mind like a pale flame. Looking up, she saw great serrated wings soaring above, briefly silhouetted against the white sails of the cutter. Jagu gasped and drew her into his arms, pressing her tightly to him, as if he could protect her with his body against the Drakhaon's fiery breath.

Crushed against his chest, she could feel his heart pounding as fast as her own. He must be as terrified as she. On the deck, the Guerriers ran to and fro in panic, hunting for their muskets.

"Hold your fire!" Jagu ordered. "The Drakhaon won't attack while we hold his men prisoner. If he sinks the ship, they'll drown too."

The great dragon circled slowly above them, shedding a dim starry radiance from its scales of midnight blue.

"But it's . . . *beautiful,*" Celestine heard herself whisper in spite of her fear. And, as Jagu had predicted, it suddenly swiveled around in the air and began to wing back toward the shore.

How to begin to write an accurate report for the Maistre of the events at the monastery?

Jagu scribbled a couple of introductory sentences, then paused.

Celestine had acted rashly, and yet her use of Linnaius's sleepdust had prevented a bloodbath. But if he penned a truthful account, he would be furnishing the Inquisition with enough evidence to accuse her of sorcery.

In his agitation Jagu pressed too hard and his pen nib blotched the paper. He reached for a rag to mop up the ink. It was hard enough writing in this choppy sea as the cutter's captain took advantage of the fresh wind off the Spines to speed away from the Drakhaon.

"Lieutenant." Philippe Viaud appeared in his cabin. "We're approaching Arkhelskoye." Jagu laid down his pen. "And we've spotted two Rossiyan frigates. Looks like they're maneuvering to cut off our escape."

Jagu rose. The report would have to wait. "We need backup. Time to fire the flare. Tell the men to take up battle stations until our men-o'-war show themselves."

He and Ruaud had anticipated meeting resistance from the Rossiyans. Three Francian men-o'-war had been waiting off Arkhelskoye to cover their getaway. The arranged signal for them to show themselves was the firing of a flare.

Before he had even reached the deck, he heard the rushing whistle of an incoming broadside and a cannonball smacked into the waves yards off their bows. The cutter rocked; he was thrown backward, grabbing at the ladder rail to stop himself from falling.

"Fire the flare!" he heard Viaud yell at the top of his lungs as he emerged.

"Where are our ships?" Celestine cried out from the rail of the upper deck.

Jagu's heart missed a beat. She was in danger from any flying splinters of timber sheared off by the Rossiyan cannonballs. And if they dared to fire alchymical missiles at them, she could be overwhelmed by poisonous vapors in a matter of seconds, her lungs seared beyond repair.

"Get below, Celestine," he shouted above the whiz of the flare as it spun upward into the cloudy sky. His voice grated, rough with fear for her safety. Guardian spirit or no, she was not invulnerable.

Another shot whizzed across their bows, closer this time, the ball hitting the water with such force that they were flung to the deck as the sea splashed up over the side.

"Let me help, Jagu."

The flare burst into emerald light above their heads, staining her white face green with lurid light as he pulled her to her feet. He felt the pulse of aethyrial energy in her as he touched her and snatched his hands away as if he had been burned. Her guardian spirit must have been awoken by the commotion.

"No, Celestine!" A show of aethyrial power might save them from the frigates, but when help was so close at hand, it was far too dangerous to risk in front of so many witnesses.

"I'm not going to let anyone take the crook from us." When she turned to him, he had to look away from the brilliance of her eyes that blazed, no longer blue but dazzlingly pale, like milky crystal.

It wasn't Celestine speaking anymore. He had to bring her back. Jagu acted on instinct, pushing her back against the bulkhead. As the distant boom of answering cannons rang out, he pressed his mouth to hers.

"Mm—Jagu!" She hit him, hard. "Have you gone mad?"

Still he held her, in spite of her struggles, gazing into her eyes. But the unnatural brilliance had gone; the shock must have jolted her back to herself. He relaxed his grip.

"They've got the Rossiyans on the run!" shouted a sailor from the rigging overhead. Rowdy cheers arose from the crew on all sides.

Jagu let go of Celestine. He was shaking. The immediate danger was past. But how could he trust her? She had let the spirit take control of her.

"Go below," he said, "and stay in your cabin until we're out of their line of fire."

She stared at him, mouth open as if to answer him back. And then as another Francian broadside thundered out across the waves, she turned and did as she was told without another word.

Dazed, confused, Celestine stood, her back pressed against her cabin door. The timbers of the ship reverberated to the deafening explosion of the cannonfire, shuddering through her body. The air stank of gunpowder fumes. She closed her eyes, trying to regain control of herself. She was trembling, but not from fear.

Jagu had kissed her, so forcefully that her mouth still felt bruised.

How *dare* he!

But if this was anger she was feeling, self-righteous fury at the way he had treated her in view of the crew, why was her body still trembling? Had he merely acted to stop her unleashing the Faie's powers? Or had she tasted something else, something fierce, passionate, hungry in that hard, lingering kiss?

And—most infuriating of all—why had her body responded so readily? Could she have fallen in love with Jagu?

CHAPTER 16

"So this is Smarna." Jagu gazed up at the ruined walls of the old citadel of Colchise, brutally bombarded by the Tielen fleet before the Drakhaoul's dramatic intervention had brought the siege to an abrupt end. The sun was burning down from a cloudless sky and he took off his broad-brimmed hat to fan his face. Flags stirred a little on the battlements in the dry heat; Francian pennants of blue and gold. He glanced tentatively at Celestine and saw her pointedly look the other way, unwilling to meet his eyes.

Since he had kissed her, she had hardly spoken a word to him. During the long voyage to Colchise, she had kept to her cabin for much of the time, under the pretext that she was writing a report on the mission. Several times he had been on the point of apologizing—but then his pride had stopped him. Damn it all, if he hadn't taken such a drastic step, she would have betrayed her secret—and everything would have been over. She should have, by all rights, been grateful. But all he had done was to drive her further away. And what was worst of all was that in acting so spontaneously, he had revealed not just to her—but to himself—a strength of feeling that he had been unable to control. So, in spite of the brilliant sunlight, he felt as if he walked under a cloud because he feared that his one impetuous act had changed things between them forever.

"So now Smarna belongs to Francia." Celestine was watching the Francian man-o'-war set sail for Lutèce with the Azhkendi prisoners securely chained in the hold. "But why do you suppose the Maistre asked us to meet him here?"

"Perhaps he has a new mission for us." She had spoken quite naturally to him and he wondered if she had forgiven him at last.

As they followed their armed escorts, Guerriers, from the harbor, Jagu could not help noticing that, whenever they passed Smarnans in the dusty streets, all turned away, as though silently refusing to acknowledge their new masters. Could these be the same citizens who had, by all accounts, welcomed King Enguerrand so warmly only a few weeks ago?

"Something's not right here," he said quietly to Celestine.

She nodded. "I don't think I've ever sensed such hostility. What can have happened?"

The Guerriers led them to a tree-lined square and into a balconied mansion built of golden stone. It had once been the Colchise residence of the princes of Smarna, hastily abandoned in the uprising when the deposed royal family fled into exile. Inside, the lofty hall was refreshingly cool; Jagu could glimpse a green courtyard garden beyond and hear the splash of a fountain. But the antechamber in which they were left to await the Maistre's summons had a sad air of faded grandeur: The gilding on the ornate cornices had all but flaked away and cracks marred the painted plaster.

"You've done well; very well." Ruaud de Lanvaux held up Saint Sergius's golden crook, touching it reverently.

Considering that the mission to Azhkendir had so nearly come to grief, Jagu was relieved to see that the Maistre was pleased with the results.

"We've never had greater need of the saint's protection." Ruaud's expression darkened. "While you were in Azhkendir, the Magus escaped."

"The Magus escaped?" Celestine echoed.

"We were attacked by one of the Drakhaouls. It swooped down into the Place du Trahoir and snatched the Magus from the burning pyre."

This was a setback that Jagu had not anticipated. He glanced at Celestine to see how she was taking the news.

"What would a Drakhaoul want with the Magus?" she burst out. "Does this mean that Eugene has summoned a daemon of his own? You remember, Jagu? Linnaius was researching the Drakhaouls in Azhkendir."

"Our duty as Guerriers has not altered." The Grand Maistre carefully placed the relic in a cedarwood box and locked the box with a gilded key from a chain around his neck. "We must keep to our plan to destroy the Drakhaouls. And now, thanks to you, we have the means to do it." He laid one hand protectively over the cedarwood box. "While our craftsmen are at work reforging the Staff, we will be laying our trap for them."

Jagu nodded. If Celestine was right and Eugene was the one responsible for setting the Drakhaouls free, the sooner the Commanderie was armed against them, the better. "So, Maistre, what is our next mission?" he asked.

Ruaud gestured to them to sit down opposite him. "The situation in Smarna," he said, "is a little . . . delicate. While you were in Azhkendir, Eugene agreed to cede Smarna to us in exchange for the safe return of the Empress. But even though the king was warmly welcomed here, matters have rapidly deteriorated since he left. Quite frankly, I find it dispiriting that the Smarnans have shown us so little gratitude, considering that we freed them from a brutal Tielen regime. But they've always been a volatile nation, so perhaps we should have anticipated some resistance . . ."

The lazy drone of cicadas in the trees outside carried into the room on the hot, dusty breeze.

"Resistance?" Jagu remembered the hostile looks they had encountered in the streets.

"I'm sailing for Francia on the evening tide"—Ruaud let out a small sigh which did not escape Jagu's notice—"but I'd like you both to stay here in Colchise to monitor the situation. The university is the center of the rebels' activities. Some of the academics led the recent revolt against the Tielen occupation force. I fear that they're stirring the students to rise up against us this time. But this situation needs handling with the utmost caution."

"Who's in command of the garrison?"

Ruaud hesitated. "Ah. There we also have a potential problem. Prosper Eguiner, a high-ranking Inquisitor."

"The Inquisition here?" said Celestine, who had been silent awhile, as though her thoughts were elsewhere. "But why?"

"A professor, called Rafael Lukan. A dangerous free-thinker whose writings on philosophy have attracted the Inquisition's notice. But we need to tread very carefully with him . . . it seems that he's an old friend of the Drakhaon of Azhkendir. One wrong move and the whole of Colchise could erupt."

"The Drakhaon," Celestine repeated under her breath.

"Haute Inquisitor Visant took the Magus's escape very badly. He saw it as a slight on the Inquisition's reputation. He's determined to demonstrate the power of the Inquisition by publicly crushing a prominent heretic. So be careful—and keep me informed of any unusual developments. Jagu, I've told Eguiner that you will assist him in the garrison, should the need arise."

"But what about me, Maistre?" asked Celestine.

Ruaud passed her a printed bill and Jagu read over her shoulder:

REPUTABLE PORTRAIT PAINTER SEEKS NEW COMMISSIONS.
Illustrious recent clients: her imperial highness, Astasia,
Empress of Rossiya; the Grand Duchess Sofiya; his
Excellency, Ambassador Garsevani. Please address all
inquiries to Elysia Andar at the Villa Andara, Vermeille.

"You want me to have my portrait painted?"

"We have already made arrangements for you to give a concert at the ambassador's residence. A little villa has been reserved for you overlooking Vermeille Bay. Your nearest neighbor will be Madame Andar and you will commission her to paint your portrait. That way you'll be able to use your conversational skills to learn a great deal about the situation here in Smarna. And, maybe the whereabouts of the Drakhaoul of Azhkendir."

"How so?" Celestine said blankly.

"Elysia Andar is Gavril Nagarian's mother."

"Maistre, isn't this a highly dangerous mission?" Jagu protested. "If you mean to bring Lord Nagarian to heel by holding his mother hostage—"

"I'm well aware of the dangers involved, Jagu," Celestine said, flashing him a defiant look.

Jagu shook his head.

"I shall need a maid if I am to play my part convincingly. Staff to run the villa." Celestine ticked off each item on her fingers. "A good quality fortepiano, not some out-of-tune, neglected instrument. And new gowns and jewelry, if I am to impress fashionable society here in Colchise—"

"All this has been anticipated. The treasurer is awaiting you downstairs."

Jagu was about to follow Celestine out when de Lanvaux called quietly, "A moment more of your time, Lieutenant."

Jagu paused, wondering what the Maistre wanted with him.

"You've proved your loyalty to the cause time and time again, Jagu. I think I can confide in you." The Maistre put his hand on Jagu's shoulder. "I have great hopes for your future within the Commanderie. I see potential in you, and that is why I'm going to share my thoughts with you." Jagu glanced questioningly into his leader's eyes. "I know you hold *her* in great regard. But you must be on your guard. Since the trial, Visant has been asking questions about her. I believe that he's set his Inquisitors to investigate her background."

This was what Jagu had long been dreading. If word reached the Inquisitors' ears about her behavior at the monastery . . .

"You know that I hold you both in the highest esteem. But I fear that she has begun to be driven more by her own desires than the greater good of the order."

"But Maistre—"

"I have serious concerns about her, Jagu. I know you would come to me—in confidence, of course—if you suspected that she was no longer acting in our best interests. Do you understand?"

Jagu felt the pressure of the Grand Maistre's hand on his shoulder. Was he being forced to make a choice?

"I understand," he said slowly, wondering even as he spoke the words aloud if he were already betraying her.

CHAPTER 17

Where was Jagu? Celestine paced the salon of her rented villa, stopping from time to time to gaze out of the window at the cliff road that wound up from the wide bay far below. The rehearsal was to have started at three in the afternoon and it was a quarter past five. Had he forgotten? That would be unlike Jagu, who was usually reliable to the point of obsession about timekeeping.

The afternoon was hot and the sheen of sunlight sparkling off the waves had been dulled by a drifting film of haze. And the constant nagging drone of the cicadas in the acacia trees had become a torment to her sensitive ears.

Since she had learned about Kaspar Linnaius's escape, she had been on edge, unable to settle to any task. They had been idle in Colchise for too long and she was restless. She had almost begun to believe that Ruaud had deliberately chosen to leave her in Smarna.

To protect me? Or to keep me from causing trouble for the Commanderie?

At last she heard horse's hooves on the cliff road. She hurried out into the courtyard, only to be assailed by the afternoon's heat, rich with the lemony perfume of the late roses in the garden.

A lone horseman rode into the courtyard; it was Jagu.

"Where *have* you been? You're over two hours late!"

He dismounted and, as the stable lad came out to take the reins of his horse, he gave her a warning look that said, "Not out here."

So she was obliged to wait until her new maid, Nanette, had brought some iced tea. Jagu, taking a long sip, eventually said, "Colchise is in an uproar." She noticed that a little muscle at the side of his eye had begun to twitch from time to time. "Eguiner has had Rafael Lukan arrested on charges of heresy. And what's happened? All the students have gathered at the university to protest."

"Why didn't Eguiner bide his time?"

"The Inquisition must be planning to make an example of him. Such tactics might work at home in Francia, but here, in Smarna?"

"I can't pretend I like this mission, Jagu. And I can't help wondering why the Maistre left us behind." Celestine took a deep breath and asked the question that had been bothering her: "Doesn't he trust me anymore?"

"I'm sure that's not the case," said Jagu, maybe a little too quickly. She did not feel in the least reassured. "Celestine," he went on, "I've been drafted in by Eguiner to help defend the citadel. I have to go back straightaway. The recital may have to be postponed."

So there was nothing for her to do. She turned away from him, not wanting him to see how angry and frustrated she felt.

"How are the sittings going for the portrait?"

She gave a little shrug. "Madame Andara is an accomplished artist. She's also extremely discreet. I don't think she's going to confide any of her family secrets to me, Jagu. Quite frankly, I think it's a waste of my time—and the Commanderie's funds."

"I'll be in touch again as soon as I have any new information." He rose, setting down the empty glass. "Be careful, Celestine. Don't do anything rash."

"As if I would!" she cried, stung that he should speak so patronizingly to her.

A puzzled, hurt look clouded his eyes. "I just meant—that if—oh, never mind."

"One of your agents has been causing the council some concern, Maistre," said Inquisitor Visant.

"One of *my* agents?" Ruaud looked up into the Inquisitor's eyes and saw that cold, keen light he recognized of old;

when Visant set his mind to a problem, he pursued it with a single-minded dedication that came close to obsession.

"We've had our suspicions for some time."

"I have no idea to whom you're referring." But Ruaud knew all too well that Visant meant Celestine.

"One of my men was in the raiding party that went to Saint Sergius. Demoiselle de Joyeuse was twice observed to use some iridescent dust that caused those who inhaled it to fall instantly into a deep sleep."

"Your man must have a strong imagination." So there had been an Inquisition agent among Ruaud's Guerriers, spying and reporting back to Visant. A discomfiting thought. "A dust that causes instant sleep?"

"There was a recipe for just such a dust in the books that were burned on Kaspar Linnaius's pyre."

Ruaud sighed. "Proof. I need proof, Visant, before I can order her arrest."

"If the Commanderie is seen to condone such dangerous arts, your reputation will be tarnished beyond repair. You must make an example of her."

"How can we bring her to trial without firm evidence?" insisted Ruaud.

"One could almost believe that she has bewitched you too, Maistre, with those angelic blue eyes."

"That is a very serious allegation, Inquisitor," said Ruaud coldly.

"Which can easily be disproved by bringing the young woman before a Commanderie tribunal. If she is innocent, she will walk free. If guilty . . ."

Ruaud stared at Visant, knowing himself outmaneuvered. *What, I wonder, do you really wish to gain from this, Inquisitor? Are you out to discredit me, so that you can become Grand Maistre in your turn?*

"Then recall her. But be prepared. If she is guilty, as I strongly suspect she is, she will try to escape. And she knows far too much to be allowed to go blabbing our secrets to our enemies."

"I think you have misread Celestine de Joyeuse's character," said Ruaud. He was sure that she would comply with his request and prove Visant wrong. "But I will have her brought back from Smarna. And then she is yours for questioning."

A knock at the door interrupted them; one of the king's household came in and bowed. "His majesty requests your presence urgently, Maistre."

Ruaud rose from his desk, wondering what this urgent summons might mean. Enguerrand had been behaving rather strangely of late and the king's obsession with defeating the Drakhaouls had begun to worry him. "Is he ill?"

"Let me take care of this little matter, Ruaud," said Visant smoothly. "All I need is your authorization."

"What?" Ruaud's mind was already elsewhere. "Oh, yes; of course . . ." He hastily scribbled an order, sealed it, and handed it to Visant, before hurrying after the servant to attend to the king.

"There must be something I can do . . ." Celestine leafed through her father's grimoire. She was almost sick with boredom and inactivity.

Was it by accident that the pages fell open at a glamour that proclaimed it would "draw out the truth from the unsuspecting"? "It loosens the tongues of the unwary, causing them to reveal all manner of secrets," read the spidery writing. "But to transmute the ingredients, to imbue them with your own life essence so that they become an agent of your will, is a risky enterprise and not one to be lightly undertaken."

This was one errand that Celestine could not entrust to her maid; she had even begun to wonder whether Nanette might be an agent of the Inquisition, sent by Visant to spy on her. So she set off alone, taking a parasol to protect her complexion from the sun, and informing Nanette that she was going to take a stroll along the cliff path to admire the view.

The blinds were pulled down in the windows of the apothecary's shop in Colchise to protect the wares from the fierce midday sun. The bell tinkled as Celestine pushed open the door, and the apothecary appeared from the back room—a wizened old man who stared at her suspiciously.

The atmosphere was dry and made her want to cough, as though a fine film of dust from his medicinal herbs hung in the air.

"Purple hellebore?" He tutted disapprovingly. "Why would you need such a rare and potent drug?"

"Rare?"

"It only grows on the lower mountain slopes around Lake Taigal. I have to import it from Khitari."

So it would be expensive. "My physician in Lutèce prescribed it. I have terrible headaches." She placed gold coins on the counter. "Nothing else will do."

The apothecary nodded and swiftly pocketed the coins. While he was busy in his dispensing room, Celestine stared at the rows of painted jars, each labeled with the names of herbs or chymical compounds. If she closed her eyes for a moment, that evocative dusty smell took her back to her father's study.

Had he ever been driven to use the spells in the grimoire? It grieved her that she knew so little about her own father, and even more so that it had to be Kaspar Linnaius, his treacherous partner, who held the information she longed to learn.

"Every time you use one of the glamours, it will deprive you of some of that essential life force that the magi call the Essence."

Hervé's warning echoed through Celestine's mind as she locked her bedchamber door and began to prepare the substances she had purchased in the little shop in the citadel.

"If you must resort to such desperate measures, do it only when your life depends on it. There is always a price to be paid for the use of magic, and you have not been trained how to conserve your strength."

Jagu arrived at Celestine's rented villa at five in the afternoon to rehearse for the recital. Her maid, Nanette, asked him to wait in the parlor.

"Where's your mistress?"

"Sitting for her portrait," said Nanette.

The instant he crossed the threshold, Jagu sensed something strange in the air: the faintest taint of magic. But before he could investigate further, he heard women's voices in the hall.

"Nanette!" Celestine called. "Madame Andar is feeling a little faint; she'll go home in my carriage."

The portraitist was leaving. Jagu opened the door a crack and watched as Celestine helped Elysia Andar across the cool of the marble-floored hall. Nanette followed, carrying the artist's sketchbook, easel, and paints. While the women went outside to await the carriage, Jagu slipped into the salon. His senses told him that some spell or glamour had been worked just a short while ago, and it was not long before he found the empty tea glass by the portraitist's chair. Warily sniffing the dregs, he detected the lingering presence of a substance that had been subtly altered by magic; it made the sensitive lining of his nostrils tingle.

He set the glass down with a bang. Celestine had given him her word never to use the grimoire again. He didn't know whether he was more angry with her for breaking her word or himself for leaving her alone for too long.

The sound of horses' hooves on gravel announced the departure of the carriage. He opened the lid of the fortepiano and listlessly tried a few notes. He had been looking forward to playing for her, hoping that they might, through music-making, reestablish something of their old intimacy. He wondered if he had been deceiving himself.

Celestine came back in; her face was a little flushed and her eyes sparkled, as though she had been drinking wine.

"How could you?" he said sternly. "How could you risk using your father's grimoire again?"

"What if I have?" she said, pushing past him to seat herself at the fortepiano. "I've learned more this afternoon than the Maistre's spies have in a year."

"You promised me, Celestine. And it's so dangerous—for you, as well as your victims." She didn't seem to be listening. "Don't you know how insidiously these Forbidden Arts work? They deceive you. You think that you are using them, but in reality, they are using *you*."

"I hate it when you preach, Jagu." She was shuffling through the music on the fortepiano and suddenly threw all the sheets up in the air. "She told me so much." Jagu bent to retrieve the scattered sheets. "She told me that Professor Lukan was like a second father to Gavril Nagarian. But best of all, she told me that there's a Muscobite scientist called Kazimir who knows how to make a potion to subdue the Drakhaoul and drain him of all his powers!"

She seemed almost intoxicated with her achievement.

"And when the Maistre asks how you came by this information, what will you say to him? You'll have to lie. And then one lie will only lead to another—and another." Jagu took her hand in his own. "Don't do this to yourself, Celestine. Don't perjure your immortal soul. Burn the book."

Celestine snatched her hand from his.

"Or if you aren't strong enough to do it, let me do it for you."

"No!" Celestine backed away from him. "It's all I have left of my father. I forbid you to touch it. If you really cared for me, Jagu, you'd understand."

He stared at her. *It's because I care so much about you, that I'm saying this.* But he could never say those words aloud. It would mean breaking his vow.

"I don't feel like rehearsing." She seized the music from his hands and banged it down on top of the fortepiano. "I'll send a report on my findings to the Maistre."

"But the recital—"

"If you want something to do, go and try out the fortepiano at the ambassador's house. It probably needs tuning."

There was no point in arguing with her while she was in this capricious mood. He turned and, without another word, left the room.

CHAPTER 18

Enguerrand waited, in the same agony of longing as a lover waits for his beloved, for his guardian angel to speak to him again.

The evening was still and close, tainted by a threat of distant thunder. Enguerrand rose from his prie-dieu and went anxiously to stand in front of his mirror. The angel had appeared to him in the glass before, superimposing his radiant image over Enguerrand's own so that Enguerrand saw himself transformed, transfigured by the angelic presence.

It had first appeared to him at sea but since then it had spoken to him only in his dreams. But every time, its sacred golden presence had filled his heart with courage and its stirring voice had repeated the same words. "*You have been chosen. Chosen to be Sergius's successor.*"

"Sergius's Staff has been reforged," he whispered. "Tell me what I must do now."

The stifling atmosphere in the room began to pulse as he gazed eagerly into the mirror. The evening shadows twisted and writhed. The angel was going to appear at last, he was sure of it.

"*You have done well, Enguerrand.*"

At the sound of that deep, resonant voice, so strong and yet so kind, his heart began to beat faster. He leaned closer, his breath misting the glass. Eyes of burnished gold burned into his until he felt as if the angel was staring into the deepest recesses of his soul.

"*But are you ready to use the Staff against the Drakhaouls?*"

Enguerrand's throat felt suddenly tight and the words that he wanted to say would not come.

"You're frightened. I understand. And that is why I have come to help you, to lend you my powers. Just as Galizur once did for Sergius."

As Enguerrand stared into the mirror he saw the angel a little more clearly: a long, leonine mane of golden hair and strong features, majestic, yet of a noble beauty. Just as he had always imagined when he was a child . . .

"You'll help me? Oh thank you . . ." Enguerrand felt all his fears melt away as he gazed into his angel's lambent eyes.

"You must defeat the Drakhaoul of Azhkendir first; he is the most powerful of all. And to that end, you must lure him to you. You still have the rubies in your possession, don't you, the ones they call the Tears of Artamon? The Drakhaouls are drawn to those jewels, as to no others."

"Not only do I have the rubies, I also have two of the Drakhaon's bodyguards imprisoned here. It's only a matter of time before he comes to their rescue."

"May I come in, sire?" He recognized Ruaud de Lanvaux's voice.

"Very well." He turned swiftly around, his back to the mirror, as if trying to hide the angelic presence—but it had faded even before his bedchamber door opened.

Ruaud presented Sergius's Staff, wrapped in white linen, to the king.

Enguerrand unwound the bindings and lifted the Staff, weighing it in his hands, as a swordsman tests the feel of a new blade.

"Well, sire?" Ruaud waited for his response. "The craftsmen did a fine job, didn't they?"

"The time has come." Enguerrand looked up at Ruaud, his face transformed by a calm, almost beatific smile. "I'm ready."

"Ready, sire?"

"To summon the Drakhaoul. I'm ready to do battle. My angel has prepared me."

Ruaud felt again that nagging feeling of doubt that had been troubling him ever since the king had told him about the angel. "Your guardian angel, majesty. Has it revealed its name to you yet?"

"He is called Nilaihah," said Enguerrand in soft, reverent tones. He was still holding the Staff across his body and for a moment Ruaud thought he caught a gleam of gold flicker in the king's dark eyes. When he looked again, it had gone; it must just have been a glint reflecting off the polished gold of the crook.

"Nilaihah," repeated Ruaud. The name was not familiar but it was many years since he had studied angelography.

"You want to send the Drakhaouls back to the shadows as much as I do, don't you?"

Ruaud looked into the king's radiant eyes. "You are very precious to me, sire—and to the people of Francia . . ." Enguerrand's expression undid him. Faced with that look of unquestioning conviction, he knew that there was nothing he could say to dissuade the king from confronting the Drakhaon.

Captain Friard knocked on the door of the Grand Maistre's study and waited for a reply.

"Come in." The Maistre's face looked drawn as if he hadn't slept, Friard noted, the fine skin beneath his eyes smudged grey. Perhaps the long journey back from Smarna in the summer's heat had worn him out.

"The king," said Ruaud, "tells me that he has been visited by an angel. A guardian angel who has told him he has been chosen to be Sergius's successor. Of course, this is wonderful news. But I . . ."

"Maistre?"

"Why am I having these doubts, Alain?" Ruaud raised his head to gaze at him with haggard eyes. "I've been Enguerrand's mentor and confessor since he was a boy. I, of all people, should be honored that my pupil has been chosen. But . . ." Again he left his thought unfinished and Friard, saddened to see him so conflicted, did not know how to reply. "I want you to do some research for me."

"Of course." Friard was glad to do anything if it would help ease the Maistre's troubled state of mind.

"It's a name. It may be Ancient Enhirran in origin, so I'll write it in Francian and Enhirran script." Ruaud dipped his pen in the shell-shaped inkwell on the desk and put down the two versions of the name.

"Ni—lai—hah." Friard spelled out the syllables.

"Don't say it aloud."

"Is this the name of . . . ?"

"The king's guardian angel. Only it's not a name that I remember encountering in my studies with Père Judicael. Of course, there are an infinite number of guardians in the hosts of heaven, so it's more than likely that my doubts are completely unjustified. But bring me every scrap of information you can find, no matter how insignificant . . ."

Alain Friard rubbed his aching eyes, leaned back on the wooden bench, and stretched. He had been researching for several days and he had moved from the vast, echoing hall of the Commanderie Library to an obscure and little-known collection hidden away in the vaults. Père Judicael had brought him here to examine an ancient text that had been brought out of Djihan-Djihar in the previous century. The book had been rescued from a burning library, and the old vellum was blackened by fire, with some of the text burned away. Scholars had argued for years over the authenticity of *The Warriors of Heaven,* whose anonymous author claimed to have recorded every known angelic appearance. There were even exquisite little illuminations in the margins. But *The Warriors of Heaven* was kept locked away, and only a few select members of the Commanderie were allowed access, for fear that unscrupulous scholars might use the information to initiate forbidden cabalistic rites.

Once Friard had reminded himself how to decipher the intricate Djihari script (which read from right to left), he began the laborious search for the name the Maistre had given him.

And at last he thought he had found the king's angel: the

poet Nilaihah. "Nilaihah," translated Friard, "has influence over wise men who love peace and wisdom."

But this was only one reference and the Maistre had asked him to bring "every scrap of information, no matter how insignificant." And one fact had been bothering Friard: Someone had scrawled an unfamiliar sigil in crimson ink beside the angel's name. He turned the fragile vellum over and scanned the next page and the next, searching for another occurrence. Frustrated, he went in search of Père Judicael, who stared at the sigil first through his spectacles then, raising them, peered so closely that the tip of his nose touched the page.

"Leave this with me," he said. "I'm certain I've encountered that sigil before; but it's an ancient and obscure script, an Enhirran variant maybe, on the Djihari alphabet . . ."

"'A poet-angel,'" Friard transcribed the translation for Ruaud, "'who has influence over wise men . . .'"

CHAPTER 19

The roar of an angry crowd penetrated the thick walls of the old citadel.

"You sent for me, Inquisitor?" Jagu saluted. The officer of the Inquisition who had summoned him was Prosper Eguiner, the man who had authorized the arrest and trial of Professor Lukan. Now that the guilty verdict had been announced, Colchise was in an uproar and the students were massing outside the citadel.

"I need every Guerrier I've got right here at the citadel. All leave is canceled." Eguiner had to raise his voice to make himself heard above the shouting of the protestors. A redhead, he was evidently finding the late afternoon's heat difficult to tolerate, and Jagu could see a film of sweat on his freckled face.

"I have a rehearsal for the recital at the ambassador's."

"That'll have to wait, Lieutenant. I need every able-bodied Guerrier in Colchise here to guard the prisoner. Have you heard that crowd? They stormed the citadel when the Tielens were here. I wouldn't put it past them to attack again."

"Was it really necessary to arrest Professor Lukan?"

"Rafael Lukan is a dangerous and heretical freethinker." Eguiner took out a spotless linen handkerchief and dabbed at his gleaming face. "An undesirable influence on impressionable young minds."

"But look at the trouble it's caused." Eguiner might be Visant's second-in-command, but Jagu was not intimidated by him.

"Frankly, I'm surprised to hear you talk that way, Lieutenant," Eguiner said, tucking away the handkerchief. "The man's a dangerous influence! We have to make an example of him."

Jagu suppressed a sigh of irritation. He had no great sympathy for the Inquisition. Their officers had never seen action in Enhirre, spending their time ferreting out evidence against unbelievers and heretics. Faced with an armed revolt, he feared that they might not have enough experience to be able to defend the citadel successfully.

"What are my orders?"

"I want you to organize the Guerriers to defend the citadel against any possible attack from the populace. The execution is to take place at midday tomorrow. I don't want anything to go wrong, do you understand me?"

"I understand. Do you have a map of the citadel?" Jagu asked. "And how many men are stationed here?"

"A detachment of fifty."

Not that many, but maybe enough, if I position them at key places along the walls . . .

As the shouting of the students settled into a regular pattern, Jagu began to distinguish words. "Free Lukan! Free Lukan!"

"Inquisitor, the First Minister of Smarna is here to see you," announced Eguiner's secretary.

"Tell her I'm busy."

"She's most insistent . . ."

Eguiner slammed the dossier shut and followed his secretary out of the room. Jagu examined the map of the citadel spread out on the desk in front of him, taking note of all the breaches in the walls left unrepaired since the last revolt against the Tielens, only a few months ago.

My mission was to work with Celestine to discover more about the Drakhaon's whereabouts. It involved infiltrating Smarnan society, playing music, and listening to the gossip of the intellectuals and the artists . . . And now, thanks to the Inquisition, the whole country's in an uproar, and I have to leave Celestine to work on her own.

The rhythm of the chanting changed. Now Jagu was

certain that he could hear, "Death to the Francian Inquisition!"

I should go back to check that Celestine is safe. Instead of which, I'm going to have to drill these Inquisition Guerriers on how to defend themselves.

An hour or so later, Jagu found himself instructing Eguiner's officers, pointing out the places on the map where the citadel was most vulnerable to attack. Then the shouting outside suddenly died away. All the Guerriers looked up.

"The calm before the storm?" said one, laughing nervously.

"Perhaps they've given up?" suggested another.

"I doubt it," said Jagu dryly. Though, the more he thought about the Inquisition's methods, the more he disliked what he had been ordered to do. Heretical as Rafael Lukan's ideas might be, execution seemed too harsh a punishment. A rumor was circulating in the citadel that the First Minister was appealing directly to King Enguerrand to intervene.

Eguiner's men had been up all night building a scaffold in the square outside the citadel. Jagu had placed armed Guerriers around the square, warning them to be ready to fire at the first sign of trouble.

Eleven was striking from the cathedral clock as he returned to the citadel. One hour to go to the execution, and the rebel students had still not made their move.

A woman screamed. Jagu seized his pistol and checked that it was primed.

"To your positions!" he ordered the Guerriers waiting inside. As he ran to guard the doorway, he heard the sound of musket shots. "So soon?" he muttered. In the square, people were running about in confusion. The sky darkened and, glancing up, he saw daemon-blue eyes staring down at him from the smoky glitter of a great hook-winged shadow-dragon. His Guerriers fired at it but their musket balls bounced off its armored scales like hailstones.

"The Drakhaon," he muttered. "I should have guessed . . ."

Two people were coming swiftly toward him; a fair-haired

young man and a bespectacled youth clutching a document case. Jagu, sensing trouble, barred their way.

"Take us to Rafael Lukan," said the man. "I have a pass signed by the First Minister."

"No one is allowed in to see the condemned man."

"But I'm his son," piped up the youth.

Could this be the truth? "I have no record of any wife or son here. Wait here, please." Jagu was forced to scan the record book.

"His illegitimate son," added the youth.

There came a sudden uproar as hundreds of students poured into the square and rushed the Guerriers. And the Guerriers, caught reloading their muskets, were not ready for them.

"Damn!" Jagu cried and in that one moment's distraction, turned away. The blow caught him on the back of the head; there was a flash of blinding, skull-splitting pain—and then, nothing.

"Lieutenant. *Lieutenant!*"

Jagu opened his eyes to see a Guerrier bending over him. He felt sick. And when he tried to sit up, he felt a violent pounding in his head.

"The prisoner—"

"He got away."

"Damn." Jagu closed his eyes. Fragments of memory began to return. "That youth. The old distraction trick. Keep the target occupied while your accomplice slips round the back and—bang! Why did I fall for it?" He groaned. "How long have I been unconscious?"

"You've been out most of the day. The surgeon says—"

"Not so loud," Jagu hissed, closing his eyes again. The sound of the man's voice had set lights dancing luridly before his eyes.

"Sorry, Lieutenant." The Guerrier spoke more softly.

"The recital!" Jagu suddenly remembered. "I have to go to the ambassador's villa—"

"The surgeon says you're to rest until he's checked you again. You took quite a blow there."

Jagu felt so queasy that he did not argue and lay back, letting the Guerrier apply a cold compress.

" 'In the light of recent unfortunate events in the citadel,' " read Celestine,

> I feel it is inadvisable to proceed with your recital. I hope you will understand, Demoiselle. It is with regret that I have decided to postpone the concert until the situation has stabilized.
>
> Yakov Garsevani, Ambassador

"Unfortunate events?" she said aloud, unable to conceal her annoyance. "Why didn't the Inquisition take Rafael Lukan to stand trial in Francia? Then they could have lured the Drakhaon there and entrapped him, using the information I charmed from his mother, far from his home. But no, the Inquisition knows best, and all my hard work is for nothing!"

Nanette appeared. "There are two Guerriers here to see you, Demoiselle," she said as two men appeared in the doorway behind her.

"We have urgent instructions from Maistre de Lanvaux," said the taller of the two.

"From the Maistre?" she asked, stalling for time; neither man's face was familiar.

"You are to return to Lutèce with us straightaway." Both wore the discreet emerald insignia on their black uniform jackets that marked them as belonging to the inquisitorial division. Visant's men.

"But I need time to pack—"

"We have orders to take charge of all your luggage."

"Let me at least send word to Lieutenant de Rustéphan."

"We must leave straightaway," repeated the first officer. There was an inflexible tone to his voice that warned her that she had been found out. But who had betrayed her?

"It was an old book . . ." Nanette's voice drifted out from her bedchamber as they led Celestine across the hall, ". . . and then the portraitist said she felt unwell . . ."

They were going through her possessions. If she called on the Faie to help her, she would only give her secret away. She would have to bide her time.

As they escorted her into their carriage, she saw other Guerriers entering the villa. She had concealed the grimoire inside a collection of *chansons,* but the Inquisitors were trained to ferret out all manner of hidden secrets.

It was stickily hot inside the carriage. Why were they waiting? And then she had a sudden horrible suspicion. Had Jagu reported her to their Commanderie superiors? He had warned her not to use the grimoire and she had ignored him. For where was he now? Had he betrayed her? Was his loyalty to the cause stronger than his feelings for her, after all?

I've risked my life many times for the Commanderie. Surely that will stand me in good stead if it comes to a trial?

A Guerrier came running over. He handed over a package to the officers.

"Demoiselle de Joyeuse," said one, "can you explain why this was found in the villa?"

The other held up her father's grimoire.

"I have no idea," she said.

CHAPTER 20

As the *Aquilon* sailed out of Colchise harbor, Andrei
Orlov found himself pacing the upper deck with his mind
on matters other than navigating the strong currents in the
bay. The sun was setting and the western sky bled crimson
light into the sea, hazed by ragged tatters of gauzy cloud.

What was the matter with Celestine? She had not even
looked at him when she came on board. Her manner had
been subdued, her eyes downcast. The two officers acting as
her escort had not once left her side. And there was no sign
of Jagu de Rustéphan. The more Andrei puzzled over it, the
more he became convinced that something was amiss.

He resolved to speak to her alone as soon as he could distract the two officers. He would get Vassian to make them
both read and sign a long document of his own devising, "a
new precaution, in these troubled times." And while they
were busy with pen and ink, he would seek out Celestine.

Celestine had not encountered Andrei Orlov since they
parted in Haeven, and the sight of him, so trim and handsome in his dark blue uniform, had made her heart race. Yet
she had not dared greet him in front of her captors; they
must not suspect that she had friends on board. She was surprised to find him already in command of a Francian warship. Where did his true loyalties lie? If she appealed to
him, would he be willing to help—or would he refuse, con-
strained by his allegiance to his new allies? She knew that
he was very ambitious. He might not want to involve himself in anything as sordid as a sorcery trial that might spoil
his chances of advancement.

Celestine tried the door of her tiny cabin. It was locked. And from the lively motion of the ship, she guessed that they would soon be out in open sea, heading back to Francia. She lay down on the bunk and tried to order her thoughts.

How could I have been so stupid as to try to hide the grimoire? At the time, she had been so certain that they would search her that concealing it in her music had seemed the best idea. *But then I was naïve enough to imagine that I could charm my way out of their trap.*

Why had she not listened to Jagu? Was it just her own stubbornness that had made her act so rashly? He had warned her and she had ignored his advice.

Why did he always have to be so infuriatingly self-righteous?

Waves slapped against the hull as the *Aquilon* plowed on through the dusk. High overhead she heard the thudding footfall and shouts of the sailors as they went about their work. Unpleasant odors arose from the bilges, seeping through the boards as the ship sailed into deeper waters.

There's no point feeling sorry for myself. I have to act swiftly or I'm as good as dead. The temptation to summon the Faie to help her escape was growing stronger with every minute that passed, but such an act would only give the Inquisitors the evidence they needed to bring her to trial.

The sound of a key turning in the lock of the cabin door made her glance up fearfully. But when she saw that it was Andrei Orlov, she could not hold back tears of relief.

"Andrei, I fear I may be in terrible danger." She tried to control her voice but the tears kept flowing. "Those two officers—"

"Don't worry; Vassian's keeping them busy with a stack of official forms that I've insisted they read and sign. In triplicate." Andrei was checking that the door was bolted behind him.

"But they're working for Inquisitor Visant. He hates me. He would do anything to destroy me."

"Tell me what I can do."

"Help me escape." She wiped her eyes.

"But where will you be safe? You can't go back to Smarna. And Francia is utterly out of the question."

Celestine shook her head. "I—I can't even go to Allegonde." Jagu had been right, of course; she had become overconfident and risked too much, without thinking through the consequences. And at that moment, she hated Jagu for having been so accurate in his reading of her.

"Muscobar," said Andrei without hesitation. "You'll be safe in Muscobar. I have friends there who will ensure that you're safe."

"Oh, but that will mean setting a new course. I couldn't put you in such a position—"

"I'll invent some excuse; new secret orders, or some such."

"You'd do such a thing for me?" The tears threatened to brim over again.

"For you, dear Celestine," he said, "anything. You have only to ask. We're heading toward Lapwing Spar. You can stay with Irina for a few days."

"Irina?" She looked blankly at him. Was she one of his wealthy relations? Or a mistress?

"Irina is Kuzko's widow. You remember Kuzko? He was the fisherman who rescued me after the wreck of the *Sirin*. No one will find you there."

"Thank you." An obscure fisherman's shack? She smiled wanly at him through her tears. "There is one other small thing . . ."

"Name it."

"A book of my father's. It's all I have left to remind me of him and they have confiscated it."

"They deprived you of your only memento of your father? I'll get it back for you, never fear."

Celestine was watching the moonlight glistening on the sea through the tiny window in her cabin when Andrei eventually returned.

"Is this the book?"

She flew to him and took the grimoire, clasping it to her. "Oh thank you, thank you, Andrei."

"It's the least I could do." She rose on tiptoe to kiss him

again, just the slightest brush of her lips against his, but his arms went round her, crushing her close. In the moonlight, his eyes burned like twilight stars and she felt a sudden frisson of warning shiver through her. She had sensed there was something different about him earlier on, but now she was certain that this was not the same Andrei she had last seen in Haeven.

"Celestine," he said hoarsely, "I can't stop thinking about you . . ." And he pressed his mouth to hers, kissing her more deeply until she began to feel dizzy.

"*Drakhaoul*," warned the Faie.

Celestine gazed up into Andrei's eyes and saw a wild, untamed flicker of desire. She realized in alarm that she was in the presence of one of the Seven.

"When?" she whispered, her hands pressing against his shoulders to hold him at arm's length. "When did this happen to you?"

"What do you mean?" There was a dangerous edge to his voice.

"I can see it in your eyes." She began to back away, her heart thudding faster. "You're possessed." She came to a halt, her back against the cabin wall, knowing that there was nowhere else to flee to.

"Captain Orlov!" Someone knocked on the door. "Why have you instructed your crew to change course?" It was one of the Inquisitors. "We're no longer on a heading for Francia."

"New orders!" Andrei called back.

"This is most irregular. I insist on an explanation."

Andrei let out a grunt of frustration. "I have to go."

"But what shall I do? If the Inquisitors find out that the book has gone—"

"I can stall them for a while. We have some excellent wine on board; this is a Francian ship, after all."

"They're Inquisitors, they're trained not to fall for such old tricks. Unless . . ." It was a desperate measure, but it might work. She pulled her ring off and pressed it into his hand. "There's some powder beneath the bezel; it's sleep-dust. Mixed with wine, it should put them into a deep sleep." She gazed up at him appealingly. "Please, Andrei? For my sake?"

He hesitated for only a moment. Then he said, "Leave it to me." Slipping the ring onto his little finger, he kissed her swiftly and let himself out.

As soon as she was alone again, Celestine sank down onto the bunk. "How far can I trust Andrei?" she whispered to the Faie. "Who was talking to me: Andrei or his Drakhaoul?" She could still feel the warning that had shivered through her whole body as he pulled her close to him. She had not felt such raw, visceral fear since the Drakhaoul of Azhkendir swooped down over the *Dame Blanche*.

"*I cannot tell for certain.*"

"What do I do if he comes back? He was so strong. He could force me to do anything he wanted and I'd be powerless to stop him."

"*I won't let him harm you.*"

As she lay shivering on the bunk, she was no longer sure of whom she was more afraid: Visant's Inquisitors or the Drakhaoul-possessed Andrei.

Jagu, still nursing a pounding headache, arrived at Celestine's villa to find the windows shuttered and the doors locked. A gardener was pruning the roses. He called out to him, "The young lady's gone. Two gentlemen in black came for her yesterday."

"Gone?" Jagu echoed. "Did they say where?"

The gardener shrugged and turned back to his roses.

Jagu spurred his horse along the chalky cliff road to the harbor, and as he rode, he cursed himself. Two gentlemen in black. Visant's men? If so, he offered up a prayer that it was not too late to save her.

Vermeille Bay stretched away into the far distance below him, the blue of the sea softened by the first autumn mists. A salty breeze tousled his hair as he approached the broken walls of the citadel. His growing anxiety simmered in his throat until he could hardly breathe.

At the harbor he went from sailor to merchant, asking,

and only receiving blank looks. At last a fellow Guerrier told him that the *Aquilon* had sailed from Colchise for Francia yesterday, carrying Demoiselle de Joyeuse, who had been urgently summoned back to Lutèce by Maistre de Lanvaux.

Why had the Maistre summoned her alone, and not him? Jagu broke out in a sweat at the news.

"Sit down and rest, Lieutenant," said the Guerrier. "You're not yet recovered from your wounds."

But Jagu knew he could not rest until he was certain that Celestine was safe. "My mission here is over." He mopped his face. "When is the next ship back home?"

CHAPTER 21

Aude de Provença was only a slip of a girl, but Enguerrand had felt an instant connection to her when she was
presented to him at court. Aliénor had invited several eligible
young noblewomen to a summer soirée at the palace and
Aude was an afterthought, eclipsed by the beauty of her
elder sister Esclairmonde. But Enguerrand had infuriated
his mother by escaping the formal dancing to go and eat ices
with Aude in the gardens, like two naughty children hiding
from the adults. Her wit and mischievous manner had en-
deared her to Enguerrand, making him forget his troubles
for a while.

A few days later, he found himself passing by the Hotel de
Provença on the way back from visiting a charity hospital.
The temptation to see if Aude was at home was too great to
resist. He was king, after all . . .

The steward, skillfully hiding his surprise at the unexpected visit, welcomed him. "Please follow me, sire."

"That wool is for your embroidery, Aude!" A woman's
voice, stiff with displeasure, could be heard as they crossed
the hall.

Enguerrand was shown into a firelit salon, where he saw
Aude teasing a tortoiseshell kitten with a length of wool,
laughing delightedly as it skidded across the polished floorboards, while her governess looked on, tapping her foot in
annoyance.

"His majesty, the king," announced the steward.

"Forgive us, sire." The governess dropped into a deep
curtsy. "Had we known you were coming, we would have
prepared—"

"No, it's entirely my fault for making an impromptu visit," said Enguerrand hastily.

"If you've come to see my sister Esclairmonde, then I'm afraid your journey has been wasted, sire," Aude said, pertly bobbing a curtsy. "She and Maman have gone to visit an orphanage today. They're doing 'charitable works.'"

"No matter," Enguerrand said, gazing at her, "it was you I came to see."

"*Me?*" she said, her brown eyes widening. And then she burst into laughter. "Why me? Everyone adores Esclairmonde; she's so beautiful and sweet-natured. Unlike me. I speak my mind. I just don't seem to be able to help myself."

Enchanted, Enguerrand found himself laughing too.

The governess coughed pointedly. "May we offer you some refreshment, sire?"

"Thank you."

But the moment the salon door opened to admit a servant carrying in a silver tray, the kitten decided to make good its escape and shot between his legs.

"Minette!" Aude shrieked and ran off after it as the servant valiantly tried to right himself and save the sliding contents of the tray.

"I'm so sorry, sire." The governess's face had turned a dark red in embarrassment.

"Demoiselle Aude is very young; such high spirits are only natural," said Enguerrand.

"Very young?" said an offended voice. Aude reappeared, carrying the wriggling kitten. "I'm fifteen, nearly sixteen." She drew herself up to her full height. "Just because I'm not tall for my age, people forget."

It was Enguerrand's turn to blush. "I beg your pardon, Demoiselle. I didn't intend to offend you . . ."

She shrugged it aside with an ingenuous little grin and held the struggling kitten up for him to stroke. "Do you have any favorite pets, sire?"

"Pets?" Enguerrand had spent most of his life studying. "My brother Aubrey kept hunting hounds, great hairy brutes; I was always a little afraid of them, I confess. But cats . . ." As he put out his hand to pat the kitten, it twisted away with a yowling cry of fear and ran off to hide beneath one of the chairs. "Oh," he said, hurt. "I don't usually have that effect on animals . . ."

"Minette can tell that you're . . . different," Aude whispered confidentially to Enguerrand.

"Different?" Enguerrand stared at Aude in dismay. Was she clairvoyant?

"He's dazzlingly bright," she said, staring into his eyes, "the spirit within you."

He caught hold of her hands, gripping them hard in his own. "You can *see* him?"

"He used to be a poet," she said, suddenly sad and distant, "but *they* forced him to become a warrior. And since then he's been angry, so angry because his true nature is a peaceful one . . ."

"Aude," Enguerrand said, his voice trembling, "I never knew that till now."

The governess coughed loudly and he hastily let go of Aude's hands. "The duchess's carriage has returned."

"If only we could talk for longer." He wanted Aude to tell him more about the daemon that had possessed him.

"*We will return for you, my child.*" Enguerrand had not spoken out loud; the words had come from Nilaihah. He saw Aude's eyes widen and knew that she had heard Nilaihah's voice. But at that moment, the duchess and Esclairmonde appeared in the salon and their intimate conversation was brought to an abrupt conclusion.

"There you are at last, Captain Friard!" came a tetchy voice.

Friard looked up from checking the next day's duty roster to see Père Judicael hobbling into the guardroom. "How can I help you, mon père?" It was rare for the old exorcist to venture out of the library these days.

"That sigil; I knew I'd seen it before. But it took me days to trace it." Judicael placed a little book into his hands and collapsed onto a chair, out of breath. "Guess what the binding's made of?" he said, wheezing.

"I have no idea. Kidskin?" The more Friard stared at the book, the more it seemed to give off an unsettling, peculiar aura. "Pigskin?"

"Human skin. Those occult signs are tattooed onto the victim's back before the flaying takes place."

Friard almost dropped the book. It had an unpleasant, greasy feel to it. It made him wonder whether the skin had been peeled from the unfortunate victim when dead . . . or still alive.

"I've marked the place," said Judicael.

Friard overcame his revulsion and opened the book. There, above an intricate engraving, was the sigil he had seen before, this time drawn in faded brown ink. Friard peered more closely, seeing that the woodcut portrayed tier upon tier of stylized, winged angels. Closer inspection still showed that many wielded spears and fiery swords and, tumbling down from the highest tier of heaven, fell one of their number. A little inscription had been scratched on the woodcut in the same brownish ink.

"Do you recognize the language?" Judicael asked.

"It looks like a variant of ancient Djihari," Friard said, scratching his head. "Is that word 'fall'?"

" 'The fall of the angel Nith-Haiah, one of Seven.' "

"Nith-Haiah?" repeated Friard, staring at the sigil.

"Written in human blood."

"How could I have been so stupid? 'Th' and 'l' are interchangeable in ancient Djihari," Friard muttered. "So Nilai-hah is Nith-Haiah. The blood-sigil is the sign of the apostate." The king's "angel" was one of the rebels. He thrust the book back into Père Judicael's hands. "I must warn the Grand Maistre straightaway."

Ruaud stared at his king. Enguerrand looked like a young saint in his pure white robes, and the Grand Maistre felt a catch in his throat as he gazed at his protégé. There was a radiance about the king, as he placed the Tears of Artamon on the altar; his eyes gleamed gold and a faint glimmer seemed to encircle his head, like a halo.

"Will the Drakhaon come, do you think, Ruaud?" Enguerrand asked. And the tremor in his voice betrayed his fear and his vulnerability.

Ruaud came closer to Enguerrand. "If you have the slightest doubt as to the wisdom of this venture . . ."

Enguerrand gave him an affronted look.

"There would be no dishonor in abandoning the attempt," Ruaud said gently.

"I won't abandon my duty." There was a stubborn glint in Enguerrand's eyes. "I'm no coward, Ruaud. I have my guardian to guide and protect me."

The summer daylight outside the chapel began to fade. *Clouds must be rolling up fast,* Ruaud thought, feeling the hairs prickle on his body; thunderstorms were common at this time of year. A fitful wind began to gust outside, high about the chapel spires.

The great door suddenly banged open. All the candle-flames guttered wildly and went out.

"Is he here already?" Ruaud swung around. A man stood in the doorway. Even in the dim light, Ruaud could see that his skin glittered as though jeweled with iridescent scales and his wild dark hair tumbled about his shoulders.

"I am here," said the Drakhaon. He began to walk down the aisle toward Enguerrand, who took a step back. "Well?" he said. "You promised that my *druzhina* would be released. Where are they?"

"Your reign of terror is over, Drakhaoul!" cried Enguerrand. He raised the gold-tipped Staff high, brandishing it like a hunting spear, ready for the kill. "Daemon, I command you to leave this man's body!" The golden crook gleamed like a crescent moon as the daylight faded from the chapel.

"I call upon my guardian angel to help me. Nilaihah, work through me—and draw out this daemon."

"Nilaihah?" echoed Gavril Nagarian.

The rose window splintered into a million shards of colored glass. Through the deadly rain of splinters burst two daemon-dragons, one scarlet as flame, the other dark as purple twilight.

Enguerrand turned, wielding the Staff, pointing it at them with trembling hands.

The scarlet Drakhaoul snatched the Staff from him, snapping it in half as if it were matchwood. The other breathed a little burst of violet flame. The golden crook melted into a puddle of liquid metal.

Enguerrand collapsed.

Disjointed words issued from his mouth as he cowered on the floor. "Why—did you—to your Chosen One? Am I—*unworthy*?"

Ruaud started out toward him but stopped as the king's body began to twitch and thrash about as though he were in the throes of a violent epileptic fit. A fine gilded mist arose, spinning around him, until the air glittered.

In the king's place, a third daemon-dragon crouched, armored with burnished scales as resplendent as the morning sun. "Why was I—so deceived?" it cried and its voice was Enguerrand's. "Save the Tears, Ruaud!"

Ruaud started out toward the altar, only to see the scarlet Drakhaoul seize the casket in its talons, hissing a warning at him that seared the air.

"Wait!" cried Gavril Nagarian. "Why should *you* take charge of the Tears, Sahariel?"

"Because, dear brother," came back the mocking reply, "*we don't trust you*." And the scarlet and purple Drakhaouls rose into the air and flew out through the ruined window.

"*No!*" Before Ruaud's astonished eyes, Gavril Nagarian transformed in a dark whirlwind into his dragon form, leaping into flight after them, the gust from the beating of his great wings sending Ruaud sprawling.

Fists thudded against the barred wooden doors of the chapel; muffled voices clamored to be let in.

Ruaud de Lanvaux pushed himself to his feet. There was no sign of the Drakhaouls—or the Tears of Artamon. Broken glass and fragments of stone were scattered everywhere. The Commanderie chapel was cracked open to the sky, a great, jagged hole gaping where the magnificent rose window had been.

And sprawled on the floor, unmoving, lay Enguerrand.

"Sire," Ruaud called. "Sire, are you unharmed?" Little remained of Enguerrand's white robes; they had been shredded to tatters, leaving the king nearly naked. Yet he could see no bruises or wounds on the king's body.

What would he do if the daemon had killed the king? And how would he explain it to Aliénor? She would blame him. She would have him and his closest advisers executed in the most prolonged and painful way she could devise.

Loud, rhythmic thuds made the locked doors shudder on their hinges. He guessed that his Guerriers must be trying to force them open.

The king let out a soft moan.

"Sire?" Ruaud helped the king to sit up. "Thank God you're alive." He took off his jacket and slipped it around the king's shoulders. Enguerrand was shivering uncontrollably; he seemed in a state of shock.

The doors crashed open and armed Guerriers came rushing in.

"Maistre, the king?" Alain Friard appeared.

"The king is unharmed."

"Thank God. Because that name you gave me, Nilaihah, it belongs to one of the Fallen. Père Judicael only just—"

"Alain, go make sure that no one has been injured in the attack." Ruaud could not bear to hear any more.

"Maistre." Friard saluted and hurried away.

"The Staff." Enguerrand's voice was barely more than a whisper. He was staring fixedly at the scattered splinters.

"It was just wood and metal." Ruaud felt a deep sense of disillusionment pervading his soul. "And we were arrogant fools to think that any of us was pure enough to inherit Sergius's powers."

All he heard in response from Enguerrand was a muffled sob.

CHAPTER 22

Steam hissed on the surface of the luminous waters. A haze of shifting mist almost obscured the surrounding rocks, which were streaked with white and jade from the healing minerals bubbling up from the hot springs.

Kaspar Linnaius rose gasping, water streaming down his face. He blinked and found that his failing sight had cleared.

A woman was watching him through serpentine eyes, her long locks of hair flowing down over her shoulders like waterweed.

"Lady Anagini," he said, bowing his head. "Thank you. You've restored me a second time."

"Don't thank me yet," she said. "I have not yet told you what price I must exact from you."

Linnaius bowed again, waiting to hear the guardian's will.

"And, as I warned you before, these are not the springs of eternal youth, no matter what the local legends may say. You've lived a long life, even for one with mage blood. I can never give you back your youth, Kaspar."

"I am content with this," Linnaius said stoically. "I only ask that you give me long enough to aid my master, Eugene."

"This is the first time that I've ever heard you express such a selfless wish," she said, floating toward him. One dripping finger gently stroked his cheek. Was she smiling? "Has your cold heart begun to melt at last?"

He did not know how to answer such a question. "So, lady, what is your fee this time?"

Her jade-flecked eyes narrowed. "You committed a crime, many years ago, Kaspar, when you stole a certain crystal from Azilis's Shrine in Ondhessar. And since that crime was committed, the barriers between the mortal world and the Ways Beyond have begun to disintegrate. Your powers—and mine—have already begun to diminish."

"You want me to put the crystal back?"

"I want you to find the aethyr spirit it contained: she who kept the balance between the worlds. The Eternal Singer: Azilis."

Linnaius's lost memories were returning to him. *Rieuk Mordiern, his green eyes burning with hatred and defiance as he gazed up at him over the dying body of his lover, his young face twisted with grief and incomprehension. Rieuk, the last living crystal magus.*

"Surely only the one who set her free can put her back?"

"If it were that simple, he would have done so many years ago. But Azilis is still joined by a bond of blood to another master ... or should I say, mistress?" Anagini's slanted eyes glinted.

"Do you mean Celestine de Joyeuse?"

"Magus! Come quickly!" A man's voice came floating through the mists. It was Chinua, his Khitaran shaman guide. "We must go!"

His voice jolted Linnaius back to more urgent concerns. "Eugene," he said, remembering. "The Emperor needs me. The Empire is under attack."

"Go, then," said Anagini, drawing the billowing mists around her like a cloak, "but don't forget, dear Kaspar, that if you neglect your part of our bargain, your powers will begin to evaporate as swiftly as the mists rising from the springs ... and then what use will you be to your beloved emperor?"

The translucent waters swirled and Linnaius found himself alone, blinking, as Chinua, his shaman guide, appeared in a narrow gap in the craggy rocks surrounding the springs.

"Chinua," Linnaius said, wading out of the hot waters into the bitter chill of the mountain air, "I need a boat."

A sea fog was blowing in across Lapwing Spar as the sailors rowed Andrei and Celestine ashore and visibility was rapidly decreasing. Celestine could just make out a ramshackle little cottage perched on the edge of the dunes.

"Tikhon? Is it really you?" Old Irina appeared, surrounded by crooning chickens. She stared at Andrei through rheumy eyes. Then she flung wide her arms and hugged him. "My boy. My boy's come back to me!"

"Irina, this is Celestine," said Andrei, returning the hug. "Could she keep you company for a few days? Until I return to collect her?"

Irina peered at Celestine and nodded. "Well, you're a pretty one and no mistake. Come in and have some tea, both of you."

Andrei hesitated. "I wish I could stay longer, but my ship's waiting."

Celestine hugged her shawl to her, shivering in the damp as the fog rolled across the dunes. She looked uncertainly at the drab little fisherman's cottage. Andrei took her in his arms and kissed her. "Just for a few days," he said, then set out over the sands to the waiting rowboat.

She stood, waving forlornly to him, until the fog swallowed the little boat up and he was lost to view.

I can't stay here, she thought as she walked back up the dunes. *I have to get to Mirom.*

Back on board, Vassian came up to Andrei in a state of some agitation. "Those two Francians, they're either dead drunk or ill."

Andrei went below to look. The officers lay on their bunks and did not respond to slaps or cold compresses, except with the faintest of groans.

He had only done as Celestine had bidden him; a draft, she had said, that would make them sleep for a day and a night. She had given him her pearl-and-diamond ring, which concealed a fine white powder within the bezel and, when no one was looking, he had added it to their wine, for a toast "to Francia and confusion to all her enemies."

Surely she wouldn't have made him poison her captors—would she?

CHAPTER 23

Ruaud knelt in the desecrated chapel in darkness. A shimmer of moonlight shone in through the gaping void of the ruined rose window, starkly illuminating the destruction wreaked by the Drakhaouls.

He clasped his hands together but he could not pray. The familiar comforting words that he had repeated day after day since he became a Guerrier had deserted him.

Ruaud pressed his hands to his temples, trying to erase the terrifying images imprinted in his mind . . .

"Maistre."

Ruaud raised his head. Enguerrand stood in the chapel doorway.

"So you couldn't sleep either." He knelt before Ruaud, his head bent. "I'm corrupted," he said, his voice heavy with self-loathing. "Tell me how I can rid myself of this curse."

Ruaud gazed down at Enguerrand's abject posture and knew that he was utterly at a loss. The king was begging him for consolation—and he had none to give. The Drakhaouls had defeated him.

"It told me it was my guardian angel." Enguerrand choked on the words. "And I believed it. How could I have been so gullible? It was just using me to steal the Tears of Artamon. And now the Drakhaouls plan to open the Serpent Gate and set Prince Nagazdiel free." He raised his head and Ruaud saw with alarm that his eyes glittered in the dark, flecked with the same gold as those of the Drakhaoul that possessed him. "Help me, Ruaud!" He reached out, clutching Ruaud's hand in his own.

Ruaud pulled out the Angelstone from around his neck; in

the gloom, the thread of gold that had deceived him burned brightly. The other threads—blue, scarlet, green, and violet—had faded. The Drakhaouls must have taken the precious rubies far away. "We must move fast, before the other daemons return," he said, determined that there was only one possible course of action. "There isn't much time."

"What do you intend?" the king asked nervously.

"To hold an exorcism."

CHAPTER 24

The first stones of the Chapel of Saint Meriadec were said to have been laid by Lord Argantel in the time of Artamon the Great. So when Ruaud told the king that the ancient chapel was deemed the most suitable place for the exorcism to take place, Enguerrand readily agreed.

Standing guard over the Holy Texts towered two massive stone guardian angels, one with an upraised sword, the other, lion-maned, holding the keys to the Realm of Shadows. Enguerrand had known their names from childhood: Dahariel and Nasargiel. And as he lay prostrate in front of the altar, he tried to keep calm by reciting the Holy Texts. But the waves of panic kept rising up, and, the more he muttered, the more apprehensive he became. *Suppose the exorcism doesn't work? Will the Drakhaoul manifest itself again? Will it force me to attack the venerable priests and exorcists gathered here to help me?*

Nilaihah had been silent for the last hours. But he feared that the daemon would not leave him without a terrible struggle. And in that struggle, it might rend him apart. He had read of such horrific ceremonies in the secret annals of the Commanderie.

Blood spattering the tiles, shreds of flesh, brain, and bone defiling the sanctuary . . .

Kneeling on the worn tiles, Enguerrand squeezed his eyes shut and begged the Heavenly Guardians to forgive and protect him.

"Make me clean again. I will do anything you ask!"

He could hear the murmur of voices and the steady tread of the exorcists approaching. One by one, the candles in the aisles were extinguished until only those on the altar still burned. Shadows filled the chapel, and in the pale light of the last candles, the worn statues seemed to take on a life of their own, as though the winged warriors were hovering in the aisles, ready to do combat with his daemon.

The exorcists, robed in black, their faces masked and hooded, stood on either side of him.

"Are you ready, majesty?" Enguerrand recognized Ruaud's voice.

"Yes," whispered Enguerrand, terrified.

The ceremony began with a low, intoned chant. Enguerrand squeezed his eyes shut and tried to pray. But he could hear a faint whispering that was growing more and more insistent, superimposing itself over the exorcists' measured chanting. And try as he might, he could not blot it out.

"Stop!" he cried. Instantly, he was seized by two of the priests and slammed down onto the hard tiles.

"Don't listen to his cries," urged Ruaud de Lanvaux, "it's the daemon talking."

"No! It's me, your king, Enguerrand. And I order you to stop this ceremony at once!" He struggled to break free but the priests were the stronger and held him down.

"Take no notice. No matter what blandishments he uses, ignore him."

But Enguerrand could hear the Drakhaouls calling to Nilaihah.

Nilaihah . . . it's time to open the Serpent Gate and set Prince Nagazdiel free. Come, join us.

Enguerrand went limp in the grip of the exorcists.

"*At last,*" answered Nilaihah.

Energy was flooding through Enguerrand's body; it sparkled through his veins and sinews, as though his blood had been transmuted to liquid gold.

"*It's time,*" repeated Nilaihah, his voice echoing like a great bell through Enguerrand's mind, "*for our final transformation.*"

Ruaud paused in the chanting of the ritual of exorcism and looked at the king. He lay utterly still, unresisting. Was it having some effect at last? Ruaud hoped so with all his heart. He took up a bottle of holy water and began to sprinkle it over Enguerrand's limp body.

"Begone, daemon. In the name of Dahariel and Nasargiel, I command you: Return to the Realm of Shadows!" He raised the ceremonial spear of the Dragonslayer, tipped with gold, and held it above the king.

Enguerrand's body began to twitch.

"It's working." Ruaud invoked more of the Heavenly Warriors. "In the name of Galizur, of Taliahad, and Sehibiel of the Second Heaven, I banish you!" His voice rose, full of confidence, strong in the knowledge that he had the power to drive the Drakhaoul from Enguerrand's body.

But an extraordinary change was taking place. The king's hair was growing, the short-cropped locks lengthening before his eyes, writhing and curling like serpents, golden and black.

"Hold him down!" Ruaud ordered the priests restraining the king. Unnerved, he continued to recite the rite, stumbling over the words.

"Enough!" cried Enguerrand. He flexed his arms and, with one sudden gesture, hurled both the priests right across the chapel. Then he leaped to his feet and stared at Ruaud.

The candles blew out.

Enguerrand's eyes glittered in the darkness. His whole body glittered, as though powdered in stardust.

Shocked, Ruaud took a step back, holding tight to the book. The stunned exorcists lay groaning in the shadows. All was darkness and confusion in the chapel—except for the light that emanated from the daemon's gilded skin.

For the daemon was beautiful. It had transformed Enguerrand to a creature of unearthly splendor. No longer in dragonform, it towered above Ruaud, golden-feathered wings furled behind its powerful shoulders.

"A—angel?" stammered Ruaud.

"*Do not call me angel. Never call me by that name again!*" Enguerrand reached out and seized the book of exorcism from Ruaud's hands. He cast it on the floor and flicked one taloned finger at it. A little dart of golden fire sizzled out and the priceless ancient book flared up, then subsided into a pile of cinders.

"Majesty!" Ruaud stared in dismay at the remains of the burned book. With both book and Sergius's Staff destroyed, he knew himself defeated; he had no resources left.

"*We are Nilaihah,*" answered the daemon. "*You will address us as such.*" The voice was still Enguerrand's, but enriched and distorted by the Drakhaoul.

"Where is Enguerrand?" Ruaud demanded. "What have you done with him?"

"*Enguerrand is no longer under your influence, priest. And you believed you were powerful enough to control me?*" Nilaihah threw back his golden head and laughed.

That cruel, contemptuous laughter was more than Ruaud could bear. He had dedicated his life to Enguerrand's education; he had worked hard to shape the young man's beliefs and attitudes, he had cared for him as if he had been his own son. And now to hear his protégé deliberately mocking him—

The Enguerrand he knew was obviously dead. This daemon that dared to masquerade as an angel had inhabited his body. And there was only one way to drive it out. He must kill the king—or what was left of him. Without a mortal body to inhabit, the Drakhaoul would be forced to flee; it would be vulnerable.

Yet in destroying Enguerrand, he knew he was signing his own death warrant. But there was no time to consider, Nilaihah was advancing upon him, golden eyes ablaze in the gloom. Ruaud seized the ceremonial spear of the Dragonslayer. With all his strength, he thrust it at the daemon.

Nilaihah gave a howling cry as the spear pierced his breast. He clutched the shaft with both hands, and tugged.

Out came the spear and the daemon's gilded blood leaked out with it, dripping onto the tiled floor, where it sizzled and steamed.

"Forgive me, my king," whispered Ruaud.

But Nilaihah did not fall. He pressed one taloned hand over the wound to try to staunch the bleeding. The other hand slowly raised the spear, pointing the bloodstained tip at Ruaud.

By now Ruaud could hear voices. His Guerriers had come to the rescue. But the doors to the chapel were locked and bolted. He began to back away down the aisle.

Nilaihah launched the spear at him. It caught him full in the chest, the force of the thrust pinning him to the wooden door.

The daemon strode toward him and pulled out the Dragonslayer's spear and cast it away.

"Enguerrand—" Ruaud tried to say his pupil's name, but his mouth had filled with blood. As he slid slowly down, he saw the dazzling form of Nilaihah rising on golden wings, making for the far window.

"What's happened here?" As Linnaius brought his craft swooping down toward the palace of Swanholm, he saw flames and smoke rising from the East Wing. Far below he saw the lines of servants and guards working to extinguish the fire, pumping water from the lake, passing buckets from hand to hand. But in spite of their efforts, the fire had taken hold; and from the air Linnaius could see the flames gusting toward the rest of the palace.

He pressed his fingers to his forehead, summoning a swift storm wind to blow rain clouds to aid their efforts. Soon the sky darkened and rain began to pour down, dampening the flames. Gaping open to the sky, a ruin of fire-blackened timbers and tumbled stone, the wing looked as if it had been subjected to an intense bombardment. And yet there was no sign of enemy troops encamped in the park or patrolling the grounds.

Linnaius made his way on foot through the rain into the palace, searching for anyone, courtier or guard, who could give him information. Dust lay everywhere and a pungent smell of smoke clouded the lofty entrance hall.

"Why is this entrance unguarded?" he demanded, his voice echoing around the empty hall. A man appeared at the far end, hurrying toward him.

"Magus!" he cried. "Thank God you've come."

Linnaius recognized Eugene's majordomo; usually spot-lessly attired, his palace livery was drenched and his face was smeared with fire smuts.

"The princess," the majordomo said, his voice rasping as he coughed the smoke from his throat. "We tried to stop him—but he was too strong for us."

"He?" Linnaius said.

"Count Alvborg."

"Oskar Alvborg," Linnaius repeated, his heart growing cold at the sound of that name; Alvborg was a rebellious nobleman who had long borne a grudge against Eugene. "What has Alvborg done with Princess Karila?"

The majordomo seemed to be struggling to get the words out.

"He—he transformed into a dragon. And then he abducted her."

"Drakhaoul." This was worse than Linnaius had expected. "A Drakhaoul has taken the princess." And the hidden text he had discovered months ago at the monastery in Azhkendir returned to his mind, laden with a new, ominous relevance.

For only by the sacrifice of the Emperor's children in that far-distant place can that Door ever be opened again and the dread Prince Nagazdiel released. And no mortal would dare stoop to such a base and inhuman act.

"No mortal would dare," Linnaius murmured as he hurried back to his sky craft, "but a Drakhaoul . . ."

"Whatever dreadful sounds you may hear, don't interrupt the ceremony," Ruaud had warned Alain Friard.

But Friard was about to disobey his commanding officer for the first time in twenty years of service. He had waited long enough. His duty was to protect the Maistre.

First there had been muffled voices, raised as if in argument. Friard had heard laughter; horrible, mocking laughter that made his skin crawl. And then the sudden, bloodcurdling cry that sounded as if it issued from the throat of a fiend in torment.

Friard tugged at the door. When he found it was locked, he pounded on it with his fists, yelling, "Open up!" with the full force of his lungs.

"What's wrong, Captain?" Lieutenant Viaud came running up, followed by several of his men.

"We've got to break this door down. The Maistre's in danger!"

And at that instant a sudden, violent thud set the door timbers shuddering.

Both officers stopped, staring at the door. Friard pointed. A pointed metal tip had penetrated the door panel and blood dripped from its sharp end. Someone on the far side had been pinned to the door, like a butterfly to a collector's tray.

As they watched, mesmerized, the spearhead was withdrawn. Seconds later came the sound of shattering glass.

"Come on, lads, put your shoulders to this door!" Friard cried. When, a few moments later, they broke the bolts and burst into the chapel beyond, they almost fell over a body lying on the tiled floor in an ever-widening pool of blood.

"Ruaud!" Friard forgot all military protocol and knelt beside his old comrade in arms, gently turning him over. The Maistre's robes were soaked with bright scarlet and more was frothing and bubbling from his lips as he tried to speak.

"Who did this?" Friard propped the Maistre's head up against his knee as Viaud attempted to staunch the flow of blood with his scarf.

"The—king." Ruaud's hand rose feebly, trying to point. "Drakhaoul—took—the king." Friard followed the direction of the pointing finger and saw that the arched window above the altar was shattered, as if someone—or some*thing*—had burst its way through. Surely the Maistre couldn't mean that the king had been abducted by a Drakhaoul?

"Find the king!" Viaud ordered his men.

"And send for a doctor," added Friard automatically, although he knew from one look at the Maistre's pale face that it was too late.

"I—I tried to stop him, Alain." Ruaud tried to speak again

and Friard saw the desperation in his eyes as one hand rose to try to grip his coat.

"We'll get his majesty back," Alain said staunchly. "You know you can count on us."

"Be caref—" Ruaud began to cough and a sudden gush of blood drowned his words. His blue eyes, which had been fixed on Friard's face, lost their focus and stared through Friard, beyond him. The hand that had been grasping at his collar fell away. "Maistre? Maistre!" Friard's voice broke. Ruaud was gone. He had died trying to protect the king, whom he had loved as dearly as a son. He laid the Maistre gently down on the tiles and drew a shaking hand over his eyes, closing the lids.

Viaud, coming back down the aisle, stopped abruptly. He knelt beside his commander's body and began to murmur the words of the Sergian prayer for the dying. Friard tried to join in but his voice was choked with tears. He wanted time to mourn the Maistre properly, but if he had understood Ruaud's dying words correctly, they were faced with an unprecedented crisis. Francia had lost not only the head of the Commanderie but her king, who had been abducted by one of the daemons he had been trying to defeat.

PART III

CHAPTER 1

One moment, all the bells of Mirom were dinning out a joyful cacophony in celebration of the birth of Prince Rostevan, heir to the Empire of New Rossiya. Then the sky began to darken.

At first Celestine thought it no more than an oncoming thunderstorm, blowing inland off the Straits.

I must find shelter before the storm breaks.

Alone and destitute, she had arrived a day earlier in the bustling capital of Muscobar and had been trudging from theater to theater in search of work. If she had been rash enough to use her real name, the concert managers would have fought for her to appear in their halls and opera houses. But she was a wanted woman on the run from the Francian Inquisition. She could not afford to reveal her true identity.

She was desperately hungry, having spent the last of her money on paying her passage to the city, and the only way she knew to earn a living was by her voice. Yet no one was interested enough in a shabbily dressed woman to bother to ask to hear her sing. Time after time, she was turned away at the stage door. "We're not auditioning. Come back next month."

If only I weren't so light-headed, I could think straight enough to work out a plan.

Around her, people were gazing up at the sky and pointing. Celestine looked up too, wondering if it might be an eclipse of the sun, not a storm after all. There was an eerie, lurid quality to the remaining daylight that made her feel uneasy. The stout flower seller on the corner of the square began to pack away, muttering as she waddled toward her cart with buckets of autumn flowers: purple asters, bronze and gold chrysanthemums. A delicious smell of frying batter drifted across from where a stallholder was cooking *blinis* and Celestine felt her empty stomach rumble.

"*Celestine. Celestine!*" The Faie was calling, the urgent voice piercing her mind like a silvered barb. Celestine looked around the wide square, wondering where she could go to speak with the Faie undisturbed. The *blini* stallholder had raised his eyes to heaven, one hand extended, as if he were anticipating rain. Celestine wavered, torn between her need for food and the Faie's increasingly frantic cries.

"*The unimaginable is happening. This darkness is leaking from the Realm of Shadows.*"

"The Realm of Shadows?" Celestine whispered. "Isn't that a sign that the world is about to end?" The Holy Texts were full of warnings about the end of the world, which would be preceded by a great darkness.

"*My father. Are the Drakhaouls trying to set my father free?*"

Why had the Faie begun to talk of her father? How could an aethyrial spirit have a mother or a father? Celestine, head spinning from lack of food, began to wonder if she was hallucinating.

The darkness was drifting across the sky from the south, like tendrils of smoke unfurling, then merging together to blot out the sun. And it was growing colder as the light was extinguished. The Muscobites began to show signs of alarm, some running, others making the holy sign across their bodies. Celestine saw many making their way up the wide steps of the church opposite, whose bells had been ringing out so joyfully only a few minutes before. As a Guerrier of the Sergian Commanderie, her first instinct was to follow them into a holy place for protection. But, she remembered with a grimace, she had forfeited her right to be called Guerrier when she had drugged the two Inquisition officers sent to arrest her.

In the eyes of the Order, I'm now a criminal on the run.

No, worse than a criminal, I'm a practitioner of the For-bidden Arts.

So she ran in the opposite direction, going against the increasing tide of people hurrying to the church as the darkness spread.

The Water Gardens were usually thronged with people at that time of day, many visiting the Tea Pavilion overlooking the lake for ices and other delicious refreshments. As it was daytime, no one had troubled to light the lamps that illumined the winding gravel paths, and Celestine had to make her way through the gathering gloom. She sought refuge in a gazebo near the pavilion. The gazebo smelled of damp and rotting wood; the autumn leaves were falling fast, clogging the still grey lake waters.

Celestine put down her little bag of belongings and sat gazing out at the darkening gardens. Her empty stomach ached.

The waitresses were leaving the pavilion, gazing up at the sky and talking anxiously about thunderstorms; a waiter stopped to lock the door before hurrying after them. Celestine crept out and tried the door handle. But as hard as she rattled it, the lock resisted all her efforts to force it. She went around the back, only to discover that the Tea Pavilion was impregnable. Built on stilts like a Khitari teahouse, with scarlet-and-black lacquered wood and a low, sloping roof, the windows overlooked the lake and were protected by carved grilles. In her frustration, she kicked at the door, bruising her toes.

She sank down on the top step, defeated, leaning her back against the unyielding door. And then she began to laugh, hard, painful, self-deprecating laughter that only made her empty stomach hurt more.

"How did I come to this?" she gasped, wiping the tears of laughter from her eyes. "Where did I go wrong?"

"*You're weak from lack of food,*" said the Faie. "*Let me help you.*" In the fast-increasing gloom, the little burst of white energy that broke the lock was bright as lightning, but no one was around to see, only the moorhens and ornamental ducks, who let out startled shrieks in the reeds below.

* * *

There was still hot water in the samovar. With shaking fingers, Celestine eagerly filled a teapot with bergamot tea, leaving it to brew as she searched the little kitchen for food. The Tea Pavilion was famed for its ice creams, but she was too cold and weak to go down into the icehouse. But the staff had left in such a hurry that she soon found apple and plum jam and some delicious little pancakes filled with curd cheese and honey. She was so famished that she crammed them into her mouth, hardly bothering to chew, even though her empty stomach soon protested at the sudden onslaught.

As Linnaius climbed out of his sky craft onto the lawns at Erinaskoe, the Empress herself came running to meet him, her eyes reddened as if she had been weeping, her hair unbound, her clothes disheveled.

"Magus," she said, her voice low and harsh, "a Drakhaoul has taken my baby. It attacked me—and took Rostevan." Tears leaked from her eyes. "Eugene has gone after it. But I fear—"

"A Drakhaoul?" Linnaius repeated. There was a sinister pattern emerging and he dreaded to think what the outcome might be.

"It looked like Andrei. It spoke like Andrei," she said, "but then it changed. It killed Valery when he tried to stop it. Why would my brother kill his best friend? Why would he steal my son?"

Why indeed? Linnaius thought grimly. One Drakhaoul had already abducted Eugene's daughter, Karila, from Swanholm. Now another had stolen Rostevan. If his worst fears were correct, they must be planning to sacrifice the children at the Serpent Gate to set free their master, Prince Nagazdiel, from the Realm of Shadows. Karila was a frail, sickly child, but he cared for her, and he could not bear the thought that the daemons were subjecting her to such an ordeal, let alone her newborn baby brother.

Astasia put her hand on his. "Magus," she said through her tears, "I know that I've spoken ill of you in the past.

But please, if you can forgive me, go and help Eugene get our children back."

"Will Lord Gavril come, Belberith?" Eugene whispered to his Drakhaoul as he gazed out over the rich blue of the Southern Ocean. "Or will he side with the other Drakhaouls against us?" For every minute that he waited, the danger to his children increased, and he was almost sick with anxiety.

"*He is here.*"

A shadow darkened the sun. Eugene turned instinctively to see Lord Gavril swooping down from the cloudless sky to land beside him on the grassy cliff.

"What do you want, Lord Emperor?"

They had been bitter enemies and there was still an unspoken tension between them. But Eugene was desperate. He said, blinking back tears, "They've stolen my children." And he never wept.

"They? The other Drakhaouls?"

"Help me, Nagarian. This is all my fault. I released these monsters. I have to destroy them, before they—" Eugene broke off, choking on the words. "I want to put things to rights again."

A glint of sapphire flame kindled in Lord Gavril's eyes. "Before they open the Serpent Gate?"

" 'Only by the sacrifice of the Emperor's children can that Door ever be opened again and the dread prince Nagazdiel released,' " quoted Eugene.

"We have to stop them," said Lord Gavril in a low, tight voice.

"It's gone very dark." Even as they had been speaking, Eugene had become aware of a change in the skies. "Is there a storm coming?"

Gavril gazed upward. "This is no storm." The black clouds were uncoiling, like a nest of shadowy serpents spilling out across the sky. "This is coming from the Serpent Gate."

Eugene could wait no longer. He clapped Lord Gavril on the shoulder. "Are you with me, Nagarian?" he cried. "You and I, together against the others?"

And he leaped into the darkening air. As he wheeled

around on outspread wings, Lord Gavril took off, shouting out, "Do you remember the way to Ty Nagar?"

"Just steer into the heart of the darkness!"

Celestine rested her head against the window frame as the darkness blotted out the last of the sun. As she was slipping into a doze, she felt a sudden charge of wild, elemental energy in the air. She flung open the door to see the trees in the darkened gardens swaying wildly in the rush of a tremendous wind.

"Kaspar Linnaius!" she screamed into the turbulent, windswept darkness. "Is all this *your* doing?"

CHAPTER 2

Alain Friard bowed as Queen Aliénor entered the ruined interior of the Chapel of Saint Meriadec, leaning heavily on her cane. He saw her gaze at the bloodstained tiles and the colored glass fragments littering the floor beneath the broken windows.

"Where is my son?" she demanded. "Where is the king?"

Alain Friard had been dreading this question. "We have found no trace of the king, majesty."

"No trace?" repeated the queen. "Your Commanderie will have much to answer for if he's been harmed, Captain! Especially de Lanvaux; I always said that man was a bad influence on my son."

"The Maistre was dying when we found him," said Friard hotly. "He said that a winged daemon had attacked him and carried off the king. I believe, majesty, that Maistre de Lanvaux died trying to protect your son."

"Winged daemon? Oh please, Captain, don't insult my intelligence." Aliénor struck the tiled floor with her silver-tipped cane. "Tielen agents, more likely. Where were your Guerriers when Enguerrand was kidnapped?"

Friard looked away, unable to sustain her accusing gaze. He knew it would grieve him to his dying day that he had not been at the Maistre's side to defend him and the king against the daemon.

"You will order all your Guerriers to search for my son, do you understand me? All other missions are to be abandoned until Enguerrand is found."

"I understand, majesty."

"This abduction is almost certainly a countermove on

the part of the Emperor's secret service," continued the queen, adding, "and if he has come to any harm, Eugene of Tielen will pay—and pay dearly."

"Maistre." Jagu stood looking down at Ruaud de Lanvaux's body in the golden light of the many funerary candles burning around his bier. The Grand Maistre's waxen face was calm in death, all signs of his final agony erased by the skillful work of the embalmers. Jagu heard a sob, and glancing at his captain, saw that Alain Friard was weeping unashamedly as he stood at attention before their leader's coffin.

"How could such a thing happen?" he asked Friard, his voice low and unsteady. "Murdered—and, of all places, in Saint Meriadec's?" He wanted answers to the questions crowding his mind; answers would keep the grief he could feel welling up inside him from spilling out.

Captain Friard saluted the coffin and took a step back; Jagu did the same, following him swiftly down the aisle. Other dignitaries, Commanderie and Inquisition, were arriving to pay their respects. He saw Friard take out a handkerchief and blow his nose. "What do you say we go drink a farewell glass to the Maistre?" he said as they emerged from the chapel. Jagu understood; in the noisy bustle of a city tavern, they'd be able to speak frankly with less fear of being overheard than in the Forteresse.

The Pomme de Pin tavern was crowded, but the two Guerriers made their way through the drinkers to a secluded corner table.

"Your usual, Captain?" The landlord brought over a bottle of red wine from Provença; Jagu poured two glasses and touched his to Friard's. "To the Maistre."

Friard nodded and they both drank in silence.

"And to his successor," Jagu said, raising his glass to Friard.

Friard glumly shook his head. "Haven't you heard? The queen's summoned Maistre Donatien back from retirement."

"But by rights it should be you—" began Jagu.

"Listen, Jagu." Friard leaned close in and began to speak in a quiet, urgent tone. "A great deal happened while you were in Smarna. A great deal that we've had to keep quiet. Don't you think it's strange that the Maistre's favorite student is nowhere to be seen? Wouldn't you expect to see him paying his respects at his tutor's bier?"

"Not the ki—"

"The word from the palace is that his majesty is prostrate with grief. But I was the first to reach Ruaud." His voice became unsteady. "I fear the king may have been abducted—by a Drakhaoul."

Jagu was still recovering from his recent daemonic encounter in Smarna. "A Drakhaoul?" One hand shot out and gripped Friard's arm. "Was it Lord Gavril? Describe it."

"It was golden—almost too dazzlingly bright to look at, the priests at Saint Meriadec's said. But that's not the first time it's been seen here."

"So it wasn't Lord Gavril."

"Lord Gavril was here too, at the Forteresse. The king used Sergius's Staff against him. But . . . *others* came."

The noisy hubbub around them seemed to recede. "Others?" Jagu leaned closer still to Friard. "Other Drakhaouls? How many?"

"Four of the Seven were here. They destroyed the Staff."

"Four?" Lord Gavril in his Drakhaoul-form had been terrifying enough; Jagu still remembered the way the air had turned blue-black around him as he flew, shimmering with the same penetrating cold fire as the creature's glittering eyes. Eyes that had burned with a bleak and relentless anger. Eyes that had chilled him to the depths of his soul.

But four of them let loose . . .

"We're powerless against them, Jagu. Is this the beginning of the end of the world?"

"So the Staff was useless. And our mission was all in vain." Jagu released Friard's arm. Friard refilled their glasses, swilling the dark wine around in the glass, staring at it—through it—before taking a long, contemplative swig.

"So is Celestine back in Lutèce?" Jagu asked.

"Haven't you heard? Inquisitor Visant sent his men to arrest her. But she gave them the slip."

"It was Visant?" Jagu's heart juddered wildly with shock.

He had been dreading this possibility for years. And Celestine had become so headstrong of late that she had become careless. "What does the Inquisition want with Celestine?"

"Ruaud thought a great deal of you, you know, Jagu." The wine was loosening Friard's tongue. "He always spoke very highly of you."

Jagu stared at the pitted, wine-stained tabletop. Hearing Friard refer to the Maistre in the past tense brought home to him the brutal fact that his mentor was dead and could no longer protect Celestine from the Inquisitors.

"We're all marked as Ruaud's men," said Friard glumly, as though reading Jagu's thoughts. "If I were a betting man, I'd wager that you, Kilian, and I will soon be sent off on some obscure mission overseas. Just like Père Laorans, all those years ago."

"Kilian's in Lutèce?" At the mention of his friend's name, Jagu lifted his head. Kilian would help him get a better perspective on matters; his clear, cynical eye would see through the lies spun by the Inquisition.

As Jagu rose, Friard caught hold of him by the arm, pulling his face close to his own. "There were three priests assisting Ruaud," he said in a slurred undertone. "They were injured when the Drakhaoul took the king. But Visant's keeping them under lock and key, 'for their own protection.' I reckon he's interrogating them, Jagu, and he doesn't want anyone else to learn what they saw."

"And that's because . . ."

"There was a circle of Galizur marked on the chapel floor when we broke the door down. When I returned to the chapel, it had been erased."

"An exorcism? You don't mean . . ." Jagu wondered a moment whether the wine was talking, but the look in Friard's bloodshot eyes convinced him that he was talking the truth.

"Enguerrand *was* the Drakhaoul. Ruaud was trying to drive the daemon out of the king's body when it turned on him."

* * *

Is this the beginning of the end of the world?

Friard's drunken words echoed around Jagu's mind as he hurried through the darkening streets of Lutèce toward the Forteresse. His ordered life was fast crumbling about him. Ruaud was dead, and creatures of darkness, the daemon Drakhaouls, were wreaking havoc.

He reached the banks of the Sénon; the wide river churned as grey as the threatening sky overhead. A lightning bolt of memory threw him back suddenly to the moment he and Kilian had first sailed with the regiment for Enhirre. *She* had come to wave him good-bye, standing just a few yards from where he was now, the dawn sun catching glints in her hair. Until that moment, he had not dared to dream that she cared for him.

He stopped, gripping the rough stone wall, overwhelmed by a feeling of regret so strong it punched the breath from him, leaving him gasping.

If this is the end of the world, what am I doing here? I should never have left her side. He hit the balustrade with his clenched fist. She had become so distant, so evasive, during the last months. She had taken idiotic risks. She had used her father's secret grimoire, even though she had promised him she would never take such a risk again. Was it the Drakhaouls' destabilizing influence that was affecting her? What was causing her to behave so recklessly?

"Celestine," he murmured into the night. Since Henri de Joyeuse's death, he had stood by her, protecting her, supporting her.

Everything is falling apart around us. She needs me—and I have no idea where she is, or how to find her.

"So it's the end of the world and you didn't even invite your oldest friend to share one last bottle of wine?" Kilian's eyes glinted in the darkness.

Jagu held out the bottle he had brought from the tavern.

"You'd better come in." Kilian pulled him inside his room and shut the door. "We can't be seen to be setting a bad example to the cadets, can we?"

"It's getting too dark to see," said Jagu. He fumbled for his tinderbox and tried, with unsteady hands, to strike a spark to light the oil lamp.

"If this is the end, then I might as well be damned." Kilian's habitual bantering tone had gone. His friend was looking at him oddly, almost as if he could not quite focus clearly on his face.

"Damned?" Jagu said, not understanding.

Kilian came closer. "You still don't get it, do you, Jagu? Although it's pretty well killed me to hide it from you."

"Come on, now, Kilian, if this is another of your jokes—" Jagu began. It was so dark that he could only just make out Kilian's face in the gloom—but he could see that all traces of malicious humor had faded from his eyes. He took a step back.

"If only it were." There was a throb of anger, almost self-disgust, in those few gritted words.

The Commanderie chapel bell began to din out, clanging a warning. As if in answer, the church bells of the city began to ring too, a frantic tocsin. Both men glanced at each other, caught in the same shared memory of the day, long ago, that the magus had infiltrated their school.

"The magus's mark?" Kilian reached out and caught Jagu by the left hand, pushing back his sleeve. The sigil gleamed in the gloom.

Jagu had been so wrapped up in his own thoughts that he had not noticed until then the tingle of fire that had begun to throb as if the magus were searing it into his skin anew. "What does it mean?" He gazed down at the mark. "Are the magi powerful enough to turn the skies dark? And why would they do such a thing?"

"It burns, doesn't it?" Kilian asked quietly. And before Jagu could snatch his wrist away, Kilian pressed his lips to the tender skin.

"K—Kilian?" Jagu retreated a step, finding his back against the wall. The growing dark, the ominous sense of impending doom, the frantic clanging of the bells, all conspired to confirm his sense that the world had gone mad.

Kilian's face hovered close to his. "Stop. Enough. Don't play games at a time like this."

"I've never been more serious in all my life, Jagu." The look in Kilian's pale eyes was enough to convince Jagu. He had never seen Kilian so serious or so intent. He was too bemused to react swiftly enough. "You'll never forgive me for this," whispered Kilian in the darkness, and kissed him.

Someone pounded on the door. "Lieutenant Guyomard! Captain Friard wants you in the Drill Hall and on the double."

Kilian slowly relaxed his grip on Jagu, who was still in shock. He had had no idea that Kilian might have hidden such strong feelings for him, feelings that went so far beyond friendship . . .

"Duty calls, even at the end of the world." And Kilian flashed him a wry, reckless grin. But Jagu saw straight through to the raw humiliation beneath. "Well, you can't blame me for trying."

CHAPTER 3

Celestine had not felt so abandoned since Maman had died. Memories of her desperate struggle to exist alone on the streets of Lutèce came crowding back.

"What am I doing here, all alone, in a foreign city?"

"*You're not alone.*" The Faie's voice issued from the traveling bag in which her father's precious book was concealed. Her pale radiance lit the gloom as she hovered beside Celestine, her eyes brimming with concern. "*I'm still here with you.*"

"But what can I do?" Celestine said. She heard her own voice as if from far away, listless and despairing. "Celestine de Joyeuse is well-known in Mirom. If I use my own name, it will only draw the Inquisition here, and it will all be over."

"*Then you must become someone else. And I can help you.*" The Faie bent over her consolingly. "*If you're willing to let me, Celestine, I can change your appearance.*"

"If I had enough money to buy henna or walnut juice, I could dye my hair . . ." Light-headed with lack of food, Celestine was not concentrating on what the Faie was saying.

"*If I merge with you, I can make other people see you differently, Celestine.*"

Celestine looked into the Faie's luminous eyes, hovering so close to her own. "You could . . . merge with me?" The prospect of the Faie sharing her mind and body stirred up disturbing thoughts. *Suppose the Faie tried to take control of me? I'd be powerless to stop her.* Celestine blinked. "Is it the darkness outside, or are you growing brighter, Faie?"

"*Become one with me and no one, not even Jagu de*

Rustéphan, will recognize you." The Faie opened her arms to Celestine, as if to embrace her, a calm smile warming her features.

The luminous figure came toward Celestine until the dazzle of light was so intense that it obliterated everything else.

A tall figure appears out of the golden mist. And then another—and another, a host of bright ones. Their bodies gleam so fiercely that she has to look away, her eyes dazzled by their radiance. Cords of flame whip from their outstretched hands and coil around her father, binding him. She hears his cry of agony as the glowing bonds bite deep into his body.

"This time you won't escape." As her eyes become accustomed to the light, she sees that the speaker is as golden-fair as her father is dark, cloaked in a glimmer of folded wings. "Your rebellion is over."

"Father!" she cries. Heedless of her own safety, she hurls herself toward him. The bright one raises one hand to stop her and she falls at his feet.

"So. You're his child." There is such contempt—and anger—in his voice that she cowers in fear.

"Take me. But spare her." Her father's face is distorted with pain; each word gasped out. "She didn't ask to be born my child."

"But she's an abomination. She's a half-breed, neither angel nor mortal. Her very existence offends the natural order." The bright one stalks around her until the penetrating fire in his eyes makes her feel as if her flesh is burning. "Child of a forbidden union. You were never meant to be." He bends down and takes hold of her face in one hand, gazing into her eyes as if reading her innermost thoughts. The touch of his fingers is hot as flame and she cries out. "She is aethyr, with her father's powers and a mortal body. When this body decays, as all mortal bodies must, where will she go then? Will she take another mortal body? What will happen to that mortal soul if she does? The balance between our worlds will be destroyed."

"Don't hurt her, Galizur, I beg you."

"You? Beg me?" The one her father has called Galizur flings her aside and goes to stand over her father. "So only now the rebel prince who has split our realm with his pride and set brother against brother, deigns to beg—and for the insignificant life of this misbegotten creature?" He raises his arm and she sees dazedly that he has drawn his sword. Gouts of flame drip from its fiery blade and sizzle as they touch the ground. "What of your followers?" He points the tip at her father's throat. "All those who followed you foolishly, blindly, faithfully, and are now condemned to eternal imprisonment? Why don't you beg for them?"

"They knew what they were doing," her father says, his proud, dark eyes staring back at Galizur. "This one is only a child. She is innocent. Her only crime is to have been born my daughter."

"I've heard enough. Take him away."

"Father!" An anguished cry tears from her throat as they bear him away into the night, their fast-beating wings stirring up a great wind that knocks her back to the ground. "Father!"

CHAPTER 4

The Drakhaouls moved toward the gaping maw of the Serpent Gate, bringing the children toward the sacrificial stone.

Eugene halted, hovering overhead, his plan crumbling to dust. If he attacked the other Drakhaouls, he would almost certainly kill his children too. But as the crimson light streaming from the Eye lit the figures approaching the yawning archway, he knew that if he did not act, there would be no future for his children anyway. For he had glimpsed the shadow waiting for the blood sacrifice on the far side of the Gate. At any moment, the Gate would open and Nagazdiel would enter the mortal world.

It has to be now.

The crimson light flickered. High above his head, Eugene saw that Gavril Nagarian was trying to pry the Eye of Nagar from the stone serpent's head. And Sahariel was out to stop him.

Eugene raised his hand, pointing at Sahariel. He loosed a shaft of malachite fire straight at the Drakhaoul's head. The shaft caught Sahariel as he slewed around in the air, searing into his neck and shoulder, half-severing one of his scarlet wings.

Sahariel let out a rasping hiss of pain. Broken wing alight, he plunged from the top of the Gate to crash onto the ground below.

The empty, uncharted sea below Linnaius's sky craft lay like a vast lake of ink. The shadow seeping from the Serpent Gate was blacker than a moonless night and it had shed a chill over the warm waters of the Southern Ocean. Linnaius shivered, pulling his cloak closer around him, willing the winds to carry the craft more swiftly.

It was disorienting navigating through pitch blackness with no moon or stars to guide him, and after a while Linnaius began to experience the disquieting sensation that, in spite of the rushing of the wind in the sail, he was going nowhere, hanging suspended in the dark of an eternal night.

Then he saw little bursts of fiery light in the far distance. He was a long way off still, and the explosions of jewel-bright flame looked like nothing more than the fireworks he had devised to amuse the guests at the Dievona Ball at Swanholm. But even from this distance, he realized that he was witnessing a battle between fallen angels. The chill dark air shuddered and crackled with each bolt of lethal daemonfire. The six Drakhaouls were fighting a desperate battle, divided between those who were determined to set free Prince Nagazdiel from his prison in the Realm of Shadows—and those who were equally determined to stop them.

"Eugene," Linnaius murmured, "did you get there in time? In time to save the children?"

"Eugene! Close the Gate." Eugene heard Gavril Nagarian's voice as if from very far away. "Close it *now*!"

Looking up into the swirling darkness, Eugene saw him winging high above the Serpent Gate, clutching the Eye.

"You and I together, Belberith," Eugene commanded. "Let's make one final effort."

"*Together*," Belberith echoed as Eugene lifted his hand, aiming at the snarling serpent's head at the crown of the arch.

"Stop." Adramelech stepped out in front of the Gate. Now that the rubies' maleficent light was extinguished, only his eyes could be seen, a glimmer of amethyst in the smoky darkness. "Destroy the Gate and you destroy your son."

Rostevan let out a faint whimper in Adramelech's arms. And Eugene heard Astasia's distraught voice telling him,

"It looked like Andrei. It sounded like Andrei. But it took our baby."

Until that moment he had not been certain. Now he knew for sure.

"Andrei?" he said. "Have you sunk so low that you would kill your own nephew? What kind of a monster have you become?"

Andrei was wandering in a dark nightmare, through a lightning-riven wilderness. He was lost.

Someone was calling out his name as if from a great distance away. And he heard the plaintive cry of a baby.

He looked down and saw, as if for the first time, the baby in his arms. He looked into the baby's blue eyes. His sister Astasia's eyes.

"What am I doing here?" he said, utterly bewildered.

The sky lit up with a brilliant burst of fire and Linnaius's little craft slewed from side to side, caught in the power of the blast. He clung on, desperately trying to regain control as he was sent hurtling down toward the ink-black sea. He managed to right the craft, skimming along the tops of the waves, just before another blinding flash of power sent the craft spinning.

"I can't even get close . . ." As he struggled to keep from crashing into the sea, he realized how pitiful his own powers as a magus were compared to the daemonic might of the Drakhaouls. How presumptuous he had been to think he would be able to help Eugene. There was nothing he could do but wait and watch helplessly, hoping against hope that Karila and little Rostevan had not been sacrificed on the ancient stone altar below the Serpent Gate.

Nilaihah came hurtling toward Gavril like a golden meteor, scattering sparks of fire in his trail.

"Give me Nagar's Eye!" The black night burst into flames of white gold as Nilaihah launched his attack.

"Look out, Nagarian!" yelled Eugene.

Instinctively, Gavril raised his hands to shield his eyes.

As Nilaihah's shaft of fire hit the rubies, the Eye of Nagar flew up into the air at the moment of impact—and shattered in a blinding explosion.

Linnaius caught a brief glimpse of the winged warriors as they clashed again, etched in flame against the night—and then came the conflagration.

Brighter than lightning, the explosion turned the black sky dazzling white. Linnaius felt his heart stop in shock—and then slowly stutter back to life. Winded, breathless, he felt the craft carried back across the dark waters by the force of the blast. He fought, but in vain; it tossed him helpless into the sea.

"*Now!*" Belberith's energy surged through Eugene's body. Green fire shot from his outstretched hand and hit the snarling serpent right in the center of the empty eye socket. The stone head burst into a thousand fragments.

Eugene fired again and again, pouring all his rage into Belberith's final assault.

The Gate fell in on itself, and a dust cloud rose, covering the clearing with pulverized stone.

"It's finished, Nagazdiel!" Eugene cried defiantly. "Yes, I opened the Serpent Gate—but now I've closed it, and it will stay closed forever!"

Linnaius's craft was light but strongly built by the craftsmen of Lake Taigal and as it bobbed up again, he clung on desperately to the side. And as he floated there, half-drowned, he saw an extraordinary sight. A great gateway had appeared on the horizon, trembling with silvered light that spilled in as if from another world. Linnaius blinked the stinging seawater from his eyes. Tall winged figures were moving, passing through the gateway, one by one. The shimmer of light began to dwindle, slowly fading, until only the darkness remained.

"They've gone," Linnaius whispered over the lapping sound of the waves. "The Drakhaouls have gone at last.

And the Serpent Gate has been destroyed. But at what price?" He dragged himself up over the side of the craft and collapsed onto the bottom, his soaked clothes leaking salt water. After a few moments, he forced himself to sit up. The Serpent Gate might have been closed at last—but where was Eugene? And the royal children?

"If he's still alive, he'll be exhausted after such a battle." Linnaius began to check the craft; it was better to concentrate on the practicalities of the situation than to think the worst. The sail was saturated with salt water but intact. And overhead, the black pall of shadow was beginning to disperse, revealing tiny pinpricks of light: the southern stars.

Maybe there was still hope . . .

Celestine came back to herself, huddled in the darkness. It had been too vivid to be a dream.

"*My father . . .* " whispered the Faie brokenly. "*I sensed his presence. But now he's gone . . .* "

"So that was *your* father?" Celestine was still filled with an overwhelming sense of loss and abandonment that she knew was not her own. "Was I seeing your memories, Faie?"

"*The Drakhaouls opened the Serpent Gate . . . but before he could escape, it closed again. It closed forever.*"

CHAPTER 5

Celestine opened her eyes to see a shaft of sunlight shining through the ivied window of the pavilion. She rubbed the sleep from her eyelids, wondering if she were still dreaming. But as she sat up, the stiffness in her limbs told her this was no dream.

"Daylight?"

"*The Gateway to the Realm of Shadows has been sealed. The Drakhaouls are finally gone—and your world is safe again.*"

Suddenly Celestine's body was racked by painful sobs that arose from a grief that was not her own.

"*I saw him. I saw my father!*" wept the Faie. "*But he was so changed that I hardly recognized him. And now he's all alone with no one to comfort him.*"

"Why is he all alone? Tell me what happened, Faie."

The Faie's sobs slowly subsided. "*I was the child of a forbidden union. My mother was mortal, my father an angel. And for rebelling against the Divine Will, he was stripped of his wings and imprisoned in the Realm of Shadows.*"

"Stripped . . . of his wings?" The image was so brutal and cruel that Celestine could hardly bear to imagine it. "But I thought that angels were creatures of light."

"*They have both a physical and an aethyrial body so that they can move between the worlds with ease.*"

"Yet you were born to a mortal woman?"

"*And because of my father's blood, I lived many years beyond the mortal span. And when, at length, my body became too weak and old to sustain me, this aethyrial form, that you see now, remained . . .*"

"Didn't you lock up yesterday, Nicolai?" The Tea Pavilion staff must have returned. "The door's ajar. Has someone broken in?"

In a panic, Celestine hurried to the back door and let herself out into the chill morning, hiding in the reeds. But the hungry ducks spotted her and set off, paddling toward her across the murky waters of the Lake, filling the air with their strident, greedy quacking. She fled, hurrying over to the gazebo, hoping that no one had noticed her.

In the clear autumn dawn of a new day, she saw her predicament all too clearly.

What a mess I've made of my life. The Drakhaouls are gone. Kaspar Linnaius is free. But I'm a fugitive, with nowhere left to run.

She slid down onto the bench, hugging her arms to herself against the chill.

"Was Linnaius telling me the truth?" she whispered. "Have I been pursuing the wrong man all this time? Was he really my father's mentor and friend? Have I thrown away everything—and all for nothing?"

Don't do this to yourself, Celestine, Jagu had begged her. *Don't perjure your immortal soul.*

Why did her heart ache when she thought of him? He had tried to stop her, and she had refused to listen to him. A bitter yearning swept through her, so strong that her blood seemed to burn.

"I hate you, Jagu de Rustéphan, for always being so insufferably, damnably right!" she cried aloud. "And now I've lost you forever. I can never go back to Francia. I have to make a new life for myself. I have to reinvent myself. I can never be Celestine de Joyeuse again."

"*Take a look at yourself,*" urged the Faie.

"You've changed me?" Celestine slowly raised her head. "But how?"

"Maela," said Celestine, staring down at her altered reflection. It was disorienting to catch sight of herself in the glassy lake and see a stranger staring back. "I shall become Maela Cassard, after my mother. I always thought it would make a good stage name." It wasn't the first time she'd had to learn to live with a new name, after all. She scrutinized her new features critically. The blue of her eyes was now the warm brown of amber, framed by darker brows and lashes, and her hair was no longer gold but a glossy chestnut. Even the tone of her skin had altered from palest porcelain to a more healthy, glowing complexion.

"How have you done this, Faie?" she asked, amazed. "Is it permanent? Can you change me back?"

"*Does it displease you? I was remembering how I . . .*" The Faie's soft voice trailed away.

"How *you* looked?" Celestine was wondering what the Faie meant. "Was that you in my dream, Faie? Did you show me your memories?"

"*But that was a long, long time ago . . .*"

Celestine went back to the gazebo. There was no one about yet, not even a gardener, but she judged it wise to collect her little bag of possessions and move on.

If only I had something else to sell. She had pawned all her jewelry but one piece to pay for her passage to Mirom. Her fingers closed around the last remaining item, which she had pinned to her dress: the jet mourning brooch given to her by Princess Adèle.

But it's my lucky charm. I can't pawn this, it's too precious.

The sky craft skimmed on above the Azure Ocean toward the western quadrant. The last smudges of darkness leaking from the Realm of Shadows had cleared, leaving the sky a radiant blue once more.

Kaspar Linnaius summoned the calmest, gentlest winds to bear his precious cargo back to Muscobar, and he concentrated his mind on weaving one breeze smoothly with another to steer them home. Beside him sat the Emperor, one arm around his daughter, Karila, his baby son, Rostevan, clasped close in the crook of his other arm. Like her brother, Karila had fallen into an exhausted sleep, her tousled fair head pillowed against her father's broad chest.

Linnaius assumed that Eugene was also asleep; his bruised face was pale and his head drooping. But after a while, Linnaius became aware that the Emperor's blue-grey eyes were fixed on him, keen as a wintry sky.

"You came to our rescue again, Kaspar," he said, his voice slurred with weariness. "How can I ever begin to thank you?"

"These last years that I've spent in your service have been the happiest of my life." Linnaius busied himself with adjusting the tiller. Never easy with expressing his feelings, this was proving even more difficult to say than he had anticipated. "But I have unfinished business that I must attend to urgently. I do not know how long it will take me . . . or indeed if I will ever return."

A long silence followed. Linnaius glanced up, wondering if Eugene had even heard him. And then a sigh escaped the Emperor's lips. Eugene was smiling at him—a sad, regretful smile. "I've been so fortunate to have you at my side all these years, old friend," he said. "But I've always known that this day would come, sooner or later. Go and with my blessing. God knows, I'll miss you . . ." His gaze shifted from Linnaius's face, staring beyond him into the vastness of the sky above and beyond. "And remember, there will always be a place at my court for you if ever you choose to return."

Linnaius bowed his head in thanks. Eugene's words had moved him more deeply than he cared to admit.

What is the matter with me? Why do I have so little control over my emotions since I returned from the Jade Springs? This is a weakness I can ill afford, when there is so much to be done.

The craft dipped suddenly and he forced himself to concentrate on the weaving of the soft, southern breezes with the fresh, lively winds that had begun to blow from the east as they flew on toward Muscobar. He was struggling to maintain control. Since boyhood he had been able to summon the translucent dragons of the air, the fierce and wayward *wouivres,* and bend them to his will. Now they were resisting him. It was taking all his energy to keep the craft aloft.

"Your powers—and mine—have begun to diminish." Anagini's warning thrummed repetitively on, like a melody that would not leave his brain.

I'll become a street singer. Celestine had been walking the pavements of Mirom all day and she was exhausted. *It's that or sell my body. And who would pay good money for such a sweaty, unwashed piece of flesh as I?*

There were prostitutes in plenty in Mirom; Celestine could not help but notice the ragged girls with hollow cheeks and dead eyes haunting the taverns by the quays, rouged and painted like dolls. Here, in the more prosperous quarters of the city, there were courtesans, immaculately dressed, flaunting their charms more discreetly as they strolled in the vaulted shopping arcades.

Do I have the courage to do what they do? Could I endure the intimate caresses of a stranger? The touch of a man's hands on my body? She shuddered. She had heard that men who paid for sexual favors often used their women badly, beating and tying them up, forcing them to perform obscene acts . . .

Celestine stared down at herself; she looked like a vagrant. Her only dress was stained and filthy from tramping the streets of the city, the hem caked with mud, and her shoes were scuffed and worn.

"If only you could be like the faie in the fairy tales and wave a magic wand to change my rags into elegant clothes," she said silently to the Faie. "And I could really do with a bath." The Muscobites favored communal bathing and Mirom had many luxurious public baths for men and women. "But cleanliness comes at a price here, and I don't have a sou to my name."

A carriage rattled by, splashing her with puddle water.

"Hey!" she cried, shaking her fist in vain as the driver continued, impervious. A gilded crest on the rear of the carriage caught the sun; it was the emblem of the Francian ambassador.

"Fabien d'Abrissard." She tried to squeeze the water from her dress. *He wouldn't even recognize me . . .*

She sank down on a doorstep, weak with hunger and despair.

Is it time to stop running? To go back to Francia and throw myself on the Commanderie's mercy?

For the fifth time that day Celestine passed the impressive pillared facade of the Imperial Theater. Built in the days of Grand Duke Alexei's father and renowned throughout the quadrant for its lavish productions of opera and ballet, the theater now displayed the gilded swan of Tielen entwined with the double-headed sea eagles of Muscobar. Around the back, the vast building was far less imposing—a brick shell stretching to the edge of a huddle of tenement buildings. And the artists' entrance was such an insignificant little door that Celestine passed by it twice without even noticing it.

She steeled herself and was about to knock when she heard raised voices inside. A stout woman stormed out, shouting furiously back over her shoulder in the Muscobite tongue and shaking her clenched fist. From within, a man's voice answered, equally heatedly. The woman turned and stamped away, muttering and shaking her head. Celestine understood well enough what must have happened. *Is this my chance?*

She put her head around the door and gazed down the passageway; like so many theaters, the backstage area was shabby, with peeling paint and bare floorboards.

"What do you want?" a surly voice demanded in the common tongue. Celestine saw a balding little man peering at her over the top of his half-rimmed spectacles.

"Work," she said, giving him her most appealing smile. "I'm a singer."

"I'm not hiring." He made a dismissive gesture. "Get out."

"At least let me sing for you—" Celestine tried to hide the desperation in her voice.

"Didn't you hear me? Unless you're good with a mop and a broom, I'm not interested."

"I'm good with a mop." The woman who'd just walked

out must have been a cleaner. "I grew up in a convent. I know how to work hard." She was so desperate that she no longer cared what she did as long as she had enough money to keep from starving or selling her body.

"You don't look very robust." He walked around her, staring at her critically. "You're thin as a lathe."

"I'm stronger than I look."

"What's your name? You're not a Muscobite, are you?"

"Maela. Maela Cassard."

"Francian, eh? What's a nice Francian girl like you doing so far from home?"

Celestine cast down her gaze, saying nothing.

"There was a man involved, don't tell me. And now he's left you? Well, I'm the stage manager here, my name's Grebin, and I don't stand for any goings-on backstage. So don't start making eyes at the stagehands, d'you understand me?"

Celestine nodded.

"I'll give you a week's trial. Starting now."

"Thank you!" Tears of gratitude filled Celestine's eyes.

The man grunted. "Save your thanks. You haven't seen what you'll be cleaning yet. Follow me."

Celestine hurried after him along a dark passageway, passing the dressing rooms. She caught glimpses of gaudy costumes hanging on rails and breathed in the stale-sweet smell of old powder and greasepaint. From farther in came the hollow sound of sawing and hammering; stagehands were at work on a vast canvas flat, painting a woodland scene. They glanced up as she passed by and one wolf-whistled.

"Get on with your work!" snapped the little man. As the passageway wound onward, a new smell made Celestine wrinkle her nose in disgust.

"Latrines," he announced, unlatching a door. Celestine took a step back, her eyes watering from the foul odor. "And when you've finished here, you're to sweep out the dressing rooms. Then report back to me so that I can inspect what you've done."

"I'll need clean water. And rags. A mop and bucket."

"You can draw water from the hand pump outside the stage door." He unlocked a cupboard and drew out a battered tin pail and a filthy mop. She stared at them in disbelief.

"Surely you can't expect me to make your theater clean with *that*." The words were out of her mouth before she realized they were far too cheeky for a cleaning girl.

"Still want the job?" He dangled the pail before her.

She nodded.

"Then get to work!"

CHAPTER 6

"A letter has arrived for you from the Emperor, your majesty."

Queen Aliénor extended one hand to take the letter from her equerry, aware that all the ministers' eyes were fixed upon her. She broke the imperial seal and scanned the neat secretarial hand, signed by the Emperor with a strong flourish. Well schooled as she was in maintaining her composure, she found it hard to disguise her bewilderment.

"Well! This is either the most ridiculous attempt to deceive us or . . ." She found herself at a loss for words and passed the letter to Chancellor Aiguillon, who took it and, adjusting his monocle, read it aloud to the ministers.

" 'I feel it is my duty to inform your majesty that your son Enguerrand is currently in the Spice Islands, in company with Lady Aude de Provença and Prince Andrei Orlov.' "

"The—the Spice Islands?" Josselin de Craon broke the astounded silence. "But that's impossible. Enguerrand and Aude were here, in Lutèce, only a few days ago. The Spice Islands are not even in the same quadrant!"

"It can take the swiftest spice clipper up to six months to reach the Spice Islands," put in Admiral de Romorantin.

"Is it possible that those priests spoke the truth?" Aliénor heard herself musing aloud. "That a Drakhaoul abducted my son and Aude?"

"With respect, majesty, the Emperor only mentions Prince Andrei, not Lord Gavril," murmured Aiguillon.

"Admiral, do we have any ships in the area?" Aliénor ignored him. "How long will it take to send a message to them?"

"It could take quite a while, depending on—"

"Then see to it without delay!" And she swept out of the council chamber, determined not to let the councillors see how worried she was about her son.

Aliénor rose as Hugues Donatien entered the room. Her heart swelled at the sight of him. *It's been too long, dear Hugues. Why didn't I bring you back before now?* He had been banished for six years, yet the mountain air of Saint Bernez Monastery had tanned his skin, lending him a look of rugged good health. She had stayed in constant communication with him, sending secret couriers who had ingeniously managed to evade Ruaud de Lanvaux's agents. But she had sorely missed Donatien's reassuring presence and wise counsel. In spite of her concerns about Enguerrand, she felt as if all would be well again, with Donatien at her side.

"Welcome back, Grand Maistre," she said and heard her voice tremble as if she were a giddy schoolgirl. She held out her hand and he went down on one knee to kiss it, pressing it with such a firm and comforting grip in his own that all her concerns began to melt away. -

"It's good to see you, your majesty," he said and his grey eyes were filled with warmth.

"Your banishment was a grave error on the part of Maistre de Lanvaux," she said, giving Captain Friard a cold and meaningful glance. "You may all leave us now. Maistre Donatien and I have much to discuss." When her ladies and Friard had withdrawn, she let the formal tone drop and went to sit by the crackling log fire, beckoning Donatien to join her. "Plaisaunces is so drafty in winter, Hugues. Besides, I think we're less likely to be overheard over here."

"We've had blizzards up in the mountains. This seems positively warm by comparison." He sat down beside her. "So, still no news of Enguerrand?"

She shook her head. "That upstart Eugene sent us a letter informing us that Enguerrand is alive. In the Spice Islands. And Aude de Provença is with him. Since then, nothing. It's the other side of the world, six months' journey by sea. How did they get there so swiftly, Hugues? And why did they run away? Did he seduce her? Were they eloping? The girl's only fifteen! It'll cause a scandal if it gets out. But how could Eugene know such a thing?" There was so much that didn't make any sense at all. "And you can't believe the terrible rumors that Ruaud's faction is promulgating, implicating my son in his murder! As if Enguerrand were capable of such a thing."

Hugues Donatien laid his hand on hers. "Dearest Aliénor, please don't worry. I'm only sorry that you've had to bear this burden alone." His eyes were grave and his tone so sympathetic that she had to bite her lip not to cry. And she had not once allowed herself the luxury of tears throughout this crisis.

"But is it a Tielen plot? Have they kidnapped Enguerrand? Or has he just run away from his responsibilities? Ruaud filled his head with all kinds of nonsense. The boy was obsessed with the idea that he was Saint Sergius's successor!"

"If this is some contrivance of the Emperor's, designed to destabilize Francia, then we will just have to show Eugene that we are not so easily undermined. There is another heir to the throne. Your daughter."

"*Adèle?*"

"Ilsevir of Allegonde *and* Adèle could rule together," Donatien corrected her gently. "Just think what a strong front Allegonde and Francia united would present to counteract Eugene's hunger for power."

Aliénor hesitated. "An Allegondan prince on the throne of Francia? Wouldn't that stir up resentment among the nobles? Especially my cousin Raimon? We don't want a home-grown rebellion on top of our other concerns."

Donatien smiled at her, his grey eyes crinkling up into a comforting expression. "But Ilsevir is the ideal man to calm the nobles' concerns. He's cultured. He's pious. He will make an excellent king."

Jagu's fingers moved deftly over the yellowed keys of the organ at Saint Meriadec's. His feet pressed the deep bass notes, building the final bars of Jolivert's "Chromatic Prelude" into a terrifying climax. He knew that if he pulled open certain stops at this moment, he could make the old stones and wooden pews resonate with the thunderous power of the last chords. He had no doubt that Jolivert had been possessed by some daemonic vision of hell when he wrote this furious turbulence of notes. As he practiced its fiendishly difficult chromatic runs, the dark harmonies brought back the terror he had felt when the skies over Lutèce turned black as night . . .

He hit a wrong note, then another. *Mustn't let my mind drift.*

Don't lose concentration for a second here, Henri de Joyeuse had warned him once as his swift-moving fingers got all knotted up and a horrible sound like the braying of a herd of donkeys issued from the pipes. "If you don't prepare for this sequence, with your thumb passing underneath the third and fourth fingers . . . pfft! Donkeys!" And he had given Jagu a swift smile as he leaned forward to mark the music with the new fingering . . .

"More air!" Jagu called down to the two bellows boys and heard them groan in response as he attacked the final passage yet again. Only when he tackled a task as challenging as that could he try to lose himself in the music and forget about Celestine. Though Saint Meriadec's was filled with memories; the first time they had ever met was here on a wet autumn afternoon. He had been seventeen, daring to play this prelude with all the brash confidence of youth . . . and she had been in the choir, a novice from the Sisters of Charity. He had never heard a voice so sweet, so clear as hers. From up in the organ loft, it had sounded to him as if a young angel were singing in the dim recesses of the old church . . .

His fingers slipped again and lost the momentum of the sequence of cascading runs.

"Damn!"

"Swearing in church, Lieutenant?" came a mocking voice from down below. "You'll have to do penance to atone for your sin."

"Kilian?" Jagu swung his legs over the narrow bench and peered down into the church to see Kilian's pale green eyes glinting up at him from the gloom. He heard sniggering from the bellows boys.

"Practice time's over," Kilian called up. "Friard's summoned us to the Forteresse. Urgently."

"Urgently?" Jagu pushed in the stops and pulled the wooden cover over the manuals. He wasn't due back until six o'clock. He hurried down the spiral stair and tossed the bellows boys a coin each. "You're off duty early today, boys." As they scampered away, he hurried after Kilian, who was already halfway down the nave. "So what's this all about?"

"We're to be sent back to Ondhessar." Kilian set off down the avenue at a brisk pace, his military greatcoat swinging open as he walked.

"*What?*" For a brief second, Jagu took the bait.

Kilian stopped, turning to face him. "Ah, you're still so much fun to tease, Jagu."

These days, it seemed to Jagu that Kilian's little jokes were forced, and that when he smiled, only the corners of his lips crinkled upward, while his eyes remained distant, even cold. But then it was hardly surprising, given what had happened on the day of the great darkness. Kilian had revealed his innermost feelings—and what had Jagu done? He had rejected him. He had done it as gently, as honestly, as he could. But there was a new awkwardness between them. Kilian had laughed the incident away as they hurried to the drill hall. "I really had you worried there, didn't I, Jagu? You should have seen the look on your face. You really thought I was going to jump your bones then and there! Well, at least my little diversion distracted you from worrying about the end of the world." Tacitly, Jagu had played along with this, bursting into stupefied laughter. "Oh, you really had me fooled, Kilian. Damn you, you'd even joke on the edge of the Abyss." But he had seen the earlier look in Kilian's eyes, both hurt and shamed. It must have cost him dear to reveal so much of his inner feelings—and dearer still to be rejected.

"I haven't a clue what all this is about," Kilian flung back over his shoulder, "but I don't think they're going to give us a raise in pay and a day off."

* * *

Jagu glanced uneasily at his fellow officers who had been summoned to the Grand Maistre's study. Of Ruaud de Lanvaux's elite squad only he, Viaud, Friard, and Kilian remained. Père Judicael was too frail to leave his rooms these days. There were others here he recognized from his cadet days, but while he had been assigned to special duties overseas, he had lost touch with many of his contemporaries.

The inner door opened and three men emerged from the Grand Maistre's private chapel. All the Commanderie officers turned to stare as Captain Friard ushered in Haute Inquisitor Visant—and Hugues Donatien.

"Gentlemen," said Donatien, smiling at them, "I have just come from her majesty and I have the honor to inform you that she has appointed me Grand Maistre of the order."

Jagu felt a sharp nudge in the ribs. "Your mouth's open," Kilian whispered to him.

"The western quadrant is still unstable. And so her majesty has asked me to do all I can to protect the safety of the realm." Donatien's smile faded. "We live in difficult times, gentlemen, and it is our duty to set an example to the people of Francia. We must be seen to be above suspicion, upholders of the Sergian Code. If there is corruption in our ranks, we must weed it out."

Jagu caught Alain Friard's eye; the captain looked utterly dumbfounded. By rights, he should have been promoted to lead the Commanderie. But Queen Aliénor had marked him as Ruaud de Lanvaux's right-hand man and confidant. *Perhaps Kilian's quip about being sent back to Ondhessar was more accurate than he could have imagined; we're all four marked as Lanvaux's followers. And Celestine . . .*

His heart felt chilled.

Celestine has never been in greater danger.

"You've served the order with distinction, Lieutenant." Maistre Donatien looked up from an open dossier, fixing Jagu with a benign and approving look. This only increased Jagu's sense of unease. "You were commended for your

bravery at Ondhessar. You and your partner saved the lives
of Prince Ilsevir and Princess Adèle. And you arrested Kaspar Linnaius together. You've worked as a team for six
years. So, where is she now?"

Here it comes. "I don't know, Maistre Donatien," Jagu
said. It was the truth, after all. Celestine had chosen to disappear. Her behavior had become more and more secretive
on their mission in Smarna. It still hurt him to think that
she no longer trusted him enough to confide in him—unless
she had been trying to save him from just such an interrogation. If he knew nothing, then he couldn't be accused of
withholding essential information from the Inquisition.

"Listen, Lieutenant." Donatien's tone was still benign but
Jagu detected a steely will beneath. "The Commanderie's
reputation is at stake. Your partner has been using the Forbidden Arts. Were you aware that she poisoned the two Inquisition agents sent to arrest her? They nearly died and
neither man will ever be fit for active service again."

"Poison?" Jagu took a step back. Had Celestine intended
to kill them? Or had she become careless in her use of the
potions and spells in her father's grimoire? She had promised him never to resort to magic again after the incident in
Azhkendir, and yet in Smarna he had discovered her using
another potion to charm secrets from Lord Nagarian's
mother, Elysia. It was as if she had begun to lose control.
Having employed one spell, she could not resist trying another, then another . . .

"She must be stopped, Lieutenant." Donatien's voice
penetrated his worried reverie. "She is a danger to herself,
as well as to others. Above all—and this is the tragedy of the
situation—she has brought the Commanderie's name into
disrepute."

Jagu found himself nodding in helpless agreement.

"You know her better than anyone. I want you to go after her and bring her back before she loses all self-control."

"But I don't even know where to start my search."

"She was last seen in Muscobar. She may have friends
there who are sheltering her."

Jagu felt as if a constricting hand had begun to tighten

about his throat. He swallowed hard. One day he had feared it would come to this. Had the spirit in her father's grimoire taken control of her, compelling her to do its will? Celestine had seemed so . . . *different* in Smarna—willful, devious, even cruel. If he could exorcise the spirit, would she revert to her true sweet-natured self? And would that be enough to placate the new Grand Maistre of the Commanderie? Or would Donatien hand her over to Visant and put her through the ordeal of a trial for heresy?

"Well, Lieutenant?" Donatien was regarding him with a penetrating look quite different from his earlier kindly expression.

"You're asking me to betray my partner?"

"I'm merely reminding you of the oath you took when you became a Guerrier. She has quite obviously forgotten hers. I'm talking about integrity, Lieutenant. I want the people of Francia to look to the Commanderie as a small but steadfast flame burning in the darkness of an uncertain world."

Then Donatien's tone softened. "The demoiselle has served Francia faithfully," he said. "We must help and support our own if they stray and help them to find their way back to the light."

The intensity of Donatien's words took Jagu by surprise. He had to admit to himself that the Maistre was right. If the Guerriers were to be trusted in such troubled times, if they were to maintain their spotless reputation as the upholders of truth, they must be seen to punish anyone who betrayed the order.

"Well, Lieutenant?" Donatien held out his hand; his ring of office glinted dully. Jagu hesitated. Then, trying to ignore the heaviness about his heart, he knelt before the Grand Maistre and kissed his ring. When he stood up, Donatien was smiling at him but it was a triumphant smile, as if the Maistre had just won a significant victory.

Jagu shouldered his knapsack and began to descend the steep stone steps that led down to the river. Seagoing barques lay at anchor beside the quay, taking on their first passengers of the day for the journey to the port of Fenez-Tyr.

"Hey, Jagu!"

He turned and, gazing upward, saw Kilian hurrying along the busy quay, pushing through the crowd, greatcoat flapping open as he ran, the rising sun turning his pale hair from ginger to gold.

"Wait!" Kilian reached him and had to lean against the mossy quay wall to catch his breath.

"Is there a change in my orders?" Jagu asked warily. He was not in the mood for one of Kilian's practical jokes.

"Damn you," Kilian said, wheezing. "Trying to slip away without saying good-bye as usual? I really don't understand you."

Jagu shrugged. Why did Kilian always read him so accurately?

"I hope you've packed a fur coat."

Jagu shot Kilian a baffled look.

"Won't Muscobar be blanketed in snow by the time you get there? Doesn't the Nieva ice over in winter? You'll be traveling to Mirom by sleigh!" Kilian said, giving him a punch on the shoulder. "But are you really the right man for this mission?" The playfulness had gone; Kilian's voice dropped to a low, intense tone. "She's not the innocent young woman you remember. She's been corrupted by the Forbidden Arts."

"I know."

"Let me go in your stead."

"But you don't know Muscobar as I do—"

"Ask yourself; do you really have the detachment to arrest her and bring her back to stand trial?" Kilian gripped him by the shoulder, gazing searchingly into his eyes.

Jagu had been asking himself the same question throughout a long and sleepless night. He pulled away from Kilian's grip and walked off without answering.

"Be careful," Kilian called after him. "She's dangerous, Jagu."

The sound of many voices shouting in unison penetrated the council chamber.

"What is that racket?" demanded Aliénor.

"It is a crowd of citizens, majesty," said Aiguillon. He looked anxious. "They are protesting about the high price of bread."

"This is Francia, not Muscobar. Francians do not revolt when life gets hard!" she said severely. "Increase the guard around the palace and find out who the ringleaders are. I want them arrested."

"They want to see the king."

"Then I'll speak to them!"

"The harvest has been poor this year, majesty. And with this severe winter, we have reports of severe food shortages in several regions."

"So what are you going to do about it, Chancellor?" Aliénor fixed him with one of her most penetrating stares.

"We spent a great deal of our revenue on the invasion of Tielen. Ships, munitions, wages . . ." Aiguillon's voice died away as the queen continued to stare at him.

"Francia needs a king," Aliénor said severely. "Why is there still no word of my son?"

CHAPTER 7

Bouts of fever racked Enguerrand's body. He lay in the village chief's hut, out of the glare of the sun, drifting between disordered dreams and lucidity.

Time and again, he relived the moment when Ruaud had turned to him, his eyes filled with disbelief, and he had hurled the spear, pinning him to the chapel door like a butterfly to a collector's tray.

"Enguerrand."

Someone was calling his name. He came back to himself to find Aude staring anxiously down at him, her heart-shaped face a blur of sun-browned freckles. She leaned closer and touched his damp cheek.

"Tears?" she said uncertainly. "Enguerrand, were you crying in your sleep?"

"I—I killed him." Enguerrand choked on the words. "I killed Ruaud. And h—he was more a father to me than my own flesh-and-blood father ever was." Hot tears leaked from his eyes and he was so weak with fever that he could not hold them back. "How could I have done such a terrible thing?"

"I don't believe that you're capable of killing anyone," Aude said. She took hold of his hand and squeezed it between her own. Outside he could hear the faint lapping of the incoming tide. But in his mind he was half a world away, locked in the bloodstained church, with Ruaud's fast-glazing eyes still staring accusingly at him . . .

"He was trying to cast the daemon out of my body. He was trying to save me. But it was too strong. And now . . . now my only friend is gone, and his blood is on my conscience."

"You didn't kill him, the daemon did. The same daemon that made you abduct me."

"Aude, Aude, I'm so sorry I got you involved in all this . . ." Sunlight filtered down through the loosely woven roof of palm leaves, making checkered patterns on his face. It hurt his eyes.

"It's an adventure," she said, sponging his face with a cool, damp rag. "And so much more interesting than having to do embroidery with Maman!"

Andrei was sitting on the white sands, lifting his hot face to the first cool breezes of evening. He was idly wondering how often spice ships came past the islands. He was even wondering if he wanted to go back to the pressures of court life in Muscobar. Life seemed so much simpler here.

"Prince Andrei?" Aude came to sit beside him, wriggling her bare toes in the soft sand. "I'm worried about Enguerrand."

"Is his fever still high?"

Aude nodded. "What can we do? None of the islanders' remedies seem to be working. He's never been strong. He was often sick when he was a child, or so my mother told me. What shall I do if he . . . if he dies? It's my duty to my country to protect him."

"Why bother?" Oskar Alvborg's voice, dry and cynical, cut in before Andrei could reply. He came out from beneath the shade of the palm trees and flopped down on the sand beside Andrei. "You're deluding yourselves if you think Eugene's going to send anyone to rescue us."

"Take that back, Alvborg!" Andrei found Oskar's abrasive manner was becoming harder to ignore.

"I can just imagine the crocodile tears that Eugene will shed as he breaks the news of our absence." Oskar continued to embroider his theme with flamboyant gestures. "The rivals for his throne, all tragically lost at sea, or whatever plausible reason he invents to explain our sudden disappearances. How extraordinarily convenient for him!"

"You should have gone on the stage," muttered Andrei.

* * *

"Hello, there!"

Andrei started awake. He had fallen into a doze when he was supposed to be watching over Enguerrand.

"We've come to help!"

Aude appeared. "Did you hear? Someone called out in the common tongue."

"I'll go; you stay here. It could be slavers, pirates . . ."

She gazed at him with apprehensive eyes and shrank back to crouch defensively beside Enguerrand's pallet.

Andrei pushed open the woven curtain of palm leaves that covered the doorway, blinking in the blinding bright-ness of the midday sun. He wished he had a weapon on hand to defend himself.

All the time he had been Adramelech's host, he had had no need of swords or pistols; the Drakhaoul had given him unimaginable power. Without that dark energy flowing through his veins, he felt pitifully weak and vulnerable.

Two men, their white robes dazzling in the noonday heat, stood outside beneath the palm trees.

"Who are you?" Andrei challenged them.

One walked toward him, his arms open, as if to embrace him. "Thank God, you're well enough to come to greet us. The islanders told us you were all very sick." In spite of his white hair, the newcomer's grey eyes were bright in his sun-burned face and his tone was brisk and lively. "My name is Laorans, Abbé Laorans. I'm in charge of the Francian mis-sion in Serindher. My companion is Blaize, Père Blaize."

"Priests?" Andrei was still suspicious.

"Missionaries." Père Blaize came over, carrying a small wooden casket, and Andrei saw that he was much younger than the abbé, although the sun had bleached his golden hair almost as white as Oskar's. "News travels slowly from island to island, but as soon as we heard of shipwrecked travelers from the western quadrant, we set out to see if we could help." He gave Andrei a broad, friendly smile that al-most disarmed the last of his suspicions.

"You're Francians!" Aude appeared at the door of the hut, her wan face suddenly bright with hope. She lapsed into her native tongue, speaking so rapidly that Andrei had trouble keeping up with her. "You must help my cousin. He's very sick."

"Don't worry, Demoiselle," said Père Blaize, smiling reassuringly at her, "I've spent years studying the local diseases."

"Please, come in." Andrei stood aside to let the missionaries enter the hut.

Andrei and Aude stood watching as Père Blaize knelt by Enguerrand's pallet and placed his hand on the king's brow, then took his pulse and raised one of his eyelids. Enguerrand seemed barely conscious, murmuring some incoherent words as the priest examined him. Andrei saw Aude bite her underlip in her agitation. *She really cares for Enguerrand, in spite of the ordeal he's subjected her to.*

"What is your name?" Blaize asked his patient. Enguerrand muttered a few disjointed syllables.

"He's delirious. He doesn't even remember his own name," Aude whispered to Andrei, but just as Andrei was inwardly debating the wisdom of revealing their true identities, she blurted out, "He's called Enguerrand."

"Well, Enguerrand, can you hear me?" said Père Blaize. "I'm going to give you some physic to try to bring down your fever. It'll taste bitter, but you must drink the whole draft, or it won't work. It's made from the bark of a tree that grows in these islands." He opened his coffer and took out phials of a cloudy liquid.

While Aude watched anxiously, Andrei turned to Abbé Laorans.

"How long did it take you to get here, Abbé?"

"The news reached us ten days ago. We set out straightaway and, thanks to calm seas and a good wind, here we are."

"Abbé, could I speak to you in private?"

"By all means." Abbé Laorans followed him out into the heat.

"Damned proselytizers," said a drawling voice. Andrei looked round to see Oskar leaning against the side of the hut, arms folded.

"There's no need for that, Alvborg. These good men have come a long way to help us."

"Oh, I don't doubt that they have. What better way to notch up a few more converts on their heavenly slates?"

"Please excuse his rudeness." Andrei had become accustomed to Oskar's constant cynicism. "We've been through a . . . a traumatic experience. None of us has quite recovered yet."

"Indeed," said Laorans, looking keenly at Andrei. "Strange occurrences have been reported in these waters. First, the darkness. Then the unexplained lights in the sky. The islanders spoke to us of winged daemons and dragons. But then, they're very superstitious at the best of times."

Andrei nodded, not wanting to be drawn out on the subject.

Père Blaize came out from the hut. "He's sleeping. My suggestion is that we wait for his fever to break, then take you all to the mission. But he's too ill to be moved yet."

"Do you think he'll pull through?"

"It's difficult to tell at this stage." Blaize looked grave. "His constitution has been weakened, maybe due to an earlier bout of fever in childhood. I've seen similar cases in Enhirre and Djihan-Djihar. A relapse can prove fatal. But tell me, can you explain the strange marks on his skin and nails? I thought at first they might be a rash or discoloration caused by the fever, although I've never seen it on any other patient before."

The telltale stains left on Enguerrand's body by Nilaihah's presence, the streaks of gold in his dark hair, the unearthly glitter in his eyes, were fading slowly. But Andrei found that he had instinctively clenched his fists, hiding his own nails, which were still a dark violet, the last traces left by his Drakhaoul, Adramelech.

"Could you take us back with you to Serindher?" Andrei asked suddenly. "That young man you've been tending is Enguerrand of Francia. There will be ships coming to search for him and Lady Aude. But I fear they'll never find him if we stay here."

"Gobain's youngest son, eh?" Abbé Laorans said, chuckling. "What an honor for our mission, Blaize: our first royal patron."

CHAPTER 8

A rumbling, like distant thunder, broke the silence of the sleeping mission.

Andrei clutched at his head. Stabs of pain, each one a spear shaft of lightning, pierced his brain. Beside him, Enguerrand moaned and moved restlessly in fevered sleep. A hissed curse came from outside and, staggering to the doorway, Andrei saw Oskar, one hand pressed to his temples, collapse to his knees in the sand. And as another lightning shaft needled through his head, Andrei sensed the other two react at the same moment.

Aude started up. "What ever's wrong, Andrei? Shall I get help?"

Andrei managed to nod before the lightning crackled through his mind again and, helpless to withstand it, he crumpled to the floor, doubled up. Why, as he squeezed his eyes tight shut against its fury, did he see the form of a winged warrior, dazzlingly bright, etched in light against the black of his closed lids?

Hallucinating . . . must be hallucinating. All the Drakhaouls are gone from this world. I saw them go.

"How are you feeling?"

Andrei looked up dazedly and saw Père Blaize gazing down at him.

"Groggy." Andrei pushed himself up on one elbow, blinking in the daylight. "What happened?"

"We rather hoped you'd tell us." Blaize grinned at him. "All three of you passed out. Before that, Aude heard you muttering about lightning and spears."

"A tropical storm?" Andrei couldn't remember. "There was rumbling, like thunder . . ."

"The skies were clear last night. But now . . ." The grin faded. "Can you come with me? I'd like you to take a look."

Leaving Oskar and Enguerrand still sleeping, Andrei followed Blaize out of the mission and onto the shore. The sky seemed overcast and as they looked out across the sea toward the distant Spice Islands, Andrei saw what looked like thick grey clouds on the horizon.

"Does that look like a storm to you?"

"It looks like . . . smoke." Andrei turned to Blaize. "You don't think—"

"Distant rumbling. Smoke. A volcanic eruption." Blaize looked at him, his habitually cheerful expression erased.

"Ty Nagar? But it's far from here. Surely . . ."

"It's not so much the eruption, it's what might follow in its wake. You're a sailor, you must have heard that tidal waves can occur after a major eruption. We have to warn the villagers. And evacuate the mission."

Andrei heard voices coming from the shore. Several fishermen came running up the beach to Père Blaize, all gabbling at once and pointing toward the sea. After they had exchanged a few words in Serindhan, the fishermen hurried off toward the village.

Blaize looked at Andrei. "We have to get everyone to higher ground."

The straggling procession wound upward through the jungle; mothers clutching babies and wailing toddlers, older children herding ragged goats, carrying cooking pots and sacks of rice. There had been no time to do anything but ring the chapel bell to summon everyone and gather up the essentials for survival.

Aude had offered to help Blaize with the mission orphans, and even though she knew only a few words in Serindhan, she soon charmed the little ones into an attentive group. They set off up the hill, clinging to her hands. Oskar, after much grumbling, hoisted Enguerrand up and followed the children.

"Is everyone out of the mission?" Blaize called to Andrei. "Where's Laorans?"

"Isn't he with you?" Andrei scanned the gaggle of white-robed mission helpers but could see no sign of Laorans's distinctive snowy hair. "I'll check the chapel. You go on ahead with the others."

Andrei flung open the chapel door and ran down the aisle, calling out for Laorans.

He found him kneeling behind the altar. At first Andrei thought the old priest was praying but as he came nearer, he saw that he was struggling to lift out some object hidden beneath one of the floor tiles.

"Ah, Andrei," he said blinking at him. "Could you give me a hand?"

"We've got to go, Abbé. Any moment now, a tidal wave will hit our shores." Andrei had almost drowned in the Straits and the terror of the approaching flood gave an edge to his voice.

"This won't take a moment. And with your strength, you'll lift it out with no trouble."

"Listen." A horrible stillness had settled over the deserted village. Hadn't the fishermen warned that the tide would be sucked out before the wave came roaring in?

"You go on, then, my boy. I'll follow."

What sacred treasure was so precious the old man couldn't bear to leave it behind? The mission funds? Andrei knelt down and felt in the cavity, his fingers closing around a metal casket. He tugged hard, and at last it came out.

"Well done!" Laorans clapped his hands together in his delight. But another sound, a faint roar, could now be heard.

"Can you run, Abbé?"

Laorans opened a side door to the rear of the altar and beckoned him through.

Andrei tucked the dusty box under his arm and hurried after him.

"There's a little path up through the trees." Laorans had to raise his voice to be heard above the sound of the incoming water. Andrei knew that he should not look back, but just put his head down and run. Yet some inner compulsion made him glance over his shoulder as the roaring grew louder. The ruthless tide had already reached the mission and he saw it smash against the white walls of the chapel, the force of the impact setting the bell clanging before the water rose to submerge it.

Ahead, Laorans stumbled over a tree root, falling headlong.

"Come on, Abbé!" Andrei heaved him up again, half-dragging him on up the hill. The relentless rushing sound of the deadly tide grew ever nearer. If they didn't make it to the top of the hill, they would be swept away. And the water was flooding in faster than Andrei could run . . .

"Reports are only now coming in," announced Chancellor Aiguillon to the somber-faced ministers, "of a violent volcanic eruption in the Spice Islands a few weeks ago, followed by a tidal wave that has devastated the coastline of Serindher and wrecked many ships."

Alain Friard glanced at the Queen Mother in the ensuing shocked silence but Aliénor's face was expressionless. At length she asked, "Is this another ruse of the Emperor's, designed to undermine Francia?"

"That was my first assumption," said Aiguillon. "But after extensive inquiries, I fear that the information is correct. I understand that several Tielen spice ships have been wrecked in the disaster, severely affecting Tielen trade."

"So Enguerrand may be dead?" Every word was clipped and precise. "And Aude with him?"

"We fear so, majesty. As well as Andrei Orlov and Count Alvborg."

Friard waited in trepidation for the queen to show some reaction to the tragic news. But Aliénor was made of sterner stuff; she had outlived her husband and elder son and although her face had paled, Friard noticed that her ringed hands gripped the arms of her chair. "I will not give up hope until I have proof positive that my son is dead. But Francia must have a king. The quadrant is still unstable and unscrupulous leaders may try to take advantage of our situation. We will write to our daughter, Adèle, in Bel'Esstar."

Chancellor Aiguillon cleared his throat embarrassedly. "May I remind you, majesty, that if it were possible for a woman to legally rule Francia, then we would not hesitate to invite you to rule in your son's stead. But . . ."

Aliénor fixed him with a look so withering that Friard winced inwardly. "You have no need to remind me, Chancellor Aiguillon. Adèle's husband, Ilsevir, is the next in line to the throne by marriage."

"Francia and Allegonde united? Surely Raimon of Provença has a stronger claim by blood to the throne. And he is a native Francian."

"Are you daring to suggest that his right supersedes Adèle's?" The queen's voice was chill with disdain. "Surely Gobain's daughter outranks his cousin?"

"But the people, majesty, may not be ready to accept an Allegondan as ruler."

"Joint ruler," corrected Maistre Donatien quietly.

"Suppose Raimon opposes the idea?" persisted Chancellor Aiguillon. "He could so easily stir up the Provençans. And he doted upon Aude. If he blames Enguerrand for her death, who knows what madness his grief might drive him to?"

CHAPTER 9

Stage Manager Grebin seemed to delight in finding new tasks for Celestine to carry out, from emptying the ash from the dressing-room stoves to tidying up the dressing rooms. He was never satisfied with what she did, merely grunting when she showed him the clean latrines, or sparkling mirrors. The seamstresses and wigmakers kept a samovar hot in the upstairs workroom so there was a constant supply of hot strong tea for the backstage staff, with apple jam to sweeten it. The women ignored Celestine, chattering among themselves in their native tongue, sometimes looking at her with pitying glances and shaking their heads.

But come Friday, they all had to line up outside Grebin's office to receive their wages.

"Now I can afford to visit the public bathhouse," Celestine told the Faie. She was so desperate for hot water and soap that she even suppressed her embarrassment at having to go naked into the steaming green waters, alongside stout babushkas and giggling young girls who splashed one another and blushed as they compared the size of their budding breasts. Celestine ignored them, scrubbing the grime from her body, then sinking into the bliss of the warm water to soak away the stiffness in her aching back from the week's hard labor. She floated lazily, gazing up at the glass roof through the rising steam.

Little flecks of white were floating down and settling on the glass.

Snow. How long can I survive sleeping in a gazebo now that winter is setting in?

* * *

When Celestine arrived early for work the next day, the theater was in chaos; dancers filled the corridors, flexing and stretching their slender limbs in every available space so that she had to weave and dodge to reach the cupboard to fetch her mop and pail.

Grebin had donned a curled grey wig in honor of the occasion and, with it tilted slightly awry, he was issuing orders with the precision of a general on the battlefield.

"They've started rehearsing a new production," a stagehand told Celestine. "*Rusalka's Kiss,* or some such fancy title. It'll be mayhem back here until the curtain goes up on the first night."

Celestine could not help stealing a quick look from the wings as a fortepiano began to play and the bare boards of the stage resonated with the rhythmic thud of the dancers' feet. It was curious, she thought, that they moved so gracefully yet their feet made such a reverberant noise.

As she was on her way to fill her bucket at the pump, Grebin appeared, his wig even more askew, and seized hold of her by the wrist, dragging her toward the costumers' workroom.

Inside, racks of costumes and tailor's dummies had appeared; the seamstresses were busily pinning braid and ribbons to a long tutu of silvery aquamarine net.

"Put Maela to work in Masha's place." Grebin propelled Celestine to an empty seat at one of the trestle tables.

"But she's a cleaning girl," complained the wardrobe mistress, looking critically at Celestine over her pince-nez.

"And Masha is still off sick with the pleurisy, Yelena. With twenty-four costumes still to complete, you need an extra pair of hands," said Grebin, hastily retreating.

Yelena beckoned Celestine over. "If you're to work in here, you must pin your hair up. Let me see your hands. Hmm. Scrub them in that basin. We can't risk you spoiling our work with dirty finger marks."

Celestine obeyed. "I can sew," she said meekly. "I was taught at the convent."

"I'll be the judge of that." Yelena picked up a length of pale blue taffeta and passed her a pincushion and a reel of thread. "I'll wager you've done nothing but turn and hem linen sheets, convent girl. Working with these light stuffs takes skill and patience. They fray easily. And if you make a mistake, it'll come out of your wages. Now show me what you can do with this underskirt."

Celestine dutifully plied her needle and thread by the frosty light illuminating the workroom.

"It's snowing again outside, and we're making flimsy costumes for water nymphs." Yelena tutted. "Those dancers will catch their deaths of cold waiting in the wings; the drafts blow through there like a winter wind."

"They'll bring their shawls," said one of the other seamstresses.

Celestine was just biting off an end of thread when Yelena swooped and snatched up her work, moving to the window to examine it. She gave a sniff. Celestine waited, silently praying that she would not be sent back to the latrines. "Stitches small and mostly even. No snagged threads or puckering. I suppose it'll do." She passed the garment on to another seamstress and handed Celestine another length of blue taffeta. "The same again. Only neater."

As Celestine sewed, faint strains of music penetrated the workroom. She looked up, listening intently. A woman was practicing, using vocal exercises to warm her voice. Minutes later, a fortepiano began to play and the unseen soprano began to sing to its accompaniment.

"No slacking!" Yelena was frowning at her from the opposite side of the table.

"Who is that singing?"

"One of the soloists, who knows? Get on with your work."

"*Rusalka's Kiss* is an *opera*?"

Yelena raised her eyes in a look of weary forbearance. "This *is* an opera house."

"Who is the composer?" Celestine could not help wanting to know more. The fragments of melody seeping in were unfamiliar yet utterly enchanting.

"Kalenik. The Grand Duchess Sofiya is his patron."

A Muscobite composer. That would explain why I've never heard his music before.

"No time for gossiping, ladies!" Grebin appeared, followed by half a dozen dancers. "Here are your first clients."

Yelena let out a sigh of annoyance and, draping her tape measure around her neck, began to issue orders.

Celestine watched, fascinated, as the dancers stripped, shivering and giggling, allowing the costumers to fit the flimsy costumes, stoically enduring the pinning and marking with tailor's chalk, turning round and round again as Yelena surveyed the results with a critical eye. The lengths of taffeta Celestine had been hemming began to be transformed with a shimmer of green and silver sequins and ribbons artfully cut and draped to look like waterweeds. The first dancers left and more arrived. The daylight began to fade as more snow fell and Grebin brought oil lamps.

"Dress rehearsals start tomorrow at nine. You'll just have to work through the night to be finished in time," he announced.

Celestine heard the other seamstresses groan in protest and looked down at her work to conceal the smile of relief. Tonight she would be warm in the workroom. The thought of sleeping another night in the snowy Water Gardens was too much to endure. And even though Grebin's brow was more furrowed and his wig more awry each time he appeared, the stage manager had food delivered to the workroom: hot cabbage soup with caraway dumplings.

"Peasant food," said Yelena with a sniff.

Celestine said nothing but spooned down the soup eagerly. It reminded her of the food she used to help prepare at Saint Azilia's: robust, tasty, and filling. The last weeks of privation had taught her that there was much to be said for enjoying such simple pleasures.

The sky craft hovered above the city as the winter sun set, painting the snowy horizon with a lick of scarlet fire. Far below, the tiled roofs were thickly rimed with snow; even the painted tiles on the onion domes of the Cathedral of Saint Simeon were coated in white.

"So this is where you've been hiding, Lady Azilis." The Magus leaned over the side of the craft, closing his eyes as he searched for that faint but telltale aethyric current of energy he had detected. "Mirom."

Linnaius landed his craft in a deserted park. He disguised himself in the long robes and fur-rimmed hat of a merchant and took to the streets of the city, prowling from square to square, in search of that elusive presence he had sensed earlier. He had been sure that he would see concert bills advertising the arrival of the celebrated Francian singer Celestine de Joyeuse, but there was no mention of her anywhere.

Did I stay too long in Tielen? I had to honor the promise I made to Eugene. I had to make sure that everything was in order at Swanholm.

Even if his successor were a mere doctor of science without a drop of mage blood in his veins, Linnaius had to be certain that he was entrusting his alchymical knowledge to a worthy successor, one who would serve Eugene loyally.

He entered a wide and gracious square dominated by a grand building boasting an ostentatious portico. Horse-drawn sleighs crossed and crisscrossed in front of its broad steps, the air noisy with the horses' hooves and the jingle of the bells on their harnesses.

Again he felt a sudden stab of aethyric energy, faint as a pinprick, yet infused with an intense, radiant power. "The Imperial Theater," he murmured aloud and set out, threading his way through the troikas.

"Where are the silver sequins?" Yelena's voice, shrill and vexed, pierced the seamstresses' gossiping. "Well? Don't tell me we've run out!"

One by one, the women looked up from their work and shook their heads.

"Oh, that's wonderful. And only seven more costumes to complete!" Yelena opened her purse. "Maela, go round to the draper's on Khazan Prospect and buy more sequins." She tossed her a coin. "That should cover it."

Celestine deftly caught the coin.

"Wrap up warmly; it'll be dark soon. And don't dawdle!"

Well muffled in her thick cloak, Celestine hurried out into the twilight. The quickest way to Khazan Prospect was to take a shortcut through a winding alley around the back of the theater. The sun was setting and the alley was unlit. She hesitated. But what had she to fear? The Faie would protect her if anyone tried to rob her.

There it was again—but stronger this time. Linnaius retreated into a doorway and watched. In the purple dusk he saw a cloaked woman emerge from the stage door and, after a quick, nervous glance around, scuttle away into the night.

He followed. She was moving much more swiftly than he and in the twists and turns of the foul-smelling alley, he almost lost her. He emerged, wheezing for breath in the sharp cold of the night air, on one of the main thoroughfares of the city, in time to see her going into a little shop.

He would just have to wait and detain her when she came out . . .

It was dark when Celestine left the draper's, the silver sequins wrapped in a twist of paper. The troika horses' hooves struck sparks off the icy cobbles as the sleighs swished past. She shivered.

What was that unsettling sensation? She glanced around, suddenly wary. Another frost haze was settling over Mirom as the temperature plummeted. It must just be the intense night cold, she told herself as she entered the unlit alleyway. She would soon warm up again by the stove in the snug workroom.

Silver eyes glimmered in the darkness.

She stopped, backing away.

"Wh—who's there?" she called, her voice trembling. She was too far along the alley to run back to the busy street. And if she called for help, who would hear her cries?

"I've been looking for you, Celestine."

Another shiver ran through her body, so intense that she feared she would not be able to stop shaking. *Those eyes of silver ice, so chill, so inhuman.* Now she knew who was blocking her way. And he had trapped her.

"Kaspar Linnaius!" she cried, as she felt her fear turning to anger. "*Show yourself!*"

"I mean you no harm, Celestine," came the hateful voice from the shadows. "I only want to talk with you."

"*He's lying.*"

The Faie had awoken to the danger.

The Magus came toward her, one hand extended. The hand that could summon storm winds with the slightest flick of finger and thumb.

Celestine continued to retreat until she felt her back graze against the blank tenement wall. There was nowhere else to go.

"What is there to talk about?" She kept her voice low in the hope that she would not betray how terrified she felt. If he had intended to kill her, he would have struck before she even knew he was there. So what did he want from her?

"I merely wish to communicate with your guardian spirit, that's all."

"*No!*" The Faie whispered her refusal before Celestine could react. "*I tell you, Magus, that we have nothing to discuss.*"

"Even though it's a matter of the greatest importance?"

"*Leave now—while you can.*"

Still he came on and Celestine raised her right hand in a vain gesture to keep him at bay.

"Leave me alone." She felt the Faie's power rushing through her, from her mind to her outstretched hand, concentrating in her fingertips. Every vein in her body burned with luminous energy. "Stay back!"

In the frosty gloom of the filthy alley, Linnaius saw Celestine's eyes begin to glimmer.

Pure white sparks of aethyrial energy shot from her outstretched hand. He snatched the ghost of a breeze from the night, twisting it around himself to repel the attack. But he was too slow to deflect the full force and the bolts sizzled through his defense, knocking him off his feet and onto the ground. Fighting for breath, dizzy, he tried to force himself to get up, slipping on the slime of ice and mud, only to drop back again.

Azilis blazed a vicious warning.

"Leave—us—alone."

Celestine saw the Magus stagger and fall. This was her chance to escape.

"He'll only come after us again." The Faie's fury still burned in her brain and she felt a second burst of fire welling up within her. *"Finish it now, once and for all."*

As the power coursed through her body, Celestine saw Linnaius push himself up on one hand, turning to her with a look so confused, so imploring, that it almost made her stay her hand.

"This is no time for weakness!" The Faie's rage possessed her and she flung another glittering bolt at him. Linnaius fell back. After one convulsive shudder, he did not stir again.

Is it all over at last? Have we destroyed him? Her fire-dazzled mind could only think of escape. She gathered up her skirts and began to run, expecting at any time to feel a flesh-shredding blast of wind catch her. "Must get away from here," she kept repeating to herself. "Must get the sequins back to Yelena. She'll be cross if I'm late."

But at the entrance to the alleyway, all the strength drained from her body and she fell, clutching at a doorpost to support herself.

"Faie, what's wrong?" This was unlike any weakness she had ever felt before, emanating from deep within her. "Did Linnaius put a glamour on you?"

For a moment the Faie did not reply and when she did, her words sounded distant and bewildered. *"What's happening to me? Why am I . . . so . . . weak?"*

The bright presence within her dimmed, like a candle-flame blown out in the wind, and the reassuring, familiar voice fell silent.

"Where have you been, you wretched girl?" Yelena rose, staring severely at Celestine over the top of her pince-nez.

"You're late! Now we'll all have to work past midnight—" She broke off. "Why, whatever's the matter? You're trembling."

"I—I was attacked." Celestine's teeth chattered. She was still shaken to the core by the unexpected encounter with Linnaius. Even enduring Yelena's wrath was preferable to what she had just experienced. "In the alley."

"Are you all right?" The other seamstresses crowded around to fuss over her. "Were you robbed?" "Did you see his face?"

"I got away." She pulled out the twist of paper containing the precious sequins and held it out to Yelena. Yelena gave a fastidious little sniff but accepted it nonetheless and unwrapped the sparkling contents.

"Go and warm yourself at the stove. Drink some tea. And don't go by that alleyway again after dark."

Celestine saw Grebin coming along the passageway toward her, carrying the dancers' flowing headdresses. "They won't do," he said, plumping the bundle of buckram and tangled ribbons into her arms. "The ballet mistress says they're too long and they get in the way. Tell Yelena they must be altered. We need them in half an—" He stopped, gazing at her quizzically. "What have you done to your hair, Maela? Bleached it? I liked it better brown." And he passed on down the passageway.

My hair bleached? Celestine stood in the dim light with her arms full of dangling ribbons and laces, not knowing quite what to do first. *Is my disguise slipping?*

This thought was so disturbing that it sent her running to the nearest empty dressing room, dumping the offending headdresses over a hanging rail and leaning close to the mirror to check her reflection. Even in the gloom, she could see that her hair was fast reverting to its natural shade of pale gold. And her eyes were blue as cornflowers once more.

"Faie?" She began to wind her fair hair up into a knot, desperately casting around for a piece of scrap material that she could use as a headscarf to hide it. "*Faie!* What's wrong with you?" There was no reply. "Answer me!"

* * *

The seamstresses stayed up all night to finish the dancers' costumes. Celestine, her hair still covered by a tightly bound headscarf, was relieved not to have to leave the theater again. The women took it in turns to sleep and sew, drinking strong tea from the samovar to keep awake. As Celestine sat slowly, mechanically stitching a seam, her eyelids began to droop, only to start awake as she saw again the Magus's face, lit by the stark, pure light of the Faie's attack.

Is Linnaius really gone at last? She had thought she would feel triumphant in the knowledge that she had destroyed him. But all she felt was emptiness. She had ruthlessly pursued her quest to avenge her father, abandoning her career, her country, even her dearest friends.

Faie? There was still no answer. Celestine's heart ached. Suppose in protecting her from Linnaius, the Faie had given up the last of her aethyrial life force?

Am I all alone now?

CHAPTER 10

The plans for rebuilding the damaged wing of Swanholm Palace lay spread out over the Emperor's desk. Eugene, in company with his architects, was comparing them with the original designs when a discreet knock announced the arrival of his secretary, Gustave.

"I wouldn't have interrupted you, imperial highness, if it were not a matter of the utmost gravity." Gustave bowed as he presented Eugene with a folded paper.

"Excuse me, gentlemen." Eugene went to the window to read by the clear snow light while Gustave hovered, waiting for a reply.

It was a transcript of a Vox message from an agent in the port of Haeven:

> Unconfirmed reports received from clippers on their
> way back from the Azure Ocean of a devastating
> typhoon or tidal wave that has wrecked many ships and
> wreaked havoc in the Spice Islands.

Eugene looked up, staring out over the snow haze blanketing the valley, yet seeing a distant shore where, were it not for the merciless heat, the sand was so white it could be mistaken for snow. "Enguerrand," he murmured. "Aude. *Andrei.*"

He had left the rebel princes behind on Ty Nagar, wanting to put as much distance as possible between them and his children. When Linnaius had returned to rescue Lord Gavril, he had offered to take Lady Aude too but she had refused, insisting she would stay with Enguerrand. And that was the last he had heard.

He looked up to see Gustave and the architects watching him cautiously. "Has anyone else seen this intelligence?" he asked.

"I believe that news may have leaked out—" began Gustave.

"Eugene!" Astasia came running in. "What's this rumor I've been hearing?"

Gustave nodded to the architects, who bowed and hastily made themselves scarce.

"A tidal wave in the Spice Islands? All the ships in the area feared wrecked?"

"There are no details yet—" Eugene began.

"Why didn't you send Linnaius back to rescue him?" She launched herself at him, beating her fists against his chest. "You left my brother marooned there. You left him there to die!"

Eugene stared at his wife, taken aback by this furious outburst. He caught her by the wrists, pressing her clenched fists against his breast. "You know well enough why I didn't bring Andrei back."

"He wasn't in his right mind, Eugene; he was possessed by that—that Drakhaoul." Her eyes burned with angry tears yet she didn't break down. "Andrei would never have done those terrible things. I was there. I saw him. It wasn't Andrei who stole our son. The daemon forced him to do it."

There was much that Eugene had not told his wife about that last, desperate battle at the Serpent Gate. Only Gavril Nagarian knew how close they had all come to annihilation and the part that Andrei had played. He looked at Gustave above Astasia's dark head. "Has anyone seen the Magus recently, Gustave?" he asked, although he already knew the answer.

"No, imperial highness."

"Then send word to all our ships in the southern quadrant to start to search for the Empress's brother and his companions. And I want to know which vessels have survived this catastrophe unscathed."

Linnaius was the only one capable of effecting a swift rescue mission. But Linnaius had disappeared. From the elegiac tone of their last conversation, Eugene feared that the old Magus was ailing and had gone to some desolate place to die. He had even set his affairs in order, initiating Professor Kazimir in his alchymical secrets so that he could continue his work for the New Rossiyan armies.

"If you can still hear me, Kaspar," he said, gazing out at the wintry sky, "I really need your help."

A soft, chill sensation brought Linnaius slowly back to consciousness. He was still lying in the alley, and flakes of snow were falling on him, forming a soft white coverlet. He managed to push himself up to his hands and knees, every muscle in his body trembling with the effort.

Azilis could have killed me. But here I am still . . . frozen to the bone, and more likely to die of exposure to the cold than a bolt of aethyric energy . . .

Slowly he crawled forward until he reached the shelter of a doorway.

So why am I still alive? He brushed the snow off his robes. *Has she put all her energy into protecting Celestine? Or has she been too long away from the Rift, the source of her powers?*

Linnaius leaned his throbbing head back against the rotting doorpost and watched the snowflakes silently falling, transforming the shabby buildings with their crystalline sheen.

She had defeated him this time, yet he was determined not to give up. He would need time to heal. But so would Azilis.

"Hey! Old man! You can't sleep here!"

Linnaius came back to his senses to see two constables of the watch standing over him, shining a lantern in his face.

"Had a few too many, grandpa?" One of them bent down and eased him up into a sitting position. "Time to go home. You'll catch your death lying in fresh snow."

"D'you think you can make it on your own?" Between them, they hauled him to his feet, propping him up. Linnaius felt a fool. But he was still too weak from Azilis's attack to do anything but accept their help.

"Where's your house?" the first constable asked loudly. Linnaius waved one hand vaguely toward the square.

"Better take him down to the constabulary."

Lying in a cell, Linnaius stared up at the cracked ceiling. If he had not felt so feeble, he would have smiled at the irony. It wasn't so long since he had been imprisoned by the Commanderie and now here he was, behind bars again, for being "incapable with drink." In truth, he was grateful to the two constables for rescuing him and giving him shelter on such a bitterly cold night. Huddled close to the little stove in the cell were three elderly vagrants and a couple of drunkards, one of them constantly mumbling to himself. The cell stank of old men's piss and unwashed bodies, but Linnaius was in no position to complain. In his weakened state, he could have frozen to death if the men hadn't stumbled across him.

Next morning, the constables spooned out a bowl of steaming hot porridge for each of the old men and sent them off into the dawn. Linnaius stood gazing up at the scarlet-stained eastern sky. The light of the rising sun had tinged the snowy rooftops a strange and bloody pink. Fortified with porridge, he set out at a dragging and unsteady pace over the frozen snow. Muscobites milled about him, all moving more swiftly than he as they hurried to work; ants, he thought, swarming past a slow, old snail. On the corner, a vendor was selling newspapers, shouting his wares aloud in a high-pitched, cracked voice.

"Tragedy in the southern quadrant! Tidal wave ruins spice trade! King of Francia lost at sea!"

Linnaius stopped. Had he heard aright? He hobbled up to the news vendor. "King Enguerrand drowned?" he said.

"I don't give out the news for free," said the vendor as other customers pushed in, jostling Linnaius, to buy their copies.

If Enguerrand was feared dead, what had become of

Prince Andrei, his traveling companion? Eugene had no love for his arrogant brother-in-law, but he would not wish the Empress Astasia to suffer his loss a second time.

Eugene needs me. Somehow I've got to find the strength to make it back to Swanholm . . .

Yelena sent Celestine back to the draper's to buy turquoise thread and ribbons.

Even though she knew she should not, Celestine retraced her steps to see if the old Magus's body was still lying where she had left him the previous night. The alley was covered with a thick fall of fresh snow, but all that she could see were the delicate prints of birds' wiry feet.

A sudden sound made her jump. Heart thudding, she looked round to see crows watching her from the fence; more were lining up on the lopsided gable of a nearby tenement. She remembered Jagu's fear of birds. She remembered the soul-stealing magus who had taken Henri's soul and his hawk. She began to back away. Could the magi use crows as their familiars?

"*He's gone.*" The Faie's voice echoed, feeble but distinct, in her mind.

"You're all right!" Celestine crossed her arms over her breast, hugging herself with relief. Her breath steamed on the frosty air.

"*We're safe—for now.*"

"But Linnaius is still alive?"

"*Forgive me, Celestine, I left you unprotected. I was just . . . so very . . . weary.*"

Linnaius arrived at Swanholm as the palace was waking to a dark and dreary dawn. He entered the palace by the secret passage that led directly to the Emperor's private apartments, passing bleary-eyed maids, who stared at him in surprise as they lugged heavy baskets of logs and coals to make up the fires.

He found Eugene already at his desk, going through a pile of dispatches.

"I came as soon as I could," Linnaius announced.

Eugene hurried toward Linnaius and took him by the arm to steady him. "Magus," he said, "please sit down. Let me pour you a drink. Aquavit?"

For once Linnaius did not refuse. As he sat sipping the powerful spirit, an expensive blend from Northern Tielen, flavored with coriander, the fog in his head began to clear.

"You've been pushing yourself too hard." Eugene was watching him with those pale blue eyes that missed nothing. "So, you heard the news about Enguerrand?"

"Am I to assume that Prince Andrei is feared lost too?"

Eugene gave a curt nod.

"And you'd like me to go to look for them?"

"Our agents in Francia have just informed me that Ilsevir of Allegonde is to succeed Enguerrand. Until now, Allegonde has remained neutral. But those damned religious fanatics, the Rosecoeurs, have just appointed Ilsevir their patron."

This was unexpected news. Linnaius knew now why Eugene looked so troubled. Allegonde and Francia united would be a considerable threat to the stability of the new Empire.

"This tidal wave," Eugene said. "Could it have anything to do with what happened at the Serpent Gate?"

Linnaius's thoughts had been running along the same lines. "It's possible that the tremendous surge of power that destroyed the Gate set off a volcanic eruption. Which, in turn, caused the wave to sweep through the Azure Ocean."

Eugene fell silent at this suggestion.

"You mustn't blame yourself," Linnaius said, anticipating what the Emperor was thinking. "If you hadn't closed the Serpent Gate, Nagazdiel would have come through into our world. And the consequences of such an act . . ."

"Even so . . ." Eugene said. Then he seemed to shrug it aside. "But you must rest before you set out, old friend."

Linnaius managed a smile. "Do I look so very frail?"

Eugene came over to him, kneeling before his chair to look earnestly into his eyes. "You've already done so much for me and my family. If it weren't for Astasia, I wouldn't be asking this of you . . ."

"I understand."

"How I shall ever make it up to her if Andrei is lost a second time . . ." Linnaius saw a brief shadow of desperation
cross the Emperor's face. He knew all too well what Eugene
was leaving unsaid.

Astasia woke suddenly, listening intently in the darkness. A
drowsy little moan came from the crib beside the bed. Ever
since Rostevan's abduction, she had refused to let him sleep
in the nursery, preferring to keep him close. Her decision
had incurred the disapproval of the elder courtiers and especially her mother, Sofiya, who constantly reminded her
that she was spoiling him and would regret it when he grew
older.

The baby let out another little cry and moved restlessly,
setting the crib rocking. *He must be dreaming.*

Eugene lay beside her, deeply asleep. She looked at her
husband in fond exasperation, wondering how he could
sleep so soundly and not be disturbed by his son's cries.

Light from the setting moon flooded the bedchamber,
and Astasia went rigid as its glimmer revealed a shadowy
figure standing by Rostevan's crib.

"Who's there?" she whispered. The silver-grey light
brightened and she recognized the pallid features of Valery
Vassian. "V—Valery?" She must be dreaming too, she was
sure of it, for Valery was dead; he had given his life protecting her and Rostevan from Andrei's Drakhaoul.

"*Help me, Astasia.*" His haunted, sunken eyes stared im-
ploringly at her as he moved closer to her bedside.

Astasia instinctively made the sign to ward off evil.

"What do you want?" Her voice trembled.

"*I don't belong here anymore . . . yet I can't seem to find
my way back . . .*" Terrified as she was by his appearance,
his words were so desolate, so despairing, that her heart
filled with pity.

"Back? To where?"

The moonlight began to fade and with it, his spectral
form began to fade away too.

"Valery, wait!"

Rostevan, hearing the fear in his mother's voice, woke up

and began to wail. Astasia pushed back the covers and ran to him, picking him up and rocking him against her. "There, there, baby, he's gone, it's all right now."

"What on earth's the matter?" came an exasperated voice from the bed. "Who's gone?"

And Astasia, to her shame, burst into tears.

"Dearest girl, you must have been dreaming." Eugene stroked her hair and, even though she pressed close against him, finding comfort in his warmth, his words did not reassure her in the least. "Waking dreams can seem very realistic."

She shook her head. "I know I was awake. And he was in such distress, Eugene. How can I help him? Should we call a priest to perform an exorcism?"

"Let's not act too hastily," Eugene said soothingly. "We don't want to cause unnecessary alarm."

"You still don't believe me!"

"There are members of Valery's family in your entourage, don't forget. What would his sister say if she heard what you were planning to do? Don't you think it would cause her distress?"

As always, Eugene had a valid reason to support his point of view. Perhaps she was overreacting. She had not been sleeping well of late, lying awake for hours, worrying about Andrei.

But if her brother was dead, wouldn't it have been his ghost that had appeared at her bedside, and not Valery's?

There was still no word from Linnaius. Eugene read through dispatch after dispatch from his agents and captains in the southern quadrant, impatiently discarding one after the other. Nothing but sad news of wrecked cargo ships, devastated villages, ruined spice harvests, and starving villagers. He had instructed Admiral Janssen of the Southern Fleet to supply whatever aid he and his men could to the survivors: food, blankets, and plenty of tools to start rebuilding.

That evening there had been a little concert in the music room, followed by *lansquenet* and *tric-trac*; Astasia and her

ladies-in-waiting took pleasure in these diversions and it reassured Eugene to see her enjoying herself. But he had left
early, rescued by the timely appearance of Gustave, bearing
a fresh batch of intelligence. Now it was past midnight; the
courtiers had retired, the palace had fallen silent and his
eyelids were drooping . . .

"*Why have you changed the colors in this room, Eugene?
We chose them together, remember?*"

Eugene's heart seemed to stutter to a halt. "Margret?" In
the dim light the slim figure turned around and he saw his
first wife gazing at him from eyes dark as shadow.

"*You said you wanted the colors of marguerites, to . . .*"

"To match your name," he said hoarsely.

"*My Eugene, the bluff soldier, struggling to master the
subtleties of interior design.*" An endearing little smile lit
her wan face.

"And you teased me mercilessly." He couldn't help smiling too, at the memory.

"*But in my heart, I loved you even more for trying because you wanted to make me happy. The painted paper
was so pretty: sprigs of daisies on a fresh white background.
Green, white, yellow. I liked to sit and read in here; even in
winter the light tones reminded me of summer . . .*"

"How can I be talking to you, Margret? Did I fall asleep
at my desk? Are you part of my dream?" Eugene was convinced that he would wake up at any moment.

"*I don't know what I'm doing here . . .*" Her voice
trailed away as she wandered aimlessly around the room.
He felt a chill descend on his heart as a gust of cold, dusty
wind blew through the study. "*It's all so different. So . . .
wrong.*" She began to shiver, wrapping her arms around her
as if to keep out the cold. The light faded, tinged with a
dingy taint of grey, as if a film of dust had descended between them. "*Help me, Eugene.*" She turned to stare at him.
"*I don't belong here. But I don't know how to find my way
back . . .*" She looked so frail, so insubstantial, that she
could have been a skeletal leaf blown in on the fitful wind.

The lantern flame illuminating Eugene's desk guttered
and died. In the darkness, he fumbled for the tinder to re-

light the wick. By the time he had succeeded, there was no trace of Margret.

So I must have been dreaming after all. Yet he still felt shaken. He wanted to remember Margret as she was depicted in her portrait: happy, smiling, and carefree. Not the confused, lost apparition his tired brain had conjured.

He yawned widely until his jaw cracked. Time to sleep. *I will accomplish nothing useful tonight; better to rise early and refreshed.* He lifted the last dispatch to file it with the others and, to his surprise, saw a fine dust fall onto his polished desktop from the papers. He touched it, raising his fingertips to examine it: tiny granules of a grey, sandy grit.

As he tiptoed into the bedchamber so as not to wake Rostevan, he saw that a night-light burned on Astasia's side of the great canopied bed. She must be so engrossed in the latest novel from her favorite writer that she had stayed awake to finish it.

"Eugene? Is that you?" She was sitting up in bed, clutching the covers to her.

"Who else would it be?"

"*He* was here again. Valery." Her violet eyes were wide and dark with fear. "I'm afraid, Eugene. Something is wrong. Very wrong . . ."

CHAPTER 11

Girim nel Ghislain's brisk footfall echoed high into the painted dome of the Basilica as he made his way to Elesstar's Shrine. At this hour of twilight, between services, there were few worshippers around, although from the glimmer of many votive candles, there had obviously been plenty of pilgrims passing through the shrine earlier. A pale-haired young Rosecoeur Guerrier detached himself from the shadows of the entrance grille and saluted.

"I came as soon as I could, Korentan," Girim said, returning the salute. "Show me."

Inside the shrine, a soft glow of candles illumined every marble niche and alcove. The priceless statue of Elesstar lay in the heart of the shrine, bathed in the pearly light. But as Girim came closer, he saw that the flawless white marble showed patches of discoloration, as if the saint's sculpted body had become corrupt and was decaying from within.

"What can have caused this deterioration? Has anyone disobeyed the prince's command?" He had asked Prince Il-sevir to issue a decree forbidding worshippers to lay even a finger on the statue. He had seen too many precious relics worn away by the fervent kisses and caresses of the faithful.

"We've kept the pilgrims at a distance, Captain."

Bewildered, Girim walked around the statue. "Then I have no idea, no idea at all . . ." He came back to Korentan. "Has anyone made any comment? What have you heard?"

"The candlelight helps to maintain the illusion, just as you suggested, Captain. As long as they file past the grille and don't come any closer, they don't seem to notice. Yet."

* * *

"Why is she decaying, Girim?" Prince Ilsevir demanded. "This is Bel'Esstar, *her* city."

"One must remember, highness," Girim said soothingly, "that it is a statue, not Elesstar's mortal remains, that we are discussing."

"Ah, but one can't help but notice the horrible semblance of putrefaction," Ilsevir said with a fastidious shudder. "People will talk. People will begin to say that the air of our city is not wholesome. That there is something rotten at the heart of Allegonde. And they will point to me, Girim. We've already had a disastrous plague-ridden summer. And now my beloved Adèle is ailing. She's already miscarried once. We can't afford any more bad luck."

"What are you implying, highness?"

"Haven't you heard the rumors?" The prince was so agitated that he began to pace the chapel. "Even though you tried to hush up the affair, the people have not forgotten the four Guerriers who were struck down here at the inauguration ceremony. There's talk at court and on the streets of the city that the statue is cursed."

"Superstitious nonsense," said Girim, forcing a laugh.

"They're saying that she should be returned to Ondhessar."

Girim could feel the prince's gaze on him, assessing his reaction to the suggestion.

"I believe it's nothing but the effects of the damp air on the marble. As you said yourself, highness, it's been an unusually humid summer." Girim knew Ilsevir well; the capricious prince was all too easily swayed by the opinions of his ministers and favorites. "I have invited two experts, a sculptor and a mason, to take a look at her. With your approval, I would like to offer them some kind of incentive to stay discreet about the whole affair."

"And where are they, these experts?"

To Girim's relief, young Korentan reappeared, followed by two civilians; both men bowed low to the prince. Ilsevir then proceeded to pace the chapel as they began their examination of the statue, only adding to Girim's growing sense of disquiet.

The Basilica clock chimed out the hour, then the quarter, each stroke making the building resonate dully. Eventually the experts finished their examination and approached the prince. From their expressions, Girim knew that the prognosis was not good.

"I've never seen anything like this before, highness," said the mason, scratching his bearded chin. "The statue appears to be decaying from within. And yet I can't find any fissure or crack where rainwater could have penetrated the marble."

"And I can assure you that the statue was thoroughly protected from the elements when we transported it here." Girim felt obliged to repeat this fact to reassure himself that he and his men had taken scrupulous care of the statue, especially during the sea crossing.

"How long before she starts to crumble away?" Ilsevir asked. The bluntness of the prince's question surprised Girim; Ilsevir was not usually so direct in his dealings with people.

The mason shook his head slowly. "If you're going to commission a copy, highness, I'd say that now is not too soon."

"Can you do it?" Ilsevir asked the sculptor.

"I believe I can," he replied. "But not here. I'd prefer to work in my studio."

Girim caught a glance from Ilsevir. "I'm afraid that will not be possible," he said. "We must ask you to work and live here. We will close the cathedral until the copy is complete. My men will bring you anything you need. And you will be most generously remunerated."

"This is to be our little secret." Ilsevir extended his hand, the signet ring glinting in the chapel candlelight. "I ask you, gentlemen, to swear on my ring, never to breathe a word of what we have discussed here today."

The men looked at one another. They glanced at Girim, who was watching them, arms folded. Then, the mason, followed by the sculptor, knelt and kissed the prince's ring.

"Will it work, do you think?" Ilsevir murmured to Girim as Korentan and the Rosecoeurs began to clear the cathedral of priests and worshippers.

* * *

When the prince had departed and the two experts had gone to make their arrangements, Girim lingered on, waiting until the chapel was empty. The candles were guttering, burning down into their sconces.

He went up to the statue and slowly reached out to touch the discolored stone.

"Why?" He dropped to his knees before her. "Why has this happened? Why have you deserted us? This is *your* city, the city you made your home." His whispered words echoed softly in the gathering gloom as, one by one, the candles burned out. "Since then, we've honored your memory. So why have you turned your face from us?" He bent slowly forward, until his forehead rested against the statue's chill marble feet. "Or is this a test of my faith?" Her bright image had illumined his life since he was a boy. His heart had been stirred by the story of Mhir, the poet-prophet whose perfect, selfless love for Elesstar had brought about her miraculous revival, through the blood of the rose that sprang from his grave. "What more can I do? Give me a sign and—" A sudden babble of angry voices started up outside and he left the chapel to see what was happening.

"I don't care what his highness says. This is a house of prayer and must be kept open to everyone." The bishop had arrived, flanked by several priests and Korentan, and his men were barring their way. "And where are we to conduct our daily acts of worship?"

"It's only for a few days, your grace," Girim said, putting on his most placating tone. "And Prince Ilsevir has put his own private chapel at your disposal, so that you can hold services there until this essential work is complete."

"A few days?" spluttered the bishop.

"And his highness has requested that you pray for the health of his wife." Girim knew that this was one request the priests would find it hard to refuse.

"Princess Adèle is still indisposed? I had no idea. Well, if his highness requests . . ."

The Princess of Allegonde's bedchamber looked out over the palace gardens, which lay covered in a crusty sparkle of white hoarfrost. From her curtained bed, propped up on pillows, Adèle could see only the grey sheen of the cloud-covered sky and the chill, wintry gardens, empty except for a single gardener pushing a wheelbarrow, and a few birds.

"Enguerrand drowned?" Adèle gazed at her husband. "But how? What was he doing in the Spice Islands? Why was he so far from home?" The bespectacled face of her younger brother swam before her eyes as she had last seen him, an earnest smile warming his customarily grave expression. "Surely it's a mistake . . ."

Ilsevir was gazing out of the window, his back to her. There must be much that he wasn't telling her, she suspected, for fear the news might make her condition worse. She sat up in bed, pulling her lacy shawl closer around her shoulders, and used a tone of voice she had often heard her mother employ.

"We are talking about *my* brother," she said sternly. "No matter how distressing the details, I need to know. Knowing is better than imagining all manner of horrible things."

He turned around. She saw instantly how confused he was, obviously at a loss as to how to broach the matter contained in the letter, and through the first waves of grief, she realized what she had long known but never admitted to herself before—that she was the stronger of the two. She might be weak in body, but she was Gobain's daughter. At heart, Ilsevir was a conflicted blend of sensitivity and self-regard, and the inner conflict between the two often resulted in his seeming unfeeling, even impervious, to the feelings of others, while internally he agonized over what might be the most appropriate, caring way to respond.

"Your mother writes that he was on his way to visit the Commanderie mission in Serindher when a tidal wave struck, devastating the whole area."

"Visiting a mission?" Adèle's eyes filled with tears. "That's so like my little brother," she said, trying to sound brave. "Poor Maman. First Aubrey, now Enguerrand. I must go to her."

"You'll go nowhere until the doctors have pronounced you fit to travel." Ilsevir came and sat at her bedside. "It's a long and tiring journey to Francia. And the mountain passes are still treacherous with snow. Write to your mother; she'll understand. Besides . . ." He looked down, not meeting her gaze. There must be something else that he was not telling her.

"How can they be so sure he's dead?" All manner of possibilities passed through her mind. Enguerrand might be lying in some islander's hut, rambling in fever, not even remembering his own name. "He might have been shipwrecked on one of the islands. Have they searched thoroughly?"

"This arrived from the First Minister of Francia." Ilsevir placed a letter in her hands; it was ornately scribed and weighted with the seal of the Francian government. "He is formally requesting our presence in Lutèce as soon as you are well enough to make the journey. It seems that as Enguerrand has left no heirs, the crown passes to you, my dearest—and to me. From now on, we'll have to divide our time equally between Allegonde and Francia. But how will the people of Francia feel about an Allegondan—"

"You're not listening to me, Ilsevir!" Adèle seized hold of his hand. "He may not be dead. We must send ships to join the search."

"But of course." He squeezed her hand in his own. "You're very hot," he said anxiously. "The doctors warned me not to overburden you. You must rest."

"How can I rest when you've told me such terrible news?" Adèle cried. Sometimes Ilsevir could be so insensitive. "My only brother—"

There came a discreet tap at the door. She broke off, remembering that there was no real privacy to be found in the palace, not even when she was ill. "Come in," she said, trying to compose herself. A lady-in-waiting appeared, eyes demurely lowered, and said to Ilsevir, "If you please, highness, Captain nel Ghislain is here with an urgent dispatch."

"Urgent?" Ilsevir let go of her hand. "Tell him I'll see him in my study straightaway." He seemed almost relieved to have an excuse to take his leave.

Adèle sighed. She had no liking for Girim nel Ghislain or his Rosecoeurs, and his influence over her husband seemed

to grow stronger by the day. "Ilsevir," she said, speaking
from the heart, "what is it about Girim nel Ghislain that
appeals to you so much?"

Ilsevir stopped, halfway to the door and turned around.
"He is a man of true vision." His eyes were shining. "His
time in the desert at Ondhessar has made him an inspiration
to us all. You should hear him speak about the revelation he
experienced when he first entered the shrine of the Eternal
Singer. I could bring him to talk to you—"

Adèle sank back on her pillows. The prospect was repel-
lent. "No," she said faintly, turning away from Ilsevir to
gaze out at the frozen gardens. She heard him pause a moment, then hurry away, his heels tapping over the highly
polished floor.

Ghislain wields too much influence over you, Ilsevir.
Tears began to trickle down her cheeks. *And if Enguerrand
is dead, who else can I turn to?*

Girim went down on one knee as Prince Ilsevir entered the
study. "Your majesty," he said respectfully, "may I offer my
congratulations?"

"News travels fast!" Ilsevir was looking perplexed. "How
did—"

Girim held out the secret letter that had been sent to him
by Hugues Donatien, watching as the prince scanned the
contents.

" '. . . Invaluable opportunity . . . unite the Allegondan
and Francian Commanderies . . . purge Francia of the in-
sidious and corrupting influences still rife in the universities
and colleges . . .' " Ilsevir looked up. His reaction would be
crucial to the success of Girim's plans. "But this is in-
spired!" Ilsevir's face was transfigured by a beatific smile.
"Maistre Donatien is right; God has given me this chance
to make the western quadrant a better place."

Girim nodded.

"Give me your blessing." Ilsevir knelt before Girim, who
extended his hand so that the Rosecoeurs' most eminent
patron could kiss the ruby ring he wore as head of the Allegondan Commanderie.

* * *

Girim went under cover of darkness to take one last look at the Ondhessar statue before leaving Bel'Esstar as escort to the royal party.

Since the chapel had reopened, the faithful of Bel'Esstar had been arriving in the hundreds to pray, with queues stretching out into the street. But not before the original Ondhessar statue had been removed in the dead of night by a squad of Girim's most trustworthy Rosecoeurs and deposited in the cellars of the Bel'Esstar Commanderie.

Lifting the cloths covering her, he let out a cry of revulsion and stepped back. The whole statue had turned the grey of mold, and the end of the nose, the fingertips, and the toes had began to crumble away. The patches of discoloration had deepened to blotches of black.

Is this a sign of your displeasure?

The priceless image of Elesstar was decaying before his eyes. And he, a hardened Guerrier, who had seen the most harrowing sights in battle, found himself unable to look at the corrupted image of his beloved saint. Hastily, he threw back the covers, hiding her.

Thank God I had the duplicate made just in time.

CHAPTER 12

The sound of strings and woodwinds tuning up wafted backstage as Celestine hurried toward the dressing rooms, her arms filled with billowing, gauzy dresses. She was amazed to see that so many dancers were obliged to change in such a tiny room. The girls crowded around two cracked mirrors, applying their eye liner and rouge as best they could. In the corridor, others sat on the floor to lace up the ribbons on their dance pumps. The room exuded a powerful odor of warm female bodies, perfume, and powder. As she stood at the entrance, many hands reached out and grabbed the costumes from her.

Yet, on her way back to the wardrobe room, she heard the strains of music from the stage and found herself drawn into the wings to listen. The orchestra had begun the overture and the enchanting melody she had heard backstage soared into the empty auditorium on violins and sweet-toned flutes. Hands clasped tightly together, she stood there, almost forgetting to breathe as the music swept her away. And as the overture finished, the singers of the chorus pushed past her, making their way onto the stage.

A sharp tap on the shoulder rudely shattered the enchantment. She turned to see Grebin glaring at her.

"What are you doing idling here, Maela?" he hissed as the chorus broke into song. "There're latrines to be cleaned."

All Celestine's delight in the music was soured. Her rightful place was there, with the singers. For a moment she wavered, indignant at the injustice of her circumstances—then she remembered that she was a nobody, without even a place to sleep.

"*Soon he'll change,*" whispered the Faie. "*Soon he'll be begging us to sing for him.*" It was only as Celestine was hefting the heavy bucket of water along the narrow passageway back from the pump that the Faie's comment struck her as odd. *Us.*

She pushed up her sleeves and set to work. Yet as she dragged the mop to and fro across the floor, the melody returned to haunt her. There was no one around to hear. She began to hum and then to sing, wordlessly, because she had not been able to make out the lyrics. Her voice was weak from lack of practice so she matched each pass of the mop to each phrase, hearing the notes echo around the tiled room until she had gained control of her breathing. Finally, as she poured the dirty water away down the open drain, she pushed her voice far into its upper register, thrilling into top notes that rang out, clear and exhilarating as an icy wind.

She picked up the mop and bucket and turned to see Grebin standing in the doorway, staring at her.

"I'm—I'm sorry," she mumbled, lowering her head as a blush of embarrassment spread across her face. "I'll get on with my chores." She was sure he would dock her pay for wasting time—or even give her the sack.

"Tell me I was hallucinating. Tell me that wasn't you singing, was it, Maela?"

"I won't do it again, I promise." She tried to hurry past him but he caught hold of her by the arm, jutting his face into hers. She shrank away, fearing what was coming next.

"Not so fast, young lady. Where did you learn to sing like that?"

"Lutèce." That, at least, wasn't a lie. "I sang in a church choir."

"Come with me." Grebin began to pull her along the passageway, the bucket clanking noisily as she hurried to keep up with him.

He opened the door to a rehearsal room. "Put that bucket down," he ordered, "and show me what you can do."

When Celestine finished singing, she saw Grebin push back his wig to scratch his shiny forehead. His face was screwed up into such a comically perplexed expression that it almost made her want to burst out laughing. She felt charged with excitement, as light-headed as if she had been sipping wine.

"So you have a voice, Maela Cassard. But you've never sung in opera?"

She shook her head. That was true; her career as an agent of Ruaud de Lanvaux had taken her into many embassy drawing rooms and concert halls, but always as a recitalist. It would have been impossible to combine the world of the opera house with the Commanderie's strict tenets.

"And you'd never heard *Rusalka's Kiss* until you came here?"

"I don't know the words. But I learned the aria listening to the rehearsals."

"A quick study too." He seized a book that had been left open on the music stand and thrust it into her hands. "This will be our next production. A romantic comedy, *A Spring Elopement*, another favorite of the Grand Duchess."

Celestine tried to hide an involuntary shiver. Gauzia had made her name in the very same work, in the role of Lise, the scheming soubrette. She looked down at the score and saw that Grebin had opened it at the first appearance of the heroine, Mariella.

"Read this."

Sight-read the aria? Celestine felt her stomach begin to flutter with nerves. The delicate pattern of black notes seemed to blur, one into another. She was being tested. If she failed to impress Grebin, she might as well give up.

Grebin struck her starting note on the keyboard and stood back, waiting.

Celestine reminded herself of Dame Elmire's advice and drew in a calming slow breath, exhaling before attacking the first phrase. The aria was lighthearted, like Mariella herself, a froth of high trills and runs. It was unlike the art songs Celestine was accustomed to singing. Yet, after ten bars or so, she began to enjoy herself. As she turned the page, she heard the accompaniment supporting her and, glancing up, saw that a gaunt, grey-haired repetiteur had slipped onto the fortepiano stool and was playing along with her.

This was turning into a performance—and she knew that she must not lose concentration for even half a beat or she would fall behind and disgrace herself.

The final run of the aria rose dizzily high; she braced herself, knowing that if she failed to reach and hold that top note, she would fail the audition.

As she let her voice float upward, she felt the Faie helping her, filling her lungs with air, brightening the tone until she reached the top. The note bloomed, then sparkled like a flower of crystal. Celestine looked up to see startled faces staring at her; people had crowded in at the open doorway. After a few seconds, someone began to applaud. "Bravo!" another cried. Grebin's ill-fitting wig had slipped over one eyebrow; he tugged it off and stuffed it in his pocket.

"We must talk, Demoiselle Cassard," he said, steering her out of the practice room through the curious throng, toward his office.

"So you learned to sing like that in a church choir?" It was more an accusation than a question.

"I was a pupil of Elmire Sorel in Francia," Celestine said demurely.

"Elmire Sorel?" Grebin was looking at her with new respect. "I heard her sing here at the Imperial Theater years ago; such a wonderful voice, such fire and passion . . ." And then the moment of nostalgia passed and he was once again his brusque, businesslike self, leaning forward across his desk to stare at her suspiciously. "Something doesn't add up here. A young woman with a talent like yours reduced to sweeping floors?"

"I told you, I've never sung in opera. I sang in a—"

"Church choir." He finished her sentence. "My dear demoiselle, you are hiding something—but what right do I have to pry into your personal affairs? Perhaps you caught a young priest's eye and had to flee a scandal . . . Whatever the reason, I'd like to offer you a contract with the Imperial Theater."

Celestine's heart began to beat faster. *Is my luck turning at last?*

"Your voice is a joy to listen to. But as you have no theatrical training, I can't put you directly into a leading role. So I'm proposing that you join the chorus as a soprano, and I'll review your progress after a month. Does that sound acceptable?"

"What would the salary be?"

"Comfortable enough for you to buy some clothes more suited to your new situation," Grebin said, looking disapprovingly at her worn dress.

Celestine found lodgings in a little boardinghouse four streets away from the theater. The furnishings were shabby and the pinch-faced landlady insisted that she pay a month's rent in advance, leaving no money for the new clothes Grebin had so pointedly suggested. Yet the room, tucked under the snow-laden eaves, was snug; the rising warmth from the woodstove on the floor below was a luxury. And the landlady's three cats took an instant liking to her, running out to greet her whenever she returned home.

Grebin set her to understudy the role of Mariella. The celebrated soprano, Anna Krylova, was suffering from a heavy cold, he told her, so she must be prepared to take her place.

And indeed, when Celestine arrived at the Imperial Theater on the day rehearsals were due to begin, Grebin rushed up to her in a panic. "La Krylova's taken to her bed," he said, "and the physicians say that her lungs are inflamed. It's serious. She won't be able to sing for weeks. You'll have to take her place. Don't let me down, Maela."

"That voice!" a woman cried out from the wings. "I know that voice!"

Celestine half turned to see a familiar face staring at her from the wings. Exquisitely painted to bring out the liquid green of her bold hazel eyes and the fullness of her lips, her auburn hair artfully curled and arranged, there stood Gauzia de Saint-Désirat.

She mustn't recognize me! Hearing her entry from the

repetiteur at the fortepiano, Celestine picked up her cue only to stop again as Gauzia stalked onto the stage, grandly holding up one gloved hand to halt the music.

Celestine stood, eyes lowered, as Gauzia walked around her, hearing the swish of her ermine-trimmed cloak over the boards.

"What's your name?"

Celestine raised her head. "Maela Cassard," she said quietly. Grebin came hurrying out onto the stage.

"Is there a problem, Diva?" he asked anxiously, glancing from one to the other. All around the theater, Celestine realized that everyone from the lowliest stagehand to the most senior chorus member had stopped what they were doing, sensing a storm crackling in the air.

"Ma-e-la Ca-ssard," Gauzia repeated, overemphasizing each syllable. Celestine forced herself to maintain her self-composure—yet the sudden appearance of her onetime fellow student and rival had reawakened a host of painful memories.

"Anna Krylova is suffering from a severe inflammation of the lungs," Grebin began to explain. "Maela has been understudying the role of Mariella and she'll be taking Krylova's place."

"I see." Gauzia stopped suddenly in front of Celestine and stared boldly into her face. "Hair can be dyed and skin darkened with walnut juice. But I know of no way to change eyes from blue to brown." She shrugged. "It must be coincidence."

"We'll break for a quarter of an hour," announced the conductor to the soloists assembled in the rehearsal room. "Thank you, Diva, that was truly delightful." Everyone broke into applause; Celestine joined in as Gauzia smiled graciously at her admirers. Yet the instant the conductor had left the room, the smile vanished and she turned on Celestine.

"Manager Grebin tells me that you studied with Dame Elmire in Lutèce." Gauzia's penetrating stare. "*I* studied with Elmire Sorel for several years, and yet I never once saw you among her pupils. I think I would have remembered a voice as distinctive as yours . . ."

"I believe I may be two or three years your senior, Diva," said Celestine. *She's trying to trick me. Has she guessed? She's trying to make me give myself away.*

"And you never sang in opera in Lutèce?"

"I sang in a church choir."

"Oh, *really*? So you won't have heard the news?"

"What news?" Celestine said warily.

"About the murder."

Celestine shook her head.

"So shocking that anyone should be murdered in church. But particularly shocking in this case. It was just before the darkness." Gauzia was obviously relishing telling the tale, lowering her voice to increase the dramatic effect. "The Grand Maistre of the Commanderie was found dying in the Chapel of Saint Meriadec. There was blood *everywhere*."

Celestine sat, rigid with shock, unable to speak. *The Maistre was dead?* "That's terrible news," she said eventually, trying to keep her voice from trembling. *I mustn't cry. Why would Maela Cassard cry over the death of a stranger?*

As soon as the rehearsal was over, Celestine put on her hooded cloak and set out through the snow to the Cathedral of Saint Simeon. There she handed to the grey-bearded sacristan the coins she had been saving to pay for her supper, and bought candles.

The monks were chanting vespers, and, as she walked through the gloom of the nave to the side chapel dedicated to Saint Serzhei, their deep voices seemed to her to be singing a threnody for Ruaud. The little chapel was already ablaze with candles, like a lantern in a dark night. She knelt to light her memorial candles and placed them one by one beneath the saint's icon, reciting under her breath the words of the Francian service for the dead.

"Dear Maistre," she whispered, "I can't believe you're gone. I can't believe that I'll never see your smile again . . .

or hear your voice." Tears began to stream down her face as memories came rushing back to her, memories from so long ago of a lost and desperate little child, suddenly swept up in the strong arms of a golden-haired knight and carried away on his charger to a white convent overlooking the sea.

"You were my fairy-tale knight, Maistre. You rescued me, you were my protector and my mentor." Gauzia's words sickened her. *Found murdered in the chapel . . . blood everywhere . . .* "A man in your position makes enemies. But who would strike you down when you were at prayer? Who would do such a cowardly thing?" Smarnan extremists, Tielen secret agents, even the monks of Saint Serzhei's shrine in Azhkendir; there were so many possibilities. "Forgive me, Maistre. I betrayed your trust in me. I didn't listen to your advice. If only I hadn't been so selfish, following my own desires, I could have stayed at your side. And then, maybe I could have saved your life . . ."

The singing ceased; the service had come to an end. She wiped the tears from her eyes as the candle smoke went wisping upward into the darkness. "But it's too late. Now there's no one left in the Commanderie to protect me. I can never go back to Francia."

CHAPTER 13

A day ago, wherever Andrei looked, all he could see was water. The sea had rushed in, flooding the whole coastline, sweeping away all traces of the village and the mission.

This morning he looked down on a scene of disorder and devastation. The sea had retreated, leaving chaos in its wake. Fragments of broken boats lay beached among the ruins of the mission chapel. Strewn all along the bay were uprooted trees, the carcasses of animals and, Andrei saw to his sadness, drowned bodies, flung up by the relentless tide to lie like abandoned dolls amid the debris.

He spent a grim morning helping the other men bury the dead. Most were strangers to the villagers; sailors or fishermen caught by the strength of the wave. As dusk was falling, the two priests, Laorans and Blaize, spoke the words of the Sergian funeral service over the mass grave, and the villagers went back up the hill to their encampment.

Andrei lingered behind, sobered and sad. The sole survivor of a devastating storm at sea, he knew how fortunate he was to be still alive.

"I've never seen anything like this in my whole life," he admitted to Blaize. "Nor do I ever want to see it again."

"What else is there to do but rebuild?" Blaize said philosophically.

It was difficult to get any rest in such crowded conditions; children whimpered and hungry babies wailed, but eventually sleep overtook Andrei. He woke to see Laorans crouched over the casket he had helped the priest rescue, carefully examining the contents by the light of the dying fire.

"What's in the box, Abbé?"

Laorans looked up at him, the flames glinting in his spectacle lenses. "Manuscripts. Ancient manuscripts whose contents are so contentious that they cost me my career in the Commanderie."

Intrigued, Andrei moved to sit down beside him. "What do they say?"

"That the children of Azilis are blessed because of the angel blood that runs in their veins. That we should respect them for their gifts, which were bestowed to benefit mankind, and not persecute them."

"And who are these children of Azilis?"

"The magi. Magus Kaspar Linnaius, for one."

"Heresy," murmured Enguerrand.

"Not according to these Holy Texts, which I discovered hidden in Azilis's shrine. My superiors thought they had destroyed them, but they burned the copy I'd made. I managed to smuggle the originals out of Francia," Laorans said with a dry little chuckle. "They were far too valuable to be consigned to the flames."

"Are they religious texts?" Enguerrand propped himself up on one elbow on the other side of the fire.

"I believe," Laorans said, his voice intense, his eyes alight with the fanatical enthusiasm of the scholar, "that they predate those we use today by several centuries. I believe that they were suppressed by the early followers of Saint Sergius. We mustn't forget that Sergius was acting under the instructions of the Seven Heavenly Guardians, led by Galizur. And that by the time the priests of Ty Nagar discovered the Rift and learned how to summon the Drakhaouls through the Serpent Gate, they had been imprisoned in the Realm of Shadows for some considerable time."

"It's still heresy," Enguerrand said severely. "Nagazdiel rebelled against the Divine Will."

"The Holy Texts we know were written by the followers of Galizur. But you, your majesty"—and Laorans gazed keenly at Enguerrand through the flames—"know so much better than I how angelic in nature Nilaihah was at heart."

Andrei saw Enguerrand flinch at the mention of his

Drakhaoul. "Is it in the nature of an angel to commit murder?" Enguerrand said after a while in a distant voice. "Nilaihah made me kill Ruaud. Ruaud who was more like a father to me than my own father ever was."

Andrei felt a pang of sympathetic guilt. "And Adramelech made me kill my oldest friend." The words were wrung out of him. It was the first time he had admitted it aloud.

"Ah, you make my heart bleed." The caustic tones set Andrei's nerves on edge as he saw Oskar sit up beyond the rising smoke. "So you killed a few people who got in your way? Learn to live with it."

"Father Blaize? You've not said a word." Andrei turned to Laorans's companion, ignoring Oskar. "What do you think?"

A distant look came into Blaize's eyes. "I found myself on a long sea voyage once with a young magus. In spite of the gulf between us, we got to know each other rather well. By the end of the voyage, I like to think that we had become friends." He leaned forward to stoke the fire with fresh kindling. "He was injured. I nursed him back to health. Should I have just turned away and left him to die? That's what *The Book of Galizur* would have had me do. Perhaps I was wrong . . . and my actions have condemned me to eternal damnation."

"*The Book of Galizur*?" Enguerrand repeated in puzzled tones.

Blaize and Laorans glanced at each other across the flames and began to laugh. "We've been away from the Commanderie for so long that we've grown used to calling the Holy Texts by that name to distinguish them from the texts I found in the Shrine."

"And what are they called?"

"*The Book of Azilis*."

Once Enguerrand had begun to read *The Book of Azilis*, he could not stop. Too weak from fever to help the other men build shelters, he sat beneath a tamarind tree, devouring Laorans's translation. At first he feared he might be corrupted by what he was reading, but as he became more engrossed, his fears faded away.

From time to time, he closed his eyes and leaned back against the rough bark of the trunk, deep in thought. Being one with golden-eyed Nilaihah had given him new insight into the origins of the ancient and bitter war that had split the Guardians of Heaven. It was only natural, he supposed, that the victors had done all they could to eradicate all traces of their opponents.

"How are you feeling, sire?"

Enguerrand opened his eyes to see Abbé Laorans bending over him, his lined face crinkled into an expression of kindly concern. It was twilight and cooking fires had been lit in the clearing. "I—I'm confused," he said. "I've begun to question everything I ever believed in."

"That's exactly how I felt!" The Abbé sat next to him. "But it all becomes much clearer when you reread the texts, I promise you." His eyes gleamed with enthusiasm in the firelight.

Enguerrand reached out and took the old priest's hand in his own. "I fear you've been very badly treated by the Commanderie," he said. "How can I begin to make it up to you?"

"So you believe, sire?" Laorans's voice quavered.

"If I hadn't seen what lies beyond the Serpent Gate, then I might still doubt the authenticity of these texts. But now, it all makes sense. And if I ever get back to Francia, I promise you, Abbé, that I'll do all in my power to see *The Book of Galizur* replaced by the wisdom of *The Book of Azilis* in all our schools and churches."

"You'll have quite a fight on your hands," said Laorans, chuckling.

"I'll be ready for them!" Enguerrand knew that he had changed since he had been host to Nilaihah; he had inherited something of his Drakhaoul's indomitable, determined nature. "And I'll have you at my side to support me."

Laorans shook his head. "I'm honored, sire, but I'm not sure I could leave my little flock, especially in these difficult times."

"Then at least let me make a copy. I'm no use to anyone until I've thrown off the last of this fever . . . but at least I could study the texts properly by copying them out."

"What an excellent idea!" Laòrans straightened up. "I'm sure that in all the confusion I managed to save pens, ink, and paper somewhere. What good is a mission without a school, after all?"

CHAPTER 14

It had been but a few months since Kaspar Linnaius had last flown across the remote Azure Ocean, yet in that time, so much had changed.

And I had not thought I would ever have to come this far again.

He passed high above the Southern Fleet in full sail, as it headed on Eugene's orders toward the beleaguered Spice Islands to aid the islanders and spice traders. But, even though they were the swiftest ships in the quadrant, it would take them at least another four weeks to complete their journey.

The calm sheen of the waters below—a deep, clear, glassy blue—was deceptive. Because, although his instincts told him that he was approaching the Spice Islands and that Ty Nagar, the fabled island of the Serpent God, lay farther beyond, he could see little below that he recognized. He had nothing to steer by, for the haze of drifting smoke from the fire cone that dominated Nagar's island was nowhere to be seen.

"Is it possible that the island is gone?" he murmured aloud. He had heard tell of volcanic eruptions so violent that they had cracked islands apart and sunk them beneath the sea. "Perhaps the distortion caused by the destruction of the Serpent Gate triggered the disaster."

Certainly "disaster" was the only word to describe the desolate scenes below. The nutmeg groves and cinnamon plantations had been washed away, along with the topsoil; only a few stumps remained. Worst of all, he could see no signs of life: The lively villages and bustling little harbors where the Tielen spice clippers used to put in to collect their fragrant cargos had vanished, with only a trail of driftwood and tumbled stones to show they had ever been there.

A terrified cry pierced Andrei's dreams. He sat up, groggy from sleep, to see others stirring around the embers of their fires. The sky was lightening toward the east although the little encampment was still shrouded in darkness.

"Forgive me. Forgive me, Maistre!" The anguished cry came again. Andrei, recognizing the Francian tongue, made his way over to Enguerrand's shelter. Aude was struggling to restrain the young king, who was thrashing about wildly.

"Don't look at me like that!" Enguerrand was staring fixedly into the darkness behind the shelter.

"Enguerrand. Calm yourself." Andrei knelt beside Enguerrand and placed a hand on his shoulder.

"Nilaihah made me do it. I tried to stop him—but he overmastered me." Enguerrand began to sob uncontrollably.

"A nightmare, or is he delirious again?" Andrei said to Aude. But Aude was also staring into the shadowy glade behind them.

"Andrei, look. There *is* someone there . . ."

Andrei looked into the gloom and saw, with a sudden chill, that she was right. The figure of a man stood there, watching. He turned suddenly and disappeared among the slender-palm trunks. Andrei gave a shout and went running after him. From the rustling sounds in the branches overhead, he could tell that the birds were beginning to wake; it must be near dawn. But the silent watcher had vanished into the night and Andrei soon abandoned his search.

"Why?" Enguerrand was saying to Aude. "Why is his soul not at rest? Why has he come back to haunt me?"

"Who did you think you saw?" Andrei sat down beside them.

"Ruaud de Lanvaux." Enguerrand turned to stare at him with sleep-starved eyes. "He tried to exorcise the daemon and I—no, Nilaihah—murdered him. His blood is on my conscience."

"A vengeful ghost?" Andrei was still skeptical.

"Why don't we have Père Laorans say prayers for his soul?" Aude suggested and Andrei saw Enguerrand's anguished expression relax a little.

"Oh yes, Aude, thank you . . ." The king lay back, evidently exhausted by his outburst. Aude met Andrei's eyes in the pale dawnlight.

"He wasn't imagining it," she said softly. "I saw the ghost too; and if it wasn't Maistre de Lanvaux, then it was a very clever spirit to copy his likeness so exactly."

Andrei said nothing, but he knew that for the practical Aude to have admitted that she had recognized the ghost, it could not have been a hallucination. As to what the ghost's appearance meant, however, he could not begin to imagine. It had left him with a chill, unsettled feeling, as if there were unforeseen consequences to the destruction of the Serpent Gate that were only now beginning to make themselves apparent.

It was exhausting working in the late afternoon, even after the fiercest heat of the day had dissipated. But to build new huts, the islanders needed timber, so even the princes of Rossiya joined in with the tree-felling.

Andrei stopped to wipe the dripping sweat from his eyes.

"Slacking again, Orlov?" Oskar jeered. He had stripped to the waist and was swinging his axe with skill, expertly splitting the wood.

"Mon père, look!" One of the little boys came hurtling past, screaming out at the top of his voice. "Look up. There's a man in a flying boat!"

Andrei dropped his axe. Oskar shaded his eyes to gaze at the sky. Aude came running out of the hospital hut. There was nothing to be seen above the tops of the trees but a line of little white clouds, fine as thistledown.

"Those children have vivid imaginations." Andrei bent to pick up his axe, wishing that he had not been foolish enough to dare to hope. Oskar began to swing his axe again with renewed fury, chips of bark flying out at all angles.

It must have been a half hour or so later when the village dogs started to yap excitedly.

"Someone's coming," said Oskar warningly to Andrei. Both men picked up their axes and went to the edge of the clearing. There had been rumors of pirates and Andrei was only too aware how vulnerable to attack the little community was.

Walking slowly toward them came a white-haired man, his long wispy beard stirred by the first evening breeze off the sea.

Andrei stared, then rubbed his eyes. Was it a mirage . . . or another revenant? The old man looked frail and walked with a halting gait, as if his bones ached, but he was no illusion.

"Magus!" Andrei hailed him. He had never thought he would be so glad to see Kaspar Linnaius in his life.

Linnaius stopped. He peered at Andrei. "Your highness is alive!" He nodded, approvingly. "This is good news indeed. Your sister has been sick with worry."

"So she sent you to look for me?" Andrei was greatly touched at the thought that Astasia still cared for him, in spite of the ordeal that he and his Drakhaoul had subjected her to.

"The Emperor charged me to search for you all."

"And what provoked this sudden change of heart?" Oskar, his shirt slung over his bare shoulders, came over to Andrei's side.

"You must be tired, Magus. Please come and rest in the shade." Andrei led the way up the dirt track as the village children followed, curious to see the old man who had arrived in a flying boat, whispering and giggling, their dark eyes round with wonder.

"They think we're *dead*?" Enguerrand raised his head from the pillow; Aude went to help him.

"The first ships bringing aid from the west are still far off. And I've been searching for you for many days, going from island to island."

"So it was assumed that we all drowned?"

"Ty Nagar is gone." Linnaius took a sip of his cinnamon tea. "From what I could see, a massive volcanic eruption split the island in two and sank it beneath the waves."

"How has my mother taken the news?" Enguerrand asked.

"Your mother has invited your brother-in-law, Ilsevir, to succeed to the throne in your place. The coronation is probably taking place as we speak."

"*What!*" Enguerrand sat bolt upright. "How dare she!"

"No one is more keen to see you restored to the throne of Francia than the Emperor," Linnaius said diplomatically. "He is reluctant to recognize Ilsevir as joint ruler of Francia and Allegonde. He has a proposition to put to you—"

"I will not get involved in the Emperor's political machinations! Does Eugene think I'm incapable of setting my own house in order?" Enguerrand, exhausted by his outburst, dropped back. "I insist that you take me straight back to Lutèce."

Linnaius sighed; he was weary of indulging these young princes and their petulant outbursts. He was tempted to remind Enguerrand that if it were not for the Emperor's intervention, there would be no hope of rescue for many weeks. "Would you prefer to wait for the Rossiyan fleet to arrive, majesty? They're still some way off and the journey back to Francia will take them at least five months."

CHAPTER 15

It was past midnight by the time Celestine reached her lodgings. She was greeted by her landlady's three black-and-white cats, who frisked about her skirts, purring and rubbing their heads against her hand when she bent to stroke them. The performance had gone well enough that evening, but Gauzia was becoming increasingly difficult, resorting to little scene-stealing tricks, conducting elaborate business behind her back as she was singing, provoking sniggers from some of the audience. She had even stooped so low as to encourage her clique of followers to chatter noisily during Celestine's first aria, leading to loud shushing, then shouts of disapproval from Celestine's staunchest admirers. Afterward, Grebin had summoned both women to his office and given them a stern lecture.

"I don't want a riot on my hands, ladies, no matter how strongly your admirers feel about your relative charms. Riots are expensive!" Grebin glared at them both. "And of course I would have to withhold your fees to cover the cost of repairs to the theater."

There were only eight more performances to be endured before Gauzia and her entourage were due to travel on to Tielborg. Celestine couldn't wait to be rid of her. Although once Gauzia was gone, there was no guarantee Grebin would give her a part in the next opera. It was rumored that Anna Krylova was making a good recovery, so Celestine fully expected that she would be demoted to the chorus once more.

She unlocked the door to her little room then stopped on the threshold. The figure of a man was silhouetted against a skim of pale moonlight. *A burglar?* She felt the Faie tense, ready to defend her.

The intruder turned toward her and she took a step back as the uncertain moonlight brightened, revealing the soft grey eyes and honey-fair hair of her dead lover. The cats turned tail and fled down the stairs.

"Henri?" she said, retreating. "What are you doing here?" It couldn't be Henri; Henri was dead. Unless this was . . .

"*Who are you?*" He stared at her. "*You sound like my Celestine . . . but I don't recognize you.*"

"Faie!" Celestine cried. "Change me back."

"*Be careful, Celestine; this is nothing but a revenant, a mere shadow of your lost love—*"

"I don't care. Change me back now." And as the Faie's glamour fell away from her, she saw his bewildered expression fade and alter, smiling as he recognized her. He held out his hands. She started forward, only to feel the Faie check her.

"*Don't go to him. Don't go any closer.*"

"Henri? What are you doing here?" Celestine ached to run into his arms.

"*I had to see you. I had to know that you were all right. There's so much I need to tell you.*"

And suddenly she knew that she could not bear to hear it. It had taken so long to heal the wounds left by his death and just the sound of his voice made the desolation of loss wash over her once more. "No," she whispered. "No, this can't be happening. You're a dream. The dead don't return."

A cloud passed across the face of the moon, casting the attic into sudden darkness. When the moonlight brightened again, the revenant had gone. But a faint, charnel taint lingered in the air that reminded Celestine of the damp crypt of Saint Meriadec's. She lit the little lamp, hoping that its glow would chase the lingering shadows from the room. Yet as its wavering flame burned more brightly, it brought her no cheer or consolation. She noticed that the table on which it stood was covered in a layer of gritty dust, as if the landlady had not cleaned in weeks. Celestine ran her finger along the wood and, as the fine particles sifted through her fingers, she heard the Faie murmuring over and over to herself, "*No. This can't be happening.*"

"What is this dust, Faie? Tell me. No matter how horrible it is, I need to know."

"*This dust has blown in from the Realm of Shadows. When the soul leaves the physical body behind, it's imprinted with its last, strongest emotion. Imprinted, almost always, with the feelings that mortal person bore for another: child, parent, lover . . .*"

Celestine nodded. A terrible sadness had begun to well up within her.

"*And those feelings are often mixed with regret. A life cut short before its time, words left unsaid, yearnings never adequately expressed. That was why I sang. I sang to ease those regrets, to soothe those unfulfilled hopes and dreams, to take away the bitterness and reveal the way through the shadows to the light beyond.*"

"'Blessed Azilia, let thy light shine through the darkness and show us the way to paradise,'" whispered Celestine. It was the ancient Vesper Prayer of the Knights of the Commanderie. Never, until now, had she understood the profound implications of those simple words.

"Who *are* you, Faie? Are you Azilis? Was Linnaius telling the truth after all?"

"*There has been no one to sing for the dead since Linnaius took me away from Ondhessar. And in that time, so many souls have become lost in the Ways Beyond, held back by their regrets and their unfulfilled dreams.*"

"So Henri came back to me, because he's become a lost soul?" The thought caused her so much heartache that she could hardly articulate the words. "I hoped that—at least—he might be at peace. I can't bear to think that he's been suffering all this time. I have to help him; I can't leave him wandering like this." As she was speaking she had begun to realize the sacrifice she might have to make for the sake of her dead lover. "Faie—if you returned to Ondhessar, would you be able to set Henri's soul free from wandering this world? And all those other lost souls?"

The Faie was silent a long while. "*But if I return to the*

Rift," she said eventually, "*I won't be able to protect you anymore. Let me stay with you a little longer.*"

Celestine gazed into the translucent eyes of her guardian spirit. In all the years they had been together, she had never imagined that one day they would have to part. But even though the thought of having to live alone and unprotected terrified her, the wish to bring peace to Henri's wandering spirit was stronger.

"I want you to help me to lay his ghost," she said. "And if that means going to Ondhessar, dear Faie, then I'll find a way to take you there."

"*Let me stay with you just a little longer.*" Azilis's voice become so soft, so persuasive, that it was like a mother's caress. "*Let me know that you, my dearest child, have found fulfillment . . . so that when I have to go back into the darkness, I have happy memories of my time here with you to sustain me.*"

Celestine felt her will wavering. Azilis must be using her powers to influence her. Had she become too attached to the mortal world? Had she found the brief second taste of life too seductive, too tasty, to give up? Every night that Celestine went out onstage to sing, she had sensed Azilis wake within her, living the music, experiencing every note, every nuance of feeling, as if it were her own. "Then I'll wait until the final performance of *A Spring Elopement* is over," she promised her, knowing full well how hard it was going to be to say farewell to her dearest Faie.

CHAPTER 16

Spring had come early to Francia, and as the royal coach bearing the Prince and Princess of Allegonde entered the long avenue leading up to Plaisaunces, pale petals drifted down from the cloudy sky, borne on the breeze from the walled palace gardens.

Adèle raised the blind of the carriage and gazed out. The people had gathered to watch the procession but they were silent, standing behind the cordon formed by the soldiers of the palace guard.

On his side of the carriage, Ilsevir waved his hand, but no cheers arose to greet him.

"They seem rather subdued, my new subjects," he observed in a dejected tone that Adèle knew meant that his feelings were hurt.

"They're still in mourning for my brother," she said diplomatically. "I'm sure they'll cheer loudly enough after the coronation." But she had noticed the significantly high numbers of guards lining the route; Chancellor Aiguillon must have anticipated trouble. The vague feeling of unhappiness that had been troubling her since they crossed the mountains and entered her home country increased. They had not even smiled at her, and she was a princess of the realm, Gobain's daughter. Did they resent her as much as her husband?

Queen Aliénor was seated on a dais in the Salle des Chevaliers, beneath the brightly colored shields and banners of the four ancient duchies of Francia. All the ministers were gathered around her, including at her right hand, Adèle noticed, Hugues Donatien, reappointed Grand Maistre of the Commanderie. In stark contrast to the vibrant banners, all were soberly dressed in mourning black.

Trust Maman to turn our arrival into a theatrical performance, she thought, wincing as trumpeters appeared on the musicians' gallery to blow a deafening fanfare. All she wanted was a cup of tea and a long bath to soak away the stiffness of travel.

"Welcome, your majesty." Aliénor rose to greet them and as all the dignitaries bowed low, Ilsevir went up onto the dais to kiss his mother-in-law. Adèle dutifully followed.

"You look peaky, Adèle," Aliénor said as she brushed her cheek with her lips. "You'd better sit down."

"It's been a long journey, Madame," said Adèle, forcing a smile, but she sat beside her mother, hoping that Aliénor would focus all her attention on Ilsevir, giving her a little time to recover.

"The plans for the coronation are ready for your approval, your majesty." Chancellor Aiguillon bowed to Prince Ilsevir as he held out a bound folder.

"Let's see." Ilsevir took the folder and opened it, leafing through the pages. "The procession to the cathedral will begin at nine in the morning . . ."

Adèle half listened as Ilsevir read aloud the order of service. She was lost in a memory of Enguerrand's coronation, and the recollection of her brother—his bespectacled face earnest and radiant, as the archbishop placed the crown on his dark head—made her eyes sting with tears.

Why did you have to go so far away to carry out your charitable good works? Why couldn't you have stayed here, safe in your own country?

"And while the bishops and other priests process up the aisle carrying the crown, the choir will sing," Ilsevir was saying. "An anthem by Talfieri, Adèle? Or one of your Francian composers?"

"Surely a Francian would be best," she said swiftly. And then, lost in the memory again, "with a Francian soloist. I'd love it if Celestine de Joyeuse . . ." Her voice faded out as she became aware that all the ministers were looking at her oddly.

"Your highness may not be aware that Demoiselle de Joyeuse is a wanted criminal," said Maistre Donatien coldly.

Adèle stared at him. "You must be mistaken, Maistre," she said. "Celestine is a good and loyal friend of mine."

"I fear that even good friends may be swayed by the lure of the Forbidden Arts. The demoiselle has been practicing dark magic."

"That must be slander! Vicious slander put about by one of her jealous rivals." Adèle was incensed that Celestine's reputation had been tarnished by such ugly rumors.

"We have proof, your highness."

Adèle turned her head away, determined not to listen to Maistre Donatien any longer; he was her mother's confidant and, she was certain now, not to be trusted.

"Official mourning for Enguerrand will end in a week's time," said Aliénor. Adèle stared at the floor. How could her mother speak so calmly and coldly about her son's death? Even hearing the words had brought the tears to her eyes again and she was fighting to hold them back, willing herself not to weep in front of Aliénor and the ministers.

There came a sudden clatter of hooves outside and the sound of shouting shattered the awkward silence.

"I demand to see my cousin! Let me through!"

The great doors at the far end of the Salle des Chevaliers burst open. The guards thrust their halberds across the opening, creating a barrier. A grey-haired, broad-shouldered man strained against them.

Aliénor rose. "Raimon?" she said in a voice sharp as steel. "What are you doing here?"

Ilsevir retreated behind his wife's chair. "Who is this rude man?" he whispered nervously in her ear.

"The Duc de Provença," Adèle whispered back. She had not seen her father's cousin in many years.

"Where's my daughter? Where is Aude?" bellowed the duke.

"Captain, would you be so good as to let the duke through?" Aliénor said to the captain of her guards.

"First you tell me, Aliénor, that Aude has run away to Serindher with your son." Raimon de Provença strode toward the dais, loudly enumerating his grievances. "Second comes the news of this tidal wave or typhoon. And then— here are the Prince and Princess of Allegonde, and talk of a coronation. I need to know: Is my daughter alive or dead?"

The raised voices, the growing sense of unbearable tension, mingled with grief for her brother and fatigue after the journey . . . Suddenly the salle began to swim before Adèle's eyes. She heard Ilsevir cry out her name. And then a roaring sound, as if of an incoming tide, rose to drown out everything else and she went under into blackness.

"Have you been eating properly?"

Adèle closed her eyes wearily as her mother started on one of her lectures again. "A glass of strong red wine a day, with a spoonful of phosphorus, will be good for your constitution. We can't have you fainting at the coronation. And we need you for the fitting of the robes tomorrow."

"Yes, Madame . . ." If only Maman would let her alone to rest.

"She looks very peaky, Ilsevir. I'd like my physician to take a look at her."

"I'm sure Adèle is just fatigued after the journey," she heard Ilsevir say and smiled to herself, touched that he had dared to defend her against her mother. If only he would stay and talk with her. He was spending so much time these days with Girim nel Ghislain and the clerics that she felt neglected.

"Nevertheless, I'm going to call in Doctor Vallot."

"Vallot? In spite of all his experience, he couldn't save my father." In the shocked silence that followed, Adèle realized that she had spoken her thoughts aloud.

"Well, I must go and meet with Maistre Donatien," said Ilsevir, retreating hastily.

"They just stood there," said Adèle when he had gone. "They stood in silence. Watching."

"What *are* you babbling about? Are you feverish?" said Aliénor sharply.

"The people. They don't want Ilsevir as king. They don't want Francia and Allegonde to be united."

"What do they care as long as the taxes don't rise too high and there's enough bread to fill their bellies? Francia alone is weak, but Francia and Allegonde united present a strong front to resist the Emperor."

Adèle lay back, knowing there was no point in arguing with her mother. But Aliénor was blind. That silent protest was a sign of a deeper malaise. Resentment was brewing in the city and could erupt at any moment into open rebellion.

The morning of the coronation, the skies filled with clouds and rain began to fall over Lutèce.

"What luck we chose the closed carriage," said Ilsevir, gazing out at the raindrops running down the windows.

"Yes," said Adèle. She felt sad and subdued. Was the wet weather an ill omen? "You look lovely," Ilsevir said softly.

"Do I?" She looked at him, surprised yet touched by the compliment. "Thank you." All the while her ladies had been dressing her in the heavy gown of blue and gold brocade, the colors of Francia, her mind had been elsewhere, wondering why she, of all the three children of Gobain and Aliénor, should be the only one still alive.

As they climbed down from the carriage, equerries hurried forward to shield them from the rain. Adèle noticed how few had gathered outside the cathedral to cheer for their new king and queen. An honor guard lined their way up the wide steps and into the cathedral: all Allegondan Rosecoeurs, she noted sadly.

And then a fanfare blared out to announce their arrival and the long procession set off. Adèle sighed. Everything in the gloomy, drafty cathedral reminded her of what she had lost: a father and two beloved elder brothers.

If only you were here to sing for me, Celestine. I think I could endure this with fortitude if I could hear your sweet voice and know you were here to cheer my spirits afterward . . .

"Ready, my dearest?" Ilsevir whispered and, looking up at him, she saw how pale he looked. She had been so bound up in her own feelings that she had neglected to notice that her husband was suffering from nerves. Ilsevir needed her support as never before. She put the past from her mind and smiled bravely up at him as she placed her hand firmly on his.

"I'm ready," she said.

CHAPTER 17

Jagu disembarked at the Mirom docks under a yellow-grey sky that threatened more snow. The crew had already begun to unload casks of wine from the hold, rolling them down onto the quayside with much raucous shouting and swearing. Merchants from Khitari in their high-collared jackets had gathered in a huddle to check on boxes of tea, and an argument suddenly broke out as one discovered a fractured seal. Wagons clattered over the cobbles, as traders in fur coats and fur-trimmed hats arrived to haggle over the *Dame Blanche*'s cargo.

The sea journey to Mirom had taken much longer than Jagu had anticipated. Winter storms in the Straits had twice driven Captain Peillac to seek shelter in little ports on the western coast of Muscobar. Cut off from any news, Jagu had fretted away his time ashore, even setting out to travel overland by sleigh. But severe blizzards inland drove him back to the ship. By the time they reached the Nieva estuary, the river had frozen over and they had to wait for channels to be cut through the thick winter ice by Tielen ships with specially designed metal prows.

Having secured lodgings, Jagu presented himself at the Francian Embassy. While he was waiting in the entrance hall, he couldn't help noticing that all the ambassador's staff were wearing black mourning bands.

"I'm sorry to keep you waiting, Lieutenant de Rustéphan." An earnest-faced young man came out to greet him, ushering him swiftly into his office. "My name is Roget de Corméry, secretary to Ambassador d'Abrissard."

"Has the ambassador suffered a bereavement?" Jagu

asked, seeing that Corméry was also wearing a mourning band.

"My dear lieutenant, haven't you heard the terrible news? The king has been lost at sea."

Jagu stared at him, dumbfounded.

"It seems that his majesty was visiting a distant mission in Serindher when a tidal wave or typhoon struck. The reports are still vague. And it's rumored—but please may I count on your discretion here—that Prince Andrei may have been with him."

"First Maistre de Lanvaux, now the king?" All the time Jagu had been trapped by the weather, he had been cut off from news of the outside world. "Are there any orders for me from the Forteresse?" he asked, trying to focus on his mission.

"A letter of credit has been sent through from the Commanderie treasurer to cover your expenses. And his Excellency asked me to ensure . . ."

Enguerrand was dead? Jagu hardly heard what Corméry was saying; he was trying to come to terms with the news. The last he had heard was that the king had been abducted by a Drakhaoul—so to have survived that assault only to succumb to the treacherous elements seemed the cruelest of fates.

"You'll need more warm clothes too."

Jagu blinked, realizing that he had not heard a word of what Corméry was telling him.

"It may be spring in Francia, but here in Mirom, the snows can still return after the thaw."

Jagu entered the vast nave of the Cathedral of Saint Simeon. A deep, dark chanting echoed through the incense-spiked air, sending shivers through his whole body. He had heard tell of the visceral power of the monks' singing, but as his eyes became accustomed to the dimness, he saw them: thirty or so long-bearded men gathered together in the golden glow of the altar candles, producing an extraordinarily deep-throated, resonant sound. He closed his eyes and let the ancient chant enshroud him. It was a music borne of the earth itself, dragged up from deep below, raw and vi-brant.

Jagu found an obscure corner and knelt, silently repeating the words of the Sergian funeral service for his lost, drowned king, though in his heart, he still hoped that Enguerrand had been washed up on some little island and was waiting to be rescued.

"How long have you known Jagu de Rustéphan, Lieu-tenant Guyomard?" asked Grand Maistre Donatien. Rain spattered against the windowpanes behind him; the view of the river and the quay beyond was obscured by trails of water.

"Over fifteen years; we were at Saint Argantel's Seminary together." Kilian gazed at Donatien, wondering what lay behind such a seemingly innocent question.

"I sent the lieutenant on a mission to Muscobar in the autumn and he has not returned. I think you may have some idea what that mission was." Donatien was still smil-ing, but his eyes gazed keenly back at Kilian.

"Demoiselle de Joyeuse."

"So he told you?"

"I guessed." Kilian could play at that game too.

"So you were close enough to know the way he thinks, acts?"

"Close enough," Kilian said lightly.

"So why do you think he hasn't brought her back for questioning?"

Kilian stared down at his boots, noticing a spatter of mud. "Perhaps he hasn't tracked her down yet," he mut-tered. "Muscobar is a big country."

"What's most important to you, Lieutenant: your vow as a Guerrier or your friendship with Rustéphan?"

Kilian knew exactly where the questions were leading; his future career in the Commanderie would depend on his answer.

Jagu, you stupid bastard. You didn't listen to a word of my advice, did you? You've gone and thrown everything away, and all for the sake of that worthless woman.

"I value his friendship highly," he said, "but my sacred vow must always come first."

"And if Rustéphan had betrayed the Commanderie, how would you feel about him then?"

"Our friendship would be over. Any betrayal of the Commanderie would feel like a personal betrayal," Kilian said stiffly. *And more so, Maistre, than you could begin to imagine.*

"You have considerable potential, Kilian." The Maistre smiled warmly at him. "I think you could go far in the Commanderie. Changes are coming. I can see you replacing Alain Friard when he retires."

"The captain's retiring?"

"Yes, and maybe sooner than he anticipates. Make a success of this mission, Kilian, and I will personally recommend you to the king for promotion."

Captain Guyomard. Kilian had to admit to himself that it had a pleasing ring to it as he hurried through the rain to the treasurer's office. And Donatien had given him carte blanche to carry out the mission using whatever means he thought appropriate.

What had love and friendship brought him? Nothing but heartache and humiliation. But promotion and the chance to become one of the men who controlled Francia? Kilian had never realized till now that he was ambitious. To rise to the top meant being ruthless, shedding old friends and allies when it was expedient to do so.

"Passage on a Mirom-bound ship for you, Lieutenant?"

"Indeed, and I'll need an extra cabin on the return journey. I'm planning to bring back an old friend of mine."

Over the next days, Jagu found himself returning to the cathedral, drawn by the power of the monks' singing. The Muscobites employed choirs of a cappella singers in their churches and cathedrals, eschewing the use of instruments for their religious services. There was no sign of women in the church choirs of Mirom, so Celestine could not have found employment there, unless she had entered a convent . . .

It was bitterly cold in the cathedral that day and Jagu sought out a tavern to warm himself. As he sat in the smoky fug, his numb fingers clasped around a mug of steaming *sbiten,* he sipped slowly, feeling the honey-spiced warmth infuse slowly through his body.

Where are you, Celestine? She had last been seen at Lapwing Spar, the southernmost tip of Muscobar. After that, he had picked up only the vaguest of clues. A fair-haired woman matching Celestine's description had auditioned for several theaters in late autumn, just before the great darkness. After the darkness, there had been no more sightings. If she was still pursuing Kaspar Linnaius, she might have gone to Tielen weeks ago.

When do I accept defeat?

Since his first visit to the cathedral, he had not been able to rid his mind of the glorious sound of the choir. One chant in particular kept weaving its way through his mind, its sonorities sad yet triumphant, like the song of a warrior who had survived a desperate and bloody battle, limping back across the battlefield, past the bodies of his fallen comrades . . .

What's happening to me? Why do I feel this way? Since Ruaud's death and Celestine's disappearance, Jagu had begun to question everything in his life. While Ruaud had been there to guide and inspire him, the Commanderie had fulfilled his need to make a stand against the darkness. But now he felt the irresistible pull of his first love—music.

Jagu had done little in the way of composition at the conservatoire, concentrating on improving his keyboard technique. Now, for the first time, he felt the compulsion to try to recapture in notes that elusive, all-transcending moment of clarity he had experienced in the cathedral.

He sat up late into the night, frantically writing, scribbling out, then writing again. It was as if the torrent of notes had been building up deep within him over a long while and there was no stopping it. It poured unchecked from his pen onto the staves he had ruled, forcing him to abandon himself to the demands of the music. It was a work for chorus and soprano soloist, growing out of the pitches of the ancient chant—quite unlike anything he had ever heard be-

fore. It was not that he had given up on his search for
Celestine; it seemed to him, as he worked, that he could hear
her singing the solo soprano part he was creating. Her pure
voice was the inspiration for his choice of words, which
were taken from the Vesper Prayer of the Knights of the
Commanderie—the "Song of Azilis." Sometimes he even
felt as if Celestine were with him in his shabby lodgings,
leaning over his shoulder as he wrote.

Day after day, Jagu worked obsessively on his Vesper
Prayer, only leaving his room to buy more paper and ink.
His landlady brought meals, leaving them outside his door
so as not to disturb him; often he forgot they were there till
hours later and had to spoon down cold beetroot soup or
tepid stew with globules of congealed fat.

After a while he began to sense a feeling of resolution. He
scanned the pages, filled with scribblings-out and corrections, reading through what he had written. The boldness
of the musical language surprised him. He had no idea that
such strength of feeling had been bottled up inside him—or
that he had the innate skills to organize the musical material. But then he had been taught by Henri de Joyeuse . . .
and he must have absorbed something of the Maistre's
technical ability in those long hours of study.

"And yet I never thought of myself as a composer then,
Maistre," he said aloud.

Passing by the little mirror over the mantelpiece, he
caught sight of himself. Haggard-eyed, with many days'
growth of stubble, he looked like a madman. If he were to
convince a Muscobite director of music to take a look at his
work, he would have to tidy himself up.

The landlady was sweeping the hall; he leaned over the
banister to ask where he could find the nearest public bathhouse.

"Across the square," she said, "on the far side, beyond
the Imperial Theater."

"What's this . . . ?" Emerging clean-shaven and damp-
haired from the bathhouse, Jagu stopped. Fresh playbills
had been plastered on the bathhouse walls. They announced

the long-anticipated appearance of the celebrated Francian diva Gauzia de Saint-Désirat at the Imperial Theater in *A Spring Elopement*.

"*Gauzia?*" Jagu stood there, lost in memories. In the five years since Gauzia had turned her back on the world of church music, her stage career must have blossomed.

Curiosity impelled him up the wide steps of the theater and through the grand colonnaded entrance, with its carved swags adorned with painted flowers and lyres. The foyer was even more impressive; an elaborate double staircase wound up to the first floor and marble statues of illustrious past performers stood in every mirrored alcove. Dazzled by the gilt and crystal lusters, Jagu suddenly caught a brief burst of song as an inner door opened from the auditorium, then swung shut again.

"Can I help you?" A flunkey in a brown-and-gold uniform barred his way.

"I'd like to speak with Demoiselle de Saint-Désirat."

The flunkey's eyebrows rose. "So would every man in Mirom, it seems," he said disdainfully. "The diva is rehearsing. If you would be so good as to leave your card . . ." One gloved hand was thrust in Jagu's face, palm upward.

"But I'm an old friend of the diva's."

"Of *course* you are. Your card?"

This was going to take more than a little ingenuity. Jagu had no cards—and even if he sent a letter, Gauzia would probably refuse to see him. As he went back out into the bitter cold, he noticed a man bearing armfuls of striped hothouse lilies, cream and pink and gold, disappearing round the side of the theater.

Bouquets for the diva.

"A moment there, my friend," he called out, drawing a coin from his pocket. "You must be very busy. Let me deliver those for you."

The florist hesitated, glancing around to see if anyone was watching. Then he thrust the bouquets into Jagu's arms and swiftly pocketed the coin.

Jagu knocked at the stage door. He held the flowers high, so that the heavily scented blooms half concealed his face.

"Flowers for the diva?" a stagehand said. "Take them straight to her dressing room."

A warren of ill-lit passages opened up in front of Jagu. Chorus members and stagehands hurried to and fro, pushing past him without even seeming to notice he was there. In the dim light, it was difficult to make out the names on the doors he passed. A gust of cold air stirred the petals of the lilies and he suddenly heard a woman's voice break into song in the distance.

He stopped abruptly. That distinct, pure tone. The unseen singer shaped phrase after phrase with sensitive musicianship. Gauzia had a richer voice, a more sensual sound, but she had never managed to rise to those elusive high notes with such unique, unearthly artistry. He knew that voice instantly, even though it was many months since he had heard her sing. He stood, back pressed up against the dusty bricks of the passageway, not knowing what to do, as the singers flitted back and forth.

Someone tapped him sharply on the shoulder. A bewigged little man stood glaring at him. "You're blocking the passageway. Deliver those flowers and get out!" Jagu looked at him blankly. "New to the job?" He let out an exasperated sigh and opened the door opposite. "In there." The room that lay beyond was already filled with flowers, and their scent was overpoweringly rich and sickly sweet.

"Who was that singing?"

The little man was already steering him back toward the stage door. "You like music, yes? You want to find out? Then buy a ticket and come to see the opera!" He gave him a firm push out into the snowy street and slammed the door shut.

"My dear Jagu, you can't possibly go to the opera dressed like that," observed Ambassador d'Abrissard.

"These are the only civilian clothes I've brought with me." Jagu looked down at the plain cut of his jacket. "What's wrong with them?"

"In Mirom, just as in Lutèce, people dress up in all their finery to attend the opera."

"My funds won't cover the cost of a new suit, let alone a ticket."

"Don't buy a ticket, for heaven's sake! I have my own box, which is at your disposal. As for suitable attire . . ." Abrissard rang the brocade bellpull and Claude, his butler, appeared. "Claude, would you say that the lieutenant and I were roughly of the same height and girth?"

Claude gave Jagu an appraising look. "Quite close, I believe, Ambassador."

"Then would you be so good as to fit him out from my wardrobe; the lieutenant is going to the opera tonight in my stead."

Claude bowed, saying nothing, but not before Jagu had seen the look of shocked disapproval that replaced his habitually detached expression.

Jagu looked at his reflection in the cheval mirror while Claude fastidiously brushed a speck of dust from his outfit. He had never worn such fine clothes; the ivory silk shirt was so soft against his skin that it felt almost sinful. From the sheen of the velvet jacket and breeches of midnight blue down to the metal buckles on the black leather shoes, his reflection gleamed.

"You would be advised to put this on, Lieutenant," Claude brought over a long, fur-trimmed coat and draped it over his shoulders, "as the frost tonight is particularly sharp." He finished his work by placing a three-cornered hat of black felt on Jagu's head, tipping it at a fashionable angle.

Jagu did not recognize himself. He was staring at a lean-faced nobleman, the man he might have become if he had been the firstborn of the Lord of Rustéphan. The disguise might work to his advantage, enabling him to continue his investigation without arousing any suspicions.

As the troika bore him away to the theater, the runners bumping over the frozen ruts, the bells on the horses' collars jangling in the frosty night, he sat back and tried to prepare himself for the confrontation to come.

When had he begun to sense he was losing her? She had

become more wayward, more willful, taking risks to get her own way, listening less to him and more, he was certain, to her guardian spirit. He could not forget the way his heart had burned with jealousy as he had watched her flirting with Andrei Orlov, despising himself more and more for not being honest with himself—or her—about his feelings.

And then it was all too late and she was gone.

As the troika slowed, the driver joining the crush of other sleighs in the broad square, Jagu saw the dazzle of bright flares illuminating the front of the Imperial Theater.

Nearly there. Why was it that the idea of running away with Celestine was suddenly so appealing?

Celestine . . . do I love you so much that I'd break my vow for a chance of happiness with you?

The ambassador's box afforded a good view of the stage and as Jagu settled down on one of the elegant little chairs, he gazed around in amazement at the lavish interior. Carved cherubs and nymphs supported every box and tier; gilded fauns and satyrs blew pipes and strummed lyres at the corner of each tier, and the central crystal chandelier was filled with hundreds of white wax candles. The buzz of conversation was so loud that he could hardly hear the musicians as they started to tune their instruments.

He scanned the program in vain for a clue; it was only natural that, as a fugitive, she would adopt another name.

Then the candles were extinguished in the auditorium and the orchestra began to play the overture. To Jagu's disgust, the members of the audience paid no attention, continuing to chatter more loudly than before to make themselves heard above the instruments. Jagu frowned at them, trying to listen to the orchestra. He was unfamiliar with *A Spring Elopement,* although the instant he caught an infectiously lighthearted melody bubbling up through the flutes and clarinets in the overture, he suddenly remembered Henri de Joyeuse's playing it.

He was so lost in the memory that when the heavy curtains parted, revealing a stage set of painted cottages and cherry trees, and a chorus of young women in pink-striped gowns began to sing about the spring blossom, his frown deepened.

What am I, a Commanderie Guerrier, doing watching this absurd, frivolous entertainment?

A sudden stir rippled through the audience and he noticed many leaning forward, raising opera glasses as—to a burst of rapturous cheering—a young woman ran onto the stage and began to sing. From her warm, rich tone, he knew her instantly. It was Gauzia, playing the part of Lise, the pert servant girl, whose mischief-making provided the flimsy plot of *A Spring Elopement.* And, as Jagu watched Gauzia flirting with the men while effortlessly singing Lise's virtuoso runs and trills, he had to admit that she was in her element in the theater. Her reputation was well merited, and from the thunderous applause at the end of her first aria, it was obvious that she had already enchanted the audience. Only when the applause had died down did the opera continue, with the appearance of Lise's young mistress, Mariella.

Mariella, in contrast to her servant, had a sad, wistful aria in which she sang of her despair at being forced to marry a rich elderly count, rather than her sweetheart, a handsome but impoverished poet. Her first phrase, exquisitely rendered, sent a shiver of recognition through Jagu's body.

Celestine.

He leaned far forward over the rim of the box, wishing that he had brought some opera glasses as he tried to make out her features. The voice, the sensitive artistry in shaping the phrases, the timbre of voice, sweet yet searingly pure, were all Celestine's. But the young woman on the stage looked nothing like her. Her hair was a rich brown and her complexion was far darker than Celestine's. But this was the theater, and all manner of magical deceptions could be achieved with lighting and greasepaint.

As the curtain fell, announcing the interval between the acts, Jagu hurried out of the box.

"Is there anything I can get you, sir?" A flunkey appeared, dressed in the same livery as the one who had dismissed him so peremptorily earlier. "A glass of white wine? Some caviar?"

"What is the name of the singer playing Mariella?"

"I believe she's called Cassard, sir. Maela Cassard."

The name meant nothing to Jagu. Was he deluding himself? Had he been so eager to find Celestine that he had imagined this Maela Cassard to be his lost love? He took one of the fluted glasses from the flunkey's tray and swallowed the chilled wine down in one gulp. There was only one way to be sure—and that was to go backstage after the performance.

"Flowers," he said on impulse. "I want a bouquet of flowers."

CHAPTER 18

"An admirer to see you, Demoiselle Cassard," called Grebin from the passageway.

"I said no visitors tonight—" Celestine broke off as the dressing-room door opened.

Jagu stood in the doorway, carrying a bouquet of spring flowers. Awkwardly, he held them out toward her. They stood, unmoving, staring at each other, she with her peignoir half-slipping off one shoulder, he still proffering the bouquet. The green, piquant scent of narcissi filled the little room.

"I wanted to congratulate you on your performance," he said. "I had no idea that you were such a talented actress . . . *Celestine.*"

He had tracked her down. He had recognized her, in spite of her disguise.

"You'd better come in, Jagu," she said. "And shut the door." She placed the flowers in a vase, turning her back on him so that he should not see the confusion in her eyes. For just to know that he was there, standing so close to her, had stirred up a host of buried emotions. Why did she want to feel his arms around her, holding her so tightly that the breath was crushed out of her? No, this could be no passionate reconciliation.

He had been sent to arrest her.

I've fended for myself all these months without you, Jagu. I've become strong. Independent. Now what am I going to do?

"So what gave me away?" she asked, forcing herself to turn around to face him.

"Your voice. I'd know your voice anywhere." His face was expressionless, but she detected the faintest husky tremor as he spoke. Skilled as he was at hiding how he felt, she knew that there was too much history between them for him to stay unmoved.

She nodded. "Those clothes suit you," she said, unable to resist reaching out to run her fingertips down the lapel of his ink-blue jacket. "It's nice to see you in a color other than Commanderie black."

"You heard about the Maistre?"

She let her fingers drop away. "I heard. I just couldn't believe it at first. I still can't believe that he's . . . he's gone."

"Your disguise—"

"Has fooled everyone but you, Jagu. Even Gauzia, though for how long I can keep deceiving her, I'm not so sure."

"I can see that you've dyed your hair, but how have you managed to change the color of your eyes?"

"Jagu, I haven't changed anything. *She's* done it all."

His expression altered, black brows drawing together in a frown. She hadn't realized till then how much she had missed seeing that familiar expression of disapproval. "So I'm not speaking to Celestine, but to her guardian spirit?"

She forced a laugh. "Of course it's me. But you must remember to call me Maela."

He gave a little shake of the head, as if he had tasted something unpleasant. "You know why I'm here?"

"Old times' sake? Because you really wanted to see me?" She couldn't resist the barbed little taunt. "My guess would be that you've been sent to arrest me."

A slight hint of color darkened his pale face and he looked down at the floor.

"And you believed that I'd willingly go back with you to Francia to stand trial? A trial with only one possible outcome? You can't be naïve enough to think that Visant would pardon me?"

He began to shake his head. "I—I don't know what I believed. I only know that I wanted to see you again."

"How touching." She sat down in front of the mirror

and began to wipe the greasepaint from her face. But his words *had* touched something deep within her, a buried memory of a feeling never completely acknowledged. But it was not the time to be swayed by nostalgia. Jagu was still a member of the Commanderie, and her enemy. As she checked her reflection in the glass for remaining traces of rouge, she caught a glimpse of him watching her, his dark eyes clouded, brooding, unreadable. And she felt a sudden unease.

Have I misread you, Jagu? Does your vow to the Commanderie count for more than your feelings for me?

She wanted to be honest with him. She owed him that, at least. She laid down the rouge-smeared cloth and turned to face him.

"Jagu, I like being Maela Cassard. I never knew before that I had a gift for opera. But every time I go out onstage, it feels like . . . like coming home." She reached out, taking his hands in hers, gazing pleadingly into his eyes. "I love everything about this life. Do you understand what I'm saying?"

"You want me to go back to Francia without you." He looked down at her hands, still clasped around his own. He seemed to be struggling with his feelings. But this was Jagu, and she was asking him to lie. She felt his fingers tighten around hers. "Hugues Donatien is Grand Maistre. He and Visant are changing the Commanderie, and not for the better."

"Then why go back?" Her voice dropped, knowing that she was suggesting something he might find treasonable. "Ruaud is dead. Start a new life here, Jagu. The Muscobites love music. With your gift, you could easily make your reputation here."

"But my vow. You're suggesting that I break my vow." His fingers tightened again until they were almost crushing hers. "And how long do you think I could keep my identity a secret? I haven't got a guardian spirit to change my appearance."

"Does your vow to the Commanderie mean so much to you?"

He snatched his hands from hers. "I—I can't believe I'm hearing you speak this way. I thought you knew me, Celestine. I thought I knew you too. Now I see how far we've grown apart."

His words hurt her. And she didn't know how to defend herself against them. "Forget this meeting ever happened, Jagu. Forget all about me. Celestine de Joyeuse is dead. Make up some story or other; she caught a fever on Lapwing Spar and died in a fisherman's hut. Or—"

"I understand." Without another word, he turned and left the dressing room.

Had she persuaded him? And if she'd finally persuaded him to pronounce her officially dead, why did she feel so empty now she had sent him away?

"Forget this meeting ever happened." Jagu took another mouthful of vodka, swilling the clear liquid around in the little glass. It was well past midnight, but there were still taverns open; the Muscobites liked to drink late into the night. Vodka was not really to his taste, even seasoned with bitingly hot red pepper. But it seemed close enough to the wound-cleansing spirit used by the Commanderie surgeons on the battlefield to anesthetize the pain he was feeling.

"Forget all about me." How could he? Yet it had felt so unnatural, talking with a stranger who had all Celestine's little mannerisms, who spoke with Celestine's voice, yet looked so utterly different. Her guardian's glamour had almost deceived him. How long would it work on others, especially Gauzia? Gauzia was no fool. She would not relish having so gifted a competitor on the operatic stage. She might already be planning ways to destroy her rival's career before it had even begun.

Celestine de Joyeuse is dead.

Celestine set out for her lodgings through the dark, silent streets.

Jagu recognized me in spite of this disguise. I can't stay here. Even if he doesn't reveal my secret, it's only a matter of time before others come . . .

Was that why she walked so slowly, dragging her feet? Or was it that—even though she had driven him away—she had not wanted to let Jagu go? The sound of his voice alone had awakened a thousand little memories.

Why had his words hurt her so much? Why did it matter to her what he thought? She had a new life, a new identity; she didn't need him anymore.

CHAPTER 19

"You've been very generous to me, Ambassador; I can't thank you enough." Jagu bowed to Fabien d'Abrissard as Claude whisked away the borrowed finery.

"So you were mistaken?" Abrissard asked, hardly glancing up from the dispatch he was reading.

"I was mistaken."

"You're a poor liar, Jagu." Abrissard looked up at last. "But events have overtaken us. I have some advice which you'd do well to pay attention to. I'd think twice, if I were you, about returning to Lutèce." He cast the dispatch down on the desk. "Ruaud counted you among his most trusted and loyal agents. I know that for a fact, because he told me so. But you and I—and Celestine, wherever she may be— have been marked as Ruaud's supporters. You see, there's a new king in Francia: Ilsevir of Allegonde."

"Prince Ilsevir?" repeated Jagu, astonished.

"And wherever Ilsevir goes, the Rosecoeurs accompany him. How do you feel about being forced to join the Rosecoeurs?" Abrissard gazed at Jagu inquiringly.

"Forced?" Jagu did not like the idea at all. "But why would I—?"

"Because the balance of power is shifting even as we speak. Hugues Donatien has been a secret member of the Rosecoeurs for many years. He will replace Alain Friard with Ilsevir's right-hand man, Girim nel Ghislain."

"No!"

Abrissard leaned forward. "And it won't be long, I imagine, before I'm replaced by one of Ilsevir's favorites. I'm no friend to the Rosecoeurs. I was always Gobain's man, and

Aliénor knows it. I imagine that Ilsevir and Donatien will purge the Commanderie of any dissenting voices as soon as they can; they may even have begun the process already."

"I could never renounce my allegiance to Saint Sergius," Jagu said without hesitation. "I could never follow the tenets of the Rosecoeurs."

"I want you to know, Jagu, that for as long as I hold office, I'll give you whatever help or advice you need."

"But you, Ambassador, what will you do?"

"Oh, I've bought a charming dacha quite close to Erinaskoe. I thought I might enjoy playing at being the country gentleman for a while: indulging in a spot of fishing, perhaps, or creating a fine garden. Of course, if the new king comes to realize that I know too many state secrets for my own good, I might have to disappear altogether." An enigmatic smile spread across Abrissard's face. "You needn't worry on my account, Jagu. Claude will take good care of me."

Celestine popped her head out of the stage door to see if the coast was clear. The fervent admirers had given up waiting to see their favorite singers at last and it was safe to set out for home.

Carriages and troikas were still crossing the lamplit square and the sound of drunken singing announced a group of revelers emerging from the nearby tavern.

"Hullo, sweetheart!" yelled one, lurching toward her. "Fancy a drink?" The beery gust he breathed in her face made her turn aside, disgusted. A drunkard was the last thing she wanted to have to deal with after the rigors of the evening performance.

"Sorry, friend, but the lady's with me," said a familiar voice behind her.

"*Jagu?*"

"My lodgings are just beyond the square," he murmured in her ear.

The drunks started hooting and whistling, but Jagu caught Celestine by the arm and began to hurry her across the square, between the passing carriages. He did not stop until they had passed beneath an archway into an inner courtyard, surrounded by tall buildings.

"You shouldn't be out alone so late at night," Jagu said disapprovingly.

"You're forgetting," she said, "that I have my guardian to protect me."

"Of course; you're invulnerable."

Was he mocking her? Away from the streetlights of the main square, it was impossible to see his expression.

"Why were you shadowing me?"

"I've been with the ambassador. You need to hear this." He unlocked the door to his lodgings and ushered her inside. She saw him look back toward the street and knew he was checking to see if anyone had followed them.

"Why, what's happened?" He had his back to her, striking a tinder to light the lamp.

"Ilsevir is to be crowned king of Francia." He turned around to face her, his expression grim in the soft glow of the lamp. "And Abrissard suspects that he will oust Alain Friard and appoint Girim nel Ghislain in his place."

"A Rosecoeur at the head of the Commanderie?" Celestine did not like the prospect at all. "But everything Maistre de Lanvaux worked so hard to establish will be destroyed!"

"I will not serve under Captain nel Ghislain," Jagu said stubbornly. "I will not swear allegiance to the Blood of the Rose."

Everything is changing . . . and not for the better. The room was chilly and she began to shiver.

"You're feeling the cold," he said. "I'll put fresh fuel in the stove. I don't have much to offer to warm you up." He opened up the little stove to place wood on the glowing embers. "I could brew some tea."

Jagu, offering to make tea? The new domesticated side to his character was unexpected and rather endearing.

"Tea, then," she said, sitting down close to the stove. "My throat's a little sore after tonight's performance; Dame Elmire would have given me a stern lecture for such poor technique."

As he filled a little kettle from the water jug and set it to boil on top of the stove, she glanced around the sparsely furnished room. It offered no clue as to Jagu's interests; she noticed a couple of bound volumes of the Holy Texts lying on the chest, alongside his sword. There was nothing to gladden the eye or the spirits; not even a spring flower. But the table was covered in sheets of paper. When she was sure Jagu was busy spooning tea into the pot, she sneaked over to investigate. Page after page of handwritten music lay before her, a mess of blots and scratched-out bars. This was just how Henri's desk used to look when he was in the throes of a new composition, littered with scraps of ideas and scribbled jottings. But the strong, well-formed hand was unmistakably Jagu's—and it had never once occurred to her that Jagu might be interested in writing music as well as performing it.

"Jagu?" She picked up a handful of music. "Did *you* compose this? This setting of the Vesper Prayer?"

He looked up from pouring tea and she saw an unusually vulnerable expression cross his face. "Don't look at that," he said. "It's not finished."

She was not to be fobbed off so easily. "These opening bars, they're for a soprano soloist. You weren't writing this for me to sing, were you?"

His hand jerked involuntarily and spilled some of the tea. Cursing, he mopped it up with his handkerchief.

"Let me try it out." He had written music for her. She wanted nothing more than to hear what it sounded like.

"It's not finished." He brought over a glass of strong brown tea. "Besides, you said your throat was sore. No more singing for you tonight. Drink this; it's from Serindher. It has a warming, malty taste."

Reluctantly, she replaced the music and took her tea, holding the hot glass carefully in her cupped hands. "Tomorrow morning, then. We can use one of the practice rooms at the theater. Gauzia never arrives until an hour before the performance. She's too busy entertaining her admirers."

"Maybe." He was looking at her so intently that she suddenly felt self-conscious.

"What is it?" she asked. "Is there a smear of greasepaint on my face?"

"I just can't get used to seeing you like that," he said awkwardly. "Can't you shed your disguise now that we're alone together?"

"It's still me, Jagu," she said, sipping her tea. *Alone together.* There was something about the way he pronounced those words that sent a little shiver through her. Yet they had been alone together countless times before. His request touched her. Would it hurt to indulge him?

"Faie," she said softly. "It's all right; I'm safe here. Change me back."

"If that's what you truly wish . . ."

Celestine saw from Jagu's startled reaction that the Faie had withdrawn the glamour she had cast around her.

"Is that better?" She felt suddenly shy, defenseless, as if the Faie had also stripped away the protective shell with which she had been shielding her true feelings.

He set down his cup, still staring at her. "The truth is that I would still love you, whether you were Maela, Celestine . . . or whoever else you chose to be."

"You . . . love me?" To hear Jagu make such a confession was so unexpected that she thought she must have misheard. "Don't make fun of me, Jagu."

"Don't you know me well enough by now? I'm incapable of joking about something so important."

"Prove it." What was she saying? The challenge issued from her lips before she could stop herself. Hadn't their relationship always been like this? Fierce arguments over interpretation, whether a piece of music or orders relating to their mission.

The next moment he crossed the room and, taking her face between his hands, pressed his lips to hers, kissing her. She began to protest, pushing against him, her cry smothered by his mouth. Then suddenly she stopped struggling, surrendering to his hunger, kissing him back, her mouth hot and eager.

* * *

All Jagu's conflicted feelings had woven themselves into the kiss: frustrated longing and helpless desire. He had expected her to push him away. But she had only pulled him closer. It surprised him how swiftly, how easily, his body responded to hers—and how urgent his need had become to take matters further. While he still had the power to control himself, he gently released her, his hands on her shoulders. She gazed questioningly up at him and he realized that she had never looked at him in such an intimate, vulnerable way before.

"I should take you back to your lodgings," he said.

"Yes, you should." But when she made no move, he began to stroke her hair.

"When you disappeared, I was afraid that I'd lost you for good," he said softly. "Why is it that you don't realize till something's gone how important it is to you?"

"More important to you than your vow to the Commanderie?"

"Since I lost you I've felt"— he struggled to find the right word—"incomplete. Like a part of myself was missing. But when I heard you were on Andrei Orlov's ship, I somehow assumed that you . . . and he . . ."

"That we were lovers?" A little blush had appeared on her cheeks. "It could so easily have happened. But I ran away. I had my reasons."

She was still so difficult to read, kissing him with such passion one moment, then tormenting him with these elusive hints and allusions. He wasn't entirely inexperienced in matters of the heart; as a music student, he'd had a couple of brief romances with young singers, but no one had ever affected him as deeply as she had.

"I wasn't there when you needed me in Smarna." To think back to those troubled, uncertain days still hurt. "I'm so sorry. When I reached the villa they told me that you'd been arrested. I went straight to the harbor but the *Aquilon* had already sailed. I followed on the next ship to Francia, only to find that you'd already given the Inquisitors the slip." His arms tightened around her. "I don't ever want to let you go ever again."

* * *

I don't ever want to let you go ever again. Those words, spoken with such intensity, at once thrilled and terrified Celestine. It felt as if every part of her that he touched was on fire. Tumbling backward onto the bed together seemed the most natural, inevitable outcome. It was such a delicious, dizzying sensation to know that he wanted her so badly . . . and to realize that she wanted him too.

Her body moved beneath his, arching upward to meet him. They had been making music together for so long that they had developed an instinctive, wordless understanding. Jagu could match the keyboard part to her vocal line as naturally as if they were one. One heart, one intelligence shaping the music together. And it seemed that their bodies moved to that same instinctive rhythm, giving and taking pleasure in equal measure until, sated and drowsy, they fell asleep in each other's arms.

The cold, pure light of a Mirom dawn filtered in through the wooden shutters. Celestine half opened her eyes, aware that she was warm and blissfully comfortable beneath the goose-feather quilt. She snuggled closer to the source of the warmth . . . and felt herself pressing up against someone else in the bed. Someone naked. As naked as she.

She lay still, fully awake now, not daring to move for fear she might disturb him. He was lying on his side, his back to her, the quilt gently rising and falling with his slow, regular breathing. His hair, untied, spilled over the linen pillowcase, black as scattered crows' feathers against fresh-fallen snow. She wanted so much to touch it, to rake her fingers through it as she had the night before in the fire of their passion, yet still she didn't dare move. But a slow flush of heat ran through her body as she remembered what else they had done in the darkness.

Will you blame me for making you break your vow, Jagu?

The brightening daylight revealed their clothes, flung across the floorboards in the abandon and desperation of their hunger for each other.

He gave a slow sigh and turned over in the bed toward her. As his arms enfolded her and she felt herself pulled back into his embrace, she swiveled around and kissed him lightly on the mouth. "Good morning, Jagu," she whispered. His eyes opened. They stared at each other.

"Um, did . . . did we?"

She burst into delighted laughter. "Don't tell me you've forgotten already!"

"Remind me," he said, "so that I won't forget again."

Later—very much later that morning—they rose and dressed. Jagu went out to buy some rolls for their breakfast and when he returned, he found Celestine studying his Vesper Prayer.

"Please, Jagu," she said. "Let me sing it for you."

"What, right now?"

"What's the point in writing music if it's never going to be performed? Come on," she said tugging at his sleeve. "We can use one of the practice rooms at the Imperial Theater!"

Once Celestine had decided to do something, there was no dissuading her. Her enthusiasm won him over. He could do nothing but smile, aware that until now he had never known what happiness was.

He had made his choice last night, and he had no regrets. He had broken his vow in making love to Celestine. He was still living on the Commanderie's money but all that would change; he would go out and find work as an accompanist.

No sooner had they entered the theater by the stage door than they were stopped by Grebin.

"Who's this, Maela?"

"My new repetiteur," she said, giving him her sweetest smile. "We're going to rehearse."

Grebin peered suspiciously at Jagu in the gloom. "But aren't you a florist?"

Taking Celestine by the hand, Jagu hurried her away along the dark passageway. "I'm . . . versatile," he called back over his shoulder.

"A florist?" she asked, mystified.

"I had to dream up a way of getting backstage to find you."

"But a florist, Jagu—" Celestine couldn't hold back her laughter any longer.

"There has to be a keyboard round here somewhere."

Her ribs hurt from laughing. "Third door on the right," she gasped, wiping her eyes.

He opened the door to the smallest rehearsal room and pulled her inside. She linked her hands around the nape of his neck, pulled his face down close to hers and kissed him.

"Someone might come in." Gently, he unwound her arms from around his neck.

As Celestine worked through her daily ritual of vocal exercises, slowly warming her voice to life, each arpeggio climbing a pitch higher, Jagu felt a sense of deep contentment seep through him. He hadn't realized until now how important a part of his life this had been.

"Why are you smiling?" she said, suddenly breaking off. "Did I make a mistake?"

"Far from it," he said. "I was just thinking how much I've missed this. You and I, working together."

"You may not still be smiling when you hear me sing your music. Of course, I shall blame you, the composer, if I make a mistake. I'll insist that it's impossible to sing and force you to change it!" She flashed him an impudent little smile.

"The opening is wordless. I wanted the voice to shine, like the voice of Azilis wreathing up to the stars through the desert night in Ondhessar."

Her face became grave and she nodded slowly. She drew in a breath and began to sing, her pure voice taking the notes he had written for her and transforming them with the unearthly beauty of her tone.

Hearing her bring the opening melisma of his Vesper Prayer to radiant life made the hairs rise on the back of Jagu's neck. He stopped playing.

"Did I make a mistake?"

He shook his head, too moved to reply straightaway. He

had imagined this moment so many times. Eventually he said simply, "It was perfect."

Nevertheless, he was glad that he had remembered to bring a pencil with him. He kept halting to make little marks on the score to remind himself where he needed to make corrections.

"You're such a perfectionist, Jagu," she said, planting a kiss on the top of his head.

Someone tapped on the door. "Demoiselle Cassard! Grebin wants all soloists onstage."

"They need you," he said, picking up the sheets.

"Meet me after the performance tonight. Not here . . . Gauzia might see you. Here's my address; it's not far." She scribbled her address on the top of the score and blew him a kiss. "Till tonight."

Celestine awoke all of a sudden, conscious that there was someone in the room. It was the empty, grey hour before dawn, the time at which the dying often fade away with the end of the night.

She lay utterly still, not daring to move. Had a burglar broken in? Beside her, Jagu lay in a deep sleep, one arm flung protectively across her body, utterly unaware. The Faie had withdrawn to the book. Could she summon her silently, by thought alone, without drawing the intruder's attention?

The shadow moved closer to the bed. Yet even in the uncertain light, she knew him, and her heart felt as if it had turned to ice.

"*Celestine?*" said Henri in puzzled tones. "*Jagu?*"

Celestine sat up, clutching the sheet tight about her to cover her nakedness. Beside her she heard Jagu stir at last and push himself up on one elbow.

"*When am I going to wake from this nightmare?*" murmured the revenant distractedly.

Her hand crept out from beneath the sheet, not stopping until her fingers pinched Jagu's arm, feeling the reassuring warmth of living flesh and blood.

"M—Maistre de Joyeuse?" Jagu sounded as dazed as

she, reverting to using Henri's full title as he had done in his student days.

"*Why can no one hear me?*" There was such a burden of desolation in his words that Celestine could not bear to listen.

"*I can hear you.*" The voice of the Faie issued from the book that lay on the bedside table.

"Faie?" Celestine said softly.

"*Go back,*" said the Faie in a tone both compassionate and commanding.

"*Don't send me back. Not there.*" The revenant's pale features twisted, warping into a look of such terror that Celestine could not bear to look and buried her face in her hands. And then she heard a voice, so pure and unearthly that it could have been the sound of a star singing. Daring to peer out between her fingers, she saw that the Faie had transformed into a creature of dazzling brightness. Her face was transfigured, her eyes closed, her arms extended as the song poured from her open mouth. A sliver of light appeared beyond the tips of her fingers, growing brighter until it opened like a doorway and radiance spilled out.

The revenant's tortured features slowly relaxed, to be replaced by a look of calm detachment. It turned and its shadowy form seemed to melt into the brightness.

The Faie's voice faded away and with it, the light that had filled the attic room.

"Is he gone?" Celestine whispered. The Faie let out the faintest of sighs. Her form was fading too as she melted back into the book. "Faie! What's wrong?"

"*I just . . . need to rest a little . . .*"

Jagu was rubbing his eyes. "Tell me that was a dream," he said shakily.

"It wasn't a dream."

"But that singing . . . and that dazzling light . . ."

How to begin to explain it all to Jagu?

"The dead don't return," he said as he lay back, almost as if he were trying to reassure himself. "Not unless their souls have been stolen . . ."

But long after his breathing had lapsed back into the

steady, regular rhythm of sleep, Celestine lay awake, trying
to make sense of what she had seen.

Gauzia closed her dressing-room door. The room was filled
with fresh flowers and their sultry scent was overpowering.
A bouquet of rose-pink camellias lay on the dressing table;
curious, she picked up the attached card to read who had
sent it. Behind her, she heard the sound of someone slowly
applauding.

She spun around to see a man sitting behind the door. He
was smiling at her. "What a superb performance you gave
tonight, Diva!"

"What the hell are you doing in my dressing room? Get
out, before I call the manager!"

"There's no need for alarm, my dear demoiselle, I mean
you no harm." The lazy smile only infuriated her more.

"Get out!" She seized the nearest object to hand—a
hairbrush—and began to advance on him, brandishing it.

"I'm here on official business," he said, not making the
slightest move to leave. "From Maistre Donatien of the
Commanderie. I'm looking for two old friends of yours. I
wondered if you might have seen them."

She lowered the hairbrush. "Old friends?" she said suspiciously. Her admirers sometimes invented extraordinary
excuses to try to get close to her.

"Celestine de Joyeuse—and her accompanist, Jagu de
Rustéphan."

"Celestine—a *friend*?" she echoed. Even the sound of her
onetime fellow student's name rankled. "What's your name,
Guerrier?"

"Guyomard's the name. Lieutenant Kilian Guyomard."
Again that lazy, knowing smile.

"Can I trust you, I wonder, Lieutenant? The very fact that
you've traveled all this way to Mirom must mean that you
have a strong suspicion she's to be found here." *Maela Cassard.* "Of course I can't be entirely sure," she said, sniffing
at a fragrant bouquet of hothouse lilies left on her dressing
table, "but I've had my suspicions about her since the start.
It's a very clever disguise. Her hair, her complexion, even the

color of her eyes. But the voice. It's impossible to disguise that unique timbre. What would make her go to such lengths to reinvent herself, Lieutenant? Is she in any kind of . . . trouble?"

"So she's here in disguise?"

He had only answered her question with another question.

"I never said I was sure." If he could be evasive, so could she.

"Maistre Donatien is very close to Prince Ilsevir. I'm sure he could put in a good word about you if you were to assist me—and the Commanderie—with our inquiries."

"Oh, really?" So he was trying to bribe her with promises of royal patronage. "That sounds rather attractive to me." She broke off one of the lilies and went up to him, tucking it into his top buttonhole. As she did so, she whispered a name in his ear.

"Maela Cassard."

CHAPTER 20

Celestine had been drowsing, her head pillowed against Jagu's bare chest, feeling so warm and comfortable that she had no desire to move. And then she heard the sound of brisk footsteps hurrying up the stairs toward her room.

"Someone's coming!"

"Your landlady?"

Celestine shook her head. "Not at that speed!"

A fist rapped loudly on the door.

"Demoiselle! Open up!" called out a man's voice in Francian.

They both spilled out of bed, fumbling for their clothes. Jagu was fastening his breeches; grabbing his shirt, he signed to her to keep quiet. The door handle rattled; the man outside was evidently determined to get in and it was only a matter of seconds before he would break the lock. Celestine tugged her shift over her head and cast around in a panic for the saffron dress she had been wearing the day before. *Please don't let it be the Inquisition.*

"*I'll protect you,*" whispered the Faie.

"I know you're in there, Demoiselle. Haven't you got a few words of welcome for your old friend, Kilian?"

Celestine, trying to pull on her stockings, stared at Jagu. "*Kilian?* Did you tell him, Jagu?"

Jagu looked at her blankly. "I didn't even know he was in Mirom."

"Well, well . . ." Kilian stood in the doorway. "Celestine and Jagu, here in Mirom together. How long has this cozy little arrangement been going on?"

"It's not what you think, Kilian!" said Jagu defensively.

"Oh, come now, it's exactly what I think." Kilian's gaze rested on the bed and the tumbled sheets. A malicious smile had appeared on his lips, but the look in his eyes was cold and unforgiving.

"Who sent you? Why are you here?" demanded Jagu, knowing to his shame that his cheeks were flaming. There was no point in denying what had happened.

"Maistre Donatien sent me. You've been gone rather too long, Jagu. He was becoming . . . suspicious."

"Has the Maistre forgotten how far north Mirom lies? My ship was icebound for weeks."

Kilian shrugged.

"So he sent you to arrest us."

"Arrest? To *escort* you back to Francia."

"Escort? Does he take me for a fool, Kilian?"

"Maistre Donatien is prepared to ask Prince Ilsevir to grant you a royal pardon on the occasion of his coronation. A gesture of clemency, if you like."

"On what conditions?" Celestine had taken no part in the conversation till that moment.

"I won't intrude on you two lovebirds any longer. The ship leaves for Francia in two days' time. I've booked passage for the two of you. If you decide to accept the Maistre's offer, meet me at the Northern Docks at dawn; the ship's called the *Héloise*."

"Will Kilian report us?" Celestine set down a bowl of tea in front of Jagu.

"I don't think he expected to find us together."

She noticed a faint blush color Jagu's cheeks as he said it. She wanted to hug him.

"But he didn't even try to arrest me." She passed him the pot of damson jam. "And he was armed. Why didn't he?"

Jagu put a spoonful of jam in his tea, stirring with an abstracted look in his eyes. "I don't know. This talk of a royal pardon. It sounds . . . feasible."

"But can we trust him?" She sipped her tea, watching him through the rising steam from her bowl. That characteristic little frown she knew so well had appeared, furrowing his dark brows; never before had she found it so irresistible. She wanted to lean across and kiss his forehead.

He was staring into his tea. "We can't take the risk." He looked up. "I fear he's become Donatien's man. He'll be back, Celestine, with reinforcements."

"But he can't officially arrest me, can he? Not while we're in Muscobar. He'd need a warrant."

"No, but he could have you abducted."

Celestine had no answer. Jagu was right. Wasn't that exactly what they had done to Kaspar Linnaius in Tielen?

"We have to split up," he said. "I'll lay a false trail to lure Kilian away from you."

"And put yourself in danger?" Her hand reached out across the table and clasped his. "No, Jagu. In the eyes of the Commanderie, you're as much of a renegade as I am—and all because you've protected me."

"You know as well as I do that there's still a chance Donatien might hand you straight over to the Inquisition." Jagu's fingers tightened around hers. "There's too much evidence against you. You have to lie low. If only for a little while."

She gazed up into his eyes. "But I don't want to leave you, Jagu. Not now, now that I've realized what a fool I've . . ." Her throat tightened but she tried to keep speaking, determined that he hear what she had to tell him. "You've been protecting me all these years. Why has it taken me so long to see how much I love you?"

He rose and went to her, wrapping his arms around her, holding her close.

"We were both fools," he said. "And it's taken me all this time to see how I've been deluding myself. Why did we leave it so late? At least we were granted this second chance. But now we're being dragged apart again."

When I lost Henri, I thought my life was over. Celestine raised one hand to caress his face, trying to imprint its lean contours into her palm and fingertips. *I'm not going to lose you, Jagu.*

He pressed his mouth to hers, kissing her again until,

dizzy with desire, she broke away, all too aware where that would lead.

"I can't just abandon my work at the opera house. I'll have to invent some excuse." Celestine felt torn; she had worked so hard to rise to gain acceptance by Grebin that she was loath to throw her new career away.

"A sudden chill, brought on by the change in the weather. An inflammation of the throat. Your physician has advised you not to sing for at least a month . . ."

"Oh and which physician is that? Doctor Rustéphan?" She tried to make light of it, although the prospect of having to be apart was weighing heavily on her heart.

"You may even have to travel to a warmer climate to recuperate fully. The voice is such a precious, sensitive instrument."

"In which time, some ambitious little ingénue will come along and usurp my place."

Jagu gave her an odd look. "For a moment there, I thought I heard Gauzia de Saint-Désirat talking."

Celestine laughed, in spite of the sadness in her heart. "Heaven forbid that I'm turning into a diva! Perhaps it's all for the best that I take a break from the stage."

"Where will you go?"

Celestine had not thought this far ahead. She was weary of being on the run. She wanted nothing more than to be with Jagu. "It was so simple back then, you and I, performing together." She turned to him. "Those were the happiest moments of my life. You don't always realize it at the time, do you? It's only when everything begins to crash down about you that you see clearly." She reached out and stroked his cheek. "I want to give recitals with you again, Jagu. Just like we used to."

"I'll have to start practicing again," he said, a little contritely.

"Then let's make a plan." If they agreed on a day and a time to meet again perhaps she would feel less anxious.

"I'll lay a false trail to confuse Kilian. I'll tell him that you've been invited to sing before the Grand Duchess at Erinaskoe."

"But wouldn't it be better if we just sent a message to the *Héloise* and both disappeared?"

"It's only Kilian," said Jagu. "Don't worry; I know the way his mind works. We were at school together, remember?"

Only Kilian. How could Jagu sound so confident? "He's never liked me, Jagu. I don't know why, but—"

"All the more reason for me to divert his attention."

"And have him blame you for helping me escape?" She shook her head.

"I can make this plan work, Celestine." He took hold of her hands, pressing them between his own. "Whatever Kilian's orders may be, I'm certain I can convince him. He's always backed me up in the past. He's my oldest friend, after all."

Why was Jagu being so stubborn over this? She snatched her hands away.

"Of course, you'll have to leave your lodgings to make it look convincing. But it'll take Kilian so long to verify the details that he'll have to sail for Francia without us. Two days, he said. That's all. And then we can rendezvous at the ambassador's residence."

"Why won't you listen to what I'm saying, Jagu? How can you be so sure of Kilian? He's Donatien's man now."

"But Donatien answers to the king. And the new king is Prince Ilsevir. Don't forget we saved Ilsevir's life." Jagu put on his jacket, turning up the collar. "Let me handle this, Celestine. Here are the keys to my rooms. You can stay there tonight." He held out the keys but when she turned away, he placed them on the table. "Well, I'll see you later then . . ."

A moment later she heard the door catch click open, then close again as he went down the stairs.

She watched from her little window in the eaves as he set off along the winding street until he had disappeared from view.

I don't want you to go, Jagu. I don't want us to have to part again so soon.

A dull pain nagged at her heart as she turned away from the window. *Is this what they call a premonition?*

The final performance of *A Spring Elopement* would take place that night. Kilian would surely not expect her to forgo her final triumphal night. And he would never dare to have her abducted from the Imperial Theater. There was no reason why their plan should go wrong . . . was there?

Jagu passed fishwives gutting the silver gloss of a fresh herring catch as he walked along the quay, searching for the *Héloise*. The raucous cries of greedy gulls filled the air as they swooped down to snatch up the discarded entrails in their sharp beaks. The pungent, oily smell reminded him of Azhkendir and their first journey to Saint Serzhei's as Père Jagu and Celestin. The memory made him smile to himself.

"Jagu with a grin on his face? Well, that's a rare sight!" Kilian hailed him. "So where is she?"

Jagu shrugged. "An imperial invitation to perform before the Grand Duchess." He had never been a good liar and Kilian must surely know it.

"Surely she's not going to ignore the chance of a royal pardon?" Kilian said lightly. "Can't you talk her round?"

"She's made a new life for herself. She's happy working at the Imperial Theater. Why make her go back to Francia?"

"And you?"

"I'm not coming back either."

"You had such a promising career in the Commanderie, Jagu. Why are you throwing it all away? Did you lose your faith? Or"—and Kilian's eyes narrowed—"were you just not strong enough to resist the sins of the flesh?"

"That's a cheap shot, Kilian."

"Well, you know me well enough by now."

"And you should know me well enough to know that I've been through a great deal of soul-searching to reach this decision."

"Well, if I can't persuade you, and your mind is made up . . ." Kilian shot him a wry, resigned smile. "How about a last drink together, then, before my ship leaves? A toast to old times?"

Jagu already felt guilty about turning his back on his comrades in arms. He wished that he could make Kilian understand that he had experienced a profound and life-changing revelation in the Cathedral of Saint Simeon. Perhaps, over a bottle of wine, he could make Kilian understand why he had chosen to turn his back on the Commanderie and dedicate his life to music.

"One last drink, then."

The dockside tavern was full of sailors from Tielen; a merchantman had just arrived from Djihan-Djihar and the crew were pouring ale down their throats as if they had been at sea for months.

"What was it Abbé Houardon used to say to us?" Jagu touched his glass to Kilian's and took a mouthful of the robust red Smarnan wine.

Kilian shrugged. "I can't have been paying attention . . ."

" 'There are many ways of serving God, and each one of you must find his own path. It may take many years but you'll find it in the end.' Well, it's taken me long enough, but I think I may have stumbled upon it here in Mirom."

"Amen to that," said Kilian dryly.

"In the cathedral. I heard the monks singing vespers. And—"

"Don't tell me you're going to become a monk!" Kilian was smiling at him. "Though come to think of it, you might be rather well suited to a life of self-denial and mortification of the flesh."

"Must you make everything into a joke?" Jagu set his glass down hard on the table, slopping some drops of wine over the top. "Must you sneer and belittle everything I do?" Maybe the wine had loosened his tongue, but he had not spoken so frankly to Kilian in a long while. He wanted to tell him about the composing. He wanted to be able to trust him like a true friend and confide in him, but Kilian seemed incapable of taking him seriously.

"There was a time when I was honest with you." Kilian's face was hidden as he held his glass up to the lantern, studying the rich red glow. "Brutally honest." His tone was light, careless, as if his words were of little consequence. "But you brushed me aside. Here, let me refill your glass."

Jagu stared at Kilian. What time was he referring to? The alcohol must be clouding his brain, for he could not think clearly anymore. He looked down at his wineglass and saw through blurred vision that it was still half-full.

"No more wine, Kilian." The words came out slurred. "I—I have to be going." Jagu tried to stand up, staggered, lost his balance, and sat down again. The din of voices in the room had become the sound of a tide rushing to envelop him, dragging him down into darkness.

Kilian looked at Jagu lying slumped across the table. He put a hand on his shoulder and shook him. No response. He put his mouth close to Jagu's ear and said his name. Still no response. The drug he had slipped in Jagu's wine had worked to perfection.

"I'm sorry, old friend," he said softly, letting his fingers drift over Jagu's black hair, "but I can't let her have you. Maistre Donatien was very insistent."

He slid one arm under Jagu's and hefted him up. "Some help here!" he called out in Francian. "My friend's had a glass too many." As he had hoped, a couple of Francian sailors soon appeared, grinning, and assisted him in dragging Jagu out onto the quay. After a few coins had exchanged hands, they carried him aboard the ship and laid him on the bunk in the little cabin Kilian had reserved, next to his own. No sooner had the sailors departed, than Kilian locked the cabin door and put the key in his pocket. Then he went up on deck to check with the captain as to when they were setting sail.

"The friend I brought on board," Kilian said, choosing his words carefully, "needs to stay here, out of trouble. If he leaves the ship . . . well, let's say that there are people out there looking for him who don't have his best interests at heart." The captain looked at him, one brow skeptically raised. Kilian placed a fistful of gold coins on the table. "Keep him safe on board here, and there's more when we leave Mirom."

PART IV

CHAPTER 1

Rieuk awoke from another incoherent nightmare to feel the ground shuddering.

A deep rumbling echoed through the Rift as though the whole dimension were about to collapse in on itself. Rieuk pressed his hands to his ears to try to block out the sound, but he still felt the vibrations shaking him until his bones shuddered.

A sere, cold wind came whipping through the trees. He covered his face with his arms to protect himself from the clouds of fine grit eddying around. The fitful wind swirled around him and blew away farther into the Rift. Rieuk slowly raised his head, sensing that he was no longer alone.

"Who's there?" he called out. Had Estael or one of the other magi come to search for him?

The arch of a great gateway glimmered, pale as if limned in starlight against the darkness. A tall figure stood in front of it, gazing around, as if it had just passed through the gate into the Rift.

A way out!

Yet even as Rieuk hurried toward it, the gateway shimmered and vanished.

The figure turned around.

Eyes—crimson as the fire at the heart of a ruby, yet dark as night at the core—scanned the darkness. Rieuk shrank back behind the trees. The creature that had come through the gateway was tall, powerfully built, with black hair streaked with flame-red streaming down its back. Its body glittered dully, as though covered in scales of jet, and its fingers were tipped with sharp, curving talons.

A Drakhaoul?

"Azilis? Where are you?" The anguished question echoed around the Rift, a rumble of distant thunder. "Why can't I hear your voice anymore?"

A dark, disturbing aura was emanating from the stranger—powerful yet bitter, poisoned with despair. As Rieuk crouched, watching, the daemon walked away into the darkness, still calling forlornly, "My daughter? Where are you?"

It was only when the daemon had gone that he noticed another faint shimmer overhead; the ghost of the emerald moon had momentarily reappeared as the clouds of dust and shadow scudded past. And by its uncertain light, he saw at last what he had been searching for: the tall silhouette of the Emerald Tower in the far distance.

A soft light suffused Rieuk's dreams, leading him slowly back to consciousness. At first he just gazed at the white walls of his chamber, recognizing familiar objects: the jewel-bright wall hanging from the silk weavers of Tyriana; the crystals he had fashioned for his own amusement into the shapes of hawks; his books of lore, collected on his travels . . .

"Am I really back?" he asked aloud. "Or am I still dreaming?"

"So you're awake at last." Lord Estael stood in the doorway.

"How—how long have I been away?"

Estael opened the shutters. The daylight seared Rieuk's sight; he turned his head away. He had become a creature of the night, forgetting how mercilessly strong the light of the Enhirran sun could be.

"We thought we'd lost you," said Estael bluntly. "I sent Almiras in after you but when he could find no trace of Ormas, we thought you were gone too."

Rieuk's time in the caves of aethyr crystal had already begun to seem like a dream; his recollection was becoming blurred and unreliable. "Was it days? Weeks?"

Estael hesitated. "Over three years."

"Three years?" Rieuk grabbed Estael by the shoulder, pulling his face close to his own. "*Don't lie to me.*"

"Time flows differently in the Rift," Estael said contemptuously. "Why else would we have put Imri's body to rest in there? Have you learned nothing?"

Rieuk was too weak to keep his grip on Estael; his hand dropped back to his side. "But Imri was dead. For the living . . ."

"Only those with mage blood can survive that long in there; an ordinary mortal would have died."

"I only had a bottle of water . . . a loaf of bread, cheese, dates . . ." Rieuk closed his eyes, exhausted by the effort of puzzling out what had happened to him. "How could I survive three years on such meager rations?"

"How long did it seem to you?" Estael's voice penetrated his stupor.

"A week, maybe two. It took me a while to locate the crystal cave. Then I couldn't find my way back; the whole landscape of the Rift had altered and I couldn't see the Emerald Tower any longer." Against the darkness he saw again the terrifying shadow of the Drakhaoul stalking through the darkness. "Until *he* appeared."

"He?" Estael bent over him. "You don't mean—"

"The Drakhaoul. He was searching for his daughter. He called her Azilis."

"You saw Prince Nagazdiel in the Rift?" Estael's tone had become urgent, excited. "We must tell the Arkhan. This is . . . extraordinary."

"The Arkhan?" Rieuk felt the old loathing rise up within him. "Are you still in thrall to that madman, Estael? Hasn't one of you had the guts to stand up to him? After all he's put you through?"

"Lord Estael!" Men's voices could be heard from outside the tower. Estael left his bedside while Rieuk drifted uneasily between sleep and consciousness.

"Rieuk Mordiern," said a stern voice. He opened his eyes to see one of Sardion's captains standing over him. "The Arkhan has ordered me to bring you to him. Straightaway."

CHAPTER 2

Kaspar Linnaius brought the sky craft slowly down, circling above the Swanholm estate, affording King Enguerrand a magnificent view of the Emperor's palace. But Enguerrand, still suffering from airsickness, was in no condition to appreciate the grandeur of his rival's home. Clutching the side of the craft for dear life, he closed his eyes and prayed for a safe landing while Aude held his other hand and whispered comforting words in his ear.

"Welcome to Swanholm!" The Emperor rose to greet Enguerrand with open arms.

Enguerrand, his knees trembling from the flight, tottered forward, and was surprised when Eugene embraced him heartily. "You're not well," the Emperor said in concerned tones. "I'll have my personal physician attend you."

"Forgive me." As Eugene helped him into a chair, Enguerrand realized how grateful he felt. He caught hold of his hand and said, "Your imperial highness, I don't know how to begin to thank you—"

"Please, call me Eugene. We'll talk later when you've recovered from the journey."

While Enguerrand and Aude were shown to their guest rooms and Gustave was making arrangements to summon Doctor Amandel, the Emperor took Linnaius through to his private apartments.

"Thanks to you, my dear Kaspar, we hold a trump card in our hands."

Linnaius nodded. He was very weary. The long journey

back to Swanholm had been difficult—partly because of his concerns over Enguerrand's frail state of health, and partly due to his own failing powers. But Eugene seemed even more energetic than usual, pacing his study restlessly as he outlined his plans aloud.

"I've given orders that no one is to leave the estate. Our royal guest's identity must remain a secret until we are ready to act. The element of surprise is still ours, and we must use it to our best advantage." Linnaius recognized that crafty gleam in Eugene's eyes; the Emperor was in his element, devising a strategy to outwit the Francian government. "But what happens next depends largely on Enguerrand."

The inner door opened and Astasia came running in.

"Where's Andrei?"

"He's safe and well in Serindher, imperial highness."

"He's alive? You've seen him?" Astasia's eyes brimmed with tears. "But why didn't you bring him back, Magus?" she cried accusingly.

Linnaius sighed. He had not been looking forward to breaking the news to the Empress. "He and Count Alvborg chose to stay behind and help the priests rebuild the mission."

"He—?" Astasia stopped, obviously at a loss for words. "My brother?"

"It's an admirable choice," said Eugene, slipping his arm around his wife's waist and steering her out of his study. "I can't think of a better way for Prince Andrei to employ his time productively. Perhaps we should appoint him as our next ambassador to Serindher . . ."

When he returned a few minutes later, he said quietly to Linnaius, "She's not been sleeping well of late. She claims to . . . have seen a ghost."

"What manner of ghost?" Linnaius inquired, puzzled.

"Valery Vassian. The one who died protecting her from her brother's Drakhaoul. Of course, I'd normally say that it's just her imagination if it weren't for the fact that . . ."

"That you've seen the ghost too?"

"Not Vassian. But Margret. Here, in this very room." A distant, troubled look had come into Eugene's eyes. "You know me well, Kaspar, you know that I'm a rational man who doesn't believe in ghosts and such superstitious stuff. I haven't told Astasia, of course, I don't want to alarm her."

Linnaius remembered how much Margret's early death in childbirth had afflicted Eugene. "And what did the ghost say to you?"

"She said she was lost. She asked me to help her to find her way back. But back where? I thought I was dreaming the first time. But then it happened again. What does it mean, Kaspar? Am I hallucinating? It's . . . upsetting."

"Lost souls," Linnaius muttered under his breath. All the while he had been in the Spice Islands, the Rift had continued to widen, and the borders between the living and the dead must have become unstable. "This doesn't bode well."

"So I wasn't dreaming!"

Linnaius paused a moment, wondering how best to frame his request. "There is one person who holds the key to this mystery. But she's a fugitive, on the run from the Francian Inquisition. If your imperial highness were to secure a safe passage to Tielen for her, I believe she might be able to put this matter to rights."

"I'll get Gustave on to it straightaway." Eugene gave the bellpull a brisk tug. "What is the young woman's name?"

"Celestine de Joyeuse."

Eugene caught Gustave trying to smother a yawn as they went through the morning's correspondence together.

"Late night, eh, Gustave?"

"Please forgive me." Gustave blushed to the roots of his hair. "It's just that—" He broke off, shaking his head. "No. I don't want to waste your time with such a trivial matter."

"I know you too well, Gustave." Eugene was intrigued. "For it to have kept you awake, it can't possibly be trivial."

Gustave seemed to be struggling with himself as to how to proceed with the conversation. "I'm sure it was a dream. I should never have drunk that second glass of aquavit just before bed. Indigestible stuff. But . . . I thought that I saw my father. Or *something* that resembled my father." His voice had become very quiet, very flat in tone. "It spoke to me. But how could it be my father? He died five years ago."

"Last night?" Eugene felt his skin crawling.

"An hour or so after midnight. About the time the moon was setting . . ."

Gustave, the most imperturbable, rational member of the imperial household, was confessing that he had also seen a ghost?

"Is that special safe-conduct order I asked you to prepare ready?" Eugene asked. "The one for Celestine de Joyeuse?"

"I have it here, ready for you to sign and seal."

When the Magus was admitted to the King of Francia's chamber, he was surprised to see Enguerrand out of bed, and sitting by the window, a rug over his legs. The feverish glitter in his eyes had gone and his skin already had a healthier glow.

"I'm glad to see your majesty looking much better."

"I owe you my life, Magus," said Enguerrand earnestly. He hesitated, then said, "Francia has treated you shamefully. I don't know how I can begin to make it up to you. But perhaps granting you an official royal pardon might be a good way to start?"

Linnaius paused before he replied. "What has brought about this change of heart, sire?" He chose his words with care. "Your Inquisition has treated me and my kind with the utmost barbarity—torturing and executing us, and burning all our books. The accumulated wisdom of many centuries has been lost on the Inquisitors' fires."

"What made me change my mind?" A distant look clouded the king's eyes. "Nilaihah? A glimpse into the Realm of Shadows? Most of all, I think, it was Abbé Laorans. I intend to dissolve the Inquisition just as soon as I have taken back my throne. And that's just the first of many reforms that I will be initiating."

Linnaius looked at the young king with genuine surprise.

"And I look forward to a new and mutually beneficial alliance between our two nations." The Emperor came in, rubbing his hands in a gesture that Linnaius recognized of old; Eugene was scheming again. "But first, we have to get you your throne back!"

"You think there may be resistance?" Enguerrand said with a touch of his old timidity.

"Your brother-in-law has the might of the Order of the Rosecoeurs behind him. We mustn't underestimate their influence. However," said Eugene, grinning, "we have a significant advantage: the element of surprise!"

CHAPTER 3

The curtain came down on the final performance of *A Spring Elopement* to rapturous applause and many encores. Gauzia departed the next day for Tourmalise, with her dresser and her coiffeur in tow, leaving Grebin exhausted but content as he counted the month's takings.

Celestine tapped on his office door and saw him writing columns of figures in a ledger. He took one look at her and said, "Don't tell me that you're leaving us too, Maela?"

"How can you tell?"

He sighed and laid down his quill. "It's that florist of yours. Or whoever he is. Ever since he appeared on the scene, you've not been the same. There's been a sparkle in your eyes, a little smile on your lips. I've seen it a thousand times before. Oh, if I could tell you the number of promising singers lost to the stage, and all in the name of love . . ."

"I don't intend to give up my singing career!" she said indignantly. "But I need to go away for a short while. Please don't take me off your books, Manager. I intend to come back."

"That's what they all say." He waved toward the door with his pen. "Off you go, then, have a wonderful life . . ."

She hesitated, then darted forward and planted a little kiss on the top of his head. "Thank you," she said earnestly. "For everything. You saved my life."

"Don't talk nonsense," he said gruffly, dipping the nib in the ink and staring intently at the ledger. "Take your wages and go." As she left the office she heard him mutter, "And the latrines have never been so clean . . ."

* * *

"What do you mean she's not here?" Kilian had run all the way from Jagu's lodgings to Celestine's and he was having difficulty making the landlady understand him. Like many Muscobites, she had only a rudimentary grasp of the common tongue.

"She is gone," repeated the landlady, retreating and slamming her door in his face. Kilian swore. He was hot, out of breath, and frustrated. He had Jagu—so why was it proving so difficult to track her down? And how long could he trust the captain and crew to keep Jagu confined to his cabin? He tugged open his jacket and undid his shirt collar as he set off for the Imperial Theater, not caring if he was not at his regimental smartest; who was there to see him?

A bribe to the old man on the stage door got Kilian backstage a second time. There was much cursing and shouting coming from the wings. The stagehands were striking the set of *A Spring Elopement* and Kilian had to keep dodging out of the way, flattening himself against the peeling wall as huge canvas flats were carried past in the narrow passageways.

"Demoiselle Cassard?" said a stagehand with a shrug. "There's no singers in today. Rehearsals don't start again till tomorrow. Stage Manager Grebin might know, but be warned—he's not in the best of moods."

"I haven't got time to chat to visitors!" came an irate voice. "There's work to be done." The stage manager appeared, a pencil stuck in his wig, brandishing another as he ticked off items on a long list with a flourish.

"I need to contact Maela Cassard," Kilian said. "Urgently."

"Don't we all?" Grebin said brusquely. "But you're too late. She's gone."

"Gone?" Kilian had difficulty controlling his temper. Had Jagu deliberately agreed to that "one last drink" in order to give Celestine the time she needed to disappear? "Gone where?"

"Young man," said Grebin, "you can either move now, or be crushed to death by a twenty-foot replica of a rustic cottage."

· Searching blindly for her would lead nowhere. Outside in the busy square, Kilian heard a church clock striking. She had outwitted him. The ship was due to sail in an hour and she had vanished.

There was only one alternative left.

The first thing that Jagu became aware of was the pounding in his head; then a lurching, rolling sensation made him feel violently queasy.

How much did I drink last night? He made an effort to sit up but dropped back, groaning, shielding his eyes against the painful brightness. Even though he lay still, the room seemed to be moving. There was a foul taste in his mouth and his tongue was furred and dry. He craved water. He rolled onto his side, trying to reach the floor. If he couldn't stand, he would crawl . . .

But even the floor was shifting beneath his hands and knees, slowly rising and falling with the regular motion of a ship under sail.

Under sail? He tried to focus his bleary eyes on his surroundings. This wasn't his room in Mirom. He could hear the sloshing slap of water against the wooden walls. Looking up to the single source of daylight, he saw a porthole. It took him several attempts to stand upright for long enough to peer out. What he saw made him swear under his breath.

The ship was moving slowly away from the quay and the tavern where he had taken that fateful drink with Kilian was already receding into the distance.

"Damn it all." He tottered toward the cabin door and tried the handle, but it was securely locked.

Exhausted by his efforts, he dropped to his knees again, pounding his fists against the wood. "Kilian!" he yelled. "Let me out!" But no one came.

They were heading toward the Nieva Estuary. Each fresh gust of wind filling the sails was taking him farther away from Mirom—and Celestine.

CHAPTER 4

Celestine began to sing softly to herself as she moved about the room, collecting her belongings, and realized that the persistent melody was the opening phrase of Jagu's Vesper Prayer. She stopped, smiling to herself, still delighting in this unexpected discovery: Jagu had a real gift for writing music.

He must have absorbed something of your skill, Henri, she thought fondly as she placed the score of the Vesper Prayer carefully on top of the folded dresses in her traveling bag with her father's grimoire.

And then she sensed that she was not alone; there was someone else in the room. All too late, the Faie woke within her, whispering, *"Kaspar Linnaius."*

The Magus stood on the threshold. "I bring an invitation from the Emperor," he said and held out a sealed letter.

Her mind went blank with panic. He must have come to take his revenge. And she was trapped, with no means of escape. "You're alive?"

"So it seems. Please, take the letter."

"F—from the Emperor?"

"Signed and sealed by his imperial highness himself," he said, showing her the Rossiyan imperial seal. It looked authentic enough, yet a magus of Linnaius's skill and ingenuity could easily have faked it.

She took it from him and, breaking the purple wax, hastily read the contents. It was an invitation for Celestine de Joyeuse and her accompanist to perform at Swanholm, with a letter of safe passage enclosed, signed and authorized by the Emperor's personal secretary.

"What does this mean?" She was still shaken by his unexpected appearance. "Why would the Emperor invite me to Tielen? Especially when I've caused him so much trouble?"

"There are others at the court in Tielen who are eager to see you again, Celestine," he said enigmatically. Celestine could not read what lay behind those chill silver eyes.

"But the singer known as Celestine de Joyeuse is dead. She had to die."

"That's all well and good as long as your guardian spirit is able to disguise your identity. But she's growing weaker, isn't she?"

How could he tell? Celestine stared at the Magus, forgetting her earlier caution. His incisive gaze pierced through her, penetrating deep into her mind. She gasped—and at the same moment sensed the Faie repel the Magus's invasion. He staggered, his eyes clouding, one wrinkled hand rising to protect himself.

"Weaker, but not so weak yet that she can't still defend herself against an inquisitive old magus," he said wryly. "All these years you've been hiding her. And now she's become too much a part of you for you to let her go. Or . . . is it the other way, perhaps, Lady Azilis?"

Celestine was so surprised by the blatant challenge that she could not reply.

"You might as well reveal yourself fully to me, my lady." Ice-silver eyes gleamed in the dim light.

"*You mustn't trust him,*" whispered the Faie. "*He's come to take me from you.*"

"I give you my word that I won't attempt to steal you again." Linnaius was staring at Celestine so intently that she realized he was looking not at her, but through her, his chill gaze penetrating her disguise to where the Faie had concealed herself. "But I beg you, Lady Azilis, to consider returning to Ondhessar. The balance between this world and the next is slowly disintegrating. Revenants have been seen—lost souls who have drifted back to this world because they can't find their path to the Ways Beyond."

"Revenants," Celestine echoed, remembering the sad, lost shadow of her first love that had returned to haunt her.

"If my Faie is Azilis, then I have no right to keep her all to myself."

"*I cannot return. I'm bound to protect Celestine.*"

"You were bound to protect this child . . . yet you may be using up too much of her life force to replenish your own failing powers."

"*I cannot break that bond.*"

"But you can break it at any time, can't you, Celestine?"

Celestine did not reply. Thoughts were chasing through her mind. It would take only one drop of her blood to break the contract . . .

"The Emperor is offering you protection of a different kind. A full pardon, his patronage, and a new life in Tielen. The Empress is very fond of you, you know."

"The Emperor is most generous." Celestine felt herself wavering, genuinely tempted. She and Jagu had not planned where to go once they left Muscobar, but with the Emperor's protection, they would be able to start a new life in Tielen, far from the clutches of the Inquisition.

"This safe passage is all you'll need. Believe me, Celestine, if you could only bring yourself to put your trust in me . . ."

"Trust you, Kaspar Linnaius? A week ago, I'd have laughed at such a suggestion. Now I don't know whom to trust anymore."

"I would tell you more, but his imperial highness has sworn me to secrecy."

Celestine still could not look directly into those chill silver eyes; every time she tried, she felt as if she were standing alone on a bare hilltop, surrounded by racing stormclouds, buffeted by fierce winds that stripped away all her defenses.

"If you're ready to leave now, I can take you to Swanholm."

"Or Ondhessar?" she said.

"Ondhessar?" the Magus repeated in surprised tones.

"*Celestine . . .*" whispered the Faie. "*Please let me stay with you a little longer.*"

"I understand now, Faie," she said. "The souls of the

dead need you to sing for them. They need you so much more than I do. Can you take us to Ondhessar, Magus?"

A strange smile passed fleetingly across his face. "Yes. Although I still have enemies in Ondhessar. I need a little time to plan my strategy."

"I need time to make arrangements too. I can't just disappear without telling Jagu."

"Then let's agree to complete our plans when you reach Swanholm."

And he was gone before she could ask any more questions, leaving her holding the letter of safe passage.

Suddenly she felt so faint that she had to sit down. "Look at me, Faie, I'm shaking!" She touched the smooth waxen sheen of the imperial seal. How ironic that Eugene should be the one to offer them a safe haven.

Celestine handed over her key to the landlady and said good-bye to the cats. Then she walked to the square, hailed a carriage, and instructed the driver to take her to the Francian Embassy. As they rattled away, she took one last look back at the Imperial Theater, smiling as she remembered Grebin's parting words.

"Oh, I intend to come back," she said. That brief taste of the heady pleasures of performing onstage had given her a craving for more. But not yet; she was far more eager to see Jagu again and tell him the astonishing news. She checked again to make sure that the precious letter of safe passage was still in her reticule.

Alighting outside the embassy, she hurried up the steps to be admitted by Claude.

"Has Lieutenant de Rustéphan arrived yet?" she asked breathlessly.

"No, Demoiselle. But the ambassador has received a communication for you. If you would follow me . . ." Claude's haughty expression gave nothing away as he showed her into Fabien d'Abrissard's study.

What manner of communication? Perhaps Jagu had been delayed.

"This is addressed to you, Celestine." The ambassador

rose to greet her, holding out a letter. She opened it and read:

> We have arrested your accomplice, Jagu de Rustéphan. He will be executed for crimes against the state unless you give yourself up to Francian justice. You have one month in which to return to Lutèce to answer the charges against you.

"They've taken Jagu. They've taken him back to Lutèce!" This was the last thing she had expected. She sat down, the letter clutched in her hand. How had it all gone so wrong? Everything had been settled for the start of their new life together: the Emperor's letter of safe passage to Tielen, the concert plans, Jagu's composition . . .

"My dear Celestine," said the ambassador gravely, "you mustn't even think of going back to Lutèce. The city's in a volatile state. Ilsevir is not popular. He's ordered his Rose-coeurs to stamp out any signs of rebellion or heresy. Aided, of course, by the Inquisition."

"Kilian." Celestine stared down at the letter, seeing the black script blur and waver as a teardrop splashed onto the ink. "Kilian, his oldest friend." *What use is crying?* she told herself angrily. *I have to rescue him.* Yet still the drops continued to fall. She looked up, dashing away the tears. "It's a trap. They've set a trap for me. They knew my weakness—and they're using it to lure me into their clutches."

"All the more reason not to walk into their trap."

"But Jagu—"

"I can protect you here in Mirom, but the instant you leave these shores, you'll be fair game for the Inquisition."

Kaspar Linnaius's accusing words flashed through her memory.

Haven't you been pursuing the wrong man? Shouldn't you be seeking to take revenge on the man who condemned your father to the stake? Alois Visant?

In that one moment, she knew that the time for tears was over. Her chin went up. "I'm going to Swanholm," she said.

* * *

"Monsieur de Corméry, it's so kind of you to take time out of your busy schedule to accompany me to Tielen." Celestine gave him one of her sweetest smiles.

The young attaché blushed. "It's—it's no trouble at all, Demoiselle, I assure you. Besides, in the circumstances, the ambassador was adamant that you not travel alone, and as I was visiting Tielen on embassy affairs anyway . . ."

In truth, Celestine was genuinely grateful to have his company to distract her from her gloom. It was a terrible risk that she was taking, traveling to Swanholm, using up so many days of her one precious month—at the end of which Jagu would be executed.

She even feared that there might have been Francian agents at the customs house in Mirom, watching out for her. But here they were, safely on board a Tielen vessel, which was sailing slowly down the Nieva toward the Straits, and no one had approached her.

Weariness suddenly overwhelmed her and she felt herself sinking to the deck. She heard Corméry's alarmed cry and felt herself drowning in waves of dizziness.

She came to her senses to find Corméry bending anxiously over her, dabbing her temples with a balsam-impregnated handkerchief. The strong, sharp scent made her wrinkle her nose and sneeze.

"My dear demoiselle, are you all right? You had me quite worried, fainting so suddenly like that."

"I fainted?" Celestine made to sit up but her head swam, so she lay back again. "But I *never* faint." She was disgusted with herself for such a show of weakness. To her embarrassment, she realized that Corméry must have had the sailors carry her belowdecks to her cabin. "It's just that I haven't slept much in the last few days." She forced herself to sound more confident than she felt. "I'll be fine after a good night's rest."

"Then I'll leave you to it," said Corméry, looking a little more relieved. But as soon as he had gone, she closed her eyes and pressed the cold handkerchief to her forehead. She felt as if she were not entirely back in her body. The odd, light-headed sensation, floating between consciousness and unconsciousness, was disturbing.

"Faie," she called quietly, her eyes closed. "Why am I so weak? Am I ill?"

"*I fear it is all my fault,*" came back the soft reply. "*Kaspar Linnaius was right; your body is not strong enough to sustain the two of us. I am using up too much of your life essence.*"

"Too much? But I've never needed your protection more than I do now. How am I to rescue Jagu if you aren't there to help me?"

"*I will return to the book to give your body time to recover.*"

Though as the ship reached the open sea, Celestine lay awake long into the night, unable to sleep for the thoughts jostling in her brain. Was Linnaius right after all? Was the Faie putting too much strain on her body every time she used her powers to disguise or defend herself? Or was he just trying to trick her?

"What am I doing here?" Alain Friard wondered as he followed his superior officers into the king's council chamber. He was surprised that the new king had included him in this private meeting, and even more surprised that Hugues Donatien had not tried to prevent him from attending. He slunk in behind Donatien, taking a place at the most obscure end of the council table. Haute Inquisitor Visant sat opposite Girim nel Ghislain, the leader of the Order of the Rosecoeurs.

"Gentlemen, we need to convince the people of Francia that you are winning the fight against the forces of evil," King Ilsevir said as he took his seat at the head of the table. "We need to restore confidence in the church. Many people saw the Drakhaouls at large in the city. Some are even saying they saw Enguerrand being abducted by a daemon. The general opinion seems to be that the Commanderie is not strong enough to protect Lutèce."

Visant's secretary was scribbling away busily, taking notes as the king spoke.

"I don't deny that the Commanderie lost the people's

confidence when Kaspar Linnaius was rescued from the stake," said Maistre Donatien. "Too many lives were lost in the panic that day."

"And since the sordid case of Ruaud de Lanvaux's murder, the Commanderie's reputation has sunk even lower," observed Visant acidly. Friard wanted to speak up on behalf of his men, but one glance at the king's face told him it was best to keep silent. "Though, if I might make a suggestion . . . it has come to our attention that there is treachery at the heart of the Commanderie itself. Two of the late Maistre's most trusted agents have betrayed the cause. We have proof. We have witnesses."

Friard was dreading to hear what was coming next.

"We must root out any sign of treachery, no matter how painful it may be," said Ilsevir sternly. "Bring these agents in and let them be tried. Who are they?"

"Celestine de Joyeuse," said Visant, "and Jagu de Rustéphan."

Friard clenched his fists beneath the table. Two of his most loyal comrades in arms. One by one, all Ruaud's elite squad were being eliminated.

"I know those names . . ." A faraway look came into Ilsevir's eyes. "The musicians who saved our lives at the opening of the Azilis chapel? Surely you're mistaken, Inquisitor?"

"The evidence against Demoiselle de Joyeuse is too compelling. As for Lieutenant de Rustéphan"—Visant turned to Maistre Donatien—"is there any news yet?"

"When the lieutenant did not report back, I sent Kilian Guyomard to Muscobar to investigate. I'm pleased to report that he has arrested him and is bringing him back to Lutèce by sea."

"So you plan to use him as bait to lure Demoiselle de Joyeuse to his rescue?" Visant nodded his approval.

Friard could take no more. He stood up. "P—pardon me, your majesty," he stammered, staring at Donatien as he spoke, "but when has it been Commanderie practice to condemn one of our own without anything other than hearsay to go on?"

"Are you challenging my authority, Captain Friard?" Visant's stare chilled Friard to the bone, yet he stood his ground, determined not to be intimidated.

"I'm defending my Guerriers, Inquisitor. I don't want to see two good and loyal agents used as scapegoats."

"Let's not argue among ourselves, gentlemen," said Ilsevir smoothly. "We must reassure the people by showing them that we are working together to defeat our enemies. I'm sure you'd be the first to agree that is our priority, Captain Friard? And to that end, I'd like to unite the two branches of the Commanderie."

Friard stared at the king, then at Donatien, who was smiling and nodding his approval.

"Maistre Donatien will be head of the new Commanderie, with Captains Friard and Ghislain as his subordinates. But Captain Friard, you will need to liaise with Captain nel Ghislain as I intend to combine the two branches into one under the sign of the Rosecoeur."

"Maistre, did you approve this?" Friard appealed to Donatien.

"Indeed, I did," Donatien said calmly. "The Rosecoeurs' methods have been so much more successful than our own, especially in Ondhessar. You have much to learn from Captain nel Ghislain."

Humiliated, Friard sat down. Everything that Ruaud de Lanvaux had worked for was being swept away by this relentless Allegondan tide. He was more certain than ever that the charges against Celestine and Jagu were false. Had Kilian defected to Donatien's side? He had never been able to read Kilian accurately, suspecting a devious mind at work behind his joking, easygoing manner. But the greatest betrayal of all was that of Hugues Donatien.

As the effects of the drug slowly wore off, Jagu—confined to his cramped cabin—had too much time alone to regret what had happened. He lay gazing at the wooden walls, cursing his trusting nature. *Why did I fall for Kilian's trick? Am I still so gullible?*

The truth was that he had been so caught up in his feelings

that he had been careless. To be in love was such a new and unexpected state of mind that he had let his guard down.

But what was the worst they could do to him for breaking his vow? Flog him? Expel him from the order? Imprison him? He could endure all that and more if only he knew that Celestine was safe. But the nagging fear that grew ever more disturbing, like thunderclouds looming on the horizon, was that Visant and Donatien merely planned to use him to get to her.

CHAPTER 5

"So the fashioning of this new Lodestar took you three years?" Sardion turned the lotus crystal over and over in his hands while Rieuk watched, hating to see the Arkhan's fingers polluting the purity of his handiwork. It was all he could do not to snatch it back. "It's very fine. Almost as fine as the original." He placed it in an ebony casket on his desk. "But matters have changed since you went into the Rift. You've seen him for yourself, haven't you?"

Rieuk was still staring at the casket that contained his Lodestar.

"Prince Nagazdiel." Sardion's eyes gleamed with that hungry light Rieuk had learned to hate. "He has come to us at last."

"To us?" Rieuk echoed uneasily.

"For years without number, my family has waited for him to return. But our mortal bodies are too frail to withstand the atmosphere of the Rift. That is why I'm sending you, as my Emissary, to bring him to me."

"Me?" Rieuk could not believe what he was hearing. Sardion wanted him to return to the Rift? "But how?"

"By offering him your body as his vessel. He's an aethyrial spirit like the other Drakhaouls; he cannot exist in the mortal world without a host of flesh and blood."

"You want me to give him my body?"

"You're the most powerful of all my magi, Rieuk. Others have tried and failed. The last I sent in was Oranir. I judged him stronger than the others . . . but he's yet to return."

"You sent Oranir into the Rift to look for Nagazdiel?" It was all Rieuk could do to control his anger.

"You still harbor feelings for that boy, even though he betrayed you?" A slow, cruel smile spread across Sardion's gaunt features. "What a fool you are."

Sardion led Rieuk deep below the palace, through a maze of passageways that ended in a forbidding chamber lined in black marble. An ancient doorway loomed beyond. The Arkhan cut a small nick in his wrist, and then in Rieuk's, smearing their mingled drops of blood on the stone. The doorway slowly opened with a grinding sound, letting a gust of chill air into the chamber.

"This is an honor afforded only to the chosen few," Sardion said, standing aside. "I shall await your return with impatience."

So I'm a fool. Rieuk stumbled onward through the gloom. *I don't know—or care—what's been happening in Sardion's court in the time I've been away. But I can't forget the years I spent traveling with Oranir. He'll always hold a place in my heart, no matter how many times he betrays me. And that's something, Lord Sardion, that you'll never understand.*

All that he could hear was the rushing of the dust-ridden wind that had blown in from the Realm of Shadows, bringing the deathly taint that leached the life from everything it touched.

"Where are you, Oranir?" he shouted into the wind, but it only tossed his own words back to him. "Ormas, can you sense Zophas here?"

"*I can sense nothing . . .* " came back the faint reply.

Walking blind into the gale, he suddenly stumbled over something in his path. A man lay sprawled on the dusty ground. Gently turning him over he saw, to his anguish, that it was Oranir.

"Ran." He cradled him in his arms, Oranir's dark head slumping against his shoulder. He had only ever called Oranir by that affectionate nickname when they were alone together. "*Ran!*" The young magus was unconscious but his body was still warm; when Rieuk anxiously pressed his fingertips to his wrist and throat, he detected a faint, slow pulse.

"You're still alive." Rieuk held him close. He didn't care that Oranir had betrayed him; this chance to see him, to hold him in his arms again, was worth more to him than any worldly reward. And then the truth of Oranir's condition began to sink in. "Alive, but for how long? How long have you lain unconscious down here? And how am I to get you out?"

Rieuk pulled open Oranir's robes and loose shirt, until he could place his hand on the smoke hawk tattooed into Oranir's olive skin. He sensed a faint pulsation, as if Zophas were dozing deep within his master.

Time has no meaning in the Rift. The atmosphere might even have preserved Oranir's life. But if he took him back to the surface, the sudden change might kill him. Rieuk knelt in the eerie half-light with Oranir's head in his lap, absently stroking the long strands of dusty black hair from his forehead, not knowing what to do to save his life.

Then he sensed it: that dark, disturbing aura he had encountered here before. The shadowy air shimmered. He raised his head to see the Drakhaoul Nagazdiel gazing down at him.

"He is strong, this young magus," said Nagazdiel in his soft, deep voice, which made Rieuk shiver, "but not strong enough to give me back my freedom."

"What did you do to him?" Rieuk choked over the words.

"I took possession of his body. But the strain was too great; he could not sustain me."

"No." Rieuk clutched Oranir to him, overcome with grief. "Ran, my poor Ran . . ." The Drakhaoul must have entered Oranir's body, draining him of his life essence to gain new strength.

"He is one of *her* children; she could restore him, if she were here. But he is weak and his hawk is weaker still."

"*She,* my lord?" Rieuk raised his head from Oranir's.

"My daughter, Azilis."

"Your daughter could heal Oranir?"

"She should be here." Nagazdiel gazed around him at the moonless waste of dying trees. "I came searching for her. I must find her." He turned back to Rieuk. "You will take me to find her. We will bring her back together." It was a command and not one to be disobeyed.

Rieuk laid Oranir gently down again and rose unsteadily to his feet. "I offer you my body, my lord Nagazdiel, if you will accept it." He had no idea whether he was resilient enough to host a Drakhaoul, but he knew that while there was a crumb of hope of saving Oranir's life, he was prepared to risk it.

Nagazdiel came toward him, his arms open wide, as if to embrace him. Fire and shadow swirled up around Rieuk, engulfing him in a smoke-shot cloud. His body burned as if he had swallowed liquid fire.

Suppose I'm too weak to host him . . . he's so powerful . . .

"*This fusion suits me well,*" breathed Nagazdiel's voice within him. "*Now take me to find my daughter.*"

CHAPTER 6

Alighting from Cormery's carriage at Swanholm, Celestine was surprised to see that one whole wing was covered with scaffolding and swarming with builders. As she crossed the wide gravel drive, the extent of the damage became clear; the roof must have caved in, taking much of the upper floors with it. She turned to Roget de Cormery, asking, "Do you know what happened? Was there a fire?"

"The official story is that insurgents kidnapped Princess Karila and in the fight to get her back, the wing was hit by cannonfire. But I heard a rumor," said Cormery confidentially, "that Swanholm was attacked by a Drakhaoul."

Celestine looked at him in astonishment.

Then they were met by the majordomo and ushered into the palace, to an antechamber to await their imperial majesties' pleasure.

Celestine, too agitated to stay sitting down, paced the parquet flooring, stopping from time to time to gaze out of the windows at the parkland. When she had last seen the view, the trees had been hung with soft-colored lanterns and the dusky summer air had been filled with music.

"Do take a glass of this excellent amber aquavit," said Cormery, taking a sip. A tray of refreshments had been brought in by a maid: a crystal decanter of aquavit and a silver dish filled with little almond macaroons. "It will help calm your nerves."

"Is it so very obvious?" Celestine forced a smile. "No spirits, thank you; they're bad for the vocal cords. I came here to sing for her imperial majesty, and if that is what she wishes . . ."

"Just don't ask me to be your accompanist!" said Corméry with a laugh. "I never managed more than 'Good night, little star.' I almost drove my music teacher insane."

The door opened and the majordomo appeared, announcing, "Demoiselle de Joyeuse is requested to attend upon her imperial highness in the Willow Salon."

"My dear Celestine," exclaimed Astasia, holding out her hands to her, "I'm so relieved to see that you're safe." And to Celestine's confusion, the Empress embraced her, kissing her on both cheeks. "There's someone here I want you to meet." She led her over to the fireplace, where a young man was sitting, with a red-haired girl beside him. Celestine let out a little cry.

"S—sire?" she whispered. "You're alive?" She was so surprised that she forgot all about court etiquette, unable to do anything but stare. Then, remembering where she was, she sank into a deep curtsy.

"Please rise, Demoiselle," said King Enguerrand. He looked thin and frail, as though he had been ill for a long while, but he was smiling at her, and the warmth of his smile made her feel as if there might still be hope for Jagu. "I know we can trust you to keep this a secret."

"But of course!"

"We cannot even risk telling Corméry yet. I owe my life to the Emperor; he sent Kaspar Linnaius to search for me and the others in my party."

"The Magus brought us all the way back from Serindher in his sky craft!" put in the girl, her brown eyes radiant with excitement.

"My cousin Aude found the journey rather more agreeable than I," Enguerrand said ruefully.

"But my stubborn brother has chosen to stay in Serindher," said Astasia with a little sniff, "to help the priests rebuild their mission. Andrei, doing good works? Whatever next?"

"I am glad to hear that the prince is in good health." Celestine could not hide an affectionate little smile as she spoke. "I owe him my life. He rescued me from the Inquisition in Smarna."

Enguerrand's expression became grave. "I've been hearing disturbing rumors about the Inquisition. They seem to have fallen under the influence of the Rosecoeurs and Girim nel Ghislain."

Celestine could not hold back any longer. "They've arrested my partner, Lieutenant de Rustéphan, sire," she cried, "and they're threatening to execute him unless I give myself up too. Is there any way you can help us?"

"Rustéphan?" repeated Enguerrand. "But you were the ones who saved my sister's life in Bel'Esstar! Why would Ilsevir seek to destroy two such loyal Guerriers?"

"Because," and Celestine hesitated, knowing that she was taking a terrible risk in revealing her secret to the king, "I am the daughter of a magus. I have mage blood in my veins."

Enguerrand was staring at her. *I've said too much.* She lowered her gaze. But then he held out his hand to her, beckoning her close. She knelt before him and felt his fingers gently touching her head, raising her face to his.

"You're truly blessed," he said, gazing deeply into her eyes, "because the blood of angels flows in your veins."

"A—angels?"

"The priest who saved our lives, Abbé Laorans, showed me the lost Holy Texts, the ones that tell the true story of Azilis and her father, Prince Nagazdiel. Now I understand that the magi are not to be feared and persecuted because of their powers; they should be honored and respected."

Celestine could hardly begin to comprehend what the king was telling her. But the one thing she understood was that he was her friend and ally.

"We have been in discussion with the Emperor," Enguerrand went on, "and we have a plan. But are you prepared to risk your life?"

"I'll risk anything," she said without hesitating, "if it will save Jagu."

A secret meeting was convened late that night. Corméry had already departed for Muscobar, bearing a dispatch box with sealed, encrypted instructions inside for Fabien d'Abrissard.

Celestine looked around the candlelit table. Enguerrand of Francia and Eugene of Tielen were sitting, talking quietly together over glasses of red wine from Vasconie. Francia and Tielen in harmony, after so many years of bitter conflict?

"Isn't this exciting?" Aude said to her. "A midnight conspiracy—just like in *The Secret Kingdom*!" When Celestine looked at her blankly, she said, "Haven't you ever read it? The Empress lent it to me; she has a fine collection of novels—"

The door opened and Kaspar Linnaius appeared.

"Welcome, Kaspar!" cried Eugene, gesturing to the chair beside his. Celestine was astonished to see the Magus break into a smile. She had never realized before how strong the friendship must be between the two men.

"I don't think the Magus is much used to smiling," whispered Aude in her ear.

"Now that we're all here," said the Emperor, "let's not delay any further. Demoiselle de Joyeuse, we have to ensure that you return to Lutèce as soon as possible."

"My plan is to try to gain an audience with Princess Adèle, and beg her to intercede on Jagu's behalf," said Celestine.

"Kaspar"—and Eugene turned to the Magus—"are you willing to transport the demoiselle right into the heart of Lutèce? It's asking a great deal of you to take such a risk . . ."

"If the demoiselle is willing to trust me," said Linnaius, gazing steadily at Celestine through the shimmer of candleflames. Celestine could not hold his gaze and, confused, glanced away.

"If you see my sister, I'd like you to give her this message," said Enguerrand, passing her a little folded paper across the table.

"And I'm coming too, to create a little distraction," declared Aude.

"Good," said the Emperor briskly. "Then here's our plan. Enguerrand and I will set out with the Northern Fleet from Holborg, making for Fenez-Tyr."

A doubtful look appeared on Enguerrand's face.

"If this is going to succeed, we need to keep you out of sight for as long as possible. We need to start rumors that you've been seen alive. If we've judged the mood of the people of Lutèce correctly, they'll be overjoyed when you return. We must increase the uncertainty for Ilsevir and his Rosecoeurs and keep them guessing. That way we can catch them off guard."

One by one, the others left the chamber until only Celestine and Linnaius remained.

If the demoiselle is willing to trust me, he had said. She felt deeply ashamed that she did not know how to begin to apologize for attacking him. But she knew that at least she must make the attempt.

"All my life," she began haltingly, "I've believed that you betrayed my father." She stared at her hands, which were folded together in her lap, unable to meet his gaze. "Now I see that . . . I misjudged you." At last she found the courage to look up into his eyes. " 'Here I am, condemned to die, and where is Linnaius?' Those were my father's last words to me. Can you understand me now, Magus?"

There was a long pause. "Yes," he said at last. His eyes no longer seemed to be looking at her, but through her at some far-distant point. "It was mere chance that I was away from Karantec when the Inquisition struck. But I was ailing, so Maistre Gonery sent me to be healed in Khitari. If I had known that you were alive, I would have done all I could to find you and bring you to safety in Tielen. But the only news that I could gather when I returned was that the magi and all their kin were dead."

Celestine was feeling more uncomfortable with every word that he spoke. "I was convinced that you had wronged my father. To be sitting here, in Tielen, talking with you, when the last time we were in Swanholm, you were my prisoner . . ." She shook her head, still trying to come to terms with the situation. "I did a terrible thing to you, Magus. And you nearly died . . ." Her voice faded away. "Can you ever forgive me?"

"You were influenced by the teachings of the Inquisition," he said gravely. "Celestine, I want you to reflect a moment and ask yourself who your true enemy is."

Suddenly Linnaius reached out to touch her face, cupping it in his hands and staring deep into her eyes. She was so surprised that she was unable to react in time and froze, hypnotized by his penetrating gaze.

"I warned you, didn't I?" he said but there was no disapproval in his voice. "You are only frail flesh and blood, and by carrying her within you, you are using up too much of your precious life essence."

There was an almost fatherly tone to his words. "Too much? What do you mean?"

"You will shorten your life if you continue in this way. The warning signs are there already. Don't you think that the time has come to set her free?"

"But how am I to get anywhere near Princess Adèle without a disguise? I have to try to save Jagu!"

"Who is speaking now?" he asked gently. "Is it you, or Lady Azilis?"

"It's me!" Celestine blazed back, suddenly defensive.

"I put it to you," he said, "that your two souls have been intertwined for so long now that you find it impossible to distinguish who is Celestine and who Azilis. That isn't what Hervé intended, is it?" Linnaius took his hands away. "I don't think for one moment that he wanted you to shorten your life by merging with her."

"How can you know what my father wanted?"

Linnaius sighed. "You've become too dependent on each other. You've given her a taste of mortal life again, and it's proved too delicious for her to give it up. And she's given you a taste of her immortal power, which is the most seductive force of all to resist."

The ormolu clock on the mantelpiece struck one in a sweet-chimed tone, and Celestine realized how worn-out she was feeling; the strains and excitements of the day must be taking their toll.

"I—I hear what you're saying," she began, trying to stifle a yawn, "but how can I let go of her when she's my only

hope of saving Jagu? Would the Emperor jettison all his
ammunition before sailing into battle?"

"We leave before dawn," said Linnaius. "Get what rest
you can; it will be a long day."

*Rough hands seize her and bind her to the stake. The ropes
cut into her flesh as she tries to struggle free. A hooded figure stands before her pyre. "Burn her," he orders the soldiers, and they set flaming brands to the logs on which her
bare feet rest.*

*"No," she whispers. Fire—such a cruel, horrible death.
As the flames lick at her skin and the smoke stings her
throat, she sees her executioner's face, his cold eyes reflecting the scarlet flicker of the flames.*

Haute Inquisitor Visant.

Still gasping for breath, Celestine opened her eyes. There
was no choking smoke, no searing flame, only the elegantly
draped bed she was sleeping in.

That dream again, always that dream of death by fire—
the cruel death that the Inquisition had inflicted on her father
and the other magi in the belief that the flames would pu-
rify the evil in their cursed blood.

The fine linen sheets were damp with her perspiration.
Since Hervé's execution, she had lived in the shadow of that
pyre. But she had never imagined that she might have to
watch as the man she loved was forced to undergo that
same cruel method of execution.

"Visant," she said aloud. *Never forget that name,
Klervie,* her mother had warned her. *He is a cruel, vindic-
tive man.*

She rose and opened the shutters; a cloudy dawn was
breaking over the green hills around Swanholm. By its dull
light, she opened her little jewel casket and took out the
one precious item she had never sold, even when she had no
money for food or lodging: the jet mourning brooch given
to her by Adèle after she had sung for Prince Aubrey's funeral.

"Dear Adèle," she said, staring at the little brooch, "you

were always so kind to me. Will you still be able to protect me now that I'm a wanted heretic?"

Jagu emerged into full daylight, blinking like a night creature, to see a contingent of Rosecoeur Guerriers waiting on the quay to escort him across the bridge into the Forteresse. Shackled like a common prisoner by the wrists and ankles, he was forced to shuffle along, hauled up again every time he tripped, in full view of the staring crowds on the quay.

The Rosecoeurs would do all they could to intimidate and humiliate him, of that he was certain. He would have to draw on resources of endurance and courage that he wasn't even certain he had within him. The only thing that he was sure of was that he would not let them get their hands on Celestine—not while he had breath left in his body.

Three men were sitting in the inquisition room, waiting to interrogate Jagu. He recognized the lean features of Inquisitor Visant. On either side of him sat Grand Maistre Donatien and, to Jagu's displeasure, Girim nel Ghislain.

"This is a sad day for the Commanderie," said Maistre Donatien. "I never expected you, Lieutenant, to betray us."

The words stung. "With respect, Maistre," said Jagu quietly, "I made my vows to the Sergian Commanderie, not the Order of the Rosecoeur."

Donatien sighed. "Such a rebellious and uncooperative attitude will do you little good. Are you not aware of the seriousness of the charges brought against you?"

"I'm aware that I was drugged and abducted against my will from Muscobar." Jagu was not going to let them intimidate him. "And if you're going to bring charges, then surely I'm entitled to a lawyer to defend me?"

Visant picked up a sheet of paper from the table and began to read aloud. "In Colchise, you let the Smarnan heretic Rafael Lukan escape an hour before he was due to be executed. You claimed that you were knocked unconscious by the rebels as they stormed the citadel, but I put it to you, Lieutenant, that you were part of the rebels' plan. Perhaps they even bribed you. In fact, you were heard to express your opinion on several occasions that you thought the Inquisition had made a grave error in arresting the professor."

That was ridiculous. "I had no connection with the rebels." They were twisting the facts to make their case against him.

"Can you prove it?"

"I was in Colchise on an intelligence-gathering mission for Maistre de Lanvaux. I was only drafted into the citadel when the students threatened to storm the prison."

"And your partner on this mission was Celestine de Joyeuse?" asked Visant.

So this was the way it was going. "Yes."

"The same Demoiselle de Joyeuse who poisoned two of my agents on the *Aquilon,* when they were bringing her back to answer charges of sorcery?"

"The same Demoiselle de Joyeuse whom I sent you to arrest five months ago," put in Donatien.

"This report from Lieutenant Guyomard says that he traced you and Demoiselle de Joyeuse to Mirom and found you living together," said Girim. "Do you deny it?"

Jagu said nothing. Whichever way they chose to put it, he was already guilty in their eyes.

"You broke your vow as a Guerrier. You disobeyed your orders." Donatien's expression was implacable. "And you were living with a wanted criminal, the very woman I sent you to arrest."

"Where is she now?" Visant demanded.

"Why don't you ask Lieutenant Guyomard?" said Jagu.

"There's no need for insolence," said Donatien. "Answer the Inquisitor's question."

"As far as I'm aware, she's still in Mirom. I have no idea why Lieutenant Guyomard failed to arrest her." But even as Jagu spoke he was silently praying that she had not fallen into Kilian's trap. It would be just like her to cast all caution aside and come after him. And powerful as her guardian was, she was surely no match for the might of the Commanderie and the Inquisition together.

"I wish to make a formal protest," he said, feeling the

leather collar around his neck pressing against his throat as he spoke. "Lieutenant Guyomard told me that if we returned to Francia, Maistre Donatien would ask King Ilsevir to grant us a royal pardon."

" 'We'? I see only you, Lieutenant."

"If you will not tell us of your own volition where she is," said Visant, "we will have no alternative but to draw the truth from you."

Jagu forced himself to concentrate his attention on the golden emblem of Sergius's crook hanging on the wall behind Maistre Donatien's head. Next to it hung the crimson rose of the Rosecoeurs, a single drop of enameled blood painted as if it were oozing from the heart of the bloom. He knew all too well what the Inquisitor intended. He had remained stoical and detached until that moment. But they would test him to the limits of his endurance and beyond. And deep inside, he felt the first real stirrings of fear.

CHAPTER 7

"We're going to fly to Francia in that little cockleshell?" Celestine stared in dismay at the Magus's sky craft. Aude and Linnaius lifted the covers and began to make ready for the journey, but she hung back, terrified at the prospect. Aude, seeing her hesitate, ran back and took her by the hand.

"Come on, Celestine, you'll enjoy it! It's the most wonderful experience ever."

Reluctantly, Celestine let Aude help her into the craft. Aude sat next to her, tucking the thick blanket she had brought around them both. "It gets really cold once you're up in the clouds." Celestine nodded and Aude squeezed her hand reassuringly. "Don't worry; it's not so far from Tielen to Lutèce. Just sit back and listen to the winds."

Linnaius shook out the sail and settled himself at the tiller of the craft. Celestine saw him close his eyes, as if listening intently. Then she saw that strange twirling, twisting movement of the fingers on his right hand she had seen him make on the *Dame Blanche,* pulling down a wind from the sky. At the same time, the sail filled and the craft began to lift.

Celestine yelped and grabbed at the side.

"It works much better if you sit still," said Aude. "Then you're less likely to tip us all out."

Celestine sank back, gripping Aude's hand as she heard the rushing of the summoned wind bearing the craft up into the sky. She risked a glimpse over the side and saw the Palace of Swanholm and the gardens, laid out far below as if she were viewing the estate on an architect's plan.

"Isn't this exciting?" cried Aude as the wind blew her ginger curls awry. "Almost as exciting as flying on a

Drakhaoul's back . . . Only I'm not supposed to talk about that," she added.

"What shall I do? Revealing my true identity to Princess Adèle means risking everything. If she can't—or won't—offer me her protection, then I'll have played all my cards and left nothing in reserve!"

"Well, I'm going to tell them I was rescued from the flood by a Tielen ship," said Aude. "I can't possibly tell them the truth. They probably wouldn't believe it, anyway. This is a kind of ship, isn't it?" she said to Linnaius. "And you are its captain, so I'm not telling a lie." She turned back to Celestine. "They'll be so busy questioning me about what happened to Enguerrand that they won't notice you, I hope."

"But what will you tell them about Enguerrand?"

"Oh, I'll go quiet and look down at the floor. I'll say that I don't know where he is—which is also true, because he and the Emperor will already be en route to the port!"

After flying high above the sea for so long, the sight of land came as an ominous reminder to Celestine of what lay ahead. She had not returned to Francia since Linnaius's trial. She glanced across at the Magus as he sat, directing and controlling the winds that carried them, and wondered if he was aware of the irony of the situation too. And then she remembered Jagu's plight, and all her other concerns seemed insignificant.

The sun was sinking, and the farmlands and orchards below were bathed in a golden haze. The trees were covered with a dusting of snowy petals.

"Spring," Celestine said softly.

It was almost dark by the time the first towers and steeples of the city appeared, black against the skyline, and the soft glow of street lanterns mirrored the stars overhead.

Linnaius followed the winding course of the Sénon, passing directly over the looming bulk of the Forteresse. Somewhere within those forbidding fortified walls, the Commanderie must be holding Jagu prisoner.

"Jagu," Celestine whispered, "I'm here. I've come to get you out."

Yet as Linnaius brought the craft slowly down into the shadows of the palace gardens, she felt suddenly unsure and apprehensive. Adèle might have changed. She might even have fallen under her husband's influence.

"Disguise me, Faie." Celestine made the quiet request as she and Aude climbed out of the sky craft. And before they set out, she placed a small package in Linnaius's hands. "Take good care of this for me, Magus."

He looked at her questioningly.

"It's my father's grimoire. You know what to do with it if I don't return," she said, gazing into his eyes. A few days ago she would not have entrusted it to him. But now they understood each other so much better. He nodded and placed the precious book carefully in the pocket of his robes.

"Be on your guard," he warned. "From here on, you'll be fending for yourselves. The next time I return, I shall be bringing your king back to his people."

Jagu had never been inside one of the Inquisition's interrogation rooms before, although he knew that they were situated in the old dungeons that lay beneath the prison tower of the Forteresse. Although sometimes, as he crossed the courtyard, he had heard faint screams coming from far below—cries that had haunted him for long afterward.

The first thing that Jagu noticed as the Rosecoeurs brought him into the room was how empty it was. His imagination had conjured all manner of gruesome images of torture: racks and iron maidens, filled with spikes to pierce the victim's body in all but the most vital organs to ensure a slow and lingering death.

All that he could see was a table and three chairs.

The Rosecoeurs forced him into one of the chairs and strapped him in around the waist, neck, and ankles.

"Note the time and the date," said Visant punctiliously, "and make sure that you spell the prisoner's name correctly."

There was a cold ache of dread in the pit of Jagu's stomach. Was Visant prolonging this just to make him feel more apprehensive? He hadn't been this afraid since the attack on Ondhessar—and then, irony of ironies, Kilian had boosted his failing courage.

"You are well-known for your skills as a keyboard player, Lieutenant, aren't you? It would be a shame to bring such a promising career to an abrupt end."

"You already know where Celestine is to be found," Jagu said, trying to keep his voice steady.

"Indeed. But I happen to believe that you can furnish us with the information we need to convict her of sorcery. We already have evidence from Demoiselle de Saint-Désirat, confirming that Celestine de Joyeuse is able to change her appearance at will."

Gauzia, again. "Firm evidence?" Jagu did not want to let Gauzia's allegation go unchallenged. "It's well-known in musical circles that Demoiselle de Saint-Désirat will go to considerable lengths to slander any potential rivals to her title."

"You were in Colchise, with Celestine de Joyeuse in late summer last year?"

"I was."

"An apothecary told my agent in Colchise that Demoiselle de Joyeuse had purchased some expensive and poisonous herbs from him on the pretext that she was suffering from headaches. But my agent later saw her slip something into the iced tea she offered to Madame Andara, the painter. Madame Andara was later taken ill. Just beforehand, however, my agent heard the demoiselle pronouncing strange words and saw a bright light issuing from her bedchamber."

An agent of the Inquisition at the villa? It can only have been the maid, Nanette. He had been assuming that Celestine was still safe in Mirom. But now the thought occurred to him that they might have captured her and were deliberately withholding the fact from him, to extract enough information to convict her of sorcery. *I can't take the risk. I can't betray her.*

Visant signed to the two Rosecoeurs; they placed a contraption on the table in front of Jagu which looked like one of the metal gauntlets once worn by jousting knights. Except there seemed to have been a bizarre modification. Protruding from every digit, Jagu could see screws, evidently designed to slowly tighten the fit around each finger until the tender flesh and bone inside were crushed.

"You may have heard of the 'Boot,' Lieutenant? Well, we call this the 'Glove.' "

The two Rosecoeurs took hold of Jagu's left arm and slit open the sleeve of his jacket and shirt, and began to force his hand into the open gauntlet.

"Wait. Show me his wrist."

Jagu had tensed, trying to brace himself for what was to come.

"What's this, Lieutenant?" Visant rose to take a better look. "What is this mark of evil here?"

Jagu looked too. The magus's mark could faintly be seen, silver-pale, against his skin.

"Are you the member of some occult organization? You'd better confess, or it will go very ill with you indeed."

"This mark was put on me when I was a boy. A magus put it there so that he could control me," said Jagu, staring coldly back at Visant. "It's all in Maistre de Lanvaux's account of the destruction of the Angelstones at Kemper."

Visant glanced at his secretary. "Make a sketch of the mark so that we can research its origins." Then he turned back to Jagu. "I put it to you that you're using this mark to summon arcane help."

"Then if I've summoned help, why has no one come to rescue me?" Jagu almost laughed aloud at the ridiculous situation he found himself in. He had told Visant it was a warning, and yet the Inquisitor persisted in his misbegotten belief that he was the malefactor.

"Your intransigence will do you no good." Visant nodded to the Rosecoeurs, who proceeded to insert Jagu's left hand into the gauntlet. The unyielding feel of the cold metal against his fingers banished all other thoughts from Jagu's mind. He knew how fragile yet complicated a thing a man's hand was. Visant wanted information and he had selected the method he knew would be the most effective for extracting it.

"And now, gentlemen, if you would be so good as to begin to tighten the screws . . ."

* * *

"Kilian?" Alain Friard caught sight of a flash of pale ginger hair as a Guerrier hurried past him. His hand shot out and caught hold of him by the arm. "When did you get back from Muscobar?"

"A couple of days or so," said Kilian offhandedly.

"And did you find Jagu? Or Celestine?" Friard did not relax his grip.

A smile of irritation flashed briefly across Kilian's face. "Celestine gave me the slip. What a complicated, devious piece of work that woman is."

Friard heard more than irritation in Kilian's tone. *He must really hate her. Whatever can she have done to cause such a bitter reaction?* "And Jagu?" he asked.

"You'll have to ask the Inquisition." Kilian tried to shake off Friard's restraining hand but Friard was not going to let him go so easily.

"What in Sergius's name do you mean, giving me an answer like that?" Friard pulled Kilian's face close to his. "What's come over you, Kilian? We were part of a team; we all worked together. Damn it, you and Jagu fought together at Ondhessar." He caught hold of Kilian's jacket, tugging it open. Through the thin linen of Kilian's shirt, he could see a dark crimson mark, shaped like a rose on his left breast. "The mark of the Rosecoeurs?" So Kilian had undergone the secret initiation ceremony.

"People change. Allegiances change," said Kilian with a shrug.

Friard, sobered and saddened, let go of him. "So I see." Kilian straightened his uniform jacket, concealing the crimson mark of his new allegiance.

Had the Inquisition arrested Jagu and put him to the question? *At least I know who my enemies are. But whom can I trust?*

As they left the shadow-wreathed gardens and approached the lamplit terrace, Aude stopped and stared at Celestine.

"Has my disguise worked?" Celestine asked anxiously.

"It's . . . *extraordinary*," said Aude. Then she recovered

herself and said with a laugh and a toss of her curls, "But no more so than anything else I've seen in the past months." They could see the royal guardsmen on sentry duty, patrolling up and down the terrace. She sucked in a deep breath and whispered, "Ready?" Celestine nodded.

Aude walked straight up to the guard at the nearest entry and said in her clear, bright voice, "Good evening. I'm Aude de Provença, and I've just returned from Serindher. I'd like to speak with Queen Aliénor."

The sentry gazed down at Aude's face in the flickering torchlight.

"Captain!" he called excitedly. "Over here!"

Aude's arrival caused, as predicted, a flurry of activity in the palace. The Queen Mother, it seemed, was away from Plaisaunces. One of her ladies-in-waiting, the motherly Marquise de Trécesson, came bustling into the lofty, pillared hall to take charge of the situation.

"Aude?" she cried and flung her arms about her. "How brown your skin is; I hardly recognized you, my dear. Thank heavens that you are alive! The duke and duchess will be so glad, so very glad." A little crowd of courtiers had already gathered, all murmuring together. The rumors would soon start to spread.

"Keep them guessing," the Emperor had said, "for as long as you possibly can."

Sooner or later, Celestine thought, keeping in the shadows, *someone will notice me.*

"How were you rescued?" "When did you return?" "Who brought you?" Aude was already being bombarded by questions as the press of curious courtiers increased around her.

And Celestine, to her alarm, began to feel very peculiar. A strange malaise began to seep through her body; she sank onto a marble bench in an alcove in the great hall, gripping the sides to keep upright.

It must be a reaction to the flight. I'm not accustomed to flying so high, that's all. This was not the time to faint and draw attention to herself. This was the moment she was supposed to slip away to find Adèle.

Little cries of amazement arose from the crowd gathered around Aude.

"What a miracle!" "How fortunate you were to be rescued so soon." "But what of his majesty, the king?"

Celestine caught Aude's eye as she tried to slip past unnoticed, and saw a sudden look of shocked surprise cross her face.

"King Enguerrand? Ah, I wish I could tell you," Aude said, playing her trump card.

Why had Aude looked at her like that? As Celestine sped off into the grand mirrored corridor that led to the royal apartments, she saw why. From every side her reflection showed her Celestine de Joyeuse. Her disguise had completely vanished.

Celestine's disguise had vanished and with it, her strength too. She felt as weak as if she had been ill for many days. Linnaius's warning kept haunting her—that she was paying the price for having used the Faie's powers for too long. Yet there was no possibility of turning back. She approached the royal apartments and noted that two of the household guards stood outside the entrance.

I can't give up now. I'll just have to bluff my way inside.

She unpinned the precious brooch from her dress and walked straight up to the guardsmen.

"I wish to see Queen Adèle," she said.

The taller of the two looked down at her, his eyebrows raised. "Do you have an invitation from her majesty?"

"No." Celestine held out the jet brooch. "But if you show her this token, I think she will grant me an audience."

The tall guard consulted his companion with a questioning look. When the other nodded, he said, "Wait there," and disappeared through the double doors.

Celestine waited, head lowered, trying not to start every time a servant or a courtier went past, silently praying that no one recognized her. From time to time, she heard excited whispers mentioning Aude's name and Enguerrand's. So the rumors had already begun to spread.

After what seemed an interminable wait, the guard reappeared and, holding open one of the doors, beckoned her inside. She hurried through and followed him past gilt-framed portraits of past rulers of Francia. At last he stopped before a paneled door, rapped softly, and opened it to admit Celestine.

A firelit salon lay beyond.

"Celestine? Is that really you?" came a soft, tired voice from a little sofa pulled close to the fireplace. "Come nearer so that I can see you."

"Your majesty?" Celestine said uncertainly. Lying back on the sofa with her feet on a little tapestry footstool was Adèle, or a pale shadow of the vivacious, pretty princess she remembered. Adèle smiled at her, lifting one hand listlessly to beckon her closer.

"Let's not stand on ceremony," she said. "Let's pretend we're still living in those older, happier days."

Celestine sank to her knees before her and took the outstretched hand in her own, kissing it. "Dear Adèle," she said, "are you unwell? I don't want to tire you . . ."

"I haven't been in the best of health of late, but I can't tell you how pleased I am to welcome an old friend! It's been far too long." She patted the sofa and Celestine sat down beside her, wondering how to begin. "Where *have* you been all this time?"

Celestine hesitated. So no one had told Adèle that she had been branded a heretic and a sorceress. There was nothing for it but to tell her the truth.

"My life is in danger. I've come to beg for your help and protection. Not just for me, but for Jagu de Rustéphan as well." Tears flooded her eyes, born of deep desperation. "Forgive me," she wept. "It's just that everything has gone so badly wrong."

She felt Adèle's hand gently stroking her hair. "Tears, for Jagu? Can it be that the two of you have fallen in love?"

Celestine nodded, wiping the tears from her eyes. "But

the Inquisition has arrested him. It won't be long before someone here recognizes me too and—"

Adèle placed one finger over her lips. "I won't let them take you. Whatever protection I can give you, is yours. But as for Jagu, if he's already in the clutches of Inquisitor Visant, that may prove rather more difficult."

"There is one more mission that I have been charged to carry out." Celestine slipped Enguerrand's letter out from her bodice and handed it to Adèle. "But please, dear Adèle, steel yourself, for it is extraordinary and unexpected news."

Adèle looked quizzically at her and unrolled the letter, smoothing it out on her lap to read it. Celestine watched anxiously, fearing that, given the young queen's fragile condition, the news might prove too much of a shock. She saw Adèle's eyes widen, then fill with tears. She gazed at Celestine. "He's alive? You've seen him? Is he well?" She wiped away a tear, laughing. "Look at us, crying like two silly schoolgirls!"

"He's recovering from a fever, but he is well, considering how close he came to drowning," said Celestine, joining in the tearful laughter. "But I wondered how this news might affect his majesty, King Ilsevir . . ."

Adèle's expression became distant, almost wistful, and the laughter faded. "Ilsevir . . ." she repeated. "There cannot be two kings. What will happen now? This could lead to civil war." She looked down at her brother's letter again. "Enguerrand asks me to say nothing of this until he makes his return. Very well. His secret is safe with me." She scrunched the paper up into a ball and tossed it onto the logs in the grate. As it flared up, the door suddenly burst open and a white-haired man in black robes came in, followed by four armed Guerriers.

"What is the meaning of this intrusion, Maistre Donatien?" Adèle could sound just as intimidating as her mother when she chose to. "How dare you disturb me without even having the courtesy to knock?"

Celestine instinctively moved closer to Adèle.

"I'm sorry to disturb you, your majesty, but this young woman is very dangerous." Donatien seemed not in the least deterred by Adèle's reaction. "I have no idea how she gained access to your private apartments, but as she is known to practice the Forbidden Arts, I can only assume that—"

"If you mean Demoiselle de Joyeuse, then I have granted her my protection." Adèle stared at Maistre Donatien, as if daring him to challenge her authority. "My *royal* protection."

"What's all the fuss about?" A door opened on the far side of the fireplace and Ilsevir appeared, in a robe de chambre of dove-grey brocade. Celestine instantly dropped into a deep curtsy and Donatien bowed. "Grand Maistre, why have you brought armed men into our private salon?"

"Sire, I apologize for the disturbance—" began Donatien but he broke off as Adèle suddenly sank back onto the sofa. Celestine, alarmed, rose to hurry to her side.

"Stay away from the queen!" shouted Donatien. Two of the Guerriers seized Celestine by the arms, restraining her.

"No," said Adèle faintly. "She . . . is not to be . . . harmed . . ."

"Adèle, what's wrong?" Ilsevir took her hand and started to pat it ineffectually. But Adèle's eyes had closed and she did not answer his question.

Donatien turned on Celestine. "You've laid some kind of sorcery on the queen, you witch!"

"I've done nothing of the kind!" Celestine cried.

"Adèle?" Ilsevir was anxiously calling his wife's name. "Get help, Donatien! Summon the royal physician."

Faie, help me. Help me now. But Celestine's silent plea went unanswered and as servants came running in response to the king's cries, the Guerriers began to drag her out of the apartment.

"Demoiselle, you're under arrest," said Donatien curtly. "Take the witch away. Take her to the Forteresse."

CHAPTER 8

"Prince Nagazdiel is here?" Sardion's eyes glittered. Through Nagazdiel's vision Rieuk could see the dark desire burning in the Arkhan's heart. "You've brought him to me at last?" He came closer to Rieuk, his hands reaching out as if to embrace the Drakhaoul within him. "My dread lord," he said, staring at Rieuk, through Rieuk. "At last I can bid you welcome. My family has watched over Ondhessar for centuries, waiting for this day to come." And then to Rieuk's amazement, he dropped to his knees and prostrated himself. "I offer myself to you, my prince. Please use my body as your vessel in this mortal world."

"Lord Arkhan, is that wise?" Rieuk began. "Is your body strong enough? Can your blood sustain a Drakhaoul?"

Sardion glared at him with his wild, hungry eyes. "You've fulfilled your purpose, Emissary Mordiern. I have no more need of you now."

"*Sardion of Enhirre, is this truly what you want?*" Nagazdiel spoke through Rieuk, his voice adding a deep, dark richness to Rieuk's natural tone. "*And once we are bonded, you will do my bidding?*"

"I was born to serve you, my lord."

Rieuk looked down with contempt at the man who had held him so long in thrall, groveling at his feet.

"*Then come closer.*" Rieuk felt the Drakhaoul concentrating all his energy to transfer himself from his body to the Arkhan's. The Arkhan began to move toward him, as if in a trance, until they stood close together, forehead pressed to forehead.

The Drakhaoul's dark energy came flooding up through

Rieuk, pouring out through his mouth and into Sardion's, in a hot, shimmering flood.

The instant the Drakhaoul had left his body, Rieuk slumped to the floor, drained. For a moment everything faded to a blur. Then he heard laughter; low at first, then rising to a manic pitch. Sardion had thrown back his head and was standing gazing down at his outstretched hands as if he had never seen them before, his whole body shaking with triumphant laughter. Little flickers of fiery energy crackled from his fingertips.

"This is—astounding! I feel so strong. So powerful!"

Rieuk caught a telltale flash of dark crimson in Sardion's eyes as the Arkhan flexed his shoulders, evidently relishing his newfound strength. Sardion extended one hand, pointing his index finger at a tall vase of beaten bronze, loosing a bolt of daemonic energy. The vase glowed white-hot, and suddenly collapsed in on itself, reduced to a pool of molten metal.

"This is the power I was born to wield!" cried Sardion ecstatically. "We will go to Ondhessar. We will show the Rosecoeurs who is the true master of Enhirre." And without a backward glance at Rieuk, he threw open the doors and strode away, calling for his guards.

"My lord, be careful, I beg of—" Rieuk checked himself. Why should he care what became of Sardion? Headstrong, cruel, impulsive, the Arkhan only cared about fulfilling his own ambitions. He had sent Oranir into the Rift as a living sacrifice to Nagazdiel, not caring what became of him, as long as he achieved his heart's desire.

"Ran," Rieuk whispered, focusing on his true purpose. He went straight to Sardion's desk, tugging open drawers, frantically searching for the ebony casket in which the Arkhan had placed the new Lodestar. He could barely detect the crystal's presence; within the gold-veined marble walls of Sardion's apartments, its clear vibrations were muted. With his good eye closed, he searched blind, relying on his senses to lead him to it, just as, long ago in Karantec, he had been drawn to Azilis's Lodestar. His heart was thudding hard against his breastbone; he could be discovered at any moment.

His fingers closed on a wooden box hidden in the depths of a drawer. He could feel the faint pulse within, shivering through the carved ebony. He drew out the box and opened it. Nestling within lay the crystal purity of the Lodestar— *his* Lodestar, that he had fashioned with such care deep in the Rift.

A burst of aethyric fire, red as blood, lit the darkening sky above Ondhessar. Rieuk looked back over his shoulder as he made his way back to the Hidden Valley, feeling the ground trembling ominously beneath his feet.

"How long can Sardion's body sustain such an outpouring of power?" he muttered. "He hasn't a drop of mage blood in his veins." He had to get to Ondhessar as soon as he could.

"Rieuk?" Lord Estael hurried out to greet him. Aqil and Tilath hovered in the doorway of the Tower, watching. "What's happening at Ondhessar?"

"Sardion," Rieuk said, trying to regain his breath. "He's taking his vengeance on the Enhirrans." He thrust the ebony casket into Estael's hands. "Please—whatever happens— guard this with your life until I return. It's the Lodestar."

"You stole it from the Arkhan?" Estael said, frowning.

"It was never Sardion's in the first place." Why was Estael still so obdurate in his support of the Arkhan? "Sardion has treated us all like dirt. It's time to make a stand against him. It's time to break free."

"Are you mad?"

"And it's my only chance to save Oranir." Rieuk pushed past the elder magi, making for the subterranean way that led back into Azilis's shrine.

"Rieuk, come back. Come back!"

He heard their voices calling after him down into the deep shaft but ignored them, pressing on into the darkness.

He had failed to save Imri. He had been too young, too inexperienced, to defend him against Linnaius. But he was older and maybe a little wiser, and he was damned if he was going to lose Oranir too.

Rieuk came out by the magi's concealed door into the empty shrine. Candles of creamy wax were burning in the little alcoves, and a bunch of fragrant white lilies lay where Azilis's statue had stood. Strange that the Rosecoeurs should still keep her memory alive here even though they had stripped the shrine of her precious relics.

He felt another burst of aethyric power shiver through the fort. He heard voices moaning, crying out in pain. The ground trembled beneath his feet again and a little spatter of stones fell down onto his head.

If that madman's not checked, he'll destroy the very place he was trying to preserve.

Rieuk climbed the steps that led up to the surface, back pressed against the wall, until he reached the entrance to the courtyard. Night had fallen, but torches illuminated the darkness, revealing a ghastly sight. Bodies lay everywhere, Allegondans in the grey uniform of the Order of the Rosecoeur. Some, still living, tried to push themselves up and crawl to safety. But the Arkhan's guards moved among them, mercilessly thrusting their spears into any Allegondan they passed, living or dead. Others swarmed up onto the ramparts, tearing down the Rosecoeurs' flags. And through the carnage stalked the Arkhan himself, his eyes aflame with Nagazdiel's power, gazing down at his victims with a triumphant smile on his lips.

"Ondhessar is yours, Lord Arkhan!" Sardion's captain of the guards went down on one knee before him, holding up the bloodstained standard.

"Burn their flags," Sardion ordered. "And strip the bodies. Cast them out into the desert and let the jackals feast upon them." He turned toward the entrance to the shrine and Rieuk shrank back inside as the fiery eyes scanned the darkness.

"And now it's time to reclaim Azilis's birthplace."

Rieuk retreated as the Arkhan made his way into the shrine.

About halfway down, Sardion stumbled, and one of the guards caught hold of him, asking anxiously, "Are you all right, Lord Arkhan?"

"Let me be!" Sardion pushed the supporting arm away and set out again down the stairs. Rieuk flattened himself against the wall, watching as the Arkhan entered the empty shrine alone.

"*Where is my daughter?*" Nagazdiel's voice rang out, harsh as the beating of a funeral gong. "*Why have you not protected her, as you promised to? Your ancestors made a blood oath to keep Azilis safe within this shrine. And now she is gone!*"

The Arkhan began to totter across the floor of the shrine, his hands clutched to his throat as if he were choking. A strange, horrible sound issued from his mouth: a gargling, strangled cry.

"H—help me." His bloodshot eyes, bulging in their sockets, gazed at Rieuk in mute appeal, one hand clawed out toward him. "Rieuk . . . Mordiern . . ."

But Rieuk could only watch helplessly as the Arkhan dropped to his knees. Sardion's face was altering: The color was fast draining from him, to be replaced by a deathly, livid hue. His skin began to shrivel and contract. And still the agonized gargling cry went on, slowly fading to a wheezing death rattle.

"*This mortal body is too weak to sustain me.*"

As Sardion crashed forward onto his face, Nagazdiel issued from his twitching frame and entered Rieuk once more. "*Now take me to my daughter,*" the Drakhaoul whispered in Rieuk's mind. "*Hurry.*"

Rieuk felt the power of the Lord of the Realm of Shadows pulsing through him. He turned as the guards came running down the stairs. At his feet lay the Arkhan's body, nothing more than a twisted, desiccated shell, as if Nagazdiel's presence had sucked all the living Essence from his veins.

"What have you done to the Arkhan, Magus?" The captain of the guards came forward, leveling his spear at Rieuk, waving on the others to follow. "Arrest that Emissary!"

The guards began to advance on Rieuk. The panicked

cry, "The Arkhan's been assassinated!" went echoing through the shrine.

"*We're wasting time here.*" Rieuk heard the frustration simmering in Nagazdiel's voice. "*Ormas, lend me your wings.*"

"Wings?"

Rieuk backed away from the guards. It felt as though a whirlwind was unraveling within him, channeling upward from the core of his being to concentrate in his back and shoulders. A tremendous pressure was building in his body. Any second now, the pressure would prove too great and his body would explode into fragments of flesh and bone. Something was trying to burst out through his spine. He gave a cry of agony as the great smoke-black wings unfurled. And then, as if he had always known how to fly, he was lifting from the ground and winging slowly up through the stairwell, aiming for the archway that opened into the courtyard.

"*Free. Finally free at last!*" Nagazdiel's cry shuddered through his body. The Drakhaoul prince had synthesized Ormas's abilities with his own to transform Rieuk's body; he had drawn out Ormas's spirit wings and transmuted them so that he could fly once more. Rieuk could feel Nagazdiel's wild delight as he soared up into the star-studded sky. The Drakhaoul had been imprisoned in the shadows for years without number; to be flying unfettered once more filled him with ecstasy.

Far below, the ground was fast receding as he rose higher toward the stars. Ondhessar looked like a child's toy fort against the expanse of the endless desert. But as Nagazdiel turned toward the north, Rieuk heard him say, "*She's fading . . . there's not much time.*"

And as they flew onward, Rieuk began to notice that they were leaving a trail of smoky darkness in their wake, as though every beat of the Drakhaoul prince's great wings was spreading the dust of the Realm of Shadows over the land beneath.

"What's that darkness over there? Is it an oncoming storm?" Enguerrand pointed toward the southern horizon, shivering.

"Can't you feel it? There's a taint of Nagazdiel's presence in the air."

"But how can that be?" Eugene looked over the side of the sky craft and saw what Enguerrand was pointing at. The clarity of the blue sky was smirched, as if clouds of smoke were billowing across the Southern Ocean toward Francia. "The Serpent Gate was destroyed; Gavril and I made sure that it was sealed forever. What do you think, Kaspar?"

Linnaius was shading his eyes to look too, keeping his hand on the tiller of the craft to keep it steady. He shook his grey head. "If Prince Nagazdiel has left the Shadow Realm, then that can mean only one thing. The Rift is widening and the balance between our world and the next is breaking down."

"The balance?"

"Azilis, the Eternal Singer, has always watched over the Rift between the mortal world and the Ways Beyond. But since she left the Rift, that balance has broken down."

Eugene scratched his head, bemused. "You know very well that I'm no expert on the metaphysical or the mythological. Could you explain it to me in plain terms, Kaspar?"

"If the balance is not reestablished, then the chaos of the Realm of Shadows will bleed into this world and—"

"And unless Azilis returns to the Rift in time, it will be too late to save our world," said Enguerrand. "The last chapter of *The Book of Galizur*. The end of all things and the return to chaos."

"The end of the world?" Eugene echoed, stricken. If it really was the end of all things, he wanted to be with Astasia and his children. He lapsed into troubled silence, wondering why in spite of all the ordeals he had undergone to prevent the coming of Nagazdiel, some crazed fool had somehow managed to set the Drakhaoul Prince free from his prison.

"I should have taken matters into my own hands." Linnaius was muttering to himself. "I should have taken Celestine to Ondhessar. And now it may be too late."

Even as Linnaius was speaking, a thin, mean wind began to whine around the craft, bringing with it a fine, dark dust that stung the skin and made the eyes water. Eugene, shielding his face, looked back again. "The darkness is gaining on us, Kaspar. Can you go any faster?"

"Faster than Prince Nagazdiel?" Was that an ironic smile lighting Linnaius's silver eyes? "I'll do what I can." And Eugene saw him close his eyes, pressing his fingertips to his forehead, muttering beneath his breath.

The craft shuddered and bucked as a cold current of air shot toward them. Linnaius opened his eyes, looking upward.

"So you came at last, old friend," Eugene heard him whisper to the empty sky above them. And suddenly Eugene saw it—a powerful translucent sky dragon, snaking straight toward them, its silver eyes radiant as stars.

"What is this monster?" Eugene cried.

"You can see him?" Linnaius's wispy brows raised in surprise. "This is Azhkanizkael—a *wouivre*, or air serpent. I suppose you could call him my familiar. He is stubborn and proud these days, and doesn't always answer my call." As if in reply, the *wouivre* tossed its great whiskered head and, coiling itself around the craft, it shot off at tremendous speed through the clouds.

CHAPTER 9

Alain Friard knew himself to be a steady, even-tempered man, not easily roused to anger. But the sounds he heard coming from the Inquisition interrogation cells that rainy night induced feelings of such deep disgust that he knew he must act or lose his mind.

He went directly to the officers' quarters and, without even knocking, flung open Kilian Guyomard's door. Kilian was lying on his bed, still in his shirt and breeches. Friard thought he could detect the smell of strong spirits.

"What do you want?" Kilian asked sullenly.

"I may not be one of the elite order of the Rosecoeur," said Friard, barely able to conceal his anger, "but I am still your superior officer. Come with me."

Kilian stretched his arms up over his head, yawning widely.

"Come *now*. And that's an order, Lieutenant!"

Kilian swung his legs off the bed and slung his jacket over his shoulders.

"Have you been drinking?"

"I'm off duty. Is it forbidden to drink off duty?"

Friard shot him a hard, disapproving look. "And tidy yourself up. You're a disgrace to the order." As he set off, Kilian slouching behind, he couldn't help but ask himself what had caused Kilian to change from a smart, keen-eyed officer to this dull-eyed, unshaven shadow since he had returned from Muscobar. Guilty conscience? If Kilian felt even a drop of guilt about what he had done, maybe there was still hope, Friard thought, marching him briskly across the rain-swept courtyard.

* * *

The guttering torch in the passageway outside the cell cast just enough light for Jagu to be able to see what they had done to his left hand. Only he didn't want to look. He didn't need to look. He knew from the dull, throbbing, grinding pain that his flesh had been slowly crushed and twisted in Visant's Glove until every bone in his fingers had been broken beyond repair.

He drew in a slow, sobbing breath.

The swollen pulpy mass that had once moved so nimbly over the keys of the fortepiano had been swathed in bloody bandages.

And Visant had promised him that the next day they would apply the Glove to his right hand. Unless he agreed to testify against Celestine.

"You were with her in Azhkendir," Visant had said, his face expressionless. "You know her secrets. All you have to do to spare yourself more pain is to tell us what you know."

"Bastards," he whispered into the night. He wanted to sleep, if only to blot out the thoughts and fears clamoring in his mind. But every time he dropped into an uneasy doze, the pain needled him awake again.

By the torchlight, Friard could see Jagu lying on his side on the narrow cell bed, his head turned away from the bars confining him, his body curled self-protectively in on itself.

Kilian made to turn away, but Friard gripped hold of him and forced him to stay where he was.

"Look," Friard said quietly. "Look at what you've done. Have you seen his hand, or what's left of it?"

Kilian said nothing. He just stared, his face unmoving.

"Is this what you wanted? Is this really what you wanted?"

"Shut up!" Kilian said through his teeth. And, twisting free of Friard's grip, he strode away down the corridor.

"*Faie!*" Celestine's whispers became increasingly urgent, echoing around the cell in which the Guerriers had confined her. "*Faie, wake up. I need you. Please!*"

"Shut your mouth, witch!" The jailer had come to open the grille of her cell; two Inquisition Guerriers stood behind him. "She's been going on and on like that all night," he said confidentially. "Calling on her familiar spirit like that. It shouldn't be allowed." He spat.

"They're ready for you now," said one of the Guerriers impassively.

They hurried her along the winding passageways of the prison wing of the Forteresse until they reached one of the interrogation rooms. Inside, seated at a table, she saw three men. In the center, she recognized the lean features and incisive gaze of Haute Inquisitor Visant. Beside him sat Maistre Donatien, and at the end of the table, a secretary, surrounded by files and dossiers overspilling with papers.

"Celestine de Joyeuse," said Visant. "Is that your name? Or should we use your true name: de Maunoir?"

"Please, can you tell me how her majesty is?" Celestine burst out.

"You place a spell on Queen Adèle, and then you have the audacity to ask how she's faring?"

"There was no spell. That's a vile lie Maistre Donatien made up to slander me."

Donatien gave a small, offended grunt, but said nothing.

"So now you're accusing Maistre Donatien of being a liar? That's a very serious allegation."

"I love the queen and I would gladly give my own life to protect her." Celestine stared defiantly back at Visant. "If you check my record as a Guerrier and agent of the Commanderie, you'll see the proof. Jagu and I defended their majesties against the magi of Ondhessar."

"I have indeed checked your record and it makes for disturbing reading. The Commanderie has been nursing a viper in its bosom. Well, Maistre de Lanvaux may have been lax enough to turn a blind eye to your misdemeanors, but he is no longer here to protect you from the Inquisition's justice."

The door to the interrogation chamber opened and a Rosecoeur guard came in. "We've brought the other prisoner as you requested, Inquisitor."

"Very good." Visant nodded. "Make him stand there. Where the demoiselle can see her accomplice."

And then, to Celestine's distress, she heard the clank of chains and recognized the prisoner that the guards had escorted.

"Jagu!" The cry was wrung from her. "Oh Jagu, what have they done to you?"

The sight alone of the bloodstained bandages was almost more than she could bear. And the awkward way in which he carried his hand, holding it close to himself as if he couldn't risk anyone even brushing against it, let her know how serious the wound was. But when he heard her voice and raised his head slowly, blinking as if the light was too bright, she saw him make an effort to control himself.

"Celestine," he said in a voice that was twisted with pain. His face looked grey, haggard in the cold light. "Why did you come? You knew it was a trap."

She wanted to run to him, but the Guerriers gripped her so firmly that she could not break free.

"What a touching scene," said Visant dryly. "The two miscreants who betrayed the order, reunited to hear their sentences."

"Our sentences?" Jagu's head whipped up. "When was there a trial?"

"There was no need for a trial," said Maistre Donatien smoothly. "As Grand Maistre of the Commanderie, I have it in my power to deal with such cases as I see fit. As you were discovered *in flagrante* and neither one of you has denied the fact, we need no further proof that you have both broken your vow of celibacy." He opened an ancient bound volume and read aloud from a yellowed page of vellum. "In the rules of our order, as set down by Saint Argantel himself, it says, 'Any Guerrier who breaks his vow must be cast out of the order so that his sin does not bring dishonor on his fellow knights.' "

Celestine heard Donatien pronounce the words as if from very far away; all her attention was centered on Jagu, knowing how much Donatien's bluntness would shame him. But

Jagu stood silent, unmoving, accepting. *Surely that can't be all?* she wondered as Donatien closed Saint Argantel's Rules.

"By the power vested in me as Grand Maistre of the Order of Saint Sergius," Donatien announced, "Celestine de Maunoir, Jagu de Rustéphan, I hereby strip you both of your rank of lieutenant. And because you have both brought shame on the order by using the Forbidden Arts, I call upon the Haute Inquisitor to pronounce sentence upon you."

Visant stared first at Jagu and then at Celestine. "The penalty for using the Forbidden Arts is death. Death by fire to cleanse and purge any traces of evil that may remain in your bodies. And may your deaths be a warning to anyone foolish enough to contemplate using alchymy or sorcery. The executions will take place tomorrow in the Place du Trahoir."

"Wait!" Celestine cried out. "Jagu isn't a magus! He's never used the Forbidden Arts. Why does he have to die?"

"Never used the Forbidden Arts?" Visant turned to her, a triumphant smile on his lips. "Then how do you explain the magus's mark on his left wrist?"

"A magus marked him; it's a sign of control." She was shocked that Visant should use the mark against Jagu in such a devious way.

"So for all these years, a magus's puppet has been a trusted officer in the Commanderie? Who knows what mischief this man has already been compelled to do by his master?"

"It's no use, Celestine." At last Jagu spoke, and the sad, loving look that he gave her made her heart ache. "They'll just twist anything we say to their advantage."

"But how can we be sentenced to death without a proper trial?" Celestine was not ready to concede without a fight. Why, at the very moment she needed her help the most, was the Faie silent?

The patter of spring rain on the windowpane was the first thing that Adèle became aware of as she drifted awake. A soft, grey-hued spring light infused her bedchamber, and for a while she lay half between sleep and waking, as if floating high above the palace. And then she heard a sigh and realized that she was not alone. Ilsevir was sitting by the fireside, reading through a bundle of papers.

"What . . . time is it?" she asked sleepily.

"You're awake!" Ilsevir dropped the papers and hurried over to her bedside. "How are you feeling?" he asked anxiously.

"A little light-headed. What happened? Did I oversleep?" Adèle's memory was still fogged with sleep.

"You fainted. I was worried," said Ilsevir, almost accusingly.

"I fainted? How feeble of me; I didn't intend to cause you any concern . . ." And then it all came back to her: Celestine, Donatien, the Guerriers, her brother's secret letter . . .

"Where is Celestine?" she demanded.

"In the Forteresse, where else? She was the cause of your fainting fit; Maistre Donatien is certain of it."

Adèle let out a cry of frustration. Ilsevir was so easily manipulated by his ministers. "Maistre Donatien is mistaken. We have to get her out of there." She tried to push herself up into a sitting position.

Ilsevir plumped up the pillows behind her. "But she's under the Inquisition's jurisdiction now. Visant has proof positive that she's been using the Forbidden Arts."

Why was Ilsevir not listening to her? "I promised her that I would protect her."

Ilsevir took her hand in his, gazing intently into her eyes. "Adèle, Doctor Vallot thinks that you may be pregnant again. After what happened before, he wants you to rest in bed and not to allow yourself to become excited or upset."

"Being pregnant doesn't mean that I have to be treated like an invalid!" Adèle said indignantly. Yet she found herself wondering: Could Vallot be right?

"Your health is more important to me than anything else." Ilsevir could say such sweet things and she loved him for it, but she wished that she didn't suspect him of keeping her confined so that she didn't interfere with the plans that he, nel Ghislain, and Donatien were hatching. If only there were someone in Plaisaunces whom she could trust to tell her what was really going on . . .

There came a tap at the bedchamber door and her maid appeared, bobbing a curtsy.

"Lady Aude has come to pay you a visit, majesty. Shall I tell her to come back tomorrow?"

"Aude?" Adèle sat up eagerly. "No, please bring her in. I can't wait to hear all about her adventures!"

"I'll leave you two girls to exchange gossip." Ilsevir kissed her cheek and rose to leave, gathering up his papers. "Remember, don't overexcite yourself, Adèle."

Aude appeared in the doorway, curtsying as the king departed.

"Aude!" Adèle held out her arms to her cousin and Aude hurried over to give her a hug. "Let me look at you!" She held her at arm's length. "How brown you are!" She pinched her cheek affectionately. "The Serindhan sun has brought out all your freckles."

"It's very unfashionable to look so healthy, isn't it?" Aude said, giggling.

"You will set a new fashion all of your own." Adèle felt her spirits lifting already, cheered by Aude's impish grin. "But what a miraculous escape." She glanced around and beckoned Aude closer. "Celestine told me all about it. Before the Inquisition took her."

Aude's hand flew to her mouth. "No!"

"She's in terrible danger, Aude. Is there anything your father can do?"

Aude thought for a moment. Then she said, "I don't know. But I'll see what I can do to persuade him. And I can be very persuasive when I want to."

Alain Friard found Philippe Viaud outside, drilling the cadets in the rain in the shadow of the damaged Commanderie chapel. He beckoned him over into the shadow of the chapel doorway.

"What's wrong, Captain?" Viaud mopped the rain from his face with a handkerchief. "You could curdle milk with that sour expression."

"I'm in the mood to curdle a great deal more than milk," said Friard grimly. "Did you hear about Jagu and Celestine? Donatien has handed them over to Visant. And Visant has just condemned them to the stake."

"That's going too far!" Viaud burst out.

"Are we going to let the Inquisition burn them?"

"Of course not." Viaud glanced out at the rain and his drenched cadets. "Lads!" he yelled. "Change of orders. Meet me in the Pomme de Pin in half an hour!"

A ragged cheer went up from the cadets as they broke ranks and hurried for shelter.

"Good man," said Friard, clapping Viaud on the shoulder.

CHAPTER 10

As soon as the guards had locked the cell door and she had heard their footfalls dying away into the distance, Celestine went over to the lock and tested it. It was a sturdy piece of metalwork and she realized immediately that it would take a great deal of energy to burn through it.

"Can you do it, Faie?"

"*If I expend my power on this, I may not have enough left to shield you.*"

"But we have to try!"

Celestine felt the Faie summoning her aethyrial energy, creating a burning core around her heart.

"*Put the tip of your finger on the lock. But the instant you sense the power begin to flow, draw it back.*"

Celestine placed her fingertip as the Faie instructed her and felt the sudden surge radiate down her arm and pass into the cold metal. The lock began to glow: first red, then turning brighter until it hurt her eyes to look at it and sparks began to fizz into the air. The smell and heat from the searing metal stung her nostrils.

"It's working, it's working . . ."

Suddenly the brightness began to fade. Even though she willed herself to stay alert, she found herself sliding slowly to the floor. Her heart was pounding furiously and there was a ringing, rushing sound in her ears.

"*Your body is too frail, Celestine,*" came the Faie's voice. "*If I go any further, it will strain your heart beyond its natural limits, and you will die.*"

* * *

As the hours of darkness passed, Celestine lay, unable to sleep, wondering why no word of pardon or stay of execution had come from the palace. Was Adèle powerless to intervene? At length she sat up and said, "Faie, give me the power to set Jagu free."

"*Your body is not strong enough to sustain another attack.*"

"But why don't you understand?" Celestine's desperation grew more intense with every passing minute. "I can't endure it a second time. I lost my father this way, I can't bear to lose Jagu too. There's no point in saving my own life if Jagu isn't there to share it with me."

"*Celestine, I am bound to protect you. I may be able to shield you from the flames, but I can't save him too.*"

"Why can't you see?" Celestine cried out. "I can't live without him. I *love* him, Faie. I love him more than life itself. You had a lover once, didn't you?"

"*Mhir . . .*" The Faie breathed his name and Celestine felt a glow suffuse her whole body. "*He gave his life to save mine. But when I learned what he had done, it was too late to bring him back from the dead.*" The glow darkened as Celestine felt the Faie's grief for her lost love flood through her.

"But if you could have gone back in time, would you have changed places with him?"

The Faie was silent a moment, then she said, "*And what makes you think that Jagu would want your sacrifice? What kind of life would you be forcing him to live; alone, without you, knowing what you had done?*"

"Celestine de Maunoir, do you have anything to say?" Maistre Donatien stood outside her cell. "You have drawn on the darkest of powers and, in doing so, you have defiled the good name of the Commanderie. If you agree to make a full public confession of your crimes, I can give you the consolation of the Sergian Church and grant you expiation for your sins."

"You're offering me consolation?" Celestine repeated, her voice raw.

"So you even reject the forgiveness of the Church?" Donatien slowly shook his head. "I see now to what depths of depravity you have sunk in your pursuit of the Forbidden Arts. I can only pray that the cleansing flames will purge the evil from your immortal soul." And he walked away without a backward glance.

"Take off your clothes."

Celestine stared at the Rosecoeur Guerriers who stood over her. One threw a rough linen shift onto the cell floor beside her.

"Take off your clothes and put this on."

What further humiliation were they going to inflict on her? She crossed her arms and said nothing, merely staring up at them defiantly.

"Or would you rather we stripped you ourselves?"

"Turn around," she said.

"You're a Guerrier, aren't you?" said one with a thick Allegondan accent. He seized hold of her by one arm, pulling her to her feet. "Why should we treat you any differently?" He caught hold of the collar of her bodice and started to tug, ripping the fine cloth.

"How dare you!" She slapped him, hard, and he struck her, sending her tumbling to the floor.

"What are you doing in here?" That lazy drawl; it was a voice she had grown to hate. Kilian Guyomard. "Report to Captain nel Ghislain in the courtyard immediately."

The Rosecoeurs hurried away.

"Have you come to gloat?" Celestine sat up, rubbing her bruised cheek. "It's all worked out just as you planned it, hasn't it, Kilian?"

"Listen." He dropped to his knees beside her, whispering, "No one is going to die today. There's a plan to rescue you, but you'll have to stay alert. When the time comes, just make sure you take care of Jagu." He handed her the shift and left the cell.

"Why?" she cried after him. "Why, Kilian?"

But all she heard was the echo of his footfalls receding into the distance.

CHAPTER 11

Hands and ankles shackled, Celestine was led out into the courtyard and forced to climb up inside a covered, partitioned prison cart—a cage on wheels. The guards pushed her to the front and pulled a heavy grille across, locking it. Crouching on hands and knees in the corner, she saw through the grille that they were dragging Jagu into the half on the other side of the partition.

"Jagu." She crawled across the dirty boards of the cart, calling his name. The cart suddenly lurched as the four sturdy horses started off, sending her sliding back into the corner. They were passing beneath the portcullis onto the bridge connecting the island with the right bank of the Sénon.

"Celestine?"

She heard Jagu's voice from the other side of the partition, and just hearing him call her name brought tears of relief to her eyes. She set out again, shackles clunking against the boards, until she could sit with her back against the partition.

"I'm here. I'm right here, Jagu."

She heard him lean back against the partition and felt her heart swell, knowing he was so near.

"We're going to get out of this alive," she said, her voice low, and fierce with determination.

After being kept so long in the gloom of the cell, she found that the daylight hurt her eyes. But as she blinked up at the cloudy sky, she saw stormclouds gathering over the far horizon. "It looks like it's going to rain."

She heard Jagu give a hard, ironic chuckle.

"If it rains hard enough, would it quench the pyre?"

"More like we'd suffocate from the smoke long before the flames were extinguished."

"No one is going to die today." She repeated what Kilian had promised her. But could she trust Kilian?

The cart rattled along over the cobbles, surrounded on both sides by an armed escort of Rosecoeurs. A crowd was gathering, trailing behind the cart toward the Place du Trahoir, but unlike the unruly, hostile mob who had jeered at her father and the magi of Karantec, these people were subdued and silent.

Celestine's thin linen shift was sleeveless and her feet were bare. The sky grew darker. A cold wind stirred the willows by the River Sénon. She began to shiver.

"Are you cold?" His voice was filled with concern. So like Jagu, to think of her before himself.

"If only they'd let us be together one last time," she said. "If only they'd let us hold each other, I think I could face what's to come."

The cart suddenly slowed, the drivers tugging on the reins.

"Halt!" The escort of Rosecoeurs marching alongside stopped. Celestine's head jerked up, trying to see what was causing the delay. Her nerves were already on edge. Ahead, at the crossroads, she spotted a patrol of Commanderie Guerriers lined up, muskets on shoulders. Their officer, his back to the cart, was arguing with the Rosecoeur lieutenant leading the escort.

"We're here to relieve you."

"This is most irregular!"

"New orders. From the Grand Maistre. You're to go on ahead to the Place du Trahoir to guard King Ilsevir. They need more troops to control the crowd. We'll take over here."

Celestine noticed that while the driver's attention was distracted, a Guerrier had crept around the side of the cart. The next moment, he clambered up, struck the driver over the back of the head with the butt of his musket, threw him out into the gutter, and leaped into the driver's seat.

"What in—" Celestine was flung to the floor as the cart went hurtling around the corner. Shots rang out behind them, musket balls whizzing close overhead, smashing glass panes in the houses. The onlookers shrieked and ran for cover.

"Stay down," hissed the Guerrier over his shoulder. "Hold your fire, you idiots. You'll hit the civilians!"

"Kilian?" She peeped through the bars at the other Guerriers running alongside, providing the most ragged armed guard ever seen at an execution. The officer who had halted the procession jumped on the cart, clinging on precariously.

"Take the next street on the left!" he shouted, clambering up to sit beside Kilian.

"Viaud?" Jagu sat up. "*Kilian?*"

"Did you think we were going to hand you over to the Rosecoeurs without a fight, Lieutenant?" cried Viaud.

As the cart careered wildly from side to side, people diving out from under the carthorses' plunging hooves, Celestine wondered if they were more likely to die in a crash than on the pyre.

And then she heard another shot ring out. Viaud cried out, grabbing for the reins, tugging the cart to a halt as Kilian swayed and slumped forward.

"Kilian!" she screamed as he toppled sideways from the slowing cart and fell into the street.

Up ahead, the street was blocked by a double line of Rosecoeurs, all aiming their muskets at the oncoming cart—the front row down on one knee, as if they were an execution squad. And she recognized the officer who was blowing smoke from the end of his pistol as he began to walk slowly, almost nonchalantly, toward them.

"Philippe, stop the cart," she begged Viaud. "I don't want any of you to die. Please. Can't you see it's hopeless? You're outnumbered."

"Viaud, see to Kilian," said Jagu, his voice hoarse. "That's an order."

Viaud's shoulders slumped dejectedly as he pulled hard on the reins and the horses slowed to a stop.

"Stay precisely where you are, Lieutenant Viaud," said

Captain nel Ghislain, "or I tell my men to fire." He reached the side of the cart where Kilian had fallen, facedown. Celestine, peering out through the bars, saw him place his foot against Kilian's body and roughly flip him over onto his back. Blood was fast welling from the bullet wound at the base of Kilian's neck and spreading beneath him, reddening the puddle in which he lay. From his pallor, she feared he might be past help. But then she heard Kilian give the faintest of groans. Ghislain crouched down beside him, pressing the second unfired pistol to his forehead.

"What little game were you playing at, Lieutenant Guy-omard?" he asked.

Kilian's lips twisted into an insolent little grin. "Just amusing . . . myself . . ." He coughed and blood began to trickle from the side of his mouth.

"Help him," Celestine begged. "At least stop the bleeding—"

"Help a traitor? I think not." Ghislain turned to his Rosecoeurs. "Arrest these Guerriers. I'll take the prisoners on to the Place du Trahoir myself."

"Kilian." Jagu's voice, low, intense, came from the other side of the cart. "I'll never forget this. Not as long as I live, I swear."

"We may see each other sooner . . . than you think . . ." Kilian's last words were abruptly cut off as he began to choke convulsively. As Ghislain took the reins from Viaud and urged the cart onward, Celestine caught one final glimpse of Kilian, his fast-leaking blood staining the muddy cobbles bright red.

As the cart turned into the Place du Trahoir, Celestine felt her courage fall away at the sight she remembered from childhood: the wooden stake, surrounded by bales of hay and logs, piled high. A dais had been erected at a suitable distance from the pyres and she could see her judges sitting there, waiting as if they were about to witness a musical performance, not an execution. Donatien and Visant were seated on either side of King Ilsevir and the Queen Mother. There was no sign of Adèle.

It's just my old nightmare again. In a moment I'm going to wake up and everything's going to be all right.

Captain nel Ghislain brought the cart to a standstill in front of the dais. Guerriers of the Inquisition stood alongside, bearing torches whose flames burned pale in the cloudy light.

"On your feet!" Two of the Rosecoeurs caught hold of Celestine by the arms and removed the shackles, dragging her to her feet. In the other section, she saw Jagu hauled to a standing position. He was in shirtsleeves, and the first glimpse she got of his face showed her a gaunt, unshaven shadow of the man she loved.

"The Inquisition has tried these two malefactors and found them guilty of practicing the Forbidden Arts," announced Inquisitor Visant.

At last his words provoked a response from the crowd; jeers and boos could be heard rising from all corners of the Place. Visant must be trying to stir them up, Celestine thought; maybe he's even planted his supporters among the onlookers.

"Celestine de Joyeuse, Jagu de Rustéphan, your crimes are doubly despicable because you committed them while wearing the uniform of the Francian Commanderie. Let your deaths be a warning to all who are tempted by the lure of the Forbidden Arts, or to those who would make a mockery of their sacred vows."

It was so dark that the torch flames burned brightly against the gloom. Celestine hardly heard the Inquisitor's voice enumerating her crimes. She could see the black tendrils of darkness unraveling from the oncoming clouds. This was no ordinary thunderstorm; the dark air crackled with energy.

"*Drakhaoul,*" whispered the Faie, waking at last.

"Something is coming!" she cried in warning. One of the Rosecoeurs struck her across the mouth.

"Don't touch her!" cried Jagu, straining against his captors.

Celestine tasted blood welling from her bruised lip but she hardly felt the pain. "Something *is* coming!" she shouted defiantly. "Look at the sky!"

"It's just a storm," said Visant dismissively. "Tie the prisoners to the stake."

"Jagu!" Celestine called out to him in desperation as they bundled her out of the cart and up onto the pyre, where the Inquisitors stood waiting. The roughness of the wood and the scratchy straw hurt her bare feet, but still she tried to reach out to touch him.

"You were partners in crime in life; now you will die together," said Visant coldly. "And may the Blessed One have mercy on your souls."

The Inquisitors pulled her arms back around the broad wooden stake, tying her wrists behind her. Then they did the same with Jagu, so that their fingers almost touched. But when she remembered the bloodstained bandages wrapped around his left hand, she didn't want to cause him any more pain.

"If your guardian's able to help us, *now* would be a good time," she heard Jagu mutter as she saw the torchbearers approaching. A strong, acrid smell of tar was rising from the pyre; they must have doused the logs in pitch to make them burn more fiercely. The darkness was growing thicker and a chill wind had begun to whine around the place, causing the torches to flare and gutter.

Something is coming.

A streak of dazzling silver, liquid lightning, slashed the darkness. Celestine saw, circling above them, a great sky dragon, bearing in its coils a small craft. The people in the crowd looked too and began to shout out in consternation as the craft broke away and slowly descended.

"Magus?" she whispered.

"It's the king!" The rumor spread among the onlookers. "King Enguerrand!"

"Rosecoeurs, defend King Ilsevir!" ordered Captain nel Ghislain. There was a rush as the Rosecoeurs pushed through the crowd to encircle the dais, priming their muskets and aiming at the craft.

But Ilsevir and Aliénor had risen to their feet and were staring at the occupants.

"*Hold your fire!*" Aliénor's command penetrated above the confused clamor. "Enguerrand, is that really you?"

Enguerrand scrambled out of the craft and hurried up the stair onto the dais. Eugene hung back, knowing that this was Enguerrand's moment.

"Madame," Enguerrand said, bowing to his mother.

"If this has all been a joke, Enguerrand, it's been in very poor taste."

"No joke, Madame, I assure you." Enguerrand turned to Ilsevir, who had gone very pale. "What is the meaning of this, Brother?" He gestured to the stake. "Why are two of my most loyal subjects about to be executed?"

"They are guilty of—" began Donatien.

"I was not speaking to you, Maistre Donatien," Enguerrand said curtly.

"Is that really the king?" Celestine heard Jagu ask dazedly. But she was distracted. The darkness was growing thicker and a wind had begun to whine around the place.

Something is coming. Something unimaginably powerful . . .

CHAPTER 12

As Nagazdiel came soaring down from the clouds, Rieuk recognized the winding Sénon far below. The physical exhilaration of flight had utterly overwhelmed him, driving all other thoughts from his mind. He had watched through Ormas's eyes countless times before, but to feel the wind against his face, to see the great city of Lutèce from this dizzying height, was the most thrilling sensation he had experienced in his life.

"*Azilis!*" The Drakhaoul had found her. They came hurtling down at such speed, weaving past pointed steeples and pepper-pot towers, that Rieuk was terrified that Nagazdiel would lose control and smash his body on the cobbles.

He took in the situation in one glance: the two prisoners tied to a stake; the dais filled with dignitaries come to gloat over the barbarous execution; the Inquisitors bearing flaming torches to ignite the pyre; the watching crowd.

"It's Celestine," he cried. "They're going to burn her!"

"Jagu, look," Celestine urged. "*Look up!*"

Flying through the ominous sky, drawing the trails of darkness behind him like a vast cloak unfolding to smother the whole city, came a Drakhaoul. At first she could only see his eyes clearly: two crimson flames searing through the gloom. But as it drew nearer, she saw a powerful figure bearing down on them on wings of shadow. And she heard the Faie cry out suddenly in recognition.

"*Father!*"

* * *

Jagu's left wrist throbbed so piercingly that suddenly he knew with absolute certainty that his magus, the one who had marked him in Kemper, had come back to claim him. Looking up, he saw the dark angel descending, swooping down out of the blackened sky like a creature forged from flame and shadow.

So he's summoned his dread lord to carry me away to the Realm of Shadows? The thought struck Jagu as so bitterly ironic that he almost laughed aloud.

"Lord Nagazdiel," Eugene murmured. "Why have you come?" And, in the depths of his heart, he felt a memory stir, a memory planted there by Belberith the Warrior, his Drakhaoul.

It was the briefest of visions that flickered through his mind, but in it he saw Nagazdiel as a tall, dark-haired Heavenly Guardian, turning to hold out his hand in friendship to him, his eyes filled with warmth and compassion.

That must have been before he was imprisoned in the Realm of Shadows. Before he became embittered and corrupted . . .

"Light the pyre!" A lone voice cried out in the stunned silence. Celestine recognized the strident tones of the Haute Inquisitor. "Are you going to stand by and let this daemon set his servants free?"

"Stop him, someone—" Enguerrand launched himself forward but Visant seized a torch from one of his terror-struck men and threw it onto the straw bales.

"Burn them!"

The straw crackled into bright flame. Celestine gasped as she felt the wave of heat hit her. And then the acrid fumes from the rising smoke blew in her face, making her eyes stream.

"Keep your mouth closed," warned Jagu through the roar of the flames.

"Faie?" she rasped in desperation, coughing as she breathed in a lungful of smoke.

"*I'll do . . . what I can . . .* " The Faie cast a translucent shield around them. But as Celestine felt herself growing dizzy, the shield began to waver.

The Faie needs me to stay strong, or we'll all be lost. I mustn't black out . . .

Rieuk saw Visant set the pyre alight. He saw how fast and how hungrily the flames leaped upward. Celestine would die if he didn't move speedily enough. And if she died, what would become of Azilis, cast adrift without a mortal host?

The sky had become so black that the flames burned fiercely bright and the dust-laden wind which had blown in his wake only fanned them higher. And then Rieuk heard a voice crying out for help—that same high, anguished, piercing voice he had first heard all those years ago when he released Azilis from the Lodestar.

"*Save her,*" Nagazdiel commanded.

There was no time to quench the fire. Rieuk took to the air again, swooping down into the intense heat and smoke to land on the pyre itself. The burning logs singed the soles of his feet, but he hardly felt the pain. Celestine's fair head was drooping. With Nagazdiel's sharp talons, he slashed at the ropes that confined her until they shredded and she fell forward against him. Clasping her tightly in his arms, he lifted from the pyre, flying with strong wingbeats over the heads of the mesmerized onlookers.

"Jagu . . ." Celestine murmured faintly. "Save Jagu . . ."

Eugene had stood watching long enough. He turned to Linnaius.

"Wind mage," he said, "can you call down a rainstorm?"

Linnaius appeared to have read his thoughts, for the Emperor saw that his fingers were already at work.

The daylight was blotted out by the fast-gathering dark. From nearby the sonorous tones of the clock of the cathedral of Saint Etienne could be heard striking noon, but the sky was as black as if it were midnight. The only light in the Place du Trahoir was the harsh light of the pyre flames.

On the royal dais, Captain nel Ghislain pushed his king to

the ground, shielding him with his body as the Drakhaoul flew overhead. Donatien threw his arms around Aliénor. Enguerrand alone stood in the rushing darkness, gazing after the Drakhaoul.

"My lord Nagazdiel," he whispered. "Protect her. Protect your beloved daughter."

Through the clouds of choking smoke, Jagu saw the Drakhaoul rising into the air with Celestine in his arms. And he could do nothing to prevent it.

"Hold on, Jagu! Hold on there, man!" Men's voices penetrated the crackle of the flames.

He was finding it harder to breathe and his senses were swimming.

"We'll get you down, Jagu!" And was that the sound of water sloshing onto the flames?

Must be losing consciousness . . .

Yet he could see black shapes looming up out of the smoke, men clambering over the burning logs toward him.

"Fire! Fire on them!" Visant ordered his Guerriers. Jagu heard the sound of shots, then screams of panic from the crowd.

A man loomed up over Jagu, slashing the ropes that bound him, catching him as he slumped forward. A stab of pain jarred through his hand, jolting him back to consciousness.

"Steady there, lads, don't forget he's injured," warned a familiar voice and he thought he recognized Alain Friard's homely features, face streaked with ash, as his rescuers bundled him down over the dying fire.

Enguerrand had never felt so angry in his life as the moment he saw Alois Visant set the pyre alight. And when the Inquisitor ordered his men to fire on the Commanderie Guerriers, he could take no more.

He drew his pistol and walked up to Visant, pressing the muzzle into his back.

"This time you've gone too far, Inquisitor."

Visant half turned, a puzzled expression on his face that

twisted into a humorless smile. "Surely your majesty is joking . . ."

"Guerriers!" Enguerrand called out to the Commanderie squad who had come running with buckets of water to Jagu's rescue.

"Sire?" One turned around and Enguerrand saw that it was Alain Friard, Ruaud's loyal second-in-command.

"Arrest Inquisitor Visant."

Friard saluted and beckoned two of his men up onto the dais. They seized hold of the Inquisitor and started to drag him down from the dais.

"You fools!" Visant cried. "You'll live to regret this. I am all that stands between you and the darkness!" He went on shouting as the Guerriers dragged him away.

"Sire, I really must object—" began Donatien, but Enguerrand turned on him.

"I am ashamed that my guest, the Emperor, has been forced to witness this barbarous display on his first visit to Francia."

"The—the Emperor Eugene?" Donatien stuttered, his face changing color from pasty white to a dark, choleric red.

Aliénor found her voice at last. "Enguerrand, what have you done?"

"What have I done?" Enguerrand echoed. "If Celestine is not set free, this darkness will never lift. She is the only one who can heal the Rift."

"Make way! Make way for the duke!" The sound of raucous shouts and the clatter of horses' hooves filled the darkness.

Enguerrand scanned the Place du Trahoir. Armed horsemen had appeared at the far side; at their head rode a grizzled, broad-chested warrior. The banners they carried, flapping in the swirling wind, were russet, black, and gold—the colors of Provença. The last of the crowd scattered as he led his retainers on, urging his charger straight up toward the dais.

"Raimon?" said Aliénor querulously. "What does this mean?"

"I've come to support my future son-in-law," announced the Duke of Provença, letting out a rumbling laugh.

Aude had been riding behind her father; she jumped down and ran up onto the dais to Enguerrand's side. Oblivious to his mother's presence, Enguerrand kissed her.

"I've never been so humiliated in my life." Ilsevir came forward, his Rosecoeur captain close behind him. His voice shook, but whether with rage or terror, Enguerrand could not be certain. "Perhaps I should remind you all that I was crowned king of Francia but a short while ago. Am I to be ignored?"

"My dear Ilsevir," said Eugene, taking him by the arm, "you and I need to talk."

"We got you down just in time, Lieutenant!" Jagu found himself surrounded by his triumphant Guerriers. One handed him a water bottle and, gratefully, he poured the cold liquid down his seared throat until he choked. He stood, wheezing and hacking, as they slapped his back and cheered.

"Thank you, lads," he managed to say, between coughs. "I owe you; every one of you." But now that he had got his breath back, he gazed up into the churning sky. "Which way did he take her? Which way did the Drakhaoul go?"

Celestine opened her eyes. She was clasped in the arms of the dark Drakhaoul as tenderly as if she were a little child being carried home by her father. And they were flying; she could feel his body shudder with every powerful wingbeat, she could feel the dark air on her face. Her eyes and mouth stung with the smoke that she had inhaled and her throat and lungs felt as if they had been seared by the pyre flames. But she was alive. Unless this was another dream . . .

And then she remembered.

"Where is Jagu?"

There was a little public garden below, shaded by acacia and willow trees; Rieuk could even hear the splashing of a fountain. He alighted and set her gently down on a bench.

She was still coughing from the smoke she had inhaled, so

he went to the fountain and brought her water in his cupped hands. She gulped it down eagerly, so he brought her more.

"*Father?*" Celestine heard the Faie's voice issuing from her own mouth. And suddenly she was filled with Azilis's yearning to be reunited with her lost father. At the same time she felt her love for her own father surge up within her, mingling with the Faie's feelings until she could no longer distinguish what she felt.

"*Azilis, my dearest child.*" The Drakhaoul clasped her to him again, enfolding her in his arms. "*I've found you at last.*"

The magus's mark gleamed ever more brightly in the gloomy alley as Jagu, bare feet slipping on the muddy cobblestones, forced himself to follow the Drakhaoul's trail. He was certain that there was a connection between his magus and the daemon that had rescued Celestine. And the more his marked wrist throbbed, competing in intensity with the constant dull pain of his crushed hand, the nearer he reckoned he must be to finding them both.

But why had the daemon taken her? He was certain that he had heard the Drakhaoul cry out a name as he came soaring down out of the darkness. And that name was "Azilis."

"Could it be?" he muttered. "Could it be that your guardian spirit is the Eternal Singer, Celestine?"

The ironwork gates to a public garden lay ahead. And the mark on Jagu's wrist burned so fiercely that it felt as if it had been painted on his skin with acid.

He passed through the ornamental gates and saw a glimmer of white ahead, through the swaying trees, their slender branches still tossed and torn by the unruly wind. He was so tired by now that he could hardly find the strength to struggle along the gravel path. But he wanted answers. And above all, he wanted Celestine.

An ornamental fountain lay ahead; stone dolphins spouted a constant flow of clear water into a wide curving basin. The sound of the flowing water soothed his jangled nerves. But, with a shock, Jagu saw the Drakhaoul standing on the far side of it, Celestine clasped in his arms, his dark head resting against hers. As Jagu limped closer, the Drakhaoul raised his head and stared forbiddingly at him through cruel, slanted eyes seared with scarlet fire.

"*I won't let you take her from me.*" And, unfurling his powerful wings, he took to the air.

"Celestine, are you all right?" Jagu's breathing came hard and fast and his ribs still ached from coughing.

Celestine seemed to be in a trance. But at the sound of his voice, she stirred and moved her head.

"I have to go to Ondhessar . . ." The cold wind howled through the trees, shredding the tender new leaves.

"Ondhessar? B—but it's so far away," Jagu stammered, crushed.

"I have to take Azilis to the shrine," she called down. "It's the only way to stop this darkness leaking from the Realm of Shadows . . ."

"And how are you going to get back?" But the Drakhaoul was winging slowly away across the rooftops and Jagu's question hung in the air, unanswered. He dropped to his knees, distraught. After the ordeal they had just been through, it was more than he could bear to lose her again.

CHAPTER 13

"So Nagazdiel is going back to Ondhessar?"

Jagu turned around to see Kaspar Linnaius walking slowly toward him along the neat gravel path. "M—Magus?" he stammered.

"I have to follow Nagazdiel to Ondhessar. I too have some unfinished business at the shrine. I have to make sure that nothing goes wrong this time."

Jagu had no idea what Linnaius was talking about, but he was determined to go after Celestine. He got to his feet. "Then take me with you."

A dry, hot wind, tinged with a breath of dusty spice, brought Celestine slowly back to herself.

Nagazdiel was making a slow descent. No stars shone in the dark sky, yet the dull glitter given off by the scales encrusting his powerful body left a shimmer in the air as they flew downward.

"Where . . . are we?" she asked drowsily.

"*Ondhessar,*" said the Drakhaoul, his voice soft, yet darkened with an aching sadness. "*This is where you were born, my daughter, the only child of a forbidden love. The love I bore for your mother, Princess Esstar of Enhirre.*"

And Celestine suddenly remembered the words he had spoken to Galizur in the Faie's dream.

"*Take me. But spare her. She didn't ask to be born my child.*"

After an eternity apart, father and daughter had at last been reunited.

* * *

Buffeted by a blast of a cold, sere wind, Celestine struggled forward, one hand raised to protect her face from the swirling, stinging dust.

"What is this terrible place?" she cried, struggling to make herself heard above the howling of the wind.

"*This is the Rift between the worlds,*" said the Faie. "*And all this chaos has come about because I have been absent too long. I kept the balance between the Realm of Shadows and the Forest of the Emerald Moon but, since I left, the darkness has leaked in and the balance has broken down. This is the reason I have to leave you, Celestine.*"

As the wind died down and the clouds of grit settled, Celestine saw a man's body lying in the gloom in front of them.

"Who is that?" she cried, coming to a halt.

"A young magus who gave his life essence to help Prince Nagazdiel." The voice came from the Drakhaoul's body, yet Celestine heard from the passionate tone that it belonged to the Drakhaoul's mortal host.

"Who *are* you?" She turned to confront him.

With a convulsive shiver, Nagazdiel's Drakhaoul form separated itself from its host and reappeared, towering over Celestine. His host dropped to his knees by the body, head lowered. She saw that he was clothed only in his loose, waist-length hair—brown, save for a silver-white streak over his temples.

"Forgive me appearing like this before you, Celestine." He spoke so familiarly to her that she almost forgot her surprise at his drastic transformation. "Lady Azilis—I beg you—please restore this young magus." He slowly raised his head and Celestine saw with shock his ravaged face, a long scar running from brow to cheek, where his left eye had been.

"R—Rieuk Mordiern?" she said in sudden recognition.

"I know you must hate me for the wrongs I did you," he said. "But this boy, Oranir, is innocent of any crimes against you. He doesn't deserve to die." And gently he slipped his arms around the young man's dust-covered body, raising it in his arms.

"*I made him a promise, Azilis,*" said Nagazdiel.

"*Celestine?*" The Faie was asking her permission.

Celestine bowed her head a moment, torn, remembering the bitter grief he had caused her. But he had braved the Inquisition's fires to save her. "You came to my rescue, Rieuk," she said at last. "How can I refuse?"

She knelt beside him and placed her hands on the young magus's forehead and breast. Closing her eyes, she felt the Faie's energy flowing through her in a clear, pure stream. And, to her delight, she saw the dark-lashed lids begin to flicker open and eyes that were black, yet streaked with a touch of flame, stared up into hers.

"Lady Azilis?" he whispered in a dust-choked voice.

"Ran!" Rieuk said brokenly.

"Rieuk?" Oranir tried to lift one hand to touch his face; Rieuk caught the hand in his own, lacing his fingers through Oranir's. The wind began to gust again. "But you . . . you died in the Rift. Is this . . . the Realm of Shadows?"

When Jagu had been serving his term of duty at Ondhessar, he had heard the legends of the Towers of the Ghaouls, but he had never ventured this way. From the air they looked like ancient tombs of some lost civilization, standing guard over the desert.

Linnaius brought the sky craft expertly down among the strangely formed towers and pinnacles of volcanic rock. Jagu marveled at his skill in handling the craft in the perpetual gloom.

"We may meet with a hostile reception," the Magus said as he climbed out of the craft, "but this is our passport." He took out from his robes a leather-bound book.

"Is that Celestine's grimoire?" Jagu asked, but Linnaius had already set off at a surprisingly brisk pace for an old man, disappearing into the gaping entrance of the nearest tower.

Jagu had no option but to follow him, biting his lip as each step he took jarred his mangled hand.

"It's been many years," came the Magus's voice triumphantly back to him in the echoing void, "but I haven't forgotten the secret way to the shrine."

"Stop right there, Kaspar Linnaius!" A flash of light illuminated the dark interior and a violent tremor ran through the ground beneath their feet, throwing them off-balance. Shaken, Jagu looked up to see three venerable men coming toward them from the upper floor of the tower. The foremost held a torch whose flickering flame was reflected in the glitter of their eyes. Jagu's mage mark began to pulse again. He knew he was in the presence of the Magi of Ondhessar.

CHAPTER 14

"Lord Estael." Linnaius held aloft the grimoire. "We have to hurry. This may be our only chance to restore Azilis . . . and our fading powers."

"And why should we believe you when you've tricked us so many times before?" The one Linnaius had called Estael came toward them. "I wondered when you'd come looking for the new Lodestar."

Lodestar? Jagu wondered what secret thaumaturgical code this could be; even in his years of training with Père Judicael, he had never heard the name before.

"And who is this?" Estael stared forbiddingly at Jagu. "He's not a magus. We only allow initiates beyond this point."

Having come so far, Jagu was not prepared to be turned away. He held up his left wrist, showing the mage mark, which gleamed like quicksilver in the gloom. The magi muttered to each other, evidently unsure what to do.

"Believe me when I say that this man's presence is essential," interrupted Linnaius dryly.

"Very well; I'll lead the way." Estael raised his torch high, revealing a tall archway that opened onto a spiral stair. "Follow me."

"This is where we must make our final farewells, Celestine." The Faie faded from Celestine's body and reappeared before her in the pale, translucent form of a young Enhirran woman. She held out her hands to Celestine.

"Is this your true likeness, Azilis?" Celestine asked, trying

to hold the aethyrial fingers in her own. "You look so much
like that famous opera singer, Maëla Cassard."

"*We made a great success together, didn't we?*" the Faie
said, smiling affectionately at her. "*We took the Imperial
Theater by storm.*"

"All this time you've been my guide and my protector,"
Celestine said, trying to hold back the tears. "But above all
you've been my friend, my closest friend, dearest Faie. I
don't know how to say farewell. It's so hard to let you go."

"*But you don't need me anymore,*" the Faie said softly.

"I don't even know how to break our bond. Don't I need
the book to set you free?" And she had left her father's grimoire at Swanholm, with all her belongings.

"Someone's coming," warned Rieuk.

A vast wasteland stretched into the darkness; Jagu could
just make out the jagged outline of tall tree trunks, their
branches snapped off and scattered across the ground.

"You mustn't stay here for long," warned Linnaius. "The
atmosphere of the Rift is treacherous for mortals, even
those cursed with a mage mark."

But Jagu had detected a familiar glimmer of light up
ahead and went hurrying toward it. Two figures hovered in
the clearing, giving off a scintillating radiance that hurt his
eyes: a slender woman and a tall man, whose bearing was
more like that of one of the Heavenly Guardians than the
Drakhaoul he had seen carrying Celestine away from Lutèce.
By their radiance he spotted Celestine, still in her charred
shift, her feet bare, like his own. Kneeling in the dust beside
her were two men, both magi, he guessed from their long
hair and glittering eyes. And he felt the mage mark begin to
burn so fiercely that, looking down at his wrist, he saw it
was giving off a faint phosphorescent light.

"You," he said in astonishment. "It was *you.*"

"Jagu?" Celestine turned and saw him coming slowly toward
her out of the darkness. She stumbled toward him and he
caught her one-handed, crushing her close to him. His hair
smelled of smoke and his face was rough with stubble but

she didn't care, pressing her mouth to his, kissing him with all the desperate passion and hunger that had built up inside her.

"*I told you; you don't need me anymore,*" repeated the Faie. Celestine unwound her arms from around Jagu.

"But how can I set you free without my father's book?" she said sadly.

"A single drop of blood is enough."

She started, hearing Linnaius's voice from the rushing darkness. The old magus appeared as another gust of wind began to whine around them, tossing his white hair and beard hither and thither.

"Are you prepared, Lady Azilis?" he asked, holding out the grimoire, the pages open, fluttering in the harsh wind.

The Faie leaned forward and kissed Celestine on the forehead. Celestine felt a last shivering tingle of aethyrial energy pass into her. "*Farewell, Celestine,*" said the Faie.

"Farewell, dearest Faie," Celestine cried. "I'll never forget you."

"Rieuk?" said Linnaius. "A single drop of blood to break the bond."

Rieuk had been watching in a daze, holding Oranir, not wanting to let go of him for fear he might slip away and be lost to him forever.

Aqil knelt beside them and put his arms around Oranir. "This is your task, crystal magus," he said. "Don't worry; Oranir will be safe with me."

Rieuk stood up unsteadily. Estael came over to him and draped his cloak around his shoulders. He placed something cold and hard and smooth in his hand. Rieuk knew from the feel of it alone that it was the new Lodestar he had spent so long fashioning.

"Are you ready, Celestine?" he asked. She nodded. He raised his hand and revealed the new Lodestar in all its clear crystal purity. He pressed the pointed tip against her index finger and a drop of crimson blood fell onto the grimoire.

"Go; be free," Celestine said. "The bond between us is broken."

"*Father!*" cried Azilis. Her slender figure burned like a candleflame stirred by the wind, flaring up brightly, then suddenly dwindling, fading away into the facets of the Lodestar.

Rieuk gazed down at the crystal and felt it come alive in his hands with vibrant, pulsing energy. It lit the darkness and confusion of the Rift like a clear beacon. And then sound began to flow from the Lodestar—that thin, high, celestial voice that he had first heard in Karantec all those years ago.

Then she had cried out to him of her urgent desire to escape the confines of the crystal, to be free. But now he heard a new sweetness, a joy, and a purpose in her voice.

Nagazdiel lifted his head and his eyes no longer burned so fiercely as he listened to his daughter's song filling the Rift with its luminous purity.

The shadowy outline of a great gateway appeared in the darkness. Nagazdiel turned and walked toward it, disappearing into the shadows. Azilis's song continued to fill the Rift, but as they watched, the gateway slowly faded from sight until there was no trace that it had ever been there.

CHAPTER 15

Jagu had kept alert until now by willpower alone, ignoring the throbbing pain in his crushed hand. Suddenly a wave of faintness washed over him and he staggered, dropping to his knees.

"Jagu!" He heard Celestine's cry of alarm as if from very far away; the world around him seemed to be dissolving into mist . . .

Someone caught hold of him with a strong, reassuring grip. A face, hawk-nosed, dark-skinned, hovered above his. "Magus . . ."

"My name is Aqil," he heard the magus say, "and I am trained in the arts of healing. I can see that you've been badly injured. Perhaps there is something I can do to alleviate your pain."

"Aqil?" The name was familiar but as Jagu wavered in and out of consciousness, it was a while before he was able to remember where he had heard it before. Hadn't Aqil been the magus who poisoned the water in the fort, forcing his regiment to retreat from Ondhessar? He came back to himself to see the magus binding his hand with fresh dressings.

"I will give you a salve to use twice a day to keep the wounds clean," said Aqil, straightening up. "I cannot undo the damage that's already been done, but I can use what skill I have to save your hand."

The excruciating throbbing had eased at last and as Jagu stared at the clean linen bindings, he even wondered whether there might be some hope that he could play again, one day.

"Thank you, Magister Aqil." Celestine helped Jagu to sit up.

"You brought Azilis back to us," said Aqil, "and for that we can never thank you enough."

"The last time we met in Ondhessar, Aqil," Jagu said, striving to find the right words to express his gratitude, "we were enemies. But I hope that this might be the beginning of a new understanding between us."

"Perhaps," said Aqil, with an enigmatic smile. "Let us hope so . . ."

Celestine and Jagu emerged from the tower into the Hidden Valley to see the last rags and tatters of the darkness dispersing, and the clear blue of early twilight revealed behind, with the first star gleaming overhead as brightly as the Lodestar.

Celestine let her head rest on Jagu's shoulder and he put his arm around her, glad just to stand together, supporting each other.

Kaspar Linnaius approached them. "I'm heading back to Lutèce," he said. "Would you care to join me?"

Enguerrand entered the Great Hall at Plaisaunces and the assembled courtiers and councillors bowed as he walked up to the dais. He loathed the thought of having to go through with this ritual, much as he loathed most of the formal ceremonies of court life. But he had to make his will known in the presence of the nobles and the council; Eugene had impressed that upon him during their recent discussions at Swanholm. "Even if it means defying your mother."

When the Emperor had come to bid him farewell, Eugene had embraced him before the court in a confirmation of the new bond between Francia and Rossiya. And Enguerrand had returned the embrace sincerely. "I shall never forget that you came to our rescue. I am in your debt."

Eugene had laughed. "No talk of debts, please!" And then his expression had changed. "In Artamon's time, the Drakhaouls divided the sons of Artamon, but in many ways our Drakhaouls have drawn us closer together. I believe that now we understand each other a little better." And with a cheerful wave, he had gone out into the palace gardens, where Linnaius was waiting for him.

As the sky craft rose up above the wind-tossed trees, Aude came to stand by Enguerrand's side, slipping her hand into his.

"I wonder if we shall ever see Linnaius again," he said to her softly.

"Banish Maistre Donatien?" Queen Aliénor rounded on her son. "I won't hear of it! I refuse to allow it. If you banish him, then I shall go too."

Enguerrand stared at her through his new pair of spectacles, seeing all too clearly the defensive, stubborn look in her eyes. He sighed wearily. Her attitude toward him was never going to change.

"Very well, dear Maman," he said, knowing full well that she hated to be addressed so familiarly in front of the courtiers. "You may retire from court to your estates at Belle Garde. But Messieur Donatien—and I remind you that I have stripped you of the title and office of Grand Maistre—you will leave Francia and never return, on pain of death."

Hugues Donatien inclined his head, saying nothing.

Enguerrand was not finished yet. "Captain nel Ghislain, I understand that the Rosecoeur garrison at Ondhessar has been decimated by the Arkhan's forces."

"According to the latest reports, your majesty." Girim nel Ghislain stared straight ahead, not meeting Enguerrand's eyes. "Though it seems that Arkhan Sardion perished in the attack."

"It's time to hand the shrine back to the Enhirrans." Enguerrand spoke quietly but placing emphasis on his words. "And to restore the Azilis statue to its rightful place in the shrine at Ondhessar."

"Now wait a moment, Enguerrand," began Ilsevir, who, until then, had stayed silent.

"We are about to enter into talks with the new Arkhan," continued Enguerrand, determined not to be interrupted.

"He is of a more scholarly, peaceful nature than his father. I believe an understanding can be reached between our two nations that will bring an end to the bloodshed. And as a gesture of our goodwill, I want the statue returned, along with the other relics."

Girim nel Ghislain bowed his head, but not before Enguerrand had glimpsed the expression that distorted his face: anger mingled with dismay.

"We are moving into a new age," Enguerrand said, addressing the court. "An age of hope, even an age of enlightenment. I want to encourage the study of the sciences in our universities. I want to encourage the expansion of our nation, working with our new ally, the Emperor." Exhausted by the effort of speaking for so long, he sat down. Yet to his surprise, he heard the sound of applause; his courtiers had received his speech with approval.

"An inspiring speech, your majesty," said Chancellor Aiguillon in his ear. He was beaming approvingly. But Enguerrand's gaze was drawn to a portrait he had ordered hung in the hall. It depicted Ruaud de Lanvaux, dressed in his ceremonial robes as head of the Francian Commanderie, with the Angelstone on a gold chain around his neck.

"I think you'd have been proud of me today, dear Maistre," he said under his breath.

"Are you certain, Doctor?" Adèle, sitting up in bed, gazed keenly at Doctor Vallot.

"Absolutely certain, majesty." Vallot said, smiling at her as he packed away his instruments.

"Oh, but now that my brother has returned, you mustn't call me 'your majesty' anymore," she said.

He looked horrified. "Forgive me, highness—"

"No, forgive me; it was rude of me to tease you so, and just when you've delivered such excellent news."

"Excellent news?" Ilsevir had just entered the bedchamber. Ever since Enguerrand's return he had been plunged into a depression, hardly saying a word to anyone, and she looked at him anxiously. "Is my wife fully recovered, Doctor?"

"I don't believe she was ever ill, highness, unless pregnancy can be counted as a disease."

"Pregnancy?" Ilsevir's face altered instantly as he let out a shout of delight. "But—but that's wonderful!" He hurried over to her bedside and kissed her. "When is the baby due?"

Adèle felt herself blushing with pleasure at his reaction. "Early autumn."

"Nevertheless, given the princess's delicate state of health, I don't recommend that she undertake the journey back to Allegonde until the pregnancy is well established and there is no risk of another miscarriage."

"I may have lost a kingdom"—Ilsevir took her hand in his—"but, God willing, it looks as if I have gained an heir."

Adèle glanced up at him anxiously but saw that he was still smiling. She squeezed his hand. The union between Francia and Allegonde had been annulled by the Francian Council and she knew that he had felt deeply humiliated. Yet the Emperor had managed to allay some of his grievances by setting up some carefully negotiated trade treaties that would bring new revenue to Allegonde.

"Is there anything you would like, Adèle?" Ilsevir said anxiously. "You have only to ask . . ."

"I really would like to tell Celestine," she said with a little sigh. "Is there no news of her yet?"

Adjutant Korentan checked his orders again. The instructions came direct from Captain nel Ghislain and were succinct:

"*The statue* is to be returned to Ondhessar straightaway. Make all necessary arrangements."

From time to time he had crept back to the secret place where Girim had ordered the disintegrating statue of Azilis to be stored while the copy was displayed in the Basilica shrine. He had felt it his special duty as a Rosecoeur Guerrier to watch over her even as she decayed. The statue was no longer a thing of beauty but to him it represented something infinitely more precious: a direct link with his beloved saint, Elesstar, carved out of marble that came from the land of her birth. It saddened him to see the ravages that the impure air of Allegonde had wreaked upon her perfection. Left in the dry desert air where she was first carved, she would not have begun to crumble away, he was certain of it.

He made his way through the musty cellar, lantern raised high to illuminate his path. Why, he wondered, did it feel as if he were lifting a sheet from a dead body?

"Forgive me, Blessed Elesstar," he murmured as he raised the heavy cloth. Then the cloth fell from his grip as he took a step back, astonished.

Pale stone glimmered in the lantern's flame.

"Is someone playing a trick?" Korentan, recovering from his initial shock, stripped the cloth away and stared. For the Azilis statue lay there as if she were freshly carved from semitranslucent marble, whiter than milk, a vision of purity in the dank, musty cellar. Tentatively he put out a hand and touched the statue's cupped hands, his fingertips grazing hers.

The prince must have arranged for the statues to be switched overnight again. How else to explain this unmarred perfection where all had been discoloration and crumbling decay? Unless a miracle had occurred . . .

Acir Korentan dropped to his knees in the dust before the statue.

CHAPTER 16

On a summer's day of brilliant sunshine, Enguerrand of Francia attended Saint Meriadec's, accompanied by the Duke and Duchess of Provença and the king's betrothed, their youngest daughter, Aude. Grand Maistre Friard arranged a special escort of Guerriers of the New Francian Commanderie, led by Captain Philippe Viaud, all resplendent in their new uniforms of black and gold.

They had been specially invited by the Maistre de Chapelle to hear the first performance of his new work, which was dedicated to his patron, the king.

The players of a chamber orchestra, strings and woodwind, were seated before the altar, between the choir stalls, bows at the ready, reeds well moistened.

The Maistre de Chapelle stood in front of his musicians, twisting his baton to and fro between his fingers. He was not yet entirely accustomed to conducting. He would have felt far happier to be back in his old place, out of sight in the organ loft, but he had come to realize that the damage to his left hand meant he might never achieve the agility and accuracy of which he had been so proud. It could take years of patient practice to meet his own exacting standards at the keyboard but he was determined not to give up.

Until then, he had decided to concentrate on composing and conducting.

Suddenly he felt nervous and unsure. Suppose he made a mistake and gave the wrong cue to the singers or players? Worse still, suppose the king hated his composition?

He turned nervously to the king, who smiled encouragingly and nodded.

Why am I in such a state? I've faced far worse than this . . .

The Maistre de Chapelle tapped his baton on the edge of his music stand and gazed warningly at the singers, gesturing to them to rise. The organist softly depressed a key to give the soloist her first pitch. The courtiers' chatter faded away as she moved forward. It was a long time since she had performed in Lutèce, and there had been rumors circulating that her voice had lost its magical purity and that her singing career might be over.

A look passed between her and the Maistre de Chapelle—a long, meaningful look. And then she began to sing.

"Blessed Azilia . . ." One long, yearning phrase issued from her lips after another, "let your light shine out . . ."

The Maistre brought in the choir—first the trebles, then the altos, until all were quietly singing the ancient vesper chant he had first heard sung by the monks in the Cathedral of Saint Simeon in Mirom. And from that solemn hymn, slow-moving like a funeral procession, the soloist's voice gradually emerged, soaring upward, her bright, glorious tone rising to the heavens like an angel's flight.

The last, aethyrial notes lingered on in the reverberant atmosphere. Jagu quietly laid down his baton. Celestine was looking at him, he knew, her eyes warm with encouragement. For a moment there was utter stillness.

And then the applause began.

"Bravo!"

Jagu had been so involved in the music that the applause took him by surprise. He turned, astonished, to see King Enguerrand beaming his approval. He turned back, automatically, to gesture to Celestine. She came forward and took his right hand. They looked at each other and smiled, happy to be repeating the old, familiar ritual. Jagu raised Celestine's hand to his lips and kissed it, to the audience's delight.

"I think they like your Vesper Prayer," she whispered to him.

"I think they love your singing," he replied. Then they turned once more to acknowledge the rapturous applause together, before returning to their places to continue with the concert.

Epilogue

"So what is this surprise?" Rieuk, blindfolded, let Oranir guide him downward through the darkness.

"It wouldn't be a surprise if I told you," came back Oranir's voice teasingly. "Not much farther now."

Rieuk stumbled but Oranir caught him, righting him again.

"Why am I fool enough to trust you, Ran?"

"It's worth it, believe me," Oranir whispered, his lips softly grazing Rieuk's ear. "We're here."

Rieuk raised his hand to pull off the blindfold. A soft green-hued radiance shimmered over the ragged trees of the Forest of the Emerald Moon. High above them, the emerald moon shone down once more, bathing them in its calm light. The healing of the Rift had begun.

"It's . . . beautiful," he said, finding his voice.

A distant thread of melody echoed through the forest.

"But look. Look over there!" Oranir pointed.

As the moonlight grew more intense, Rieuk saw that a sapling had sprung up in the clearing since he had last visited the Rift. And as they set out toward it, he felt Ormas wake within him, fluttering up to perch on his shoulder. New leaves were unfurling on the slender branches of the young tree. They were shaped like lotus flowers, and they gave off a strange, yet irresistible perfume—with something of the spiciness of cloves mingling with a bittersweet honey-eyed scent.

"*I know what this is, Master.*" Ormas took to the air, circling above the young tree. "*It's a haoma tree.*"

"A young haoma tree." Rieuk gazed gratefully at Oranir.

"*They're coming,*" Ormas cried excitedly, taking off into the sky. "*My brothers are coming back!*"

And as the two magi followed him, they saw other hawks winging in, dark as smoke against the delicate green of the moonlit sky. They circled high overhead at first, then suddenly swooped down to skim above their heads.

As Rieuk lifted his head to watch them, he saw one that darted closer than all the others, almost as if it recognized him. As it passed by him in graceful flight, he caught sight of its brilliant eyes gazing at him. Brown eyes, flecked with dark gold, like tortoiseshell.

Rieuk stood, his mouth a little open, an unspoken question hanging on his lips.

"Imri?" he whispered.

The tips of its wing feathers brushed the top of his head softly, almost like a caress. And then it was gone, darting away to join the others in their ecstatic, eternal winged dance.

Author's Note

The full story of the events that culminated in the battle at the Serpent Gate is explored in much greater detail in my trilogy The Tears of Artamon. The first book, *Lord of Snow and Shadows,* introduces Gavril Nagarian, unwilling heir to the throne of Azhkendir and its cursed heritage, who soon finds himself locked in battle with ruthless Prince Eugene and his dreams of empire. In the second, *Prisoner of the Iron Tower,* we first meet Celestine de Joyeuse and her accompanist, Jagu de Rustéphan, as Francia is drawn into the conflict. The third book, *Children of the Serpent Gate,* sees the disastrous repercussions as Eugene's ambitions threaten not just to bring down his empire but to bring the world itself to an end.